DEAN ING

BLOOD OF EAGLES

TOR

BLOOD OF EAGLES

Copyright © 1987 by Dean Ing

First printing: April 1987

A TOR Book

Published by Tom Doherty Associates, Inc.
49 West 24 Street
New York, N.Y. 10010

ISBN: 0-312-93010-0

Library of Congress Catalog Card Number: 86-51591

Printed in the United States of America

0 9 8 7 6 5 4 3 2

For Ted and Carl,
each with some eagle
in him.

PART ONE

MAY 1944

Chapter 1

ELBAS Hamid lay motionless, feeling sun-warmed stone under his hard empty belly, his head and shoulders projecting over a sheer five-hundred-meter abyss, his head cocked for the faint growl of Nazi machinery. Except for a distant eagle on solitary patrol above the canyon, nothing moved. The boy behind Hamid thought that in profile, with his big prow of a nose, his mustache sweeping out like talons etched against the heavens, the partisan leader must have some eagle in him.

At the moment Hamid's ears caught only the blade-sharp keening of the wind above this pass in the Dinarics—and of course the measured breathing of the boy protecting his back. Two years before, in the spring of 1942, these savage mountain peaks of northern Albania had fairly shook with the clatter and squeal of mechanized German equipment. Hamid's little band had been stronger then; had already fought the invading Italians to a standstill with their mountain men, stalwart Gheg tribesmen. And a few Tosks from the southern lowlands as well, to give them their due. Tosks might copy Turk ways and religious practices, but they too were Albanians who shared the Gheg thirst for Fascist blood.

The German reinforcements had been tougher to swallow, sweeping into the little Balkan nation with crack mountain divisions and even a tough little Mark IV tank expressly modified for mountain warfare. It had taken the Albanian shock brigades two full years to stop the Nazi advance. Now, in mid-May of 1944, Hamid knew that the Germans were losing on several fronts. He did not much care, so long as he saw them retreating on this one. If the Englishmen had still been around now to supply ammunition and news, they could have told Hamid that tiny Albania, of all European nations invaded by the Nazis, was the only one finally to hurl them back without foreign troops.

Hamid would not have been surprised. The Gheg was—had always been—master of the Dinaric Alps, the toughest mountain guerrilla the world had ever known.

The boy heard it first, and squeezed gently against Hamid's ankle. Far below along the primitive roadbed, still beyond their line of sight; not the creak of leather saddles, but a thin metallic squeal. Hamid half turned, the slow measured movement of one who knew better than to move quickly when outlined against the sky, and gestured for the monocular.

The boy, Pal Kraga, had his father's high cheekbones and straight nose, and looked younger than his fifteen years. Hamid tried not to show impatience as the boy unslung the thong from his throat with meticulous care. The monocular had once been Zeiss binoculars, sawn in two after the elder Kraga took it from the neck of a dead German. Now Kraga, a minor diplomat returned from Serbia to fight as a partisan, occupied a shallow grave near Shkoder—fertilizing homeland soil, at least—and had passed on little more to the youth than his whipcord features, the Zeiss optics, and an English revolver.

The monocular was too precious, and Hamid had requisitioned it; but he was wise enough to let the boy carry it for safekeeping. In time of peace this whiskerless lad would still be under the protection of the *bessa* pledge, a year too young for the ancient threat of Gheg blood feuds. But even feuding families stood together against the Germans. Most had thrown in with Tito's communists, but republicans developed their own ragtag BK army, the Balli Kombetar, National Front. The BK ranks had now thinned to a few little groups of survivors, yet they still took their toll of Germans. Younger boys than Pal

Kraga were veterans in this campaign, the most glorious blood feud in Albanian history. Now the Germans were in steady retreat, but to let them do it with all deliberate speed was not the Gheg way. The Gheg way was to kill them all; tomorrow if necessary, today if possible. Hamid had lost count of his own kills; even the boy had made bones the day after his father's death, promoted from unarmed courier to sniper. The boy might never live to develop a guerrilla leader's gift of quick decisions under fire. But given time, the boy learned well; and with a scoped rifle he was very, very steady.

During the next two endless minutes, Elbas Hamid picked out the separate sounds of different vehicles still unseen: the staccato chug of an air-cooled staff car, the rumble of lorry engines straining along the narrow rocky surface of the road-bed, the moan and chatter of something that had to be Caterpillar treads. Hamid fully expected that his first glimpse of this retreating group would be of Climbing Toads, the Gheg epithet for the astonishingly agile little German tanks that had dealt so much misery to honest men. Typically, during their long retreat from Albania's capital city of Tirana, the Nazis would put a Toad or two at the head of a column, and another as rear guard, with troop lorries in the middle and Schmeisser-armed motorcycle couriers coursing like sheepdogs, engines yapping, along the flanks of the column. But those lorries sometimes carried supplies too, food and ammunition and loot. A week's ration of supplies for a company of Nazis would last Hamid's little band for months.

Hamid wondered briefly why this motorized column was avoiding the main road from Lezha past Shkoder. Whatever the reason, it was playing into the hands of his BK band. Elbas Hamid's command, including himself, now numbered exactly six men and five boys. He expected to lose two, perhaps three, in this engagement against perhaps ten times their number. He also expected to win. It was not a foolish expectation: they were, after all, Ghegs.

Hamid grunted in surprise as the first vehicle edged into view some three kilometers away; it was a staff car. It boasted a light machine gun on an improvised mount, and moved at

scarcely more than a good walking pace for a man like Hamid.
Too far off to tell, even with the powerful Zeiss, but the little
car's occupants were almost certainly privates. No great loss if
they set off a mine dug into a rough mountain track.

Hamid's partisans had set no mines, but that meant little.
General Hoxha's Albanian communists, damn their eyes, might
have done it without warning Hamid's republican partisans.
The communists had Soviet munitions and men to spare,
especially Shehu's gang, the Seventh Shock Brigade. These
days, Mehmet Shehu was as likely to open fire on decent
Catholic BK partisans as on the Nazis. Clearly, the communists felt the war was sufficiently won to begin clearing out
republicans, in anticipation—but that was a strategy for many
tomorrows, and Hamid's immediate problem deserved his full
attention.

The second vehicle, and two more behind it, were heavy
lorries with canvas stretched tight over high bows. There
might be a score of troops under each tarp, or cases of iron
rations. With the first shot, he would know. Then the Climbing Toad appeared, its short-barreled cannon capable of hurl-
ing a projectile the thickness of a man's wrist into a crevice a
mile distant. Hamid grunted again, and the boy inched up to
peer past his arm. Behind the Toad was only one more lorry;
no motorcycles, no more tanks. A puzzle; certainly not the
usual method of German deployment here. Perhaps the tiny
dot atop the Toad was the protruding head of some Nazi
general, safely touring the Dinarics from the thickest armor
available. Hamid thought about it until the column passed
behind a distant crag. At this pace they would be at the river
crossing within the hour.

Hamid knew his ridgeline trails as an eagle knows its
nest. "With my Luger and the Enfield," he said to the boy, "I
can make echoes enough for a dozen, and make life short for a
few Germans. Leave me the mule and run. Tell Petar what we
have seen. There will be no time to dig a trench across the
trail, so he must detonate the satchel charges to cut a trench
this side of the river crossing. Petar must emplace three sharp-
shooters ahead of the column. The rest of you will flank the

Nazi pigs, with the youngest above and the more experienced below near the riverbank where the enemy will try to escape. Now, repeat what I have said.''

The boy did so, speaking with his barely detectable Serbian accent so unusual for a Gheg—but what was one to expect of a boy whose family had lived among Serbs for so long? ''The youngest will snipe from above while we men wait near the river,'' the boy finished, poised for his long run.

Elbas Hamid grinned. ''You and the other men,'' he agreed, handed back the little Zeiss monocular, and sent the boy on his way with a gesture. Alone, he made his preparations with care. He carried two grenades in addition to the English rifle and the captured Luger. The enemy column, when it reappeared, would be almost vertically below; near enough that Hamid's long right arm might make them mistake the first grenade for a mortar round. By the time the Germans realized they were under attack from a lone sniper and pressed on, many minutes might have passed; or longer still, if Hamid managed to disable that lead lorry on the narrow road. He had one advantage: the Toad could not elevate its cannon to fire nearly straight up. Dynamite would have been better than grenades, but that was one munition Hamid's band had used to the last stick.

Five minutes later, from better cover between the crags where his muzzle flashes might not be seen, Hamid hurled that first grenade. The vertical distance was so great that he had the Enfield scope snugged to his cheek before the explosion, just behind the little command car. He was half aware of its gunner, sagging across his unfired weapon, as he drew a bead on the windshield of the lorry behind. It was not the best of shots, perhaps because he had misjudged the flatness of an Enfield's trajectory when firing at such a dizzying downward angle. He worked the bolt action and tried again. A star appeared midway down the lorry's windshield, and now other things were happening, none of them good because the lorry did not stop.

Sometimes the Nazis flipped back tarpaulins to reveal heavy machine guns inside lorries. This time the big trucks disgorged helmeted men with weapons, but no packs. Hamid cursed; packs always slowed a man down, even men of the German First Mountain Division. They were already returning fire; here, there, everywhere, with no idea how many Albanians they faced. And those lorries kept grinding along as though Elbas Hamid were of no importance.

Hamid wriggled backward and grasped his second grenade, clearing its safety with a snap, and risked another look below before coming up to his knees for a long toss. This time he heard exclamations and wondered whether they had seen him or the grenade. He was not long in doubt; now a stuttering burst, probably from a Schmeisser, spanged among the rocks near him just before the grenade dropped between the lorry's wheels. The explosion was oddly muffled, the taut canvas of the lorry shuddering. Hamid saw the lorry tilt slightly, then lurch to a stop; knew that his grenade had blown both dual tires on the near side, and also that he had taken a hit just below his left buttock. A ricochet or a stone chip, perhaps, but not in a place where a tourniquet would help. He worked his way backward, slinging the rifle onto his back, then progressed upward in a series of squatting leaps to the trail just behind the ridgeline. Whatever damage they'd done to his leg, they hadn't severed the heavy muscle.

Twice he fired the Luger, each time from a different point, and though he understood no German, he was aware that the shouts meant that the Nazis were pursuing two operations at once. One operation involved changing those shredded tires; the other was aimed at Elbas Hamid himself.

He had risked enough, accomplished enough; changing those tires would take a quarter of an hour, and he would be needed at the river crossing. Hamid took one last risk, straining to topple a trunk-sized boulder that might start a rockslide or, at least, crush a few Nazis climbing for him. Then, without waiting to hear the boulder's dusty progress, he mounted the mule and urged it southward.

Unlike a horse, the mule was not so stupid as to lope on such a trail, even while smelling Hamid's blood, and it moved in a careful canter while Hamid hugged its neck. The German fire was still fairly steady, receding as he put more distance from the column. With any luck, none of them had seen his escape. Presently Hamid shifted upright, standing in the right stirrup as he felt back along his upper thigh. Oh yes, it was bleeding a freshet, all right; his entire leg was sodden with blood. Hamid did the only thing he could: he leaned so that most of his body weight pressed the long gash against the saddle, and murmured encouragement to the mule.

By mountain road, the river crossing lay twelve kilometers to the northeast; by mule and ridgeline, only seven. Elbas Hamid was still conscious enough to whistle, his left boot dripping blood, as the sentry spied him a half hour later.

Petar Murra was supervising the placement of flat stones over the satchel charges so the force of the explosion would cut downward into the roadbed, when Hamid eased himself down from the mule. Obviously the boy had brought the message; he was probably somewhere below now, familiarizing himself with boulders along the riverbank with the other experienced snipers. Five minutes spent memorizing every feature of your cover could buy you a longer life.

Petar donated a villainous frown as his leader hobbled to sit and watch the final preparations. "Can you fight, brother Elbas?"

"Unless I faint like a woman from this miserable scalp wound," said Hamid, shucking off his trousers.

Petar Murra did not smile at the joke, which suggested one's head in his backside for being wounded unnecessarily. "Hysen; Jorgo: bring adhesive and pack sterile fleece into this thing." Both men knew that the only way that fleece could be sterile was by pouring a bit of raki into it. The infernal sting might help push away the cobwebs from his brain after the loss of a quart of blood. Hamid was already dizzy, needing a moment to understand why their youths were stacking freshly cut brush to hide the low cairns of stone across the roadbed.

Hamid knew that he would have to pass his command on to bandy-legged little Petar Murra, and said as much while lying face-down, grunting as their oldest member, Hysen

Kosovo, packed the wound. "Perhaps I should be above with the boys," he added.

Scowling as always, Murra accepted command by giving an order to his leader. "That rifle of yours will do more damage if you are firing from across the river," he said. "Give the fatherless Nazis another source of fear. Can you mount that mule? Then hide it with the other two beyond the crossing and see if you can find high cover." He turned away toward the twin fuses that led under a pile of stones, then looked back. Petar Murra had many scowls, and this one was affectionate. "Pace yourself, brother; an unconscious sniper will be of no use to us."

Hamid needed help from Kosovo to remount. Before kicking the mule's flanks he watched Murra running the fuses under roadside debris. "If you wait much longer, they will certainly hear the explosion."

"Assuredly they will," Murra said. "Jorgo Babani has volunteered to time the fuses so that the explosion may take a few Germans to hell."

Hamid nodded and reined the mule forward. It was suicidally risky for Jorgo, a thickset young man of great courage, but Petar Murra was now commanding. If the Germans did not stop at sight of the brush pile, and if they failed to see the smoke of the fuses, and if they failed to see Jorgo wriggling down among the rocks to cover, then perhaps the satchel charges would perform a double service. Hamid collected their other pack mules and led them to the crossing, where the river swept ankle-deep over bedrock before plunging into deeper currents.

Finding a defile suitable to hide three mules across the river was no simple task. Hamid chose the first ravine that seemed climbable, remaining mounted as long as possible to husband his flagging energy. The mules accepted their rocky corral with philosophical calm as Hamid secured them, and he limped back to the face of the canyon. No time to seek better cover now; even without the monocular or the rifle scope, Hamid could see the German staff car chugging down the grade a kilometer distant. The rest of the column could not be far back.

The sturdy Babani lay in full view of Hamid, two body lengths below the roadbed, watching the progress of the staff car, judging, risking. The murmur of rushing water was near enough to mask the sounds of machinery, but Hamid clearly heard the echoing crack of a rifle from somewhere above him at the same instant he saw Jorgo Babani's heavy torso jerk. The damned Germans must have sprinted to the ridgeline trail above him.

Young Babani slid into a crevice, apparently lost, and now Hamid was already making his way upward, choosing his cover carefully to remain unseen by the Germans on both sides of the canyon. Astonishingly the motorized column continued its slow progress; was it possible they had not heard the shot? What matter anyway, when they had field radios?

And then Hamid, hauling himself upward painfully, saw a brown fleece cap move above him. Nazi troops did not wear Balkan headgear. Nor did the collaborator Chams from the south, as a rule. One of the renegade Cossacks, perhaps, who had thrown in with Germany against Stalin. Hamid was still wondering as he eased the rifle from his shoulder and aimed. The distance was under two hundred meters and, from evidence of a few stones trickling down, the sniper was shifting position.

Hamid risked a look over his shoulder and saw Petar Murra creeping on his belly toward the unlit fuses. In another ten seconds it would be too late, for two Germans were already darting from the halted staff car toward the barricade of brush and stone. Hamid dared not wait any longer and turned his attention back to the Cossack sniper, who would have an easy shot at Murra.

As the man's upper body leaned into view, Hamid saw the homespun coat and the handlebar mustache very like his own, and suspected the worst even as he squeezed the Enfield's trigger. Shot through the lungs, the sniper vented only a grunt of surprise. Then he was tumbling from his perch, inert as a bag of grain, and slid, bounced, tumbled again to lie fifty meters above Hamid. If there were more snipers, they could pick off his BK youths on the opposite heights with ease.

Hamid knew he was bleeding again, knew also that his immediate concern must be any other snipers above him. It was beyond belief that Hoxha and Shehu had turned their coats, but the man he had shot bore every possible resemblance to another Gheg mountaineer. When general firing broke out across the narrow canyon, Hamid saw that the pair of Germans had been cut down and spotted the low-slung Murra trying to drag poor Jorgo Babani backward toward the river. And *still* those lorries continued to grind forward, idiotically, though now German troops were pouring from under the bows to seek cover among the rocks.

Near fainting, Elbas Hamid reached the fallen sniper; wrenched the torn woolen coat from the man, saw the fleece cap lying in a crevice above. He was turning the man's pockets out when the man opened his eyes, seeming not to see Hamid.

"Recount to Shehu that I tried, comrade," he said in Albanian. Did he imagine that Hamid was his rescuer?

Not so roughly now, Hamid laid the man's broken hands over his breast. "That you did," he replied.

"They must not stop the loot shipment short of the bridge," the man whispered, "after all our . . ."

Then the mountain spoke, a single deep cough that Hamid felt through his boot soles half a heartbeat before he heard it. Petar Murra had done his job, and so had Hamid. The communist sniper was no longer breathing.

Hamid ducked low as he thrust the man's belongings in coat pockets, for a hunk of stone from that explosion could brain him from five hundred meters. As echoes of muted thunder died down the canyon, he retrieved the fleece cap and began to work his way toward the top of the near ridge wearing the man's most conspicuous clothing. It might buy him a few seconds when they spotted him. Hamid surprised himself by staying conscious all the way to the ridge. He was surprised again when he found no others there.

A lone Gheg sniper, trying to foil the BK ambush? He had very nearly succeeded, but now a smoking trough yawned impassably deep in the roadbed. The only bridge on the river lay another ten kilometers or so to the northeast, and evidently some of Hoxha's men had plans for intercepting that column. So much for communist plans: Hamid lay prone in good cover and drew a bead on a German, four hundred meters across the canyon, who was climbing steadily toward the BK lads. The mystery could wait.

Hamid shot the climber first, then saw one of Murra's men darting toward the staff car and its machine gun. By now the German column had stopped, the machine gun of the Climbing Toad hammering upward at muzzle flashes from above. Hamid's next round went into the exposed fuel tank of the lead lorry, and through the scope he saw fuel pooling beneath. He needed two more rounds against the heavy chassis before he got the spark he wanted, and suddenly the lorry was wrapped in orange flame. He might burn a year's rations with that vehicle, but it would give his brother Ghegs a chance to use the staff car weapon. Hamid saw one, then another of the boys fall casualty to the tank's machine gun.

Now the rear-guard lorry was in reverse, churning dust as Hamid recalculated his windage. As he found its windshield in his scope, he saw the glass shatter from a series of impacts. He would remember to heap praise upon the boy who managed that shot—slender Nendori Iskander, no doubt, with his long-barreled Luger and its rapid fire. The lorry did not stop immediately, but turned sharply as it reversed, its rump slamming into the mountain before it stalled. Between its front fender and the fifty-meter drop to the river was enough space for a small vehicle to pass. Certainly not enough leeway for the remaining lorry, or the Climbing Toad. The tank gunner had abandoned his machine gun, probably to get that damned cannon into play, and Hamid considered firing a few rounds into the open hatch to see what ricochets might do. The burning lorry was now a pillar of fire, forcing the Albanian gunner away from the command car.

Sixteen rounds left for the Enfield, and at least thirty Nazi troops still firing at his people; he swung the rifle in search of other targets. The damnable Toad was probably not heavy enough to force its way past the stalled lorry anyway, and could not pass the others to continue forward on the narrow road.

Thin shouts from some arrogant German voice had an electric effect on the troops, who now began an orderly retreat toward the rearmost lorry. Hamid saw that some of the men were pausing as they passed the intact middle lorry, as someone tossed small objects from its tailgate. Hamid judged where the gamesman might be, behind the canvas, and fired twice. No more objects came flying from that quarter. And then the Germans astonished Hamid again.

With unspeakable courage, fully in the open, twenty-five Germans began to literally manhandle the stalled lorry, pushing it toward the river. As God was his witness, Hamid believed that they would do it. Or might have, without the steady firing from Petar Murra and the others. Hamid fired and saw his target fall in front of the rear dual wheels. Two men snatched their fallen comrade up, and Hamid shot one of them through his tunic. Germans were flopping like netted ducks on Lake Shkoder now, thanks to their following of lunatic orders. Hamid wondered whether the burning lorry carried food or ammunition. Surely not the latter, else the Germans would have fled its vicinity by now.

A figure appeared in the turret of the little Toad then, waving and shouting until a bullet caromed from the light armor. Then the figure popped below again, dropping the armored hatch. Some of the foot soldiers tried again to move the blocking lorry, but others were now hotfooting it down toward the river and imagined safety. Rounds were now cooking off from the command car's weapon, scant meters from the burning lorry; a great pity, as Hamid's men could have used that stuff.

The intact lorry was abandoned now, more Germans falling as they faced Petar's men in the rocks below. The armored Toad was now nudging a front fender of the stalled rearmost lorry, thrusting forward, tearing away dull sheet metal. Yes, the hated Toad could scrape by to safety if the lorry kept shedding parts. Then Hamid's heart leaped as a small figure emerged from the rocks and ran straight for the stalled lorry. It was Hysen Kosovo, the only grandfather of the group, not the brightest of men but one who knew his duty. Kosovo could drive a heavy lorry—and now he proved it, dumping the inert driver into the dust, leaping into the cab, moving quickly while the lorry shuddered resisting the slow passage of the Toad as it inched along, one set of Caterpillar treads a hand's breadth from the edge of the roadbed.

The lorry rumbled to life. A German soldier stood up, took dead aim at Kosovo, and fell sprawling, shot from above. The Toad, moving backward, edged around the ripped front end of the lorry to find good purchase and a clear road ahead. And then Hysen Kosovo found a forward gear, the big lorry lurching forward against the flank of the Toad, forcing its treads inexorably over the brink. Hamid trained his scope on the little tank's vision slit, wondering why the gunner had not once fired that cannon, and saw his scope fill with the top of the Toad as it began to slide down the embankment with a ponderous grace, treads still scrabbling for purchase. Old Kosovo leaped from the lorry as its dual rear wheels nosed it forward. The lorry tipped and swayed, stalled once again, poised more off the road than on with its steel chassis grounded at the precipice lip.

Finally one tread of the tank did find traction, which was a great mistake, for the tank was already tipped perilously, and in seeming slow motion, with a great roaring of its engine and screeching of iron on stone inside a cloud of dust, it rolled on its side. Then on its top, then a complete roll, then once again, coming to rest on its side not ten meters from the riverbank. Hamid wanted to add his voice to the cheers from across the canyon, but could not make his throat work properly. The BK band of Elbas Hamid had never bested a Climbing Toad before.

By the time Hamid got the distinctly nervous mules across the river again, the last few rounds had been fired through the heads of wounded Germans. For a wonder, his wound had quit bleeding. For a second wonder, the BK had lost only four men—not two men and two boys, for the least of their snipers had to be considered a man—but four *men,* in this strange battle. For any but Hamid's tiny forgotten group, the spoils would have been worth those losses.

The partisans found that the burned-out lorry had been lightly loaded with iron rations, a half-dozen soldiers, and upwards of a hundred paintings. The old canvas and richly carved, lacquered wooden frames had burned so merrily that little more than carbonized sticks remained. The Iskander boy, who often sketched on whatever was handy, seemed ready to weep. "Stolen from our cathedrals and museums," he said with a sweep of his arm. "Why did the merciful God choose us as the destroyers of our own fine works?"

"It was lost to us either way," Murra shrugged. "Look on the bright side, nephew." He nodded toward the undamaged lorry, in which more rations and cartons of nine-millimeter ammunition were being counted. Hearing an exclamation, Petar Murra stumped hurriedly to the uptilted tailgate of Kosovo's lorry in time to see old Kosovo goggling at his own fists, or rather their contents. He held thick banded stacks of paper money. A heavy metal chest, cinched to tiedowns on the bed of the lorry, held a man's weight in crisp new bills. No doubt the German troops had drooled at that cargo squatting among them.

Petar Murra made a gesture and Kosovo tossed him one bundle. Hamid limped over and tugged a few bills from the packet. "Greek currency," he murmured. "All freshly minted, therefore all false. And yet . . ."

"Yet we could buy new guns from Hoxha's men, who need not know if we wrinkle the bills up a bit," Petar said. To Kosovo he added, "Pass it out to our men, let them carry a bundle apiece. The rest? Cache it in oilcloth, Hysen, and do not forget where you put it."

The burial squad, composed of younger members, were covering their dead friends with hardscrabble, laying their comrades to rest in the trench they had blown in the roadway. Elbas Hamid knelt at the trench a moment, crossed himself with a prayer for their valiant souls, and found it very difficult to rise afterward.

Pandeli Toma, nearing manhood and almost as tall as

Hamid, steadied his leader. "You might lighten your pockets, uncle," he teased gently, feeling the heavy mass of Hamid's coat pocket.

Hamid sighed and pulled two clips of Russian ammunition from the pocket. None of their weapons used such rounds, though the communist shock brigades had clips to spare. Hamid grinned and dropped the useless ammunition at the roadside. It was one of Shehu's men he had shot; let Mehmet Shehu wonder which of his thieving bands had waylaid thirty-eight Germans and a Climbing Toad! And stole more drachmae than a man can count away from the oh-so-glorious revolution. The BK had won a double triumph this day. Had it been worth the lives of four republicans?

In the other coat pocket he had thrust coins, a clasp knife, and a tattered oblong that had once been a man's wallet. He cared little for the dead man's name, or the browntone photo of a woman and two children, but the folded letter was something special. It seemed to be only a brief handwritten letter from a kinsman, but Hamid remembered a fragment of lore from the days when the BK was on better terms with Hoxha's brigades. He searched for certain words, and was not disappointed; the kinsman had wished a better tomorrow for *rintje*.

The names of two Albanian communist organizations, at the start of this war, had been Work, *Puna,* and Youth, *Rintje.* Elbas Hamid knew a primitive passport when he saw one: he held a free passage for himself through communist lines.

A curiously muffled shout from below drew the men's attention. It was Koci Ahmeti, a usually taciturn fellow whose head now poked from the hatch of the upturned Toad. He was struggling to pass some heavy object to the Kraga boy, and he was laughing. Hamid did not feel able to climb down so far, and sat at the verge watching as the youths hauled something very like a folded blanket from the hatch. A blanket of brown canvas, stitched with many pockets—or perhaps a new type of antipersonnel device filled with explosives.

"Are our nephews so eager to trigger a land mine?" Hamid's question sobered them.

Pandeli Toma lifted one end of the canvas with both

hands. "Can explosives be so heavy?" But he spoke to the Kraga boy, who drew his little Gheg knife and worried carefully at one of the stitched pockets while, from inside the tank, Ahmeti leaned out to watch.

Petar Murra was calling orders to the others, draining fuel from the upturned lorry to fill the tank of the one good vehicle. Yes, the path is now clear for us to drive that prize back with our wounded, including myself, thought Hamid—and then all those thoughts left him as young Toma drew a single, flat, finger-thick rod the length of a pistol barrel from the canvas. It gleamed as if afire, challenging the afternoon sun with its own burnished yellow.

"Toss it to me," Hamid called.

"I cannot," said Pandeli Toma, whose youthful energy Hamid envied as the boy bounded up the stones toward his leader. Toma placed the little bar in Hamid's hand. Hamid knew instantly, even before he had cut into the soft metal, that he was holding a bar of purest gold. It had been crudely minted, probably melted down in desperate haste by Nazi pigs who could not haul heavy religious artifacts intact. The benevolent God only knew how many of them lay in that tank. The sniper had spoken of a loot shipment. Elbas Hamid drew a deep breath and began calling orders.

Chapter 2

THE Climbing Toad, as it turned out, had never fired its cannon because the cannon had no ammunition. The interior racks for cannon rounds, instead, had been filled with rolled canvas blankets sewn with hundreds upon hundreds of finger-sized gold bars. Each blanket weighed as much as a child of ten, and over thirty of those blankets had been entrusted to the men in the tank. Some of the blankets had flown loose during the furious rollovers of the Toad, and had crushed the occupants like bugs; no wonder Ahmeti had laughed. The two dead men bore identification of the Sicherheitsdienst, Nazi Party Intelligence, which explained why they wore excellent civilian clothing of the sort once boasted by King Zog and foreign sportsmen in Albania.

Now Elbas Hamid guessed why the Toad had been sandwiched in the column for supposed safety. The men in the tank had authority, but not experience in mountain warfare tactics. When Hamid recalled the dying sniper's mutterings, he decided that Hoxha's well-fed communists were still waiting for that column—and they almost certainly knew of the gold. For a ton of gold, Shehu or his general, Hoxha, would murder every BK sympathizer in Albania, no matter that they all fought a common enemy. It was all very well to intercept a ton of gold, but what were they to do with the infernally heavy stuff? They numbered only seven now, plus the three tired mules. And the lorry, which Kosovo could drive, but— Hamid dreaded the wasted time, but called a council anyway.

While the Iskander boy climbed a hundred meters as sentry, and the other youths lugged brown canvas blankets up to be strapped against the lorry's bed, Hamid conferred with his adults. He began by telling of the communist sniper; it would be suicide to proceed north. There was only one contrivance capable of moving that gold: the lorry. And only one direction it should be driven. The lorry would quickly outdistance the mules, said Murra. Not so, Kosovo replied: with no turn-around for several kilometers back, the lorry must be driven a long distance in reverse and would take God's own sweet time, not to mention swilling fuel. The mules would actually be faster on the road during that initial period. They might cover twenty kilometers in an hour's time.

Petar Murra, who had survived strafings, hated and feared aircraft as few others could. He worried that the Nazis might send a Fieseler patrol craft winging overhead to check the column's progress at any time, and his fear was reasonable. Further, for all they knew, more of Hoxha's men might be cantering along the ridgelines now in anxious patrol. It was agreed, then, that they must have the gold cached in some secure spot within the hour. But what spot?

It was Koci Ahmeti, a cart driver in prewar days, who provided the solution. "As a boy, I once brought supplies to a copper mine ten kilometers down the river from here, before this road was widened," he said.

"The first place they will search," Murra scolded.

"It was an open pit," said Ahmeti. He added quickly, "But I lost a cartload over the precipice once, and nearly fell into a cave while retrieving my goods. Two kilometers or so farther from here than the mine."

Hamid: "A large cave?"

Ahmeti, dryly: "I was hurried, brother." Even Murra chuckled at this. "But it was certainly large enough for our purpose, and the entrance was well obscured by green brush growing in the cleft."

Hamid nodded. Water trickling from slits in the mountain often supported spots of greenery on brown slopes. "Are you certain you can find it again?"

"If I cannot, are we any the worse off?"

It was a good point. Hamid saw Petar Murra's slight shrug and nod, and slapped his hands against his knees. "We have delayed enough, brothers. Make sure our packs are all stowed in the lorry. We can carry the false Greek money after all. Send a boy ahead with the mules. With luck, Kosovo will overtake them past the turnaround. The rest of us can ride in the lorry."

Murra insisted on riding the lead mule himself, with the Kraga boy on the last mule for an added pair of eyes. It was not necessary to add that if Murra met with gunfire, the boy might still return to warn them. In another five minutes, with a bad moment when Kosovo scraped past a tailgate, they had left the scene of their ambush. Murra and the boy were soon out of sight, their mules trotting stolidly ahead. At least the smoke from the burned lorry no longer signaled against the sky.

The turnaround appeared within twenty minutes, sooner than they had expected, yet something in Hamid kept his nerves aquiver. If one sniper had watched them, another might be doing so even now. Yet they dared not wait for darkness. Hysen Kosovo cursed and jockeyed the great vehicle around, peering past the remaining shards of windshield, and then pursued the mules with repeated clashings of gears. A few minutes later, Ahmeti pointed to a bowl-shaped depression across the narrow canyon and slightly below them. The tailings pile from the mine featured a few ancient timbers and gleaming stones of a faint greenish cast. A bit farther, Petar Murra hailed them with his familiar two-note whistle. He had seen the mine too. The mules were hidden nearby with the boy.

Ahmeti did not want anyone slowing him down, as he put it, when he descended what was now a two-hundred-meter slope to the river. From below, he would have a much better chance to spot that cave as he proceeded downriver. Hamid agreed because they could keep Ahmeti in view. Murra chose the Iskander and Toma youths to make solitary patrols in both directions on mules along the near-side ridgeline trail. Gunfire from their heights would mean trouble. Murra rode the third mule as rear guard, stopping often to study the ridges. Hysen Kosovo drove slowly with Hamid beside him, and the Kraga boy perched atop the cab hanging on to canvas. The boy's young eyes could track Ahmeti in early evening shadow far better than his elders could.

Several times, the boy tapped his boots on the cab roof to indicate that Ahmeti had fallen behind, perhaps to study the slope. Each time, Kosovo switched off the engine to save fuel. They had covered at least three more kilometers at a fast walking pace, and the river was now farther below, when the boy swung down to the roadbed, waving from the lip of the road. Kosovo killed the engine and sighed. Hamid eased himself down as though his backside were fine porcelain and was joined by Murra at the overlook.

The boy sighted along his pointing finger. "He is climbing—there," he said. "Should we unload now?"

"Not until we know what our brother has found. Memory is tricky after so many years," Hamid said. He could see several patches of green dotting the slope below, outwardly no different from a thousand other patches on many a mountain slope.

Petar Murra peered upward. "That young lackwit Nendori should have signaled us if he has kept pace," he muttered. High above, the sun still splashed against brown crags. Their signal mirrors were ideal for moments like this, yet no repeated bright dot-dash, their "all clear" signal, reached them. A rapid sequence of flashes would warn of danger, and a few other sequences completed their repertoire. To receive no flashes at all might mean nothing; or it could be the worst possible news. "If this good beast is up to it, I should reconnoiter above," the stalwart Murra judged.

Hamid juggled priorities. Koci Ahmeti faced a fifteen-minute climb to reach them even if he found the cave. Those canvas blankets could be dragged downward two at a time with ease—though not by the wounded Hamid. Two men and a youth on those slopes, with Hamid watching helplessly from the lorry: yes, because Petar Murra was correct. They had to know what was going on above. "Do not spare the mirror, I beg you," Hamid smiled, and clapped his friend's shoulder. Murra and his tired mule were gone moments later, following an animal trail upward.

Within ten minutes it became clear that Ahmeti had found his cave, for the men could now see him clambering up the slope, then detouring much nearer to disappear a second time. Without a word, Elbas Hamid crawled into the lorry's bed and began to shove blankets of treasure off the tailgate. The treasure, a full ton of gold, lay at the verge and Hamid was pilfering their packs for cordage when Ahmeti appeared thirty meters below them.

Koci Ahmeti's face was ashen as he leaned on a great boulder and called upward. "Not one cave," he said, panting, "but two. The second is there," he added, nodding upriver, saving his arms. "Perhaps the same cave. There is room," he gasped out, and then dropped his head, his chest heaving.

Even a Gheg has limits, thought Hamid with affection. He himself, for example, could not even do much work. As he thought on it, echoes of a sharp report clattered through the clear, thin air.

The boy pointed upward. The sun was still touching the ridge, and a rapid volley of flashes met their gaze from perhaps a kilometer behind them.

The mirror had made his decision for him. "Drag it to the nearest cave and hide it well," he said to Ahmeti. To both of them he said, "We must not disturb the turf and stones near the verge. Hoxha's trackers are Ghegs." And with that, he hefted a canvas roll and heaved it as far as he could.

The roll struck heavily, then slid to a stop near Ahmeti where the great boulder detained the occasional small rockslide. On loose rock such a means of lowering this cargo could easily start a rockslide. But turf anchored the stones. It was primitive, but workable. Old Kosovo tried to copy Hamid's heave with poor success but Kosovo and the boy together, swinging each blanket as children swing a playmate by hands and feet, exceeded Hamid's distance. And after every toss, they glanced upward and back along the winding scar of road.

The boy and Kosovo then picked their way carefully over stones to reach Ahmeti, who had recovered enough to carry a canvas roll over his shoulder as he descended, angling upriver slightly. Hamid stroked his mustache and smiled to see the boy shouldering a roll equally well, while Kosovo followed with difficulty. Hamid limped to the cab and retrieved his scoped rifle, then sat down between boulders where he could see both the ridge and the returning laborers. No vehicles crawled into sight on the few segments of road he could see. But anyone who sighted them would remember where the lorry had stopped. Hamid wished that he could drive a lorry, and cursed uncertainty.

The boy was first to return, wasting too much energy in his leaps upward, and Hamid cautioned him about it, ending with, "Could you heave the rolls down to them, nephew?"

"I could try," the boy answered, and hurried across the stones above some point Hamid could not see. The boy called down to his fellows, then hefted the roll which arced from sight. A moment later the boy was selecting another packweight in gold, perspiring and beaming. "This is faster," he panted, and hurried off again as Hamid scanned the heights to no avail.

The next shots that sounded along the canyon seemed no nearer, but suggested battle: a single round, several rapid reports that could have been of heavier caliber, then more reports at irregular intervals. It was over in ten seconds or so, and Hamid snugged himself into the rocks with his English rifle.

The boy gave no indication that he had heard anything, save that he was now carrying a roll over each shoulder. Kosovo came hurrying back as quickly as old knees would allow and did as the boy was doing. From their timing, Hamid judged that the upper cave could not be more than a hundred meters below the road and that Ahmeti must be near, or above, the entrance.

And now a rider appeared high on the animal trail, repeating a whistled note that was Petar Murra's signature. He was not sparing the mule. Hamid peered through his scope hoping to see boys following, knowing that the light would soon be too dim for his scope to be very effective. Exhaustion or injury made Murra lean so far that Hamid feared he would fall.

It was probably exhaustion that precipitated the tragedy below, as well. The boy had disappeared toward the cave and now Old Kosovo staggered off with the last blanket but, instead of heaving it down, elected to carry it below. Hamid glanced up to see Murra only a few hundred meters away, and it was at that moment when he heard Kosovo's despairing cry.

Hamid left the rifle where Murra could use it and ignored the pain near his rump as he moved down the treacherous slope. He saw no evidence that trackers could use; indeed, he saw no one at all until he picked his way to the point from which those heavy canvas blankets had arced from sight. Here he paused, indecisive, on the brink of a slope that was almost a sheer drop for thirty meters or so. An agile man might negotiate it—but he could see the boy, face etched with terror, clinging fast to the brink of another drop-off below, swinging one leg up even as Koci Ahmeti scrambled forward to grasp the boy by the armpits.

Hamid turned and called up to Petar Murra, whose right sleeve was dark with blood. "Trouble here! How much time have we?"

Murra spat dust. "Minutes at most; Iskander and Toma died under communist fire, but the advance patrol is in hell."

"Can you drive that lorry, brother?"

"Yes, but I do not understand those levers."

"Leave the mule and my rifle; drive away as fast as you might, before someone sees the lorry stopped here. Scatter handfuls of that Greek money a kilometer up the road; it should give them pause."

"And you?" Murra's tone was full of doubt.

But Hamid, despite his wound, was already picking hand- and footholds on his way down. "If we find the lorry nosed against the mountain ten kilometers distant, we shall whistle for you. If not, we shall meet you at the Drin bivouac in five days. You must be the hare Shehu's hounds will chase, brother Murra.''

Hamid heard Petar Murra call Godspeed to the four of them and continued, stumbling like a man full of raki. But there were no longer four partisans to cache the gold. Hamid very nearly dropped into the narrow dark slit of the cave entrance before he saw it, and by that time the Kraga boy had dragged himself to it as well.

Ahmeti had already started to skirt around the precipice which had nearly claimed the boy, but stopped, crossed himself, and shook his head. "Ah, Hysen," he called softly, "I said that you would dare once too often." Retracing, he nodded below and said to Hamid, "Old goats become brittle, brother. Hysen Kosovo has splashed his brains on the mountain."

"My fault," groaned the boy, unlacing his left boot to study the swelling there. "I led him to it."

Hamid crawled to the precipice; saw for himself that old Kosovo, all but hidden in a crevice, had split his skull open in his fall; crawled back to the high, narrow opening into which Ahmeti had already disappeared. Hamid blinked as he moved into the cool dimness and through a pungent odor of decay that was not entirely unpleasant. He paused, hearing the struggle of an engine as it labored to start. Twice Murra stalled the vehicle, and then they heard it roar away, and Hamid met the boy's frown with, "Petar is drawing our enemies away."

The mouth of the slit in the mountain was floored with the debris of many small rockslides, but a few paces back there was only stone. Hamid found the roof higher, and heard faint chitterings echo from somewhere above. The wall nearest him was crusted with some chalky substance. He sniffed his hand: bat dung. He imagined the tiny creatures, made loathsome by legend, roosting for ages in crevices above, their droppings gradually building on ledges until the stuff coursed down the stone. And yes, at the foot of the wall lay a trove of bat guano, slowly making its way back into the mountain.

Now Hamid could see Koci Ahmeti on his knees, up to his armpits in a hundred times a thousand years' deposit of dung, scooping into the damp guano, sneezing and cursing as he worked. Hamid: "Is there no better cache?"

Ahmeti: "Can we take the time to find one?"

Of course Ahmeti was right. The entire cache of gold would take up no more space than a coffin, and who would ever think to search for it here? Hamid agreed, dragging the canvas blankets near Ahmeti, and within minutes they had deposited the gold in Ahmeti's trench. Hamid knew he was taking an extra risk, but he slashed open several pockets of the last blanket and pocketed five more of the little gold bars. It was short work to shove the grainy dung back, to smooth it by hand, and to spread the excess along the vein of it that time and seasonal rains had created.

The Kraga boy, by that time, was on hands and knees with them, stifling his sneezes. Hamid stood up with a great effort. "Petar has left my rifle and his mule on the road. We must use them both if we are ever to see the Drin bivouac again."

They were all filthy with bat guano by now and, as they stood once more at the entrance in early evening light, Koci Ahmeti made a joke that might be roughly translated as nightsoil and night toil.

"Here," Hamid said, handing each of them two of the gold bars. "Do not imagine that this is a reward for that miserable jape, brother Koci. If we are captured, those bars are your death warrants."

The boy hesitated, then offered his gold to the men. "I cannot walk," he said. "I shall be safe here, and can guard the gold. In a week, perhaps . . ."

Koci Ahmeti fixed the boy with a glare. "Forget your penance, Pal Kraga. Hysen Kosovo's end was not your doing." He put his shoulder under the boy's armpit and began urging him forward, adding to Hamid, "The boy tried to catch Hysen like a bag of beans. He nearly succeeded, and could have died in the effort."

Hamid, encumbered only by his wound, was first back to the road and offered a callused hand to the boy. The trail above seemed innocent but that could change on the instant.

He retrieved his rifle and the pitiful spare clip beside it; handed both to Ahmeti. "Have you enough wind to walk, brother?"

"If this poor beast will let me ride his tail," Ahmeti said, and helped Hamid onto the mule. The boy flopped across the mule's back, grunting in pain as he arranged himself behind Hamid. In a moment they were moving up the road at a fast walk, Hamid and the boy riding double, Ahmeti grasping the mule's tail to assist him up the gentle incline of roadbed.

They had not gone a single kilometer when the boy, watching behind as Hamid watched the heights above, gave his warning. "Deploy, deploy," he called, slithering from the mule. Hamid responded instantly, sliding off the other side, and saw Ahmeti, off balance as he released the mule's tail, spin and snake the rifle sling from his shoulder. A single horseman in homespun clothing, over a hundred meters behind them in the road, had dropped his reins to steady his aim. His first round took away the throat of Koci Ahmeti, who sprawled backward and uttered dreadful gargling sounds as he died. Hamid, using the mule as a shield, found his big Gheg revolver and backed into the rocks lining the roadway.

The boy never lost his resolve, even at the last. On hands and knees, he scrambled for the scoped rifle lying at Ahmeti's side, grasped it, rolled aside an instant before a rifle bullet horneted past him. "Climb, uncle," he piped softly in a voice high with fear. "Have I not the right to face my accuser?"

Hamid knew that his sidearm was useless at this distance. The enemy rider dismounted with an athlete's bound and disappeared into the rocks. Hamid's mule trotted several meters in the wrong direction, back toward the sniper, and reared as the next shot tore into its breast. Its hindquarters failed first and the mule sat for a long moment in a ridiculous position, forelegs stiff and quivering, before it fell sidelong in the dust. A few kicks, and it was still.

The Kraga boy seemed determined to die like his Gheg ancestors. "Seek cover," Hamid hissed; "have I taught you nothing?"

In reply the boy snapped the rifle to his shoulder, evidently spotting a target—an experienced target which had spotted him first. Hamid saw the impact squarely in the boy's breast, and the dust that flew from his jacket before he was slammed backward by the slug against stones that should have been his shield. The boy pitched sideways and fell as if his body had turned to gelatin. Hamid drew himself down into the rocks as far as he could, his revolver cocked, and listened for telltale signs. When he risked a look between stones he saw blood leaking from the boy's nose and mouth. He had seen it before when a Gheg's great heart had been blown apart within him, burst like a melon.

Then, in utter disbelief at first, Hamid heard the clop of a shod horse, moving nearer at a casual trot. Perhaps it had shied from the gunfire. But peering from his cover with his chin in the dirt, Hamid saw that the horseman had remounted and was approaching openly like an idiot, his Russian rifle lying across his saddle pommel. Hamid's only possible conclusion was that Hoxha's man had been so intent on poor Ahmeti that he failed to see two riders on the mule. Which made Hamid's job absurdly simple.

Hamid waited until the man was dismounting near Ahmeti's body, glancing toward the body of the boy in suspicion, and taking slow two-handed aim, Hamid shot him through the stomach. The man staggered, tried to bring his weapon up, and took Hamid's next round through the cheekbone. He fell across Koci Ahmeti without a twitch.

Alone now with no responsibility to any but himself, Elbas Hamid took no further risks of pursuit. He took the man's rifle and limped to the waiting horse, a lathered dun gelding. He moaned as his left foot found its stirrup, then set off at a trot toward the lorry. With enemy coat and hat, horse and rifle, he might survive nightfall.

Ten minutes later, he rounded a bend to see the lorry stopped dead in the road a kilometer farther on. It was not nosed into the mountain and it swarmed with men dressed in the partisan fashion. Hamid led the gelding back a ways, wedged its reins between boulders, and moved through the twilight taking his time, using what cover he could. He drew near enough to hear bits of conversation, in Albanian, and saw two men roll the body of Petar Murra down and down toward the river. Communists were not religious men given to burials— but then, Hamid himself had left several good Catholics lying dead and unburied this day. A man with a scarlet armband and a holstered pistol tossed something and caught it, talking to one of his fellows, and Hamid recognized one of the little gold bars. Oh yes, they knew that Petar Murra had seen those canvas blankets. What they could not know was that one tough, determined BK man was still alive to tell of it.

Elbas Hamid made his way back to the gelding, glad of the arrogance that kept Hoxha's men from sending a swarm of sentries up onto the heights. It was dark when his mount crossed the ridgeline trail, but he knew it would have been insanity to use that trail. He forced the gelding onward until he could not see beyond the next silhouetted crag, and only then did he dismount. He buried his two gold bars beneath a stone, on the off-chance that someone would find him lying on a stone bed with reins in his hands. The next morning he pocketed the two bars. Now he had a safe-conduct pass and a story: he had taken the bars from one of the BK republicans after a firefight the previous day. With half-truths and that safe-passage paper, he might yet reach Albanian lowlands.

He showed that paper twice during the next five days, but never had to submit to a search once. While moving toward the west alone, Hamid entertained himself with fantasies of wealth, while admitting to himself that they were fantasies. He harbored no illusions about retrieving that gold anytime soon. It might, in fact, lie covered in batshit for all eternity. At least he had denied it to Nazi and communist alike, unless he was interrogated and broke under torture. He resolved to put the hoard out of his mind until some future day when Albania was once again a God-fearing republic, free of domination by Serbs and Russians. Yes, it was best simply to forget it.

PART TWO

AUGUST 1944–MAY 1985

Chapter 3

NO one who has seen a ton of gold disappear into a deposit of bat guano is likely, ever, to forget it. Elbas Hamid's dreams were haunted by the stuff for the next year, and these visitations increased as he grew increasingly certain that the Nazis would not return. His days were increasingly filled with the living nightmare of the new—thoroughly communist—Albania. Hamid found that his cousins had been hunted down and butchered by communist troops in the search for him, because someone in Enver Hoxha's ranks had made a careful postmortem of Hamid's ambush on the Fierze. Hamid's group had been the only BK band still operating in that region. His wife, under protection of the traditional *bessa,* had nonetheless died in a mortar attack on his village near Dibre. He turned his face away from the village and vowed to remember its ashes.

Floating through the Albanian lowlands posing as a ragged, deaf-mute Tosk amid a human flood of the displaced and homeless, Hamid lost thirty pounds and this, with the peppery wisp of beard, added years to his appearance. In a way, starvation helped him, for he bore little resemblance to the man he had been only a year previous. He soon learned that his name graced a wanted list for crimes against his own state. Perhaps it was a fair charge, he reflected, while making his way down the coast toward the island of Corfu. Albania's emergent leader was none other than General Enver Hoxha, and Hoxha's only god was Stalin. Hamid heard that Mehmet Shehu had also survived the murderous infighting, still Hoxha's closest ally within Albania's Stalinist government.

Hamid did not know precisely how Shehu had managed to explain the loss of that gold, but any bright Albanian could have guessed. Mehmet Shehu would execute the survivors of his own patrol and plausibly deny that the gold ever existed, while seeking the plunder by every means possible. If Hamid were identified before he found sanctuary with the West, he would lose his fingernails and teeth during Shehu's interrogation. He vowed not to be taken alive and kept his hawk nose turned toward Corfu, where rumor placed several ships of the British Fleet. At night, wrapped in his communist rags, Hamid sometimes fondled his two finger-sized gold bars as if they were his own private parts.

At some point in his travels—Hamid could not recall when—he began to discount his original idea of pinpointing the gold for republican Albania. There was no such place. If Hamid was any judge, Albania was already becoming a Stalinist hell, and the exiled King Zog had a gypsy's chance of returning in anything other than chains. Besides, the communists were right about Zog and his retinue: they had always squandered money like drunken Turks.

Whose gold was it, then? Those hastily minted bars, hundreds upon hundreds of them sewn into rotting canvas pads, were anonymous. They belonged to the man who held them. Many nights, Elbas Hamid dreamed of a shepherd seeking shelter in that cave from some wild Dinaric storm, a man as penniless as Hamid himself; or, equally likely, perhaps a lad no older than the valiant, sacrificed youths' of the little partisan group. Bat guano made excellent fertilizer, and it was not unlikely that the faceless shepherd of his dreams might try to sell the stuff. And then, when the shovel struck something curiously like a leaden blanket within the stinking muck . . . It was at this point when Elbas Hamid would waken, soaked in perspiration despite cooling breezes off the Adriatic. If his entire band of partisans had paid for that hoard with their lives, then by rights it truly belonged to the survivor.

Hamid told himself that when he retrieved the gold, he would seek out the kin of his murdered partisans and share the wealth. It was exactly the thing a good Albanian Catholic needed to add righteous fervor to his mission. He would never forget their names—for that matter, he had seen some of them posted in listings of "enemies of the people" as if they were still alive, and he knew that Mehmet Shehu and Enver Hoxha would never forget, either. It was almost a comfort to know, absolutely and unerringly, the nature of one's enemy. Shehu was a Tosk but still an Albanian to his marrows, and the loss of that gold to a rival group would impoverish the man's very soul. Not even a cash repayment of equal value would slake his thirst for vengeance. That was the way of the born Albanian fighter—and both Shehu and Hoxha were certainly that.

And so was Elbas Hamid, who waded out into the Strait of Corfu on a chilly night in 1945 with a stolen bicycle inner tube wrapped twice around his almost meatless ribs for flotation. The lights across the strait were those of larger vessels than anything communist Albania owned. If he could avoid a bullet from the shoreline patrol, he had an even chance of a favorable current to sweep him to the West with its humane and laughably naive ways.

According to records of the British Secret Intelligence Service, one Elbas Hamid of the republican Balli Kombetar became the three hundred forty-seventh partisan to be positively identified by the British SIS on Corfu. Two American OSS men listened carefully to Hamid's story of his odyssey; one of them had recently made a similar escape, and judged Hamid's account accurate in all respects. Here was no double agent sent to the West, but a man they might use in the near future. The Albanian received decent clothing, excellent food, and a star ranking for his knowledge of the Dinaric Alps. SIS records did not reveal anything about a ton of gold bars for the very good reason that Hamid never mentioned them.

Soon, word reached Tirana that Corfu harbored a time bomb of Western influence, and the mining of Corfu's waters was only the first of Enver Hoxha's gentle persuasions. Meanwhile, the SIS and OSS treated their Albanians well, kept them separated in teams, and trained them for missions back into their homeland. Elbas Hamid regained twenty pounds and improved his mastery of Greek while disporting with the serving wenches of Brit-managed bistros on Corfu. He always seemed a bit distant, with the reserve of a wealthy man fallen on hard times. For this was, of course, exactly how Hamid viewed the matter. More than once while in transit, he smeared grease on those gleaming golden bars and inserted them, oh, so tenderly, past his anus into the large bowel. What the spy-runners did not know would not hurt them. And it only hurt Hamid when he sat, or coughed while carrying those golden suppositories.

His caution served him well. He managed to avoid his first scheduled SIS mission, to Durres, thanks to a rotting molar which he had treated himself for a year, ignoring the discomfort in the Gheg way, lancing the swelling now and then to drain the pus from his gums. He merely claimed excruciating pain on the eve of the mission and was getting expert dental care on Corfu at the moment his team deflated its rubber boat a few kilometers up the Albanian coast from Durres. A great pity, but Durres was too far from the canyons of the upper Fierze River.

The team may have been intercepted on the beach by pure accident; in any case, one of the men escaped. It began to seem that Albania had more armed coast-watchers than she had coast. The SIS sacrificed several infiltrator teams before admitting that it might be easier to bring them in from the Pindus Mountains of Greece, or as chutists dropped by night.

When Corfu came under direct attack by Albania, the SIS pulled its operation back to Malta, near Sicily. Elbas Hamid became one of many Albanians groomed for espionage there. He was viewed as something of a prize by case officer Fred Taylor of the newly formed CIA, who took Hamid's easy smile for easy friendship and imagined that they were close.

Hamid studied hard to excel. Every time he parachuted from a war-weary Lysander training plane while Taylor watched,

Hamid told himself he was jumping toward a pit of bat guano.
He never refused a jump and that, too, went into Taylor's
reports. When the CIA urged the mission to Lezha, Hamid
made certain that his health was good. He knew the town well,
and the mission required infiltrators to seek allies among Gheg
tribesmen nearby while dispensing the good will and the better
antibiotics of the West. And with all that time on his hands, a
mountain man might do a bit of hunting up the canyons of the
Fierze.

If Fred Taylor was successful, Hamid would be picked up
by a dead-black Lysander on a given night near Lezha. If
Hamid was entirely successful, he would retire among friendly
Italians in Venice or Trieste and diddle his toes in the Adriatic
for the next thirty years without once thinking of Taylor.

Hamid did not know that Trieste was of equal importance
to the CIA as a jump-off point for Western teams into Albania.
But someone in London knew altogether too much about the
SIS plans in Malta. His name was Harold "Kim" Philby,
whose work in British Intelligence included a detailed over-
view of the Balkans. Some of the Old Boys in the SIS already
knew that Kim Philby was enamored of other men. They
would not learn for years that he was also enamored of the
Soviet Union, the highest-placed Soviet agent ever unmasked
in British Intelligence. It would be years before a CIA man
would smoke out the Soviet mole in MI-6 and see Philby
scuttling to Moscow. Meanwhile, Albania rolled up Western
teams almost at will, forewarned of every detail by Philby,
sometimes including the original names of the team members.

A great deal of intelligence work is done thousands of miles
from points of contact, as Philby proved. Some of that work is
no more dangerous than clipping news releases, and fitting
snippets of information together to see if it makes a realistic
picture. With CIA help, the SIS often fed selected releases to
its Albanian teams to keep them current on Balkan affairs.

Two days before his mission to Lezha, Elbas Hamid read
a copy of a clipping which had been translated carefully into
Albanian from the original Italian. The SIS knew that an
Italian dateline was more likely to be believable to an Albanian

than one from any Balkan country. Indeed, they sometimes faked such bulletins. This one, however, had been honestly translated.

PESCARA, Italy (*La Bandiera*, 17 March 1952)—Italian officials today delayed their response to demands by Albania's First Party Secretary, Enver Hoxha, for the return of three Albanian nationals. The men rowed to Pescara and freedom on Wednesday last, after their escape from an Albanian fishing vessel.

The escaped men, whose names are being withheld, claim that they prefer exile in Italy but would accept relocation to Titoist Yugoslavia, where a half million ethnic Albanians now reside beyond the reach of Hoxha's stern rule. Since the breach between Tito's Yugoslavia and the U.S.S.R. in 1948, relations between Yugoslavia and Albania, a Soviet client nation, have approached armed conflict.

The fishermen told reporters in Pescara that they hoped to trade knowledge of a new Soviet submarine base at Albania's Vlore seaport, for unlimited Italian visas. Informed sources say that this news would certainly ensure firing squads for the three men if they are ever returned. In the past two years, the Albanian news agency has reported summary trials and executions of several hundred Albanians after attempts to escape that small, self-exiled nation. The attempt to flee is itself an act of treason, according to Albania's head of the Sigurimi secret police, Mehmet Shehu.

A decision on the fate of the fishermen is expected soon. Officials hinted that emigration to some other Western nation is always a possibility, in keeping with similar policies recently instated by Yugoslavia's Marshal Tito.

Elbas Hamid read between the lines. The British and Fred Taylor wished to reassure him that, no matter how he managed to get back out of Albania, he could expect to hoist a glass of raki in a Maltese bistro again. Lysanders had been known to miss a landing zone, but Shehu's secret police had been known to miss a briskly moving target. All the same, Hamid decided to keep that poisoned needle Taylor had issued him where he could get to it at any moment. Taylor had given him wonderfully forged documents, but Taylor would never grasp the full significance of Hamid's capture. The only men who could grasp it, thought Hamid, were Mehmet Shehu and perhaps Enver Hoxha himself, if Shehu had been ass enough to share the true story of the stolen gold with his leader.

Two nights later, Elbas Hamid—with the gold bars taped to his left wrist—and two others dropped from the sky into broken country near Lezha. The aircraft made it back. None of the team was so lucky. Fred Taylor read the strident news release from Tirana a week later and knew that this was one item he would not pass to his Albanian teams in training.

TIRANA, Albania (People's News Agency, 30 March 1952)—Minister Mehmet Shehu of the Sigurimi today announced the liquidation of a band of emigre criminals near Lezha after their prompt detection by decent citizens. Minister Shehu displayed a pointed suicide needle taken from the throat of a traitor believed to be one Elbas Hamid, noting that this was typical of the despicable monarchist warmongers of the West. The two other criminals were shot, as all spies can expect to be shot, while trying to escape.

Fred Taylor managed to forget Hamid's ready smile in a week. He needed longer to reconcile the fact that those goddamned Sigurimi gumshoes knew that the team had come from the West. But that needle of Hamid's had been smeared with an alkaloid used exclusively—well, almost exclusively—by the Yugoslavs. How had Shehu's people known of this added deception? Maybe poor Hamid had talked first, and had used the needle later. Hell, maybe the Sigurimi had used it on him! Or maybe Elbas Hamid had been turned; was in fact still smiling and spilling his guts freely to everyone in Tirana who would listen. That last scenario seemed very unlikely; it clashed with everything Taylor knew about Ghegs.

Somewhere, thought Taylor, the bloody Sigurimi could have an agent in place under deep cover; a mole far beneath the cricket grounds of Brit Intelligence, or maybe even inside the Company, the CIA itself. Probably the Company, he hazarded; the Brits are lots more experienced at this shit than we are. And are they ever fond of saying so!

Another year and another ninety staunch Albanians were expended before Fred Taylor received a change of station to Trieste, a city spanning both sides of the Italo-Yugoslav border. He was damned glad of it, for now he was no longer forced to coordinate every last detail with the Brit MI-6. By the end of 1954, Taylor and his Chief of Station actually had a few small Albanian successes to crow about. They weren't throwing the commies out of Albania yet, not by a damn sight, but they'd run a dozen singleton agents in and back out of the place with only nominal losses—which was to say, fifty percent. By comparison, aside from a few local Albanian uprisings quickly quelled by Sigurimi gunfire, the big Anglo-American operation in Malta had achieved only the death of tough anticommunist partisans: nearly three hundred of them since 1948, if the horrendous truth were ever known.

And as long as he was mulling about truth, Taylor mentally stirred what he had learned of Trieste. After endless postwar wrangling, the city had been split between Italy and Yugoslavia. The truth was that it worked like old people fucked: a spasm here, a withdrawal there, and nobody wanted to think about tomorrow. In Trieste's Zone A, the Italian part that included Taylor's Albanians, there were still more than fifty thousand Slavs running loose and every last one might be selling information to Tito. Thank God, Taylor's few remaining Albanians were a clannish lot, especially the feuding Ghegs who sometimes turned to bagging members of rival families when things got too tame. No point in asking them about it. Old joke: how to tell when an Albanian was lying? When his lips were moving. And then there were Taylor's Italians, a bag as mixed as Albanians themselves. At least the Italians were more trustworthy—or were they just smoother liars?

A Trieste Italian often spoke several languages and had more cover stories than Sidney Riley. Some of them commanded the Albanian tongue, and a few had marched into the Dinarics for Il Duce before getting their asses thrown out by the Ghegs. Taylor had feared the worst when he sent these singletons into Albania because the Sovs were building new submarine pens there and Shehu's security forces were tighter than ever. But the accents of the Italians seemed to be no problem; in such a hodgepodge country as Albania, dialects changed from village to village. His Italians went in alone and sometimes came back loaded with information. He eventually retired a few like old Mazza and sturdy Bellini from field work after they had proven themselves in several singleton missions apiece. Taylor kept them in Trieste to interrogate defectors, and Vicenzo Mazza became an expert at nailing doubles— agents sent by the other side to infiltrate the CIA's Albanian ops. Alessandro Bellini, a much younger man, sometimes got too intense for cat-and-mouse interviews, but once trained for debriefing he knew too much to be risked for still another drop into the Dinarics. After several successful missions, Bellini was kicked upstairs for the good of the Company.

Left alone, Fred Taylor might have made a success of the Albanian thing. One of Mazza's missions tipped the West to the power struggle between Hoxha and a fellow named Xoxe, who was a bit too friendly to Tito for Hoxha and his cronies. Bellini's last foray—Taylor had given up hope weeks before the man returned through Yugoslavia posing as a *Croat*, for God's sake—revealed that some of those Gheg mountain boys were still spoiling for a march on Tirana.

But the Albanian operation had never been cost-effective. Taylor's chief hinted that the little country was to be part of a deal cut with the Sovs, with representation in the U.N., though everybody knew Albania would vote the Stalinist line. In short, the West was giving up on Albania and its submarine pens. Taylor did what he could to place his best agents in decent jobs, and left Trieste for good.

Fred Taylor was back in Virginia in 1961, an analyst on the Balkan desk with two kids, a mortgage, and a Buick station wagon, when he dropped a clipping on his blotter one day and began to laugh. Damned shame, he thought, that he couldn't have passed this one on to his field agents a decade before.

TIRANA, Albania (ATA, 21 May 1961)—First Secretary Enver Hoxha has served notice to the revisionist traitor Khrushchev that Albania will not stand idly by and permit the dismantling of naval bases that are, and should be, Albanian property. Khrushchev has recklessly smeared the memory of Joseph Stalin in his own country, as our new Chinese comrades agree, but he will not be permitted to erase Comrade Stalin's naval bases with the same ease.

Elements of the People's Militia are in place at Albanian bases in Vlore and Sazan. Further attempts to remove revolutionary assets placed in Albania by Comrade Stalin will be met with Albanian artillery at point-blank range. This includes the submarines, tenders, and radar equipment placed here under Stalin's farsighted benevolence before his untimely death and character assassination from the likes of Khrushchev. If the renegade Soviets imagine that the People's Republic of Albania will hesitate to send these vessels to the bottom of the Adriatic, let them move one vessel a millimeter from its Albanian pen.

Hand that sonofabitch Hoxha his due, thought Taylor, still chuckling; given his new alliance with the Chinese People's Republic, Hoxha could force Khrushchev to part with some obsolete subs. The Sovs couldn't march on Albania without going through Tito's Yugoslavia, and that wasn't in the cards. A show of force from the Black Sea? Maybe, but Albania's new ally, China, might do some forcing of her own on the Mongolian border. And Taylor knew what the Sovs knew: Hoxha and his asshole buddy Shehu never backed down.

Never. Albania might not know what to do with a handful of subs, but poor old Nikita Khrushchev wouldn't get all of them back. It was the price he paid for dumping on Joe Stalin's tomb when there were statues of Stalin twenty feet high in Tirana.

Fred Taylor was as retired as a Company man ever gets in 1978, with two BMWs, a split-level not far from Langley, and a professorship in Foreign Affairs at George Washington University. That was the year when he had his last laughs over the Albanian situation. Some of his best chuckles came while reading an essay by a grad student who really should've been an English major. The effort was titled, "Whither Albania?" reminding Taylor again of the Brits back on Malta; a triumph of style over substance. And that equaled a failure of substance.

The essay said, in part: "It is clear that China's future depends on better accommodation with the West, no matter how much this rankles the old man of Albania. One must conclude that Enver Hoxha, a hard-line dictator of the old school, was senile in severing relations with the Chinese, his last possible source of aid."

Oh sure, you little prink, thought Taylor; Hoxha's my age, so he's senile. And every ship's captain who ever went down with his ship was senile, every Jew who refused to recant. And let's not forget David, of course; going up against Goliath was an obvious case of early senility. Anybody who draws a goddamn line and sticks to it, even if it's Stalin's line, is judged three rounds short of a full clip by American kids who don't know what real commitment means. Hell. Pity none of our kids ever spent a year in some place like an Albanian village, where you suck absolute commitment in with your mother's milk. But no Americans were permitted to set foot in Albania, nor Sovs, Yugoslavs, nor journalists of any kind whatever. And if a tourist wore his hair too long, they scissored it at the border. If they suspected you were anything but a tourist, they might stick those scissors in your throat.

He shook off memories of Elbas Hamid, remembering him as larger than life with that villainous mustache and hawk nose always quivering in total commitment to something he had lost in Albania. He resumed reading:

"Albania remains the only nation to keep alive the uncompromising philosophy of Joseph Stalin. By turns she has rejected the leadership and the aid of Yugoslavia, the Soviet Union, and Communist China. In each case, Mr. Hoxha has rejected billions in aid for the privilege of following the most harsh principles of Marxism. The result of all this is that Albania, determined to exist on her own meager resources, is by far the poorest country in Europe. Dedicated Balkan scholars conclude that Albania may remain a pariah among nations for generations to come."

Which was so much bullshit, thought Taylor. Enver Hoxha was seventy years old, and nobody lives forever. As soon as Hoxha died, there would be some changes in Albania. There had been a time when one of Taylor's men had both the means and the opportunity to terminate Hoxha, as the old company cowboys used to say, with extreme prejudice. Who had it been? Mazza, one of his Italians. But Mazza had had no orders about it—who could have imagined he'd be in Shkoder with a backpack full of French plastique at the same time as Hoxha? That explosion would have set some changes in motion.

Correction: change would begin to be possible. You didn't expect a flip-flop—what was it the pop psychologists called it—snapping? Right; you couldn't expect the country to snap from one dogmatic extreme to another overnight, but you could expect Albania to sound less like a junkyard dog within, oh, five years of the passing of Shehu and Hoxha.

Fred Taylor picked up his blue pencil and began to print neat characters in the margin of the essay. "The really interesting time," he wrote, "often comes immediately after the passing of the strong man." In Albania, he thought, it could be a time of paroxysm. He considered adding that insight to his marginal note, then shrugged. Why add to the kid's bad habits by teaching him to use high-valence words like "paroxysm" in an academic paper?

Taylor spent much of his Christmas vacation in 1982 writing a paper solicited by a think tank which, he knew, was funded by the CIA. Andropov was making overtures to Hoxha again, and so were the Chinese, presumably hoping to gain fresh access to those sub pens adjoining the Mediterranean. But Hoxha was having none of it. The big surprise was the arrest and "suicide" of Mehmet Shehu late in the year. Taylor flatly discarded the Albanian charge, that Shehu's entire family had become a nest of Western agents. More likely it was some falling out between thieves—perhaps Hoxha's discovery that Shehu kept a numbered Swiss account, or some other little failure on Shehu's part.

The failure wouldn't have to be recent, either; Enver Hoxha could hold a grudge like a miser hugged his gold. Taylor assumed that whoever kept tabs on the Balkan desk at Langley would have the best guess, and avoided wild guesses in his paper. The thrust of his essay was that both China and the Sovs would do backflips to get those sub pens, and that the West might be well advised to see that Enver Hoxha stayed healthy forever. If his successor leased those sub bases, the Mediterranean might be less healthy for the U.S. Fleet. Taylor resisted a ludicrous impulse to title his paper "Whither Albania?" and accepted five thousand dollars for the job.

In April of 1985, Fred Taylor was making plans to visit his son in Bangor when he spotted a piece in *The Washington Post*. He read it without much residual glee, because Taylor had given up hopes that the human race would develop a rational approach to coexistence. The Albanians, for example, still paraded their childish defiance to world powers.

BELGRADE, Yugoslavia (Balkan News Agency, 13 April 1985)—Albania today rejected Soviet condolences over the death of Enver Hoxha, the world's longest-serving head of state and the virtual dictator of communist Albania for over forty years. The Soviet condolences were officially "turned back as unacceptable," said an Albanian spokesman, who added that Albania will have nothing to do with the Soviet Union.

The body of Hoxha will lie in state in the nation's capital, Tirana, until Monday when he will be buried in

Albania's Martyrs of the Homeland cemetery. Hoxha died Thursday at age 76 after a long history of diabetes culminating in a heart seizure.

Hoxha was a fierce Stalinist who boasted that Albania remained the world's only stronghold of true communism. Under his tough leadership Albania virtually withdrew from foreign trade, a nation seldom visited and known chiefly for its uncompromising ferocity. Hoxha severed relations with Moscow in 1961 charging that the Soviets were seeking accommodation with Western powers. In 1978 he severed links with Peking on similar grounds. Hoxha discouraged outsiders and prohibited Albanians from accepting presents from abroad. In 1982 he masterminded the overthrow and reported suicide of his long-term comrade, Premier Mehmet Shehu, later charging the ex-premier with treason.

No successor was announced, but Belgrade sources expect that Hoxha will be succeeded by his protege Ramiz Alia, 60. Diplomats in Belgrade expressed hope that, with Alia's accession, Albania may end its long self-imposed exile by seeking better relations with neighboring Greece, Yugoslavia, and Italy.

Taylor judged, as before, that years would pass before the Albanians began to exhibit something like a new posture. He wondered if he had underestimated them when, taking his ease in Bangor in late May of 1985, he happened across an item in *The Economist* which lay on his son's coffee table. Too bad, he mused, that American taste ran to *Time* and *Newsweek* when the Brits were still translating editorials like this one for their general public.

TRIESTE, Italy (*Novo Giornale* editorial, 16 May 1985)— Without daring to offend irascible Albanians by public statements, Italy's ministers on both the left and right privately show pure relief at the passing of Mr. Enver Hoxha. Nothing could be worse, they say, than a neighbor bristling with arms and insults who utterly refuses for two generations to forgive old wounds at the hands of the Fascists. Before Mussolini, Italy and Albania were good neighbors, and Italian tourists are still treated with something almost like guarded acceptance. With Mr. Alia at Albania's helm, our officials harbor new hopes for trade with this small, fearless oil-rich nation facing us across a few miles of open water.

But it appears that something could be worse: a resumption of Albanian ties with either the Soviets or the Chinese People's Republic. Those submarine pens on Albania's Adriatic coast are a vast temptation to these powers seeking a military base on the Mediterranean. Experienced Balkan-watchers note a subtle shift in releases from ATA, the Albanian news agency, in past weeks from scorn of Soviets and Chinese to something approaching even-handed criticism.

For their parts, both Soviets and Chinese are wooing Mr. Alia with the very greatest subtlety. Nothing else is likely to win a naval base; the Soviets cannot march on Albania without going through Yugoslavia, and no one with any sense craves general war with the Yugoslavs. The Chinese are, of course, even worse situated for such aggression. In this case, Mr. Alia can gain material aid from both powers, playing them against each other without yielding Albania to either of them. This is an eminently sensible course—but Albania is still a nation of hostile mountain tribesmen, quick to take offense, slow to forgive. Her leaders have ignored "sensible" courses for two generations and could do so again.

On the other hand, sources in Belgrade hint at much-improved relations between Yugoslavia and the little nation on her southern flank. This can only be a good sign; the Balkans are still the Balkans, a potential source of armed conflict at any time. As a gesture of good faith, Belgrade and Tirana have begun to discuss their border problems, including exchanges of long-obsolete confidential information. Some of those old files carry the dust of more than forty years, and must be of only historical interest. But it is a start; perhaps Italy can do the same. It may be the beginning of general trade between Italy and Albania after all these years, an alternative to Albanian dependence on the Soviets. It is difficult to see how such exchanges could harm anyone.

Old Taylor thought about that for a long time. Albania's musty files might tell the Yugoslavs much about the fate of many a spy team. Could vintage Yugoslav files possibly be worth the exchange?

PART THREE
JUNE 1985

PART THREE

July 1985

Chapter 4

GILMAN, California, had never known real upward mobility until the coming of the semiconductor industry around San Jose, a half hour's drive north. By 1985 Gilman and many another small town had developed a benign tumor, a real estate boom reaching outward from Silicon Gulch, and Tarzan could have swung antenna-to-antenna from Gilman to the Golden Gate. Most of the new housing developments were not little boxes made from ticky-tacky; they were big boxes made from integrated circuits, $300,000 mortgages, and blind faith, built within sight of the San Andreas fault. A lot of the new people lived around Gilman now. A lot of them voted Republican. Some of them inhaled their entertainment through straws. Few of them had more than a sketchy notion of the recession that gripped the rest of the country. Thanks to this fallout from the San Jose region, many of Gilman's people were average but insulated, decent but screwed-up, living their dream of the Mercedes, the Jacuzzi, the Marantz.

Gilman's city fathers watched the swelling of the tumor and did their best to develop the town as a sleepy bedroom community without destroying its unique status as garlic capital of the world. They might have succeeded without the kids.

Stenciled curb legends warned "NO SKATEBOARDS," but there was no foot traffic in the fierce afternoon heat of

Gilman to restrict the boy. He rode the skateboard in a sleepy slump-shouldered boneless glide, pushing off with his right leg now and then, swerving without apparent effort around minor obstructions. Though he moved at the speed of a long-distance runner, he did not exert enough effort to break a sweat. It would have been hard for a casual observer to imagine why the youth's progress out Tenth Street, away from the center of town, was of such vital interest to the three men in the brown four-door Ford Galaxie.

The boy's arms were tan, slender but well muscled, and his elbow scabs implied frequent contacts with solid objects. The holes in his jeans were big enough to pass a child's fist, and the sleeves of his scrubby tee-shirt had evidently been burned off. Across the back of the tee-shirt was a death's head drawn in indelible black flowpen with "Society Threat" lettered below. The boy's straight dark hair was cut short in a crewcut gone to seed. Only his Nike footgear and the battered, high-tech skateboard suggested that he was anything but one of the migrant workers in the little California town. Until recently, Gilman's leathery old-timers had paused to gape at sights like this. Now they only muttered "punker" and spat. When they no longer spat, Gilman's punk contingent would probably think up some new provocation. All in all, a harmless game.

The men in the brown Galaxie had a more serious game in mind. Here in the southwest side of town, Gilman's older bungalows gave way to ranks of new townhouses behind adobe walls, and only an occasional parked car broiled at the curb. No other traffic moved along Tenth for the moment. After a quick consultation Danilov, the big man in the back seat, leaned forward and gripped the door handle as Nelson, the driver, moved his gear selector. Within three seconds the big sedan had shot past the youth, veered across the sidewalk, and stopped in grass almost touching the high adobe wall. Both near-side doors flew open, the long-armed Danilov grasping for the boy's waist, a little fellow named Roberts in front leaping to intercept their quarry.

The boy had swerved toward the narrow grassy strip as he

saw the car cannonade over the curb. By some magic known to skateboarders alone, he flicked a foot back behind the skateboard's rear wheels and popped his little vehicle into the air. It happened to catch Roberts squarely in the chest as the boy snatched at his skateboard and ducked. The big man in the jogging suit just behind him took a handful of tee-shirt which tore loose as the boy pivoted and darted away.

Squalling tires, slamming doors, and curses in plain American told the boy that he was still pursued. He tossed the skateboard down ahead of him expertly, bounced one foot atop it, and spurted across the street. Tenth Street was open and deserted, so he popped the curb to the sidewalk and thrust off at a sprinter's pace toward a set of low-roofed buildings a block away. An old flat-tired Datsun, the only vehicle parked nearby, prevented the Galaxie from angling straight to an intercept point, and by the time the driver felt the *whump* of his left front tire over the curb, the boy had swerved from sidewalk to street again. Shade trees, still only the thickness of a man's calf, stood like leafy fenceposts between the sidewalk and Tenth Street. They were just thick enough to rattle a Galaxie's rivets, and to avoid them the driver accelerated along the sidewalk, left wheels spitting grass.

The boy risked a glance back, saw the Galaxie about to pass, and stopped with unbelievable agility. Now he was sprinting over the curb behind the sedan, now leaping onto the skateboard again as he fled up a broad walkway toward the low many-windowed buildings. The Galaxie's driver killed the car's forward motion by cranking the wheel as he tapped and released the emergency brake, provoking a hard slide with wheelspin. It seemed to the boy that the big Ford was near enough to run him down and he changed direction again, fleeing along the high stone wall with "GILMAN HIGH SCHOOL" picked out in stones of dark colors.

The Ford driver cut across an expanse of lawn. He saw the broad steps leading downward toward a perimeter alleyway and realized that, while the kid could hardly go off a six-foot ledge over sprawling junipers on that fucking toy of his, he could probably negotiate those steps. But a Galaxie's big fat tires could do that, too. He gunned the sedan ahead, going around the boy because nobody wanted the kid in pieces, and plugged the stairway with the car, braking savagely. Something below the car clanged, scraped, and now the exhaust note was a louder rasp.

The boy angled straight for that six-foot drop, and suddenly it was obvious that he *could,* by God, clear it and the junipers with ease, landing on macadam in a deep knee-bend still with the skateboard under him. While the Galaxie had progressed in a series of curves, the boy's path had looked more like sharp angles. He darted up that broad alleyway with the Ford thundering in pursuit and, building up speed with hard thrusts of his right leg, aimed for five steps leading upward to an atrium of sorts. Nelson gaped in disbelief as the kid sailed straight up those steps, the skateboard platform scraping in a series of gliding impacts, and for an instant the kid disappeared.

Ignoring the furious curses of his passengers, Nelson hauled the big sedan around, seeing the black sheen of macadam that swept upward into that atrium. The driver saw now that he was in the courtyard of a high school automotive shop area, faced by closed garage doors on three sides. With no other way out, the kid would have to come past them now. And behind those walls, the kid could yell his goddamn head off while Danilov stuffed him into the Galaxie. Roberts and Danilov exited as if steam-propelled while the kid was trying a locked door.

The man on the other side of that door had been in the shop for an hour, working quietly in the natural light of high windows. Stuart Ransome was a man of medium height with good shoulders, longish arms, and big callused hands. His hair was of the no-particular-hue labeled ''chestnut,'' short and curly over a broad forehead, and before a Washington State defensive back broke it, his nose had been as straight as that of Michelangelo's David. His chin was good but the mouth would never have satisfied a classicist; the jargon term was ''ungenerous,'' though he was generous enough with its smiles. Ransome never forgot that a high school teacher was a role model so, winter and summer, he ran a bit, did the calisthenics he loathed, and looked it. Ransome moved with the kind of graceful economy that permitted an oil change without staining his pair of worn tan cords or the Birkenstocks he wore without socks. His tee-shirt was edged in blue, and in flowing blue script across the cotton stretched over his pectorals was the suggestion, "Let's Talk About Sex," with the telephone number of the L.A. Free Clinic. It had been a joke, a present from a lady down south. It was also a piece of quality goods which, nevertheless, Stu Ransome never wore around students, any more than he would have worn it to work at Lockheed ten years before. A bit of routine hobby maintenance when alone was exactly the time to wear such a thing.

Stu inhaled the faint odors of warm dust and engine oil without complaint, pausing as he heard the approach of a big engine somewhere outside the shop windows. Stu had just loaded the shop's grease gun and was walking toward his Corvair-engined Baja Buggy when he heard distant drumming of a fist on a locked garage door. Despite the heat, Stu had opened only the high shop windows. While it was perfectly jake with the school board for a shop teacher to work on his own summer projects there, a few crochety bastards in Gilman would complain about it anyway. Stu knew the drill after nine years at Gilman High, and kept his hobby profile low. Now he heard the protest of tires on hot macadam and, under the hammer of a gutted muffler outside, shouting. Sounded like a kid in trouble.

Stu sighed and ambled toward the shop door with its glass portal and integral wire mesh. Before he could reach for the knob he saw, for half a second, a familiar face pressed against the glass. It was already gone when he opened the heavy door and looked out. "Mark? Hey, what's the—" Then he stopped, staring into the face of a big burly type in a jogging suit not twenty feet away. Sweat had plastered the jogging suit to the big man's rib cage. Between Stu and the other man the boy crouched, holding the skateboard like a club, preparing to swing it in a sidearm sweep as he watched the burly stranger. A smaller man was wrapping a light nylon jacket around his left arm as he flanked the boy.

A third man sat watching from a brown Ford, and suddenly he was whirling the car in a tight rum-runner's switch. "Fucker's got a Mac Ten," screamed the driver. "Come on, come *on!*"

"It's a setup," Roberts blurted, and was instantly off and running toward the car, the boy spinning toward Stu, the big jogger tossing a look over his shoulder before he, too, ran for the Ford with the lope of an inside tackle.

The boy brushed past Stu and into the shop, and Stu nearly dropped the grease gun while slamming the door. Under the echoes of the door slam in the shop, Stu heard a deep voice baying, "You must wait!" a moment's near-silence punctuated by heavy foot slaps, then the roar of a big car accelerating hard and the heavy slam of a chassis over some obstruction. Five seconds later the place was so quiet Stu could hear labored breathing somewhere in the shadowed far end of the shop. Two of those men had sounded as American as light beer. The big one? Only three words, barked out fast, but maybe not by an American.

Stu looked down at the grease gun in his hand. Yeah, it might look like a weapon, if you were both hurried and paranoid. Could those guys be plainclothes police, chasing Mark Paladino? "They're gone, Mark," he called softly. "You want to tell me why the hell you're so popular?"

Mark Paladino eased up from behind an old oil drum with a tire iron in his hand, still platter-eyed from his encounter. "Swear to God, Mr. Ransome, it beats me." He placed the tire iron on a scarred wooden workbench and blew out his cheeks as he walked into the light, the skateboard in his left hand.

Stu Ransome faced the youth using his best shop-teacher scowl. "This is no time for bullshit, kid; they thought my grease gun was heavy artillery. If those guys were cops, this place could be wall-to-wall riot guns in five minutes."

"I haven't *done* anything, Mr. Ransome! Anyway, cops don't try to haul you into cars without a word or flashing a badge, do they? Assholes ran me off the sidewalk right there on Tenth in front of God and ever'body, tore my best shirt, chased me two blocks, nearly ran me down—'' He took a deep breath. ''I don't know, man. You ever see the fuzz pull any shit like that?''

Stu sucked a tooth. ''Not recently,'' he grinned. ''You haven't been pushing Kona gold, demonstrating against Reagan—you know,'' he finished.

''I'm clean as a shop towel.'' Mark fed him one of his own standard shop jokes, showing both hands in a shrug borrowed from his father. ''And I never saw those guys before, honest.''

''You didn't pop an allie in front of that Ford to get them chasing you?''

''Jesus, no, man—I just grabbed bio-air over a lot of steps, but they'd already tried to grab me.'' Staring down now as if the skateboard held some secret: ''I think they coulda creamed me if they wanted to.''

Stu recalled the big man's stance, arms wide, dark eyes calm under heavy black brows as he waited for the second man's flanking movement. His face had held not rage, but calm anticipation. ''I think they wanted you in that car, Mark.''

''Tell me about it!'' The youth was recovering his usual demeanor, the go-to-hell disdain of the punk rock kids. ''Bunch of pervs, you ask me, man.''

Stu reached out, squeezed Mark's shoulder gently, steering him toward the sound-insulated cubicle which was Stu's office. ''Could be. I don't think they were law. In any case, we ought to phone the police.''

He flicked on the cubicle light and was checking his telephone list when Mark Paladino said, very softly in the stifling little room, ''Maybe you better call my dad first.''

Stu glanced up, saw the boy lick his lips. ''Want to change your story, Mark?''

A hesitation, a long breath as Mark Paladino met Stu's gaze. Then: ''I'm being straight with you, Mr. Ransome. But I know my old man, he'd turn blue if you called the oinkers. Let him decide, huh?''

''Fair enough. I've forgot his number; will he be home?''

''Just like always,'' the boy said, and recited a local

number. Stu dialed; offered the receiver, but saw the boy shake his head with the ghost of a wry smile. "He'd believe it from you."

"Don't know if I believe it myself," Stu muttered, then changed his cadence with the third ring. "Hello, Justin? Stu Ransome, at Gilman High. Right; well, we've both been busy, I guess. Look, Mark is here with me. He's pretty shaken up right now but we thought we should call you before we contact the police."

Stu saw the boy look toward the ceiling as if help were hanging there. Sure enough, Justin Paladino misunderstood. "No, no, hold it, Justin," Stu said, forcing a chuckle. "Mark hasn't done anything, at least he says he didn't; but from what I gather, three men just tried to haul him into a Ford sedan on Tenth Street. He made it here to the school with the Ford on his tail and they took off. But I saw 'em; they seemed to mean business, and I believe what Mark says. And from the way they were trashing that car, I don't think they were cops." Pause. "Sure, he's right here." With that, Stu elevated his brows and offered the instrument to Mark.

Mark made a grimace that bared his teeth and showed every cord in his neck, but took the receiver. The boy's voice now held a very careful reserve, coming from deep in his chest, perhaps a subconscious ploy to appear manly. Or perhaps not so subconscious. "Hi, Pop. Yeah, I'm fine. It's like Mr. Ransome said."

The next few minutes told Stu a lot about the current relationship between Justin Paladino and his only son. Mark wanted approval, but was loath to ask for it. And Justin Paladino was a strict disciplinarian of the old school, from the old country. Stu had met the elder Paladino over a year previous, soon after the boy had turned in an exquisite model for a class in Technical Miniatures—a good weasel phrase for model building.

The problem was that Mark's model had been much too good. It wasn't the first time a kid had enlisted help from a parent, and Stu was always victimized by mixed emotions at these times. Too few parents gave a damn about such things.

But this model had been extraordinary by any standard. Slender Mark Paladino had more thumbs than Mickey Mouse, and his in-class work was the usual slapdash product of kids who wanted results instantly. Stu had accepted the model gravely, without comment, when Mark brought it in. The model had begun as a Pocher kit, one of four finely detailed model cars imported from Italy by Tyco and then sold cheaply by K-Mart. Mark's was the 1932 Alfa Romeo Spyder, a superb model roadster over a foot long, but someone—damn sure not young Mark!—had envisioned it as a restoration project inherited by rust.

The Alfa had been mounted on heavy plywood disguised as dirt. The rubber tires had been scuffed, one tire was flat, and the engine cowl had been unceremoniously stuffed into the cockpit. The engine had been assembled in the car, then partially taken apart, and the upholstery was ripped as if some lilliputian driver had brushed past the seat back too many times. The blood-red paint was faded and peeled, and several spokes on the wire wheels were sadly bent. Tiny wrenches lay on the running board with a defunct starter no bigger than a pencil eraser. From any angle, it appeared to be the skeletal remains of a wonderful machine abandoned by a six-inch Philistine.

After studying the tableau long past school hours, Stu Ransome had called the boy's home intending to suggest less thorough help in the future. He'd wound up in an hour-long conversation with Justin, instant friends through a shared interest in the modeler's craft. Evidently, in Europe a modeler learned many tricks worth sharing.

Stu had visited the Paladino place twice; had found Justin Paladino a single parent of middle age, a man of patience and subtle understanding, who spoke excellent English and was clearly concerned over the widening gulf that separated him from his young and thoroughly American son. Stu always suspected that Mark's final project, a Baby Bowlus sailplane that bettered three minutes over Gilman High's athletic field, was as much Justin's work as Mark's. But Mark's classwork showed real improvement, and Stu Ransome was content.

Then Mark, perhaps with a bit of coercion from his father, had taken the basic course in auto mechanics, again under Stu Ransome. During that semester, Mark had gone punk and made no secret of the fact that any friendly banter from a teacher was an embarrassment. No doubt this minor rebellion had not gone unmarked in the Paladino home; in any case, Stu neglected his visits to Justin Paladino's old frame bungalow near the creek on the east side of town. Had it really been so long? Studying Mark's facial hair and the swell of well-defined triceps on his arms, Stu Ransome suddenly felt older than thirty-five. Christ, he thought, turn your back for ten seconds and they're grown men . . .

Now, finishing a detailed account of his recent scare, Mark added, "They would've had me if Handsome Ransome had been slower." Mark darted a quick glance in Stu's direction, flushing as he considered his words too late. Evidently, Gilman High's kids did not realize that teachers were familiar with their own nicknames. "Mr. Ransome thinks we oughta goose somebody in the cop shop. I figured, knowing you—" He trailed off.

After a long pause, Mark nodded into thin air. "Okay. I said *okay*, for chrissake! Will it kill you to say I did right? —Thanks, Pop. That didn't hurt a bit, did it? —Sure." The youth set his jaw, thrust the receiver out. "For you," he said in obvious relief.

"It's me again," said Stu into the instrument. He had expected to hear nervous tension in the accented voice, but nothing quite like this. He was acutely aware that Mark was watching and listening carefully. "Nope, no weapons that I saw. —Hell no, Justin, the administration frowns on us keeping guns here; that's what the police are for, I hear tell."

Listening again, Stu frowned, then swept the expression away as he met Mark's gaze. "I'd give 'em a call if I were you. —Well, if you're sure. Tell you what: I'll run him home myself since you can't pick him up. —Yeah, that's true, but I could let Mark out through another entrance and pick him up with the Saab; he could hunker down in back. —No, not in the trunk, in the back seat! Jeez, Justin, calm down. —Sure, but it won't be dark for five hours yet. —No, it's okay, I needed to put a new distributor in this old Corvair engine anyhow, and Mark can help if I really taught him anything last year. Now, will you do me a favor in return? Tell me why those three goons are after Mark; I know damn well you must have a pretty good idea.''

Stu saw the boy shake his head and step out of the cubicle. He grunted a few times into the receiver, watching Mark peer through the armored glass in the distance. At last he said, ''You don't have to tell me about custody fights, I've got a twelve-year-old girl I haven't seen in years. But let's pretend I don't know anything about it, Justin. I'm on your side, but I can't afford to get caught between her lawyers and yours; okay? Right. See you about dark, then. Yeah, the same blue Saab; it doesn't look like much, but it won't get arrested for loitering.''

Stu replaced the receiver and stood for perhaps a minute, thinking it over. If the ex–Mrs. Paladino had to kidnap her own son, those rough types wouldn't be connected with the law. But with all those cultural imperatives Justin had brought with him from Italy, maybe the father himself had taken the boy illegally, years before. In which case— Stu shrugged off the endless permutations. This was the kind of crap Wiley Reed knew inside out and backward; plenty of time to ask later. Right now, he had some maintenance to do, and a fumble-fingered punker to do it with. Mark would piss and moan, but Stu figured the kid would decide it was worth the grimy fingers when that flat-six Corvair mill sang through its little glass-pack mufflers like an operatic basso.

Yeah, thought Stu, when in tune the Corvair resonated like a regular Boris Christoff. Karen would enjoy the comparison. She'd enjoy it a hell of a lot more than Stu was enjoying the comparison of Christoff's voice with that of the big yazoo in the jogging suit. Boris Christoff had been as Russian as they come.

Chapter 5

TWICE, on the pretext of stretching his legs, Stu Ransome strolled outside while Mark Paladino, using his skateboard as a mechanic's creeper, searched for Zirc fittings and pumped grease into the joints of the hybrid VW Baja rig. The brown Galaxie had left its marks, all right: rubber burns on the steps out front, and gouts in the grass near Tenth. The car itself was nowhere in sight—but it might be parked on a side street, waiting. Stu felt his Birkenstocks sweat-slick on the soles of his feet and hoped the bastards lacked air conditioning.

Errant breezes from the high windows and sips from the shop water cooler made the heat bearable, especially for Mark, who seemed to lack sweat glands and took Gilman's furnace temperatures for granted. Around seven o'clock, Stu crammed big exhaust hoses over the Corvair mufflers to carry the exhaust outside and finished his tune-up. This was the part kids liked—almost as loud as your average rock group—and Stu explained various details to the youth as he worked. The vacuum advance for the timing of the little air-cooled aluminum engine wasn't like that of other GM Sixes, and it was notoriously finicky about low-octane fuel, so the distributor settings had to be ju-ust right. But stuff a late-model, four-carb Corvair mill into a VW Bug with shortened body panels and you had a poor man's Porsche. With its external rollbar and most of the engine exposed to view, its lines were ugly as a pile of troll turds but worth all the trouble if, like Stu, you also had Porsche brakes and fat Goodyears on wide rims. The heavy black rollbar cast a dark stripe across the gleaming yellow paint of the car, and quartz-iodine rally lights were clamped atop the rollbar over the car like the eyes of some great insect. Stu rarely used those flamethrowers on public highways; if they didn't peel paint from four hundred yards, they could leave other drivers with the UFO experience. There was nothing quite like a yellow Baja rig, Stu believed, to keep the respect of Gilman's youth.

By eight o'clock, the sun splashed bright reflections through the windows high on the far shop wall. Mark Paladino put the exhaust tubes away. "My gut says it's midnight," he said. "My old man'll have supper fixed."

"Oh Lord, that's right." Stu hurried off to his cubicle. "I'm going to catch some flak from my lady for this," he added, and punched a number from memory. Three minutes later he returned, flicking his left hand as if shaking water from it and grinning at the boy.

Mark grinned back. "She the bimbo with blonde hair and brunette skin I saw you with at the school Open House?"

"Yep—and be careful who you're callin' a bimbo."

Shrugging, the brown eyes innocent: "A great bod, man, unattached but makes everybody think about attaching: bimbo."

"Fair enough. Definitions change, I guess." The same kid who watched his language in a model-building class tended to make up for it in a shop environment. By objecting, Stu would only alienate the boy. Stu put away his wrenches, screwdriver, and timing light, then locked and trundled his chest of tools away.

Mark leaned on the car's rollbar. "Aren't you gonna take this out for a shakedown? You always tell us . . ."

"Do as I say, not as I do. But come to think of it, I can take the Baja rig where no bloody two-ton sedan can follow. I could leave the Saab in the lot. But you'll have to scrunch down in the seat, kid."

"Suits me."

There was no question that Mark Paladino, for all his punker nonchalance, liked their exit from the shop. After double-checking the other entrances for security, Stu toggled the overhead garage door and waited for it to open fully, enjoying the direct breeze on his face. Then he waved the boy into the front passenger seat, let the engine's cough steady to an idle, and strode over to the door switch again. The door needed roughly ten seconds to rumble down to its automatic lock. In that time Stu swiveled back into the driver's seat, engaged first gear, and had the yellow Bug smoking its tires into the atrium. Thanks to the old ZF limited-slip differential unit, Stu could virtually pivot the vehicle around on one rear wheel while keeping the revs up. He did it in the atrium, just to be certain he saw the overhead door close completely. Then he eased off the pedal a bit, straightening the undersized steering wheel, and let the Baja rig shoot down the macadam incline. Holding the wheel steady with pressure of one knee, he shrugged into his safety harness with its three-inch lap belt and double shoulder restraints.

Then Stu Ransome gave full play to his fantasy, pretending that the brown Galaxie was waiting somewhere along Tenth. He upshifted and, instead of heading for the street, set out across the quarter mile of playing field that stretched away from the school, big tires carrying the featherweight car across the grass without leaving ruination in their wake. He angled across a perimeter ditch and upshifted again on pavement, checking both rearviews continually, and in moments was cruising south beyond the town limits toward Garza Junior College. Presently he turned off, following an old pockmarked road that led north again. No brown Ford appeared in the rearview.

Stu tapped the youth on the shoulder. "You can sit up now," he called over the rasping burble of twin exhausts, then added in exasperation, "And buckle up, for God's sake! Haven't I taught you guys anything at all?"

Making his reluctance obvious, Mark Paladino found the heavy nylon webbing and, after studying Stu's restraints, locked his belts in place. Seconds later he was glad he had done so, as

the car leaped ahead in third gear. Stu knew the narrow road
well, having used it many times to check tire adhesion. Knowing the boy was watching him as well as the bends in the road,
Stu gripped the wheel with false intensity, frowning as he fired
the yellow VW through tight corners and upshifted while
exiting each one. He was taking no real chances, but Mark
Paladino could not know that. It was Stuart Ransome's view
that any sixteen-year-old would enjoy a bit of rapid motoring,
and he made the mistake of overdoing it. Two minutes later he
spewed gravel entering a good two-lane road, ran the tach up
to its 5400 rpm redline in third, then shifted into fourth and let
the car settle back to a legal pace.

Mark swallowed twice, then said, "Holy shit, man. How
many times you had this thing in orbit?"

"Just blowing out the cobwebs, Mark. Every time I get it
over redline it throws that goofy fanbelt, but wouldn't you say
it's in tune?"

"I'd say your personal guitar is missing a few strings,"
Mark responded grimly. "If anybody asked, Mr. Ransome,
sire."

"Didn't you want me to wring it out for you?"

"I'm not fucking crazy! I just wanted the best chance of
getting home in one piece, and I'm still not sure I will."

Stu kept his expression noncommittal and nodded, selected a cassette from a box near the shift lever, thrust it into
the tape deck. "Your dad made me promise we'd come in
around dark, and we've still got a half hour. Want to take a
rat-run up to Heller Pass?"

Mark shrugged. "I know you're hot snot in a race car,
man. Just don't kill me; okay? Will you do that little thing?"

Stu grunted and took the state highway west, somewhat
more sedately as the blacktop became a steep mountain road
with frequent blind turns. He was enjoying himself, nodding in
time with the beat from a pair of rear-mounted Altec speakers.
Fifteen minutes later they reached the summit, where Stu
turned the yellow VW around at the Watsonville overlook. He
shut off the engine for a moment, turned down the volume on
the tape deck, rolled down his window to revel in the mingled

scents of pine and towering eucalyptus. Sighing: "Beautiful; sometimes I think about building a cabin up here," Stu said.

"I can't even think with that choir crap you're playing," Mark complained. "That supposed to be music?"

"*Catulli Carmina,* by Carl Orff," Stu replied, and snapped it off. "Good music to drive by."

"Sounds like fifty wops yelling in hell." Something in Mark's gaze dared Stu to point out that Mark himself was Italian.

Instead, Stu said, "It's Latin; drinking songs from the Middle Ages. Downright dirty if you understand it—or so I'm told."

"You and my old man can get off on it then," Mark said. "It bores holes in me, man." Mark gave one grudging look off toward the coast, now in twilight shadow. The youth was plainly uncomfortable. "Hadn't we better get back?"

"Yep." Stu let the VW coast downhill for a few yards, let in the clutch, and began easing the car toward Gilman. He found it hard to admit that Mark Paladino was the more sensible of the two of them, in his distaste for spirited driving. "I guess we don't have much in common, Mark. Me and my Baja rig and Carl Orff; you kids and your vans and heavy metal."

With something like horror, Mark snorted: "Heavy metal? Aw, man, that's airhead shit. Anybody with one brain cell to rub against another is into hardcore punk."

"I'm not sure I know the difference."

"Listen to the words then," Mark replied. "Heavy metal is loud and obnoxious and macho-dumb; punk is loud and obnoxious and smart."

Stu admitted that he spent very little time listening to hardcore punk lyrics. "What's the punker message, Mark? Seriously," he urged, seeing mistrust in the boy's face.

Mark thought about it, watched the big pines slide by on his right, and said after a minute of reflection: "Racial equality. Don't get fucked up with drugs. War is obsolete. Think for yourself, don't be sexist, and above all, don't let the system make you a carbon copy of your parents, because boy, they are *really* fucked up. They even hired Ronnie Reagan to make sure we *stay* fucked up!'' Mark stuck his chin out defiantly. ''Western Union don't send those messages, man, that's hardcore. Of *course* you never listen.''

''Come on, kid, I'm listening now. Why 'of course'?''

''You tryin' to start a shouting match like my old man? Because I don't care much one way or the other.''

''I'm not competing. I'm listening. Let's try it again: why d'you say I never listen?''

After several heavy breaths: ''Ah, fuck it. Look, you were an''—he drew the next word out, breathing it in bogus awe as if it were an incantation from which the magic had long ago evaporated—''en-gi-neer at Lockheed. You took all the courses the system said to take, maybe did your hitch in Vietnam killing people. You got a job in Silicon Valley building hydrogen bombs or whatever; you became part of the system. Now you're a secret agent for the system whether you know it or not, flexing your big muscles for sophomore cowboys, building macho cars and hoping we'll all follow you like little ducks in a row. Well, man, they shoot ducks. No, thanks.''

Stu grunted assent and made no reply until the highway straightened out as it entered the broad valley floor, flanked by small wineries and rows of grapes on the nearby hills. Stu flicked on his low beams in the dusk and breathed the faint musk of garlic that seemed to identify Gilman better than any city limits sign could. When he no longer smelled that garlic around Gilman, Stu reflected, maybe it would be time to move.

At length, Stu said, ''Mark, I can't speak for anybody else, but for me you've offered me a bowl that's half strawberries and half bullshit. I can't swallow it all, but I won't spit it all out either. I was an army brat; my dad was Corps of Engineers, so I was with him in Germany for a few years in the late fifties. Then he came stateside again, but we moved around a lot. By the time I'd taken enough lumps to make some friends, zip, off we'd go again.''

''So?''

''Well, when you don't have many friends, you take

sports and hobbies and books pretty seriously. For me it led to mechanical engineering at Oregon State, on an athletic scholarship.''

"A conflict in terms," Mark quoted quickly.

"I've heard that. I agree with it in a lot of cases. Anyway, I make no excuse. You can't make me feel bad about catching six passes off Southern Cal cornerbacks, Mark. I took my lumps and liked it, and God knows the girls in Corvallis liked it, and I made my grades because I *didn't* want to be shipped away to Vietnam and get my butt shot off. But if I wasn't anxious to grab a rifle, I figured I ought to be learning how to be useful some other way. I ask you: was that macho-dumb?''

A shrug. But not a disagreement.

"Well, then, was it obnoxious and smart?"

A snort that was almost a laugh. "Okay, it was somewhere between skinhead and punk. Take one giant step forward,'' said Mark.

"You're right about my being co-opted by the system for a while. I married a small-town debutante and got a job at the Lazy L, Lockheed to you, making more money than was reasonable in seventy-two. Four years later I was damn sick of it. No, I wasn't making bombs, but yes, I was on a project that developed a new offensive missile. We called it *de*fense, but it wasn't, it was *offense*. This country had no real defense, by an open decision at the top, and that scared the hell out of me.''

Mark's sly smile was accusing: "But you did it anyway."

"Guilty as charged. But then I started spending my evenings getting a Master's with a teaching credential at San Jose State, so I could get out and do something for the future, instead of against it. My wife was furious; it raised hell with her social calendar around Los Gatos when I wasn't available as an escort. I felt guilty about not seeing Amy except when she was asleep, but guiltier still building more offensive threats.''

"Amy your wife?"

"Our daughter. Holding her while she slept sometimes, I'd get to thinking about the world she would inherit from me. It kept me going until I could get a job as a teacher.'' A sigh, as Stu reached Gilman's chief arterial and turned south. "And no sooner had I landed a job in beautiful downtown Gilman than Liz decided I was downwardly mobile. She took Amy and her family's help, and disappeared. To Florida, as it turned out." He was doing exactly what he had promised he would not do, offering a justification that directly challenged Mark's view. "But I didn't go back to the missile industry, even though it might have given me my infant daughter again. Now that we're starting to build real space defenses that might save millions of civilian lives, I get tempted sometimes. I might go back yet, one day. And I would stay as long as I thought I was doing more good than harm."

"Meanwhile, you teach kids to tune up their damn Z-28s and Firebuzzards," said Mark. "Skinhead macho. Congratulations."

Suddenly Stu was chuckling helplessly, shaking his head. "You are one tough little sonofabitch in a debate, Mark. I hate those belchfire V-8s more than you will ever know, but they're what Gilman's new rich give their kids, and I work with what I'm given. I take kids who won't do *any* goddamn thing that doesn't give absolutely instant reward. I teach 'em a little about deferred gratification—uh, working for a delayed payoff."

Quickly, angrily: "I understand a few long words when you talk real slow. You're talking down to me, Mr. Ransome, sire. Again."

Silence, as Stu turned east toward the edge of town. Then, "Boy, you guys grow up fast. You're right, and I apologize. I don't mind if you keep me honest."

"Shit you don't," Mark muttered.

"Okay, so it bothers me a little. But don't stop."

"Don't worry."

"And when you're not around, I'll listen to some punk lyrics," Stu said, smiling.

"Wouldn't hurt you any," Mark countered as the VW turned past a high oleander hedge and through heavy link fencing toward the one-acre plot of Justin Paladino. The hood of a blue Chevrolet coupe was just visible, parked alongside the garage facing the drive, and Stu felt a touch of deja vu;

Mark had earned a B for tuning that Chevy in the school shop. Justin's other vehicle, a trucklike Toyota Land Cruiser, was nowhere in sight. Then, as they drew abreast of the little bungalow, Mark peered toward the garage. "What the fuck has he done to the breezeway?"

Stu braked near the garage and jerked around as a bulky shape materialized from high shrubs to stand at his side. "Jesus, Justin; you ought to wear a bell or something!"

Justin Paladino, a sturdy balding figure in tan khakis, carried a rifle in the crook of his arm. At the moment his heavy brows were furrowed as he scanned the entrance to his place with a slow swiveling of his head. He spoke gruffly, with the faint accent of one who had spent much of his life in his adoptive country. "I had intended my friend to drive his Saab into the garage to let my son out, Mr. Ransome. I did not see my friend in a Saab, I saw two men in a very strange Volkswagen." A heavy sigh. "If Mark was visible on the street, there is no point in your going into the garage now."

"I'm really sorry," Stu said, shutting off the engine and opening his door. Still cradling the rifle, the older man trotted with silent steps along the grassy verge of the drive into the dusk. A moment later Stu heard the squeal of a big gate, and then Justin Paladino reappeared with the same glum expression.

Mark approached his father with a stride that seemed somehow formal. "My fault, Pop. I got muscle cramps, hiding down there on the floorpan." The lie was formal, too.

In the reflections of a red evening sky, Stu saw Justin Paladino's face alter swiftly from irritation, through something like pain, to fondness. "Yes. I was only thinking of your safety, Mark." The father embraced his son in a brief one-handed bear hug, then turned to shake Stu's hand. "You understand my concern, Mr. Ransome?"

"Sure. I don't understand why I'm 'Mister,' though. Never was before."

Paladino's chuckle was brief, nervous. "Worry forces us into old patterns, Stuart. Please be an honored guest at my table," he added, waving them toward the kitchen steps.

Mark was still squinting toward the garage until his father

placed a gentle hand on his back. Stu saw that the breezeway was covered by thin leaning panels of plywood, an addition since his last visit a year before. As they went through the rear door into the coolness of the kitchen, Mark mentioned the change. "What's all that plywood doing out there?"

"They would have hidden you, coming from the garage to the basement steps," said his father without elaborating. He stood the rifle near the door and clapped his hands lightly, beaming at the new arrivals. "Enough of this," he said. "Mark, when you take your bath, you might put on a shirt."

"I've got a shirt," Mark growled, and then looked down. "Oh yeah. It's beyond punk now, I guess." Stripping the torn garment as he moved down the hall toward his room, he revealed the well-developed laterals of a youth on the edge of manhood.

Stu washed up at the kitchen sink, not missing the fact that every shade was drawn over every window he could see. A single lamp was lit near the dining area, facing so that its light bounced off the windowshade. Plenty of light, thought Stu; but it wouldn't reveal the moving shadows of the people inside. Not just a whole lot of flies on old Paladino, he decided.

Stu leaned against the pantry door, sipping a pale varietal Pinot Noir that Paladino evidently bought by the case, and talked with his host as Justin made final preparations for a late dinner. Justin folded his sleeves back with precision, showing masses of curly black hair on corded forearms. His wrists and fingers belonged to a farmer, yet his nails were carefully tended and Stu had seen those stubby fingers tease miracles from X-acto blades and balsa. A man of such precise habits, thought Stu, must have his hands full with a kid like Mark. Still, the sounds from the bathroom suggested that Mark Paladino was taking his bath according to instructions.

Justin seemed determined to treat the school confrontation lightly as he tested the fettucini on the stove, but it was clear that he wanted every detail. Stu furnished them all, including his suspicion that the burly devil who had sweltered in a jogging suit was not an American.

"From where, then?" Justin Paladino drained the pasta, swirled a thick pat of butter onto it with practiced motions; set the knife down carefully; smiled wonderfully with big even teeth, his dark eyes merry under the straight brows. "It probably does not matter. But at times a few words are enough to suggest, say, a Romance language, or Slavic or perhaps Greek. An East Indian will have entirely different vocal patterns."

"I heard three words, Justin."

"Three words can say much. Accept the word of a man who has taught at—schools of language."

"If I had to take a wild guess, I'd guess Slavic."

The barest flicker of Paladino's eyes, then a shrug and again that disarming smile. "My once-wife had a weakness for exotic people and probably has it still. Do you think the Ford was rented?"

"Not as easy to tell as it used to be. I never did get a look at the plates. Sorry."

Now Justin was applying olive oil and lemon juice to a salad that carried a hint of grated Romano. "Please do not think me crazy, Stuart, but from past experience I expect more attempts on my son. You feel certain these men did not want to harm him?" Paladino handed the salad to Stu and made a gesture toward the table, set for three.

Stu slid the big bowl onto the table and returned. "From the way he talked, Mark seemed to think they could've run him down instead of grabbing him. And I didn't see as much as a pocketknife on any of them. I don't think they wanted to hurt him."

"No. They wouldn't, of course," Justin murmured. "But they might not be so gentle with his father."

Stu jerked his head toward the rifle that leaned against the wall. "I'd think twice before using that thing, Justin. Or even waving it around inside the city limits."

"We are in the country here. And we Italians have appropriate ways of dealing with rabbits in our gardens." Justin smiled. "You know that I am a careful man, Stuart. I have had hours to think on this. The sheriff cannot provide us with constant surveillance and I cannot keep my son behind a chain link fence all summer. I need some legal opinions as well, but I do not know an attorney in Gilman."

They discussed it briefly, and Stu furnished the name of Ron Curry. Justin washed his hands, dried them on a clean towel, rearranged the towel with its edges aligned on its rack. Speaking softly now, he said, "Caution tells me to place Mark out of reach for a few days. I know that my legal position in this matter is not good; are you certain you want to know more?"

"I don't think so. I know you're a good father; that's enough for me."

Justin gnawed his upper lip once, seemed to catch himself at it, and drew a heavy breath. "Would that, and a great deal of money, be enough for you to put my son in hiding through the weekend? I know it is an imposition. There is simply—no one else I can trust, Stuart."

"If you trust me, then don't bribe me. And I'm not too sure Mark would want to go wherever I take him. He's not a little kid anymore, Justin."

The shoulders slumped as Justin turned away. "I had no right to ask," he said.

"God*dammit,* Justin! I didn't say no; I meant it's more up to Mark than to me."

"He will obey if I tell him to go with you. He will be surly—"

"That's news?"

"—But he will obey." Justin reached into his pocket and withdrew a sealed envelope. "You must feel free to keep him where you think best—Gilman is much too small—and so you will need money. I do not want you to tell me where my son is until we are face-to-face again. No matter what I might write, or say on the telephone. No matter what," he said again. He shook the envelope toward Stu. "I can afford it, and it is not a bribe. You must take it, Stuart."

Stu jammed the envelope in a hip pocket with a growl of frustration. "This is crazy. God, I hope," he said.

The sound of water gurgling from a tub penetrated from the hallway. Speaking more quickly now, Justin went on. "I dealt with this problem once before. I will contact these people in my own way, to convince them that they will fail. Please do not come to this house again. I will call you every night.''

"I'm not always home," said Stu. He was damned if he would sit with sandwiches by the telephone waiting in his duplex apartment for Justin's call.

"You can tell me when to call, on your answering machine," said Justin.

"I haven't got one."

"You now have the money to buy one," Justin replied simply. "Consider it a favor to me."

"Thought of everything, haven't you?"

"If I had, these people would not have found me. There are many ways to pick up an old trail."

"You gonna lay down a new one?"

Justin showed his big white teeth again as he turned toward the kitchen drainboard. "Hardly. But if even *I* do not know Mark's whereabouts when I face these people, I shall feel much better about negotiating." Then he flipped back a thin cotton dishtowel from a shallow bowl containing what was evidently a green olive paste and stirred it, sniffing as he wafted one hand above the bowl. "Pesto," he said, noting Stu's interest. "Used sparingly like a sauce for the pasta. It is best at room temperature."

"More Italian peasant lore?"

Justin nodded as he carried the bowl to the table. "You will rarely find it in a restaurant. In Pisa"—he lifted one hand, waggled it—"perhaps."

Mark shuffled into the dining area wearing scuffed red tennis shoes and what looked like the bottom half of a tan flight suit, complete with huge pockets and Velcro closures at the ankles. He was drawing a fresh tee-shirt over his head, a bright yellow garment with crimson lettering across its front. "Dinner ready?"

A snort of exasperation from his father. "I have told you about that *insensato* shirt, Mark."

"It's a joke, for Christ's sake," Mark said.

Stu squinted at it. "I can't even read it."

"The lettering is Cyrillic." Justin lifted the bowl of pesto with one hand and pointed to the three scarlet words in a bored lecturer's singsong. "Komitet Gosudarstvennoy Besopasnostiy," he said. "A bad joke."

"KGB," Mark said, his smile asking Stu to share. "I got it in Monterey while Pop was teaching there. Getting too small for me now," he added, tugging at its waist.

Justin waved them to the table. Stu slid into a seat where, a year before, he had studied model plans with Justin Paladino. Mark's tee-shirt was only a little too tight; at the rate kids grew, it would've been bought within the past few years. Stu's idle guess was that Justin Paladino had moved directly from Monterey to Gilman. Funny how you could know a man for years without knowing anything of his background . . . "You never told me you were a teacher, Justin."

"Sure. For the Army," said Mark with faint scorn.

"A school of languages," Justin said quickly. "In the north of Italy during the war, one became fluent in many tongues, or starved."

The Army's School of Languages at Monterey had a hell of a good rep, and the connection suggested that the feds thought well of Justin Paladino. Stu forked a mound of salad onto his plate, enjoying the interplay of fragrances. He took a helping of fettucini and watched as Justin spooned a modest dollop of the dark pesto from its bowl. "You use that pesto like it might be full of cayenne," Stu observed.

"Only pine nuts, olive oil, Parmesan cheese, a bushel of basil, and spices," Justin said gravely, smearing it generously across his pasta. "It has few enemies. Trust me."

Stu tasted the stuff carefully, then again. Eventually he took three helpings. Its mealy texture and olive color gave little hint of just how deliciously it met the tongue. "Times like this," he said to Mark, "be glad you can afford your own Italian chef."

The youth grinned back and nodded, his face full of fettucini, and Justin Paladino beamed.

Chapter 6

IT was past ten o'clock when Stu Ransome agreed to Justin's scheme for picking up the boy later, instead of simply driving away with him. It was nearer ten-thirty as he parked the yellow Baja Bug in the carport of his duplex. He wondered briefly if old Paladino was a mental case. Moving cautiously in darkness, cursing his case of nerves as he scanned the stillness of his back yard, he let himself in at his kitchen door. After setting the lock on the inside he showered quickly, snatched a pair of fresh briefs from his top dresser drawer, and cradled the telephone receiver between his shoulder and ear, finger poised to punch a familiar number. Then he replaced the earpiece. Where had he heard that wiretappers recorded the numbers you called, as well as the conversation? Wiley Reed, maybe—and Wiley should know. Okay, if the Paladino place could be called from anonymous locations, why do less for Karen?

He slipped into ventilated nylon running pants and a light net tee-shirt before snugging on his best blue Adidas runners and securing the laces. Then he fished under the bed, drew out a battered TWA bag, and carefully folded a pair of lightweight gray slacks into it, chose supple black loafers, black socks, and a plain yellow short-sleeved shirt of Pima cotton with the patina of silk. He thrust his wallet into one of the loafers and

Justin Paladino's envelope into the other, resisted a sudden temptation to open the envelope and count the money, then put his loafers beneath the folded slacks and stood for a long moment, staring at the open flight bag. Of course there was room, but the Beretta was heavy. And it committed him to full acceptance of deadly force.

"No way," he muttered, zipping the bag. It was bad enough that he was dressing for trouble, without carrying fourteen rounds of heavy unregistered trouble in a TWA bag. He wrapped a Kleenex around his keys to keep them from rattling and sealed them behind Velcro in the pocket of his running pants, paused at his kitchen cabinet to withdraw a tiny flat tin of anchovies which went into the flight bag. Finally he turned off the lights, let himself out, and tested the lock. Twenty feet away in the next duplex, Marty Prufer's bedroom TV murmured softly, a reassurance of life as usual in Gilman. Momentarily, Stu smiled at the ease with which he had become caught up in old Paladino's foolishness, and strode toward the sidewalk.

The dark shape that glided from Prufer's hedge made him jump like a deer, and Stu gave chase as far as the curb. "Serves you right, Thurber," he breathed, chuckling as he watched the furry streak disappear into the next yard. Prufer's cat, Thurber, had set him in motion and he let adrenaline have its way, telling himself it was only for exercise. Besides, if you ran during a summer in Gilman, late evenings or early mornings were the times to do it. Stu enjoyed his six aerobic blocks to the Saab, still parked in Gilman High's lot, and he was pleasantly atingle when he arrived. He let the little two-liter turbo warm up for thirty seconds or so, in no great hurry because the Paladino place was only five minutes away. He drove to the south edge of town before returning on Monterey Highway, and was satisfied that he was alone. Only then, following Justin's instructions, did he pull up to a pay phone.

The first number he punched was Karen Cavender's. "It's me," he said when she answered at the fifth ring. "At the Gilman 7-Eleven on Monterey. Look, the problem with that student? Well, it isn't going away. —No, I ate with the

Pal—uh, my pals. Damn, this is irritating; I don't know whether I'm playing kid games or what, but I seem to be caught in somebody else's game of domestic cloak and dagger. There's one chance in a million that someone else is listening to us, so just humor me. I'll tell you about it in a half hour.''

He listened a moment, and chuckled. "Sure, tonight, unless you've made other plans. I wouldn't blame you, love. —I'm leaving shortly. Expect two of us. —That's part of what I'll tell you later. 'Kay; bye.''

He fished for another quarter, and slapped his forehead to jostle his traitor memory. Justin Paladino's number was unlisted. Damn, damn; a prefix about four years old in Gilman would be what? 847. Right; suddenly he recalled the rest and punched it in, and had to wait only two rings.

"Is Betty there?" He felt more like an idiot than ever as he asked it, loitering under bright lights and asking for a nonexistent woman. He heard Justin tell him he had a wrong number, replaced the receiver, and drove east to Llamas Creek Road. Presently he slowed and flicked his high beams while approaching the old WPA bridge, some two blocks from the Paladino place. Seconds later he saw a slight form rise up from the low concrete pillar carrying a Nike bag in one hand, a skateboard in the other.

Scarcely had the Saab stopped when Mark Paladino swung into the front passenger seat and stowed his load in the footwell. "We meet again, Mr. Bond,'' said Mark in a mocking stage-British drawl as the Saab accelerated away toward the freeway interchange.

"Buckle up,'' Stu said. "This Lotus is a submarine too, remember.''

Mark did as he was told, laid his head back on the headrest, and sighed. "Beats me why you go for this shit, man.''

"It's your sparkling personality. How could I refuse?''

They fell silent then, letting the little turbocharged coupe pull them up the South Valley freeway toward the glow on the horizon that was San Jose. Not until they had passed the townlet of Coyote did Mark speak again: "I could split in

San Jose, you know. I know some dudes up here. You don't have to humor my old man just because—why are we turning off?''

''Coyote Road runs almost to Cloud Drive,'' Stu replied, ''which is where we are invited to spend the night with a certain blonde bimbo who, incidentally, will give you a Mohawk with her bare hands if she hears you call her that.''

''While you applaud.''

''We skinhead machos are great fans of violence,'' Stu murmured, swinging the Saab through the gentle bends of Coyote Road. ''Anyway, I am not humoring anybody. I am doing a favor for a friend who is worried sick about his only son.''

''Worried? He loves this kinda crap. Some guys rent pussy once a month. My old man becomes a werewolf every few years; thinks the peasants are closing in with pitchforks, from the way he acts. Then we have to move again.''

''Like from Monterey to Gilman,'' Stu mused out loud.

''I can't believe he told you that,'' from Mark.

''No. Wild guess. And forget I said it. If Justin wanted me to know these things, he'd tell me.''

Now they were skirting a hill, nosing to the left up a steep suburban drive. The lights of San Jose stretched north to San Francisco, south to Gilman, through a summer night mercifully free of smog. ''Doesn't matter what I want to tell you,'' Mark said. His tone made it more statement of fact than accusation.

''Mark, your dad's been making decisions for—what, sixty years?'' Stu heard a grunt of assent and went on: ''He's a cautious man and if I've got to choose who's pulling my strings, I choose sixty over sixteen. Now before you tell me how cautious *you* are, show me your elbows.''

Stu had not heard the youth laugh for almost a year; a high, delighted cackle, its last notes dropping to something reminiscent of Justin Paladino's own soft chuckle. ''You got me, sheriff,'' Mark admitted. ''But what's a little road rash if it teaches you to beat a big-inch Ford?''

''You've made your point,'' Stu agreed, topping the hill

and pulling into a driveway. "But if those guys are going to stay beat, let your dad work it out. And he put you in my care, so don't go running out on me; okay?"

"Right." Mark stood with his bag and skateboard while Stu fished his flight bag from behind the seat, then followed on a cement walk toward the front of the little stucco house. In the near distance below them, the valley freeway sliced through San Jose's south hills, cradling a solitary southbound car in a moving cocoon of light. Mark hurried to catch up. "Hey, what's her name again?"

"Bimbo," Stu replied, "since you enjoy living dangerously."

Karen Cavender met them at the door padding in flat strap sandals, her straight blonde hair curling under on each side over a belted housecoat that merely hinted at good hips and ripe cleavage. Beneath indirect ceiling lights her dark skin glowed as if lit from within, a striking contrast to the yellow hair. Her eyes might be a bit too tilted, her mouth a bit too generous, to be thought pretty; but rarely did any male between fourteen and eighty forget that Karen was present. Perhaps it was partly her voice, with its faint husky vibrance, that Mark recognized as much as anything.

Stu got a brief kiss, a welcoming peck that suggested long familiarity. She smiled at Mark and stuck out her hand as he stepped into an air-conditioned living room that seemed, somehow, Japanese in flavor despite the bookcases along two walls. There were no Oriental trappings but with the exception of one high-backed wicker chair the furnishings were low, spotless, and severe, oriented toward the center of the room. Mark took her hand, standing as tall as she, and glanced uncertainly at Stu Ransome.

"Karen Cavender, meet a young friend of mine from the wilds of exotic Gilman: Mark Paladino. I promised his father Mark could crash here tonight," Stu said in one breath, artificially jolly.

"No problem," Karen said, and made herself ravishingly beautiful with her smile as she closed the door.

Mark's memory had not deceived him; when she smiled,

that full lower lip and the small even teeth it revealed were—he said it aloud: "Dev-a-*stat*ing."

"They grow up fast in my classes," Stu answered Karen's sidelong glance. "So be careful; you could give a man whiplash with that smile."

Karen glanced at the youth while jerking a thumb in Stu's direction. "Now you see why I keep him," she said to Mark, and snapped off the television. "So sit already. Can I scare up something from the fridge?"

"Something light," Stu said, collapsing on a folded futon the color of summer grass. Mark shrugged amicably and chose a low Danish chair.

"He means Oly Gold," Karen said over her shoulder to the boy as she swept toward a massive Dutch-door refrigerator, just visible in the kitchen. "If he asks for something substantial I bring a Heineken. The man keeps me penniless, I tell you; penniless."

"Whatever he's having," said Mark in tentative request. He visibly relaxed as Karen moved back to them, unscrewing bottle tops with deft motions. None of them acknowledged that, with the beer, Karen accorded Mark an adult's status.

Karen sat down cross-legged next to Stu, tucking the housecoat in. "I've paid for my story, guys. I want it. What's all this about cloak and dagger? Or should I ask?" She looked from one to the other.

Stu raised his brows at the boy, who took a pull at his Oly Gold, smacked, and said, "Dungeons and Dragons is more like it. My old man wants me out of town until further notice."

Stu shook his head, his expression pained. "You aren't an unwanted child, Mark. I vouch for the lady. If she's going to help, she needs the whole truth."

"So do you," Mark said, as though to himself. "You tell it, then."

Stu's account used up a second beer, with few interjections from Mark. Karen asked only a few questions, but they were good ones. Why had the police not been told? Had anyone tried to serve Justin Paladino with papers? Was the boy's father aware that a sixteen-year-old could generally choose the parent he preferred? In each case, the answers lay with a man whose absence was, itself, almost a physical presence in the room.

"Sounds like Mr. Paladino could use Wiley," Karen remarked, "if he can afford it."

Mark's "Huh!" was rich with irony. "He can afford it. He's a nickel pincher, but don't let that fool you."

Karen's smile was faint. "You don't know Wiley's fees."

"You don't know my old man's bank balance."

Stu felt that this tack could become uncomfortable for them all. "Wiley Reed's a private investigator, Mark," he offered. "Karen works for him part-time."

"No shit! You're a P.I.?" His brow was wrinkled, but Mark was grinning.

Karen waved a hand gracefully as though erasing a message printed on a slate between them. "No, nothing like that; I'm a librarian. But Wiley's an old friend and he needs an answering service because he lives in a camper, and—uh," she began to laugh gently. "It gets complicated. Let's just say Reed Investigations pays me to research things, sometimes. And I take his calls."

"Speaking of Wiley," said Stu, and strained to reach his TWA bag. "Lint! Front and center," he called, with a rising-note whistle that startled the youth.

"What the f—heck! Is the guy here?"

"Lint is Wiley's cat," Stu explained, and whistled again, peering toward Karen's hallway. Meanwhile, he fitted a metal key to a tab on the small oval can he had taken from the bag.

"Lint is Lint's cat," Karen corrected. "He lived with Wiley for a while but he seems to prefer a house that isn't on wheels."

The lean gray tom that strode from the hall was no beauty, with half of one ear missing and a tail that had once been much longer. "Christ, he's punk," Mark breathed, and was captivated instantly.

Lint may have been no one's pet, but he marched gravely to Stu Ransome and bumped foreheads with the man before sitting down, his big yellow eyes expectant. Stu said, "Down, Lint." The cat blinked. He was already sitting. "Inside out, Lint." The cat ignored him and yawned. "Up, Lint."

Immediately the cat sat up, forepaws folded primly, eyeing the object in Stu's hand. Stu rolled away the lid from the anchovies, pulled a brown sliver from the can, gave it to Lint. While the cat chewed, Stu watched. "This bloody cat responds to maybe half a dozen words and a few gestures," he said to Mark, and gave the cat another anchovy. "Either Lint is a genius, or cats generally play stupider than they are."

"I never thought of you as a cat person, Stu," said the boy. Rites of passage are many and protracted; the use of the first name went unremarked, but not unnoticed.

"He's not," said Karen with fondness. "He's a teacher, Mark."

"Dime a dozen," Mark said. His wink was one beat late, suggesting that he had spoken without weighing his words, but was not in the habit of apologizing.

"I mean a *real* teacher, somebody who really wants to know how things get learned. People, cats, planaria worms— even an occasional teenager." Karen's tone was dry, but still good-humored. "He might even teach you something if you let him."

"He already has: buckle up when he's driving," Mark smiled, draining his beer. Karen donated another ravishing grin, offered one hand, palm up, and Mark slapped it gently.

Stu teased another anchovy from the can, trying not to smile. "I don't get no respect," he said to the cat.

"Yeah, you do," Mark replied softly. "My old man— well, you're the only guy he trusts. And he—it's not fair, goddammit."

Karen studied the youth for a moment. "How about his other friends around Gilman?"

"What other friends? His tomato plants? His books and models and that old Land Cruiser?" Mark Paladino yawned hugely. "He's pretty much a hermit. He'd like it fine if I didn't have any friends either."

"And now you know why," Stu replied, stifling a yawn

of his own. "Not many men would give up everything for a kid."

"Yeah," Mark said dryly, and set his empty bottle down.

"You two are asleep with your eyes open," Karen said, getting up. She offered a hand to Stu, who took it and grunted to his feet. "Mark, the futon opens up; you can crash on it here. Or you can sleep on a good couch in my study. Wiley uses the couch sometimes. Suit yourself."

Mark looked from her to Stu Ransome. "Wherever I won't be, uh, in the way. I didn't bring my pajamas."

"Skivvies are fine," Stu said. "No big deal, Mark. You can use the john in the hall. I sleep with Karen in the back bedroom; it has its own bath." He tossed a faint smile toward Karen. "Among other things."

"Among other things," Mark quoted, every inch a high school junior for the moment.

Karen's aspect was still cheerful, but as she took Stu's hand en route down the hall she looked back, studying the boy carefully. "You're not used to—informality like this, are you?"

Mark shook his head. "Or honesty, either. It makes me— ashamed, Karen. I'm not complaining," he rushed on. "I just feel, oh, like I owed you. Like my father owed you," he amended.

"Your dad is paying," said Stu, and pushed open the door to the back bedroom.

"My dad is why I owe you some honesty," Mark said, standing slump-shouldered in the living room. "He's not always the straightest arrow in the bag."

"We can talk about it tomorrow," Stu mumbled.

"I can't sleep if I don't tell you now," was the dejected reply. "You think you're hiding me from my mother's goons, right?"

"Something like that," Stu said, already half asleep.

"Wrong. My old man has some connections from the old country that he's been running from, as long as I can remember. He won't even go into an Italian restaurant. I don't have to ask why; I've read about the Cosa Nostra."

Karen's voice was suddenly very small, her hand gripping Stu's tightly. "Mafia?"

"Bingo." The boy turned and began to unfold the futon.

"You're guessing," Stu prodded.

"Not about my mother," said Mark Paladino, and turned toward them with a look of bleak misery. "She died right after I was born."

Chapter 7

THEY lay silently on their backs for a half hour, breathing quietly, willing the night breeze to freshen through the open window, arms folded with hands under their heads. Then, on the off-chance that Karen was truly asleep, Stu whispered, "He couldn't wait 'til tomorrow to drop that one on me. No-o-o."

Karen's reply was almost a whisper, bubbling with amusement: "At least now *he* can sleep." The feathery touch of her fingertips on his arm suggested that she might entertain other notions.

"I never felt more like running across the ceiling in my entire life," he said, sat up abruptly, and snapped on the nightlight below the level of Karen's kingsized bed. She heard the angry buzz of a zipper, a rustling, and then Stu lay back holding an envelope above him in the dimness. He tore it open, and a cascade of well-used paper fell across his chest. Hundred-dollar bills.

"What on earth?"

Craning his neck, he retrieved the bills. "Eighteen, nineteen, twenty; just wondering whether I'd die rich. You think I could buy off the Mafia for two thousand bucks?"

"I think Mr. Paladino has proved that he knows he's in serious trouble. Call it good-faith money."

"Faith? We are *all* in deep yogurt because Justin Paladino lied to me! First thing in the morning, I'm going to— Hell, I don't know what."

"I've been giving that a lot of thought, my love. First, no one knows where Mark is, so here he must stay for the time being. Second, you go back home to Gilman and carry on as usual, and keep your eyes open until we know more."

He rolled over, propping his head with one hand, and gazed at her. "You don't screw around with the Mafia, Kare. I won't involve you, and that's final."

She raised one languid arm, pulled his head down to hers; gave him a lingering gentle kiss. Massaging his scalp, holding his mouth an inch from her own, she said, "I like that boy; he reminds me of me, ten years ago. Yes, thanks to Wiley I *do* know a little about what he calls the Families here on the coast. They still have scruples against shooting women. That figured prominently in my decision," she chuckled. "And I am already involved, and that is also final."

He pulled back to lie flat again. Presently: "I told Justin to contact a lawyer I know. Maybe I should've told him about Wiley Reed instead."

"Or maybe you should trust Mr. Paladino for a day or so. I'm not averse to seeing Wiley with a little cash, but— Stu, has it occurred to you that *Mark* might be lying?"

A long pause. "Sheeeeit," he said at last. "Maybe I can sleep on that."

"Maybe. Will you tell me why you're holding that money like God's own poker hand?"

He laughed softly. "Waiting for you to call, I guess."

She reached down, found him, and now the huskiness in her voice was full of promise. "I'd much rather raise, fella. How'm I doing?"

"Uh—you ever make it on a pile of money?"

"Nobody ever offered. But if I am not very much mistaken, I feel an offer impending."

"Mmm." He rolled toward her, stuffing the wad of paper under her pillow. "You never got this kind of payoff from the tooth fairy," he murmured, nuzzling past a fall of blonde hair to reach her ear.

"Nor this kind of service," she replied, and turned her head to find his mouth again, opening herself to him, giving; taking.

Presently they lay quiet, except for occasional chuckles as though one of them had said something delightful. He said finally, "At least I've found something I can sleep on."

"Like hell," she said, giving his shoulder a gentle shove. "Anybody ever tell you it's like a Turkish bath under you, mister?"

"Turkish regiment, yes. Turkish bath? I forget," he said, and rolled away again. They laughed together, quietly, and then they slept.

The next morning promised to be another scorcher. Stu managed to break the yolks of all three eggs—"sunnyside all over" in Karen's opinion—while assembling breakfasts with toast and orange juice. They ate in the sequestered sunlit patio behind her house and agreed, before Karen left for city college, that Stu would return to Gilman.

Mark accepted his fate grimly. "I've been campused before," he said. "Maybe the cat will keep me company. Should I answer the phone?"

Karen had a better idea. "I'm running late, but Stu can show you how to play my answering machine back. And you can hear the incoming message anyhow, if you're standing near. If either of us has anything to tell you, we can do it without mentioning names." She paused in the sliding doorway to the kitchen with egg-smeared dishes in hand. "You know, I could get to enjoy these shenanigans. You should bring your friends more often."

Stu, dryly: "Just like old times, hm?"

Her laugh was half lost in the homely clatter of Melmac in the sink. "Sort of; but here we have telephones." Stu leaned back in the patio chair, enjoying the touch of early sun on his throat before it became a midday torch, and missed the questioning look from the boy. Presently Karen returned with keys jingling, kissed her forefinger, placed it on Stu's chin, and waved goodbye as she stepped from the kitchen into the gloom of her garage. A moment later they heard the hum and rattle of an automatic door, then the marbles-in-the-disposal warmup of a small diesel.

"Jeez, she needs a valve job," Mark said as the car pulled away.

"VW diesels always crank up like that," Stu murmured, eyes still closed. "Ain't I learned you nuthin'?"

"What'd you mean about old times, Stu?"

Stu stretched hard, popping his shoulder joints, and was silent for a moment. Then, "I guess she wouldn't mind. Karen's family used to be a great example of how more equals less, and she hid out for several years to get away. Her father was, uh, still is, Doyle Cavender. Ring a bell?"

"Nope."

"Before your time, I guess. A technical editor, wife and two kids in Sunnyvale, nothing out of the ordinary until he lost his job at United and took a job with a little-bitty computer software company about 1971. The company grew fast, and pretty soon Cavender was bossing a lot of people. They paid him partly in stock for a while; Karen says she remembers how it pissed him off, but of course he wouldn't remember it that way."

Mark shook a forefinger in the air sardonically. "Fate's a coincidence that fucks you over; genius is a coincidence that works out. That's from *Flipside,* I think."

"Pretty good. What's *Flipside?*"

"Punk media, man," Mark replied in don't-you-know-anything tones. "So what happened?"

"Old Doyle was a fierce bridge player, and so was the company president, so when the company was bought out and the president started up a new company, he took Doyle Cavender with him. Maybe they understood each other's signals," he chuckled. "I guess you had to be there to understand how power can snowball at the start of a big new industry. All of a sudden Doyle Cavender was giving interviews to *Fortune;* hobnobbing with the Ferrari set; moving up to Atherton."

Stu fixed his gaze on the boy and lowered his voice. "So many people told him he was brilliant that he decided it was true. What it really amounted to—and I'm quoting Karen's mother—was that Doyle Cavender just happened to have his umbrella upside down while it was raining chicken soup."

Mark laughed. Stu continued, "The old girl is Manhattan Jewish, and a lot of it rubbed off on Karen. Makes for interesting relationships. *Any*how, Karen and her brother had been comfortable in Sunnyvale, but they took to lah-de-dah in Atherton like two frogs on the freeway. Her dad decided the whole goddamn family had to be models of success, or else. For Karen, it was 'else' at the age of fourteen."

"Lotta families do that to their kids. It's worse than being ignored," Mark grumbled.

"Her mother was hitting very expensive bottles, her dad was hitting her mother, and Karen hit the road. Wound up in a commune near Felton while her folks were turning the Bay Area upside down looking for her. See, it never crossed the old man's mind that his half-Jewish princess might not be hiding out among the rich."

"Right under their noses," Mark grunted. "Man, I know dudes been hiding out *in their own houses* without seeing their folks for a year. You know, a quick sneak through an upstairs window once or twice a week just to rustle a meal, use the VCR while everybody's out raking in money, maybe grab a few bucks. Parents leave money on the table. Weird. Makes you sad, you know?" Mark's voice had trailed off in reverie, but now he quickened his tempo: "How'd they find Karen?"

"They didn't, for five or six years. Karen changed communes a few times; kept thinking she'd find one that did what communes were supposed to do. She did some drugs. Those were the days when she learned how to use a system without getting pinned down in it. That's what I meant about being like old times. I gather she got pretty sharp at it."

Mark snorted. "Then she couldn't've been into anything heavy, man."

"Not for long." Now Stu shook his head; blew out a heavy breath. "You know what scared her straight? When she realized she was valuable to two different communes because, among freaks of all ages, she was the only one who could write a coherent letter begging money from other parents and friends. She wrote a hell of a lot of letters. And then one day she walked out without a word, got a job in Santa Cruz waiting tables. Even finished high school there.''

"Waiting tables, with her old man living in Atherton?''

"That's Karen,'' Stu replied, as he might say "That's life.'' "So then she moves up to South San Jose, gets a job, enters SJ State as an English major, does work-study in the library, and falls in love with the place. And after all that time, Doyle Cavender hires his umpteenth private investigator, who happens to be this Vietnam vet from Oklahoma with a wooden leg named Wiley Reed.''

"His wooden leg is named Wiley,'' said Mark, deadpan. "I just want to keep this shit straight.'' He saw a mocking threat in Stu's level gaze. "Okay, okay. Don't stop now. I may want to believe some of this, one of these days.''

"Wiley's like the Immaculate Conception,'' Stu grinned. "You either take him at face value or not at all. Well, Wiley starts from square one, and finds Karen in about ten minutes because she's of age, using her real name. Karen begs Wiley not to tell because she doesn't need the hassle. Wiley gets her story, and gives her an update on her folks, which is roughly that Doyle Cavender has lost ninety-six percent of his ass on decidedly dumb investments and no longer seems to think he is the lost son of Albert Einstein, but Cavender still has just enough money to hire Wiley Reed at two hundred a day plus expenses. And that touches Karen's tough little heart, so she lets Wiley arrange a meeting.''

"And she goes home and all is forgiven,'' Mark prompted.

"Not really. She gets along with her folks now, but once you leave home, Mark, somehow you can never quite *be* at home there again. Karen's got good instincts: she didn't try. She took a Master's in Library Science on her own hook about the time I met her. She did some stuff for Wiley, the kind of research she's good at, and they'd learned to trust each other, and eventually he put her on his payroll. So now Karen has two jobs. Call it a job and a half,'' he amended.

"Hold it,'' Mark said teasingly. "How'd you shoot this Okie out of the saddle?''

Stu had been toying with his breakfast napkin. Now he paused. After a moment he smiled carefully. "You are too old for a spanking, and too young for a backhand. But you could learn a little discretion.''

The boy swallowed, looked away. Nodded. "I was out of line,'' he admitted.

It was the first time Stu had heard anything resembling a real apology from Mark Paladino in a year. He held up one hand, palm out in an Indian peace sign, and freshened his smile. "We met at a garage sale where Karen and I were fighting over the same book,'' Stu said, getting up. "She knows what every damn book in the world is worth, so if you're mooching through her shelves here, treat every book like it's rare. Because it might be,'' he finished, going indoors.

Stu needed only shoes and socks to finish dressing. He went through the drill with Karen's answering machine, which Mark quickly mastered, and cautioned the boy against leaving the house and its secluded patio. Ten minutes later he was tooling the little Saab down Coyote Road alone.

Cutting over to Monterey Highway, he stopped in Morganton, Gilman's rival as a bedroom community. The banks were not yet open but the boom in Silicon Valley made hundred-dollar bills commonplace, and Stu handed over two of them at a place called Solid States, a specialty store for people too rich for Radio Shack. The answering machine used two cassettes and a multidigit remote code instead of a hand-held coding device. He kept the receipt for Justin Paladino. Then, on an impulse, he called Paladino intending to say something to the effect that Betty was doing just fine, oh excuse me, wrong number.

No answer after eight rings. Stu drove south, then east as far as the Llamas Creek Road, and spotted the back of the Paladino place a hundred yards from the road. Paladino's old Chevy sat in the same spot, but the forest-green Land Cruiser was nowhere to be seen. Well, maybe he'd sold it. Or maybe he was driving it around Gilman; in an argument with most other vehicles—a brown Ford Galaxie, for example—the Toyota would be sturdy as a tank. Stu continued back across town, pulled up behind his Baja Bug, and after fifteen minutes with the set of directions, had the answering machine plugged in with a cheery greeting for any caller.

His loose schedule for the day involved checking out some new diagnostic equipment for the auto shop, and mail-order chores to broaden Gilman High's supply of the little Estes model rockets for the September crop of sophomore modelers. The new Estes catalog lay in a welter of folders next to the recliner chair in his living room, and Stu had windows open and blinds up to catch any vagrant breeze when the telephone rang in the kitchen.

Stu walked to the kitchen entryway and leaned against the framing, waiting as his new machine went through its paces. Then he heard a familiar voice, apparently freeze-dried and reconstituted. "Uh, Stu? Marty Prufer. Didn't know you had this damn machine, don't tell my boss I said so but I hate 'em. Just wondered if you'd made connections with your cousin, name of Harry. I saw him and his buddy at your back door about dawn, and you know me: early riser. Tell Harry I'm sorry I scared him when I called out the window. Anyway, I figured you must be up at Uvas Reservoir fishing, that early. Harry said he'd leave a message you couldn't miss, but he'd get back to you anyway. Just wanted to let you know, pal. We IBM automatons are human, too. Uh—see you."

Stu was tempted, but stayed where he was until Marty, somewhere in a San Jose IBM facility, hung up. Stu had enough cousins to go around, God knew, but none named Harry. He walked outside and stood in the drive, stroking his chin. His first confirmation of Prufer's claim was a small, spade-shaped indentation in the soft earth under his bedroom window. A herringbone pattern, probably the toe of a jogging shoe, its heel having rested in the tangle of bluegrass that seemed always on the verge of dying or taking over the hedge.

Moving around to his back yard where the smoke-blackened old barbecue rig stood, he saw no slit screens or other evidence of predawn visitors. Maybe they'd left a message in his mailbox, he decided, wheeling to test the idea. And then, passing the Baja Bug, he happened to glance through a window and saw what looked at first like burlap hanging from the driver's headrest. Stu cursed himself for not locking the car; cursed again as he opened the driver's door and squatted outside, rubbing gooseflesh from his upper arms on a warm summer morning. A razor-sharp blade had slit the headrest from end to end, in a single pass, at just about neck height. In the seat itself, roughly where a man's family jewels might be, someone had cut two jagged circles the size of plums from the upholstery.

Stu stood up, scanning his surroundings carefully, and strode inside the house on stiff knees. Sure as hell, a message he couldn't miss. He could repair the upholstery with a vinyl kit in minutes, but that and other things could be done at Gilman High. This time Stu dressed as if for a fishing trip, in jeans, dark long-sleeved tee-shirt, and J. C. Penney's best high-top caulked hiking boots. His fishing knife was the traditional item with one long blade and a hook-removing utility blade. It went into his left front pocket, Justin Paladino's money into the right. His last item lay cold against his belly beneath the tee-shirt, on safety, with over a dozen nine-millimeter parabellum messages in the clip and one jacked into the chamber.

It was entirely possible that these people did not know he had two cars. Stu had his Big-4 bag full of necessaries crammed into the Saab fifteen minutes later. He was on the brink of calling the Gilman police, but dammit, he had promised Justin he wouldn't. Still, that was before he learned he was dealing with organized crime. *If* he really was—and in this maze of thoughts, Stu Ransome parked the Saab in Gilman High's rear parking lot and walked warily through the school's spacious inner quadrangle. The shop building boasted four doors for foot traffic. Stu used his master key and marched straight to his office telephone.

Paladino did not answer. Stu slammed the telephone back down on his desk, clumsy with haste, and found a second number. The receptionist at Calvin and Curry answered on the second ring. Mr. Curry was on another line; would he hold? "Tell Ron it's Stu Ransome. It's urgent that he call me the minute he's through. If this number is busy, keep trying," he said, and gave her his office number.

Next he called Karen's place and waited an interminable twenty seconds for her recorded voice to finish its spiel. At the beep he said without preamble, "Two men were at my apartment around dawn, so they've got to know who I am. Slashed the VW seat cushions to scare me, and it worked. I'm gonna be pretty mobile for a while, folks. It's barely possible they'll be able to check on close friends of mine so don't show yourself to *any*body you don't know. If somebody comes after you, hightail it on foot to the nearest cop shop and tell them the truth. Don't be afraid to yell your head off on the way." He replaced the receiver, hearing a faint ping that was probably heat expanding the big overhead shop doors. He drew the Beretta and walked silently to the little atrium door where this whole damned business began for him. Nothing.

The phone rang while he was setting the Beretta's safety. He reached it in two rings, gaped at the voice, and then found himself breathing heavily. "Justin, how the hell did you— never mind, I can guess. You've put me into a Mixmaster, old buddy. Unless you want me going to the cops in the next ten minutes, I suggest you come to the high school quadrangle where we can talk."

He listened for a moment, then: "He's where I think he'll be safe. It was you who said we'd only discuss that face-to-face. —Damn right things have changed. If you want to know how much, be in the quadrangle in ten minutes. —Okay, fifteen," he finished, and broke the connection.

Knowing that Karen normally called home to query her answering machine at noon, he decided against a direct call that could frighten her unduly. By the time she heard his message played back at noon, he might have more to say. He was searching in storage boxes for a vinyl repair kit when the phone rang again.

"Thanks for the call, Ron," he said. "No, I've sort of dropped out of baseball this summer; you guys are doing okay without me. Actually I called you about Justin Paladino. I take it he's already contacted you." He listened for a moment. "He's put his son in my care while he deals with some very unpleasant people. It may be a custody fight, or it— I see. Nope, Justin's a very careful guy. Doesn't have many friends, but— Whoa; sounds like you're trying not to tell me something. —He already called me here, so I assume he's been talking to you in the past few minutes. —I'm seeing him right away, this morning, or so he said. I'm beginning to think you mustn't bet on what Justin says. —Right, I will. —I understand; even you shortstops have ethics." He laughed at Curry's reply, said goodbye, and replaced the receiver carefully. Whatever Ron Curry could not tell him, he was left with the unsettling idea that Paladino was not seeking help against organized crime.

He checked his watch, then strolled into the quad, squinting into the cloudless robin's egg blue. Gilman High's chief concession to the sun was a wide, slat-roofed gazebo in the quad, hardly more than a roof on poles. It took Stu a moment to realize that the bulky figure sitting atop a table in the gazebo's geometric center was Justin Paladino.

No telling how long Justin had been sitting there, patiently scanning every path between the low buildings that defined the quad. The man had asked for more time when he needed less. Time to study the layout, perhaps. Stu moved toward the gazebo, feeling prickly heat, feeling naked as well.

Justin was eating red grapes from a paper sack, withdrawing them one at a time, chewing and swallowing each one in patient ritual before he took another. "You are upset, Stuart," he said, nodding as though to himself.

"I am petrified," Stu corrected, hitching his backside up against a wooden table, folding his arms and casting a look around the quad. "How long has your wife been dead, Justin?"

The older man continued to nod as he bit into another grape. Then, "Many years," he said, gazing away to the hills where scrub oaks competed with high grass in a mottled pattern. "I did not kill her, if that is what—"

"Christ! Who said you did?"

"I could not know what you might have heard during the past twelve hours," Justin said. "I am under great strain, my friend, and I had much to do. It is easier when I know that Mark is in your care. Where?"

"If you're still vulnerable, are you sure you want to know?" Paladino shook his head. Stu then described the trouble with his upholstery in a few terse sentences. "Mark and I both think that's more consistent with the goddamn Mafia than with your ordinary garden-variety kidnappers."

A flicker of something, perhaps recognition, passed across Justin's swarthy face. "Yes," he said at last, and put the sack down on the table. He made the shift with care, but the damp kraft paper sagged as though someone had placed a brick among the fruit. "So my son has made that connection."

"Which means you lied. Mark and I and someone else I value a great deal, are all at risk. How'd they find out who I was?"

A shrug. "How many shop teachers work here? Or perhaps they traced your license plates. Whatever you think, Stuart," he said, speaking quickly, "they are really after me; they have been for years. If they must hold my son to get me, they will. I need a few days to disappear again, and you were my only hope to keep Mark safe. I do not know whom to trust."

"That's fucking obvious; you sure haven't trusted me. What's in that sack besides grapes?"

For the first time, Justin Paladino coped with a startle response. Then, relaxing: "My revolver. You cannot understand how much power these people have, Stuart. They have separated close friends before, and on shorter notice than this."

Stu sucked a tooth, considering, then stretched the cloth of his shirt across his belly. He waited while Justin studied the flat outline of the automatic under the fabric. "If I was out to get you, Justin, I'd have done it somewhere else. I don't even like toting this bloody thing."

"This is not an ideal ambush, I admit." As if to validate the innocence of the setting, a boy chased a golf ball into the edge of the quad a hundred yards distant, then bounced it away again. Paladino's mouth stretched in a shy smile. "I am satisfied of your loyalty, Stuart, now that we are together. I shall make it worth your trouble. That, at least, I can do."

"That house of yours: I bet it's crawling with alarms," said Stu, and saw a lift of eyebrows that seemed to confirm it. "Now, then, either you tell me the truth or I drop Mark off at the creek near the house with eighteen large bills and a telephone recorder I've already bought, and that's the end of it for me. I may do it anyhow; and I intend to check details."

Chapter 8

STU raised his hands; let them fall to his sides. He burst out angrily, "Why can't you go to the police, for God's sake?"

Justin Paladino paused, studying the peaceful slopes to the west, before he answered. "I did, once—no, three times, to be completely truthful. Stuart, the name Alessandro Bellini is not uncommon in Pisa, in the north of Italy. Alexander is a popular hero, and Bellini is like Johnson or Smith. It was my name—and that of a partisan much older than I, and also of several others. For reasons you appreciate, I am carrying all the identification I have," he added, reaching into the inside of his jacket for a pack of envelopes secured by a rubber band. Something turned over in Stu's breast; he recognized the rubber as special four-millimeter Pirelli strip that he and Justin had ordered to fly models, a year before, when life had been simpler.

Paladino selected an envelope with *discendenza* printed carefully across its edge; offered it. Stu could read little of the thing, but it appeared to be the birth certificate of one Alessandro Bellini, recorded 11 Novembre 1926. The paper was old, without the scrollwork and engraving common in America, but it boasted a convincing number of signatures of Pisa officialdom. "You won't mind if I keep calling you Justin," Stu remarked as he returned the thing.

"You Americans tore down much of my country, but you were generous. I was an orphan, one of those children to whom new languages come easily, and the wife of an American colonel took me under her wing, as they say. I had never traveled much before, but with them I did; Trieste, the Tirol, and so on. I picked up more languages that way.

"When the colonel was reposted to America, they did what they could for me but it took years before I was permitted to emigrate. By that time I was making my way as a translator. They needed translators in Cambridge, near Boston, which also has many Italians. I would not have cared if I had been the only Italian in America, of course," he added with his sudden candid grin.

Stu: "No little odd jobs for the Mafia in Italy?"

"Never. We were happy in Cambridge—though she would be alive now if not for those ferocious winters. I met my wife while she and I were helping programmers to edit early attempts at machine translation. This was at M.I.T., though we were paid by an Air Force contract. Rita Teodori was from Koritza; an Albanian, very orthodox. Almost a Catholic," he said with a sigh. "The Albanian tongue is, ah, polyglot, but interesting. You can verify our marriage, I suppose."

"I intend to," said Stu.

"Sunday, June twentieth, 1965, in the Albanian Orthodox Church—in Boston," Justin said evenly, answering the challenge. "It was during that time that I realized how important computers and semiconductors would be. I made careful investments, watching the growth of computer studies around Cambridge, and I suppose I was lucky. I am now what you would call well off.

"Those were the happiest days of my life, Stuart. Rita had certain female problems, some sort of yeast infection, and did not become pregnant for, oh, about three years. Mark was born in 1969. Then I arrived home in our apartment one night—January of 1971, I think—to find that three men had picked both of our locks. It seems they knew I always returned earlier than Rita because she would always pick up the baby from the sitter." His sigh was almost a moan.

"These men—they insisted that I was another Alessandro Bellini, who was very familiar with the Balkans and supposedly had information they demanded. My wife was from a Balkan country, which weighed heavily against me. I could not even make up a plausible lie because I had no idea what this other Bellini was supposed to know. They forced a dagger between my teeth, and held it against the roof of my mouth," he said, swallowing, "while one of them cut me."

Justin Paladino, his eyes locked with Stu's, loosened three buttons of his summer-weight shirt; pulled the panels of the shirt apart. Stu counted five old scars, like the petals of some cancerous flower, radiating across the pale flesh. Stu Ransome closed his eyes and shuddered.

"They told me in great detail what would happen to me and my little family if I did not reconsider, or if I tried to disappear," said Justin, buttoning his shirt again. "Then they left, promising to return. You can imagine my wife's fear when she saw what they had done to me."

"I thought the Mafia left women and kids alone," Stu said.

"Perhaps they only said the worst of those things to frighten me. In any case, Rita called the police while I was too weak to stop her. My memory for faces is good. Since the police had already come to my apartment, I cooperated. After all, I was an alien who could be deported. I still am."

"You were never naturalized?"

Justin shook his head; brought out an old-fashioned wallet thick with currency and searched its small pockets as he continued. "I looked at photographs for days, and identified two of the men. At that point, the Boston police were joined by agents of your Department of Justice. The Sicilians had committed worse crimes than merely carving up an alien, but my testimony would be sufficient to have them deported. The police had promised protection for me. And I believed them, until Rita"—he paused, seemed to lose his way, then resumed as he blinked rapidly—"Rita disappeared a few days later. The authorities placed a policewoman in charge of my son and put many men in cars around our apartment house in bitter freezing cold. Do not ask me what they hoped to accomplish.

"I received a call the next day from the men who took my wife. They told me where to find her. Rita had been trussed, gagged, and placed in the trunk of a car within a block of our apartment. Evidently they had intended to release her after luring me to the car as her replacement. But those unmarked cars full of men in brutally cold weather frightened her abductors, who simply walked away from the car and disappeared.''

"I don't know if I want to hear this, Justin," Stu managed to say.

The Paladino accent was thicker now, with repressed fury. "Can you believe the monsters told me they were sorry? A policeman forced the trunk of that car and found my wife there. She had frozen to death during the night," Justin said hoarsely, and added in a voice full of disgust, "I am sure you can find her obituary if you must. Did I kill her? Perhaps I did," he said, nodding sightlessly into fourteen years of self-recrimination.

"But I would not kill my son as well. I agreed to testify against the men who had tortured me but the authorities admitted I would have to change my identity. Mark and I were sent to a place—oh, perhaps not so terrible," he said, as if chiding his memory. "A desert prison of sorts called La Tuna. Most of the inmates there were—well, Joseph Valachi walked the fence perimeter every day. He was not exactly friendly, but he was typical.''

Stu's head jerked up. "The Mafia informer Valachi?"

"He died of natural causes while we were there," said Paladino, nodding. "Eventually it was decided that La Tuna was not the sort of place where an innocent witness and an infant boy should spend their lives. In any case, the men I was to testify against were never found. Under something called a Witness Relocation Program, I received help in getting new papers; a new identity." He had been holding a creased green card in his hand, and now he passed it to Stu. "This is proof that I am entitled to permanent residence as an alien.''

The little card carried the picture of a younger Justin Paladino, but with the same intense gaze and strong nose; a thumbprint; physical details that tallied; and a fresh surprise that didn't. "You had more hair then," Stu said, smiling as he returned the card. "And another name."

"Ah: Signore Carlo Lambert," Justin said with wry amusement. "Many Italians from my own Tuscany region have French names, and I thought a French surname would add a layer of misdirection. The Federal Marshals told me that they could not be expected to help me further, once I assumed my new identity. You will find that Signore Lambert taught at the Army's School of Languages for a number of years."

"That's where Mark got his KGB shirt?"

A snort instead of a smile. "That, and anything else he wanted. I fear I have spoiled him, Stuart."

"It can't be easy, being a single parent," Stu replied. "Didn't he know anything about your background, or how his mother died? He seems to think you're a Cosa Nostra man yourself."

"He was told that Rita died of complications after his birth. I know now that I should not have told him that, but what is done, is done. You would be surprised how a child assumes that his upbringing is normal, no matter how strange," Justin said. "I taught him to be wary of strangers." Another snort: "But it was my own stupidity, a chance encounter in a restaurant in Monterey one night, that ended the life of Carlo Lambert."

Stu said nothing, waiting, watching the quad entryways. Justin placed his papers in his jacket, speaking dreamily, seeming almost to enjoy the memory of his panic. "To hear your old name called by a voice from the past is most unsettling, Stuart. I turned to see a man I recognized vaguely from my days in Boston. He was smiling, but I could not—you would say, 'place' him. He sat down with a woman much younger than he, without saying anything more. I turned away and tried to be calm, but Mark was asking me why the strange man thought I was someone else. I spilled most of my coffee. We left as soon as possible. The last time I glanced at the man, I thought I recognized him as the devil who had forced that knife into my mouth. Had I been alone, I might have killed him.''

''With that revolver?''

''With a fork, if necessary,'' said Justin softly. ''I had no weapon with me; I—my God, Stuart, I was having dinner with my young son in a decent restaurant! But Mark *was* with me. I rushed him to my car and drove away, I did not care where, so long as I could get into the hills where I could evade anyone following. I found myself in Salinas. I took a motel room, and made Mark promise he would not leave it. And then I drove back hoping to find the man at the restaurant. I nearly drove off the cliff in my haste, but all for nothing. He was gone, of course. I drove back to my little rented house in Monterey and took everything I had to take, and when I left that night, Carlo Lambert ceased to exist. I made certain I was not followed to Salinas. I tried to contact the people who had provided my papers after La Tuna. They professed to have no record of me; I was alone. The next day I drove Mark halfway to Los Angeles and then returned to Gilman. It seemed as good a place as any,'' he said in tones implying that no place was very good.

''What did you intend to do about that guy if you'd found him?''

Justin Paladino's nostrils flared. ''What do you imagine? I had sought help from the authorities three times, and each time something had gone wrong. They had already washed their hands of me, years before. I knew that the entire weight of this country's justice system was not enough to bury such men as those who killed my wife.''

''So you'd do it yourself, without being sure who he was?''

A long silence. Justin reached down, pulled a grape from the bag, popped it into his mouth. ''Possibly. I think I would have tried to make him identify himself somehow but,'' he sighed and swallowed, ''we will never know.''

''You hope,'' Stu rejoined. ''Are you really going to face those guys now?''

"When I am ready," Justin said, and took another grape with steady fingers. "I have responsibilities to Mark, in the event that this does not work out for me." A pause, glancing sidelong at the younger man: "Would you accept the responsibility of Mark's guardianship in the event of my death?"

Stu's "Ohh shit" was a protracted growl. Quickly, then: "He's a good kid, Justin. I'm not hedging on that account, but—hell. I don't suppose there's anyone else you can turn to."

"No one," said Justin with finality. "And if I should simply disappear, the attorney Curry assures me, it would be well for someone to have his power—I mean to say, power of attorney in my behalf. I have chosen you, my friend. The thing is done."

Stu jerked erect. "Without my knowing about it? Ron Curry didn't tell me a damned thing when I called him."

"No. I was—wrong in that, I suppose; I shall remedy that when I call him." The heavy brows contracted as though squeezing the next words out of him: "Complete trust, Stuart, is a difficult thing for me."

"If I have your power of attorney, Justin, I could clean out your bank account. You know that?"

"So I am informed. That is why I signed the paper," Justin said. "You also have certain rights to my property. If I should die or disappear, Stuart, I wish you to do one thing with my son."

Stu wiped perspiration from his forehead. "In for a penny," he muttered. "Go ahead."

"Restore my car with Mark's help. The Toyota—" He shrugged, then grinned. "Yes: it, too. It is ugly and old, but serviceable—rather like me," he said shyly.

"Your alter ego?"

"Exactly. My spirit could rest knowing that you and Mark were involved in such—companionable efforts, using my money. I have given this much thought, Stuart. It is a thing you do well, and an extended project which bonds men together. Do it in my memory."

"When you talk like that you give me the creeps. You're not dead yet, Justin."

"You and I developed bonds of friendship on much briefer projects than these. Would you do it?"

"You damaged those bonds by lying about all this. For the sake of our friendship, keep playing straight with me. But yeah, sure; I'd do it." The idea did have merit: a year-long restoration on that Chevy might do wonders for Mark's outlook on long-term goals.

Justin Paladino eased his bulk from the table; retrieved the heavy sack, cradling it in his left arm. "I expect to be out of town briefly," he said, "but I shall keep in touch by telephone." He scanned the quadrangle. "One more thing, Stuart: do not, under any circumstances, go to my home or allow Mark to do so until I have told you, face-to-face, that it is safe."

"Why wouldn't it be?"

Justin turned and said as if to a child, "It would not be safe because it would be very, very dangerous." After a moment's thought: "If you find it absolutely necessary to enter the house, first turn off the water pressure. Is that clear? Not the electricity but the water. The cutoff is near the driveway entrance. I do not think you want to know more." He turned and began to walk away.

"I still think the police could help," Stu called, and saw a stolid shake of Justin's head. "Okay, but keep me posted every day. I'd like to know you're still suckin' wind, wherever you are." This earned a nod.

Stu watched until the older man disappeared toward the parking lot, then reaffirmed a decision. The police might have only official connections with organized crime, but a private cop was something else again. He heard the burble of a rugged engine echo from behind the fine arts building and glimpsed Paladino's boxlike old Toyota as it turned toward the street. Then he walked back toward the shop building. Somewhere in the near distance, a motorcycle engine coughed to life and stuttered off sedately. Stuart Ransome was not paranoid enough to connect the two events.

Seated in the old swivel chair in his office, Stu considered at length before dialing Karen's number. It was still a half hour before noon, when she usually queried her tape machine. After waiting for the beep, he said, "Me again. Look, I think it's time we brought Wiley in on this business. I can do my paperwork just as well at your place as here, and with air conditioning. I've got to do some upholstery work at home, but I'll shoot on up there afterward. Anytime Wiley wants to drop by, tell him he's got a client. The sooner the better," he finished.

His next call was to Ron Curry, who seemed relieved and much less cagey. Yes, Paladino had signed power of attorney to the man most likely to swing at an inside pitch. Yes, Paladino had also made a will, a very simple one; Curry couldn't discuss that until he got the man's permission. And by the way, was old Paladino considering a long trip?

Stu bit back an urge to unburden himself. If some mobster got close enough to slit his throat, Karen and Mark already knew enough to steer the authorities in the right direction. And the Beretta under his shirt was a powerful booster to confidence. "He doesn't tell me everything," Stu replied vaguely. "But he said he'd give you permission to tell me what you two cooked up."

That would be very helpful, said Curry. They shared a joke then, and Stu rang off. He left the building holding a manila folder crammed with paperwork and a vinyl repair kit, a few minutes after twelve, and parked two blocks from his apartment. With luck, the Saab might remain anonymous.

Stu raided his slumbering old Amana for a half pint of cold peach yogurt and dallied inside until he realized he was waiting for the telephone to ring. But the sooner he finished his chores and drove back to San Jose, the sooner he could talk with Wiley Reed. He left his back door open so that he could hear the phone and set about repairing the damage that a very thin blade had done to his Bug's upholstery. It took longer than he had expected but presently he squatted outside the Bug's open door, worrying with his teeth at the vinyl cement drying on a forefinger as he studied his neat patchwork. He did not see the faint scatter of dried red earth which lay beneath the right rear shock absorber mount, and so he did not roll under the Bug to see what had rubbed that soil loose. On the other hand, he left the Baja Bug in the drive after washing up, and so the tiny radio location device taped to the shock mount continued to report that Stuart Ransome's car was not in use.

He walked back to the Saab, going by a different route from the one he had taken earlier, watching in vain for any parked car that might mean surveillance. He saw no one, discounting the two boys who sat at curbside, heads together, tinkering with a shiny black Yamaha bike. Another time he might have paused to help. Another time he would have noticed that the boys were Asiatic. Another time he would have wondered for only a moment when a distant concussion shook the town.

But this time he stepped his pace up to a trot, hurrying to the Saab, careful not to burn his forearm on the blistering metal as he opened the door. Before he had driven three blocks, Stu could see glimpses of gray smoke now rising across town. He knew, somehow, that the explosion and the smoke were not merely from *near* Justin Paladino's little bungalow. He drove to Llamas Creek Road, and presently he saw the utter ruin of what had been an ordinary clapboard house on an acre of land with an old Chevy ruminating on its sins in the sun. Now the roof of the house squatted like a napkin folded over rubble, and white-painted planks lay like wind-scattered straws around the foundation. The roof of Justin Paladino's garage lay like some great folding door over the Chevy sedan. It occurred to Stu that someone had neglected to turn off the water pressure before entering Justin's place.

He did not slow down, but watched the progress of two small fires until the road curved toward Heller Pass Highway, and then he swung the Saab over to the freeway. He was too immersed in his thoughts to notice the shiny little Yamaha bike with two small helmeted figures that followed a quarter of a mile behind as he turned onto Coyote Road.

Chapter 9

WILEY Reed's GMC pickup sat in Karen's driveway, listing to starboard so that the high camper body seemed ready to topple. Stu made a note to suggest overload springs as he hurried inside, suspecting that Wiley liked the scruffy camper as it was. It would be ridiculous in a chase, but then, Wiley wasn't that kind of P.I. And it certainly provided homey, innocent-looking camouflage for a man using a 400-millimeter lens. Stu heard quick footsteps and the sound of a sliding door as he tried the doorlatch. "Wiley? It's Stu," he called through the open window. Behind him, a motorcycle puttered up the hill.

"Hold your horses," was the reply as a deadbolt snicked. The door swung inward to reveal a swarthy, erect six-footer of perhaps forty years with longish black hair, prominent cheekbones, and the kind of eyes that must have greeted Hernan Cortes at Tenochtitlan. Wiley Reed smiled as he did most things, lazily, off-handed as though contemplating a nap. "You got the boy nervous as a toad on a hot skillet, Stu," he said, swinging the door shut again. His smooth stride gave no hint of the prosthetic limb fitted just below his left knee as Wiley Reed led the way to the patio, stopping at the refrigerator to hand Stu an Oly Gold. Mark sat very straight in his patio chair, smiling nervously at Stu, drinking something brown and full of ice. Probably, Stu guessed, the iced coffee Justin favored while poring over model plans. Well, Justin would be working on different plans now . . .

"Mark, here, wouldn't let me in 'til I knocked on wood," Wiley said, and rapped on his left shin. The hollow *thunk* was convincing, though the prosthesis was really fiberglass. At that moment Mark twisted in alarm and half stood. They all heard the arrival of a car outside. "That'll be Karen," Wiley said with his easy drawl. "When I called, she decided to take a half day off." Mark Paladino resumed his seat.

Moments later, Karen let herself in, rattling keys with a cheery "Hi, guys. Don't overthrow any regimes until I make me some tea."

Shaded by the roof peak, the four of them sat outside and sampled vagrant breezes as Stu went over the latest developments. Wiley scribbled with a yellow pencil in a small spiral notebook as he listened. Mark's expression was unreadable until Stu described the death of his mother, and then the boy shook his head slowly.

Karen, studying the youth: "Mark, if this is difficult for you—"

"No, no," he said quickly. "I wish my old man had laid the truth on me a long time ago; it—makes a difference."

Wiley was studying his notes. "Some of this tallies with a lot of ancient history, like the M.I.T. machine translation studies, Chomsky—" He trailed off and waved a negligent hand. "You know."

"I didn't," said Karen. "Where an Okie Indian picks up all that stuff is beyond me, Wiley."

"Aw shaw, shit, shucks." He kicked at an imaginary pebble, then squinted at Stu. "You were on a roll, and I want to see where I come in."

Stu resumed. At one point, Mark snapped forward. "Yeah, I fall asleep alone watching reruns in this grunjy motel. Next day my dad drives all over hell, won't hardly talk to me. Has this bitchin' big six-shooter stuffed in a side pocket of the Toyota. Tells me there are some escaped convicts around, says he's just being careful. Anyway, we wind up in Gilman, and I gotta get used to 'Paladino' when I'd always been Mark Lambert in Monterey. My dad dropped a lot of bullshit on the school registrar, and I guess it all went down. But not with me, man. That's how criminals act. Sure he's my father, but—I mean, hell! What was I supposed to think?''

"The worst, of course," Wiley said. "This is one resourceful dago; be a pleasure to meet him. Does he know I draw two notes per diem plus expenses?"

"Relax; I'm your client. I can rent you for a few days here and now," Stu replied, and resumed his account up to the point where he felt the distant concussion wave spread across Gilman. "Mark, don't worry about your dad; he'd already left the house, and I'm sure he didn't intend to go back for a while. But I drove along the creek road, and I'm afraid your house is in pretty sad shape."

"That goddamned dynamite," Mark burst out. "He had nearly a case of it in the basement. Used a few sticks to root up some old eucalyptus stumps once. Great. And how about all the stuff in my room?"

Stu's gaze held wry amusement: "What room? Mark, the house is an acre wide and three feet high. Sorry."

Wiley, slowly: "But Mr. Paladino never told you in so many words that he booby-trapped the place? Chances are, somebody else set off his little surprise, and I'm not in the accessory-to-murder business."

Stu exchanged looks with the P.I., then shook his head. "He only told me it would be dangerous for me to go there," he said carefully. "For the record."

Wiley took a pull on his beer; saw the gray tomcat pad up to brush his leg; leaned to scratch Lint's forehead. "About time, you ol' turd-snatcher," he said fondly. "A flea collar, yet; these people gonna turn you into a yuppie, you don't watch out." Then he scratched his own chin and turned coal-dark eyes toward Stu. "Truth is, I don't see just where I fit in."

"You fit in where we *find* the truth," Stu said. "Mark, I'm sorry to say it, but we don't really know all this is straight stuff."

"Okay, then let me say it," Wiley rumbled softly, glancing at the boy. "Is Paladino an innocent man, or isn't he? Why are the West Coast Families really after him? If there's a contract on him from back East, it sure isn't the usual kind. There's still a few button men around, even if Fratianno and Spilotro are out of business. They would, um, just put Mr. Paladino down and fly back to Philly or Detroit and that'd be the end of it. These people want to sit down with him—but what are they after? And we can't just ask the old fella because he doesn't like to show his cards."

"And the first question," Stu put in, "is whether you could help out. Maybe as a go-between."

"Nope, that's the second question. The first question is how I can take a man's money for runnin' checks he doesn't want run. I don't like it, Stu."

"It's my money," Stu insisted, planting a forefinger atop the table between them. "Justin gave it to me to help Mark, and if you know a better use for it, tell me."

A pause, and a long swig of beer. Karen sipped her tea and smiled faintly, with the patience of one who had long since given up trying to tell Wiley Reed what he should or should not do. At length Wiley placed the empty bottle precisely on the tabletop circle of moisture; belched. "It's your money, bubba. You wanta spend it on some clapped-out gumshoe whose contacts are fair to poor with people whose names end in vowels, it's your problem. I may not learn a damn thing, but I'll spend your money. Tell you what: I'll give it three days, maybe a flight to Vegas or L.A. but only if I have to. Meanwhile, Karen can work back in the other direction."

She cocked her head. "How do you mean?"

He tore out a fresh page, began to copy brief phrases on it. "If our friend Paladino—who is not my client; *you* are," he acknowledged, nodding at Stu, "—is on the up and up, he'll know details about things that Karen should be able to research. How bad was Pisa hit back in the forties? Get a description of La Tuna; I've heard of it but that's about all. Any records of his wedding or what happened to Mrs.

Paladino—uh, Mrs. Bellini, I mean. An old Monterey phone book, if there's one in local archives: any record of—"

"Unlisted number," Mark said.

Wiley shrugged; nodded. "I hope this double-checking doesn't put your nose out of joint, kid. Just remember, it's in your own interest."

Mark, glumly: "I know. My old man's got more stories than Scheherazade."

Wiley laughed, a soft repeated grunt that would have been at home in a bigger belly than his. "If it'll help, I'm already satisfied on some of this. Stu saw something we call a green card—an I-151, the old-time permanent alien residency card. Anyway, it's damn sure not Uncle Sugar who's after him, they don't work this way. He busy with taxes every April, Mark?"

"Sure, just like everybody."

"Then he has a Social Security number. I'd say he's legit as far as he can be." Wiley finished his scribbling, handed the little sheet across the table; stood up. "This'll keep you busy awhile, Karen. I'll be in touch. I got me a strong suspicion that if you videotape the six o'clock news, we'll know more about what went down at the Paladino place today. And I could ask around. Stu, it's just possible that some badges may show up at your place to ask about that. Since Paladino didn't actually say he rigged the place with explosives—and maybe he didn't—you don't have to voice any suspicions. You don't even have to talk about Mark, 'cause you only *suspect* he's here. He might go anywhere if he takes the notion." The prosthetic leg was more evident as Wiley mounted the two steps into Karen's kitchen. Then he poked his head out again. "Almost forgot. You want to cough up a retainer now?"

Stu stood and fished into a pocket, withdrawing the wad of bills which prompted a brief whistle from Wiley. "Hell, I'd mug you for that myself, if I couldn't see the whacker under your shirt. You want to keep it better hidden, Stu." He took six bills, stuffed them into a front pocket. "Karen can write you a receipt. Want some advice?"

"Shoot."

"*Don't* shoot. Don't even carry it; not unless you practice regularly, which you know and I know, you don't."

Karen, with some heat: "And what is he supposed to do if he's cornered by these people?"

"Same as I do: talk ree-al nice. If I get next to anybody who knows about this thing, he'll know whose side I'm on—but you can bet *I* won't be carryin'."

"Not where it shows, anyway," she muttered.

He winked, said, "See y'all," over his shoulder, and let himself out by the front door.

Karen studied the paper in her hand as she sipped her tea. "Stu, you might program the VCR for the news. You remember how?"

He did, and found a fresh videotape, kneeling before the little Mitsubishi recorder in the living room like a supplicant as he programmed the machine. He saw the top of Wiley's old camper disappearing down the steep slope toward Coyote Road, felt the muzzle of the Beretta against his gut, and decided that Wiley was right. If Justin was the only one those people wanted, and if he was really preparing to meet them, and especially if any police called on Stu, he'd be wise to put the weapon away. Not too far away, though; he could not forget the repairs to his Baja Bug.

Presently Karen and Mark came inside bearing three tomatoes, an onion, and a zucchini squash from her patio garden. Mark, though no stranger to kitchen chores, laughed as he helped prepare the bacon for a dish called Forbidden Zucchini. "*Occult Cookery*; where'd you get this cookbook? The cartoons remind me of something," he said.

"Wouldn't be surprised," Karen replied, still addressing Mark, tossing one of her delirious smiles to Stu as he wandered to their vicinity. "The author used to do a great comic strip: *The Spirit*. Before your time, I'm afraid."

"The hell," said Mark, watching Karen slice long strips of firm-fleshed squash, flipping pages of the cookbook. "Old comics never die. Mel Crenna's got a couple of those in mint condition."

Stu straddled a kitchen chair, his forearms crossed over

its back, and enjoyed the interchange. Evidently punkers could be very shrewd collectors; the Crenna kid, judging from the numbers companionably argued by Karen and Mark, owned a small fortune in old comic books. Galvanized by a sudden thought, Stu injected without much hope: "If he's got any old model airplane kits—no, I guess not."

"I could ask, next time he takes us to a rock gig. He visits his mom in Gilman, but he lives in Los Altos."

"I will bet you a Kulmbacher, the best dark beer ever brewed, that he doesn't." Mark's quizzical frown asked him to elaborate, and Stu complied: "Your generation is into quick payoffs. Comics, video games, prefab models. The old kits—Cleveland, Megow, Scientific, Ideal—flew like angels but they took—"

"Deferred gratification," Mark crowed, raising a triumphant finger on high. "Did anybody ever tell you how you ride that into the ground?"

Karen saw the storm brewing. "Whoa," she said, pointing with her kitchen knife toward Stu. "Class is not in session, my love. I agree that Mark's generation is in for hard lumps if they don't learn how to sweat for future goodies. I found that out the hard way. But today's kids will learn it, too. And the harder you push, Stuart Ransome, the harder they'll fight it. Topic closed," she said with emphasis, browning diced onion with bacon and spices in a big iron skillet.

"You run a tight ship, woman," Stu grumped, and began to set the table while Karen dropped zucchini strips into the skillet.

After lunch, Karen helped tidy the kitchen and collected research materials—a clipboard with paper, a pocket-sized recorder, and a roll of dimes for the Xerox machines—before she paused at the front door. "How does salmon in lemon sauce sound for dinner?"

"I have some trout in my freezer," Stu replied. "I can bring them."

"You're leaving too?"

"Depends," he said, and saw no particular alarm in

Mark's face. He saw no point in creating any. "I've left some paperwork after all. I'll be back here by six or so."

"Trout amandine then," she said. "Okay, Mark?"

"Sounds great," said the boy, and responded to her wave.

Stu remained for another half hour, waiting until he was certain that Mark Paladino's case of nerves had subsided. He finished the Estes paperwork, sealed an envelope, saw Mark scratching Lint's bony flank as the boy turned the pages of Karen's copy of the *Ananga Ranga*, and stood up. "That stuff'll rot your mind," he grinned, adding, "Look what it did to me."

Mark glanced at him sidelong. "You're kidding."

"Yeah, I am; but you could die laughing. Nothing is funnier than a Hindu sex manual that takes itself too seriously." He stood and stretched, checked his watch. "You'll be okay here with your attack cat?"

"I guess. Couldn't I go with you?"

"Rather you didn't. We ought to play it safe until your dad gets a chance to defuse the situation," Stu said, palming his keys and heading for the door. He set the lock, heard the latch thunk behind him. Moments later, he was in motion toward Gilman.

He swung off the Valley Freeway just north of the town and took the creek road again. A dozen cars were parked along the gravel shoulder as he neared the Paladino place and Stu stopped as well, reluctant to leave the Saab. A police van was driving through Justin's gate, headed into town. Orange plastic fluttered in the breeze, a limp cordon strung on stakes around the ruins of the house, festooned with small signs too distant to read. Two dozen gawkers stood outside Justin's Cyclone fence, their cars clotting Justin's street. In Justin's driveway sat a fire truck. The fires had evidently been extinguished before doing much damage, and a small clump of figures busied themselves near what had been Justin's outside basement door.

A faint flash lit the basement entrance, probably a police photographer at work, and Stu decided against moving in for a closer look. He put the Saab in gear and drove to his own place, wondering if he would ever see Justin Paladino again.

This time he drove past his driveway, then turned up the alley and jounced along, passing his back yard, parking on the street around the corner. No suspicious cars nearby, no lurking strangers; he walked back down the alley and entered his yard with a squall of bad hinges on the wooden gate. It occurred to him, as he unlocked his kitchen door, that Paladino wasn't the only one who might rig a house with explosives. Or a car, for that matter. But who would gain from that? The hell of it was, Justin seemed to be escalating the trouble rather than defusing it.

Standing silently in his kitchen, Stu looked past the dining area into his living room. He'd half expected the place to be trashed but, he reflected, that had been a product of sloppy thinking. People ransack an apartment when searching for inanimate things, and these guys were after live bodies. In which case— Stu drew the Beretta and, with all the stealth he could muster, began to check each room. He moved in a careful duck-walk, squatting low and feeling like an idiot, perspiration runneling from his hairline. He checked the back bedroom last, with its stacks of magazines and hobbyist equipment, his sturdy little Kaypro computer sharing the top of a card table with a month-old scatter of relays and escapements from a model radio-control unit. The closet was innocent, too, crammed with vintage model kits and accessories. Even the dust was undisturbed; and this gave him an idea.

Stu flicked on the fluorescents and hauled a cardboard box from the closet, choosing a vial labeled "desert tan" from his stock of model paints. It was ocher, finely powdered. A faint dusting of the stuff would be barely visible to anyone not looking for it, and without a similar supply of ocher, a disturbance could not be repaired. Filling a small camelhair brush with the powder, he gently flicked the tip of the brush above the sills of both back windows, laying down a telltale that might have been tracings of ordinary dust. Then he moved through the house, repeating the process at each window. The knobs at his doors received the same treatment; the wooden thresholds as well. He could step over the rear threshold and simply swing the back door shut without touching the outside knob. He left the door ajar, put away the ocher and brush, then checked his new machine for fresh messages. Nothing.

He had, of course, forgotten no paperwork. But patience had never been Stuart Ransome's strong suit; and now he admitted to himself that he had returned to Gilman in the hope of learning something, anything, that might—well, lead to positive action. *You mean accelerate the pace, fool: admit it. Waiting is the hard part. Yeah? Harder than getting your balls cut off?*

To quench this dangerous internal dialogue, he withdrew a package of six pan-sized, frozen trout from his Amana's freezer and stepped outside, letting the back door swing shut. He squatted behind the Baja Bug's engine compartment for perhaps a minute, running his gaze over the engine accessories. The ugliness of this kind of bodywork was that the engine innards were mostly exposed. The beauty of it was that you could squat beside it and do maintenance—or check for any new wires that might have been attached; wires leading to a detonator, maybe.

Satisfied at what he saw, he lay on his back and eased beneath the high-clearance Volkswagen underpan. Somewhere he had read that detonators were sometimes attached to mercury-switch motion sensors. No external wiring, no need to get inside the car; you just secured your little package beneath the driver's seat or the fuel tank, attached one wire, and left the premises. When the vehicle began to move, or turned a corner— Porky Pig time. "Th-th-th-that's all, folks," he recited softly to himself.

But the underpan was just as he had left it. He did not check that rear shock absorber mount. Instead, feeling the frustration that quickly turns to anger, he wedged the Beretta next to the old canvas toolkit beneath his seat, rolled the Bug's windows down, and then backed it to the street, heading in no particular direction. He might have gone by Ron Curry's office, but what for? Or he could have dropped in on Fran O'Grady at the *Times-Dispatch*; slender, quick, and fortyish,

Fran would already have every official detail about the Paladino place plus a dozen shrewd inferences.

But there was no way to pump Franny O without her knowing it. And anyway, he knew damned well that he was driving the Baja Bug for the express purpose of seeing if he would be followed.

Stu need not have worried on that score. Either way he went down that street, one of the two waiting cars parked several blocks away would have noted the transmitter signal, which could be picked up from a third of a mile under good conditions. Even if he had used the CB unit in his Baja Bug, he would not have noticed any interference because of the frequency spread. In any case, Stu rarely used his CB anymore, and disliked thinking about how much the thing had cost him.

The men sweltering in the stakeout cars had no such dislike. They did not even dislike shop teachers in general or Stuart Ransome in particular. They did dislike facing what might have been a submachine gun, without superior firepower of their own. They detested any public face-off that might bring public servants. And above all, they loathed what had happened at the isolated little bungalow of Justin Paladino.

Stu drove up Animas Boulevard, then turned left at Heller Pass Road, following the route he had taken with Mark. West of town he saw an International pickup turn off behind him, and relaxed until he noticed a black Camaro coupe, a quarter of a mile back with two occupants, keeping pace. Behind the Camaro, too far for identification, a maroon notchback followed. Stu stepped up the pace abruptly. The Camaro pulled in at a small winery and Stu relaxed again until he noticed that an old maroon Mustang notchback had gradually halved the distance behind him. It, too, had at least two occupants. As he entered the first of the bends heading up to Heller Pass, Stu was crowding the speed limit and what he saw in his external rearview sent a flash of heat up the back of his neck. That black Camaro, or its twin, was now close behind the Mustang.

Time was when you could easily outrun an American muscle car on a winding road; no more, if it was well driven.

Stu crammed the gear lever into third and hurled the Baja Bug up the macadam slope, turning the wheel against oversteer as the big rear tires slid out on tight turns. In two minutes he had lost sight of the Mustang, but the winding road prevented him from seeing more than a few hundred yards back. He allowed himself, in driver's parlance, eight-tenths driving, where ten-tenths was his absolute limit.

The Corvair engine gave him almost the same power-to-weight ratio as a hot Camaro; his short wheelbase and big tires were a definite advantage over the bigger cars on this road. He considered flogging all the way to Watsonville, but at the summit overlook was a county park with several winding roads where Stu and Karen had spent more than one lazy afternoon. If he could make the turnoff without being seen, his followers would probably roar past the overlook and be well on the way toward Watsonville before realizing his maneuver—if, indeed, they cared.

Braking hard, shifting down twice, he put the rear tires into a wicked slide as he drew within a few yards of the turnoff. Then the Corvair belted him up the slope onto county park property, not hard enough to provoke a telltale dust cloud. He pulled off and craned his neck, hearing the thunder of two big engines somewhere near. When the black Camaro hurtled into view first, taking every inch of road as it flashed past headed for Watsonville, Stu entertained a fleeting notion that the cars were simply having a little rat race of their own. Then the chunky Mustang's tires squalled under savage braking and, as the driver spun the car end-for-end near the overlook, Stu recognized the man whose huge black-haired forearm gripped the window ledge on the passenger's side. That was the forearm that had tried to gather Mark Paladino in.

The Baja Bug's tires showered debris twenty feet as Stu flung the car forward. Behind him, the Mustang spurted gouts of gravel like rocket exhausts, fighting for traction. Somewhere ahead, on park property, lay a turnoff that skirted the park on a twisting summit road. He might lose the Mustang by careening through the park's cloistered drives but this was summer, and too many innocent campers would be at risk. The summit road turnoff, inside the park boundary, was better for his purposes: a rutted, forlorn affair, maintained as a fire lane. The Mustang's driver had expertly killed his forward momentum by that moonshiner's reversal, but he was a good ten seconds behind now. The Camaro? Maybe its driver had merely raced the Mustang for kicks.

Forcing himself to keep his pace half sane, Stu bore to the left, keeping one eye on his rearview as he sped beneath the sweet, pungent canopy of redwood and eucalyptus. He honked a warning at two children who played in a meadow just ahead and then found the turnoff he sought. The chromed mouth of the Mustang gaped several hundred yards behind. Stu ignored the fist-shake of a jogger as his left fender shredded foliage on the opposite side of the road.

How had they known he'd turn at the county park? That damned Mustang had been braking before they could see him. Well, he'd wanted to see if he was under surveillance, and he sure as hell was. *Happy now? Bitch, bitch, bitch . . .*

Stu had forgotten the old park access trail that forked from the summit road, but remembered when he saw it. With a demonic laugh he twisted the steering wheel hard and whirled down the primitive roadbed. Once a logging trail, it was scarcely a road at all now, with shrubs growing in the path that hugged a ravine as it led down toward the outskirts of Gilman. The Baja Bug nosed downward, rebounded from a huge root, and was momentarily airborne, its oversized shocks cushioning the slam. Stu's rearview was now full of dust, a smokescreen that trailed him down the curl of road.

The summit road would have been an advantage, but this madman's descent would rip the living guts out of any vehicle that lacked high ground clearance—precisely where a Baja Bug excelled. Stu used second gear, letting the Corvair engine do most of the braking for him, and forged down the incline away from the big trees at the summit, flashing past scrub oaks. Dust filled the Bug's interior as he bottomed his suspension in a rut.

He risked glances behind, navigating sharp bends, straddling horrendous trenches made worse by years of erosion. At the fourth hairpin he spied the Mustang; it had managed the first downslope but one front wheel had gone over the unprotected lip at the turn, throwing the car sideways. With both rear wheels in a gully and its chassis resting on baked hardpan, the Mustang was as immobile as a sequoia.

Stu eased to a stop. He watched the big passenger climb out holding a dark object near his face and staring up the slope behind him. And then Stu saw a gleam of chrome flash through underbrush far above. The distance was nearly a thousand yards and its mass was mostly hidden by foliage, but Stu realized that the black Camaro was now stopped at the trailhead. Determined men would need a while to get that Mustang back up the slope to a decent surface, and Stu thrust his fist aloft in wild elation. There was no way they could catch him now.

Yeah, but they've tipped their hand and they'll be mad as hell. If they'd just wanted to follow me, they wouldn't have come on like that at the park entrance. No, those bastards want me between a rock and a hard place. The big one's using a walkie-talkie. Jesus! And they know where I live . . . He was trembling as he had not trembled since that time when he was thrown from a raft on the Rogue. You could claim it was the cold water, but you knew it was the fear. And hating yourself for it only made it worse.

He saw the Mustang's driver pull a longish object from the car, then flop across its hood. The big fellow's arm snaked out across the hood and wrenched the object away, then handed it back with angry gestures. The smaller man stood up, facing Stu down the ravine, holding the device at his side. It was almost certainly a weapon, and Stu got under way with a spew of hardscrabble. He would be visible for much of his descent but still found himself weak with relief. The big man seemed to be running his show, and gunfire did not seem to be part of his plans. *So why does he have weapons in his car? Maybe for the same reason I carry the Beretta. Jesus, he's big; the NFL has pass-rushers smaller than that . . .*

Some three miles below, the old trail met a good access road, one end of which fed into Heller Pass Road. The Camaro could have started back by this time; Stu took the other direction and came barreling into Gilman from the northwest. Though his own place was unguarded, Gilman High's maintenance people doubled as watchmen, which made his decision for him. He fought off an impulse to stop on Roxanne Street and march into the police station. Instead, he drove straight to the school shop and damned his fluttery fingers as he unlocked the shop's atrium door.

After wheeling the Bug inside to a corner which could not be seen from the glass door port, he brought the overhead door clattering down again. He dry-washed his hands to quell his shakiness, telling himself he was safe for the moment.

Only I have to go home to put a new message on the damn recorder. If I had it here— He knew what his next moves must be, and saw that the first would have to be made before his pursuers returned to Gilman. Two minutes later, the sidearm tucked against his belly button, he was running steadily on foot toward home. There was nothing like a good run in hundred-degree weather, he found, to flush the butterflies from his gut. By the time he vaulted the back fence in his alley, he was sticky with sweat but steady again.

The faint dust on his doorknob was undisturbed. He checked for fresh messages, found none, and erased the greeting he had taped. Then he taped another: "This is Stu Ransome. I'll be out of the state for a few weeks. This machine isn't recording very well but I have a better answering service at a racing shop near San Jose where"—he paused to compose a phrase only his friends would understand—"they do the special work on my car. Call that number; they'll take the message."

Justin and Karen both knew he did his own mechanical work at the school shop, so they would know to call him there. For others less friendly, it should sound like a dead end. He had no time for freshly dusting that back-door knob, but flung himself over the fence again and, a minute later, slid into the furnace of the Saab's seat. He stuck the Beretta beneath his seat; fished his baseball cap from the rear footwell and his orange-lensed Suntiger glasses from the glove compartment. It wasn't much of a disguise, but it might serve if the black Camaro was back in town.

He took Monterey Highway to Morganton, sauntered into Solid States again, and delighted the sales clerk by taking a twin to the answering machine he had bought the day before. This one had a different query code. He sighed and jotted both three-digit numbers on his Social Security card, then looked at the rapidly dwindling sheaf of bills in his hand. "Easy come, easy go," he muttered, obtaining vast respect from the clerk, who took him seriously.

Late afternoon traffic was now clogging the main thoroughfares. Stu let the flow carry him into Gilman, hoping that there really was safety in numbers. He parked the Saab in the new development near Gilman High, walked to the central quad carrying his new purchase, then crossed to the shop building and let himself in by the quad door.

He needed little time to set up the machine, but somewhat longer to compose his message. "Hello, anybody, it's me. I got chased to Heller Pass about three-thirty, by four guys—two in a maroon Mustang, two in a black Camaro. I think they wanted to sit on me but muscle cars don't work on logging trails. The passenger in the Mustang was the same big hunk of meat who tried to grab a young friend of mine, so I think they're out to snag me if they can't get anybody better. I am getting closer every minute to the cop shop, folks, I don't like this bullshit one little bit. If you have a message, wait for the beep."

He was halfway through the quad before he remembered the trout. He returned, found the plastic bag full of fish almost thawed in the Bug's passenger footwell, and hurried out again. Had he been thirty seconds slower, he would have heard the telephone's shrill echo through the eaves of the empty shop.

Chapter 10

VIKTOR Danilov spat on his hands and rubbed them with a fine linen handkerchief as he watched Ray Nelson untangle the tire chains they had linked as an emergency tow cable from the Camaro. It had taken them ten minutes to inch that low-slung black monstrosity down the trail backward as a tow car, and another half hour of backbreaking work to drag the Mustang around so that its rear wheels could find purchase.

Without Danilov's great sloping shoulders and heavy arms at the Mustang's rear bumper, they would never have finished the job. He drew some satisfaction from the expressions on their faces: surprise, respect; perhaps even a little awe for anyone who could clear a Mustang's rear wheel off the ground. A furious man whenever fury was likely to bring results, Danilov had surprised his American helpers again with his calm acceptance of this predicament.

He waited until the chains were stowed before addressing them in rather good English. "So." He paused for effect, refolding the handkerchief carefully, staring at the others in turn: Allen Connor, the gaunt, balding, sunburned specimen who spoke little and drove the Camaro; his younger brother, Ken, who combed his blond hair to hide the same pattern baldness; and little Ray Nelson, disheveled and still in a dull rage over his failure to control the Mustang. "You have underestimated this man, or exaggerated your own abilities."

"Aw bullshit," said the Camaro driver without much heat. "Either one of us coulda caught that asshole if we had the same equipment."

Danilov's gun-turret gaze rested on the speaker. "It amounts to the same thing. You chose your equipment, Allen, and now he will be alert for these cars."

"A pair of high-center rally Broncos will do it," Ray Nelson put in. "I can boost one or two in San Jose."

"You mean, steal them," said Danilov scornfully. For the dozenth time, he reflected on the paradox he was expected to resolve. To achieve his goal he needed men native to the locale, men who would not shrink from kidnapping an alien. In short, men beyond the law who were intelligent enough to cage the quarry. The paradox was that few free-lance outlaws had the brains of a plate of noodles. "No, you will not; you will trade these in properly. Stolen vehicles draw too much attention."

Ken Connor snorted. "It was that fuckin' Roberts who drew the attention. I told him not to case that house without askin' you first."

"He has paid for his foolhardiness," Danilov said, "with his life and Carma's."

"You hope," the younger Connor replied.

"It was not my stupidity, but theirs. I have told you from the first that my government does not wish to provoke a crime wave on an ally's soil. Italy wants only what is hers—Paladino— without fuss or bloodshed."

But Ken Connor would not leave it at that. "Carma's folks were guineas, and he had some doubts about you. Just before he got out of my car at Paladino's place, he said you sounded an awful lot like a goddamn Russian."

"*Ethnic* Russian," the big man boomed, "as many another Slovene!" More quietly: "Italy and Yugoslavia share a border, Ken; I speak the tongues of that border, just as Paladino does. Must I show you my papers yet again?"

"No, just show me Paladino so we can get this shit over with."

His big callused palms upraised, Danilov barked, "Enough! Paladino has shown that he will kill to escape Italian justice, but as you see, he dares not turn himself in to your authorities. He will lie, or run, or kill as it suits him; and I am beginning to doubt if he cares much about this man, Ransome."

Ray Nelson: "Maybe he don't care all that much about the kid, either. You ever consider that?"

"Yes, but I do not believe it. I know something of this man. The father will be tractable if we hold the son."

Now Allen Connor spoke; and when he did, the others always listened. "Just remember what I told you before: I won't kill a kid for some wop runaway. Bust him up a little? Okay."

"I have children of my own," Danilov replied truthfully, and added the lie for leavening: "Under no circumstances would I harm the boy, nor do I want Ransome or even Paladino injured enough to need medical help." He heaved a great sigh and glanced at little Nelson. "Killing Ransome here would have been worse than pointless; the weapons will not be used unless I say so. Is that clear?"

Nelson: "I'll remind you of that if we manage to get this Ransome guy's ass in a crack. Don't be surprised if we have to soften him up a little. He didn't scare off with Carma's warning, and near as I can tell, he'd drive that fuckin' Volkswagen down the Grand Canyon just to give us the finger."

"I accept responsibility for that stupid chase, though it was on your advice, Ray. Now we will be more subtle. We must give Ransome more time; let him lead us to Paladino or the boy without further chases." Danilov opened the passenger door of the Mustang. "We will meet at the motel, and then Ray can spend more millions of lira to purchase appropriate vehicles."

Riding at his ease back to the valley freeway and thence to the motel on San Jose's outskirts, Viktor Danilov lapsed into a silence that Ray Nelson left undisturbed. A generous measure of truth, spread like olive oil over the surface of curiosity, would diminish the ripples made by necessary lies. Danilov was good at it, and suspected that Justin Paladino was equally adept. He wondered how much of the truth was known to this Ransome fellow. All of it? If so, Ransome would soon be babbling out his troubles to American authorities. On the strength of this possibility, Danilov would move out of the motel to a safehouse on San Jose's east side. He would continue to put these lackwits up in a luxury motel because they were his tripwires.

If authorities came calling, they would converge on the motel. If they made themselves known to the motel's assistant manager, Danilov would soon be warned. The man was also well versed on the subtle meanings of loitering strangers, or innocent-looking vans parked within shotgun-mike range of a room, or tourists wearing conservative ties who insisted on occupying a particular room next to another, even more partic- ular, room. If any of these things happened, Danilov would fly to Rome and leave a trail convincing enough to assure the Americans that he had given up his quest.

On the other hand, Paladino—it was handy to think of him as Justin Paladino, though his file bulged with other names—had never been the sort of man to tell whole truths. More likely, he would offer Ransome a tale as dense and savory as good Italian sausage, slippery with oil, stuffed with finely ground lies, spiced with enough truth to avoid a rancid smell. And if he swallowed enough of it, Ransome might think he had good reason to avoid his own authorities.

Given Paladino's situation, Danilov himself would have done much the same. Not, of course, for the Italian govern- ment; that part of Danilov's story was a carefully woven fabrication. It would tear quickly under the probing of federal agencies, but with men like Nelson and the Connor brothers it provided a cloak. Besides, they *wanted* to believe. The thick wads of Danilov's currency gave each of them five thousand reasons for believing; or would, when Paladino was sedated and in Danilov's hands for a drive to Mexico. Once he turned the man over to his contacts there, Danilov could wash his hands of this entire affair.

Perhaps Paladino would be interrogated in Mexico; more probably he would be smuggled alive to Europe. Briefly, Viktor Danilov permitted himself a trace of regret for Paladino's fate. The man had covered himself well, and for so long that most men in his position would have forgotten how to be vigilant. It had been Danilov's decision, after a week's surveillance and utter certainty as to Paladino's real identity, to crush him immediately by kidnapping the boy. Who could have believed the little ferret would be so elusive on a wheeled toy?

Now Paladino was thoroughly alerted, and had given his own counterthreat with a report heard across Gilman. If he and the boy were together, they might disappear again, this time permanently. Danilov did not think father and son were united because Carma, set on sentry duty, had seen a youth's shadowy figure slip from the Paladino place to hitch a ride at night just outside Gilman. Too bad Mario Carma had been too slow to grab the boy. And Paladino himself had remained in the house that night. It was not precisely clear how this man Ransome fitted into the puzzle, but at the moment he was Danilov's only likely avenue to either of the Paladinos.

Well, there were other ways to learn more about Stuart Ransome. Danilov knew better than to present himself to a private investigator with his needs, but with the right story, one of his men could do that. Nelson would never do. Ken Connor? Perhaps, but Allen Connor had the look of a solid citizen and seemed the most intelligent of the lot, despite his criminal record. Yes, Allen might do. It might cost upwards of a thousand dollars and several days before Danilov had a solid report on this new loose end, Ransome, including his friends and haunts. Meanwhile, an electronic bug hidden in Ransome's apartment might yield even more information. It was a thing he should have done before this. Ransome must be allowed to relax his vigilance. If he did not lead Danilov to one of the Paladinos on his own within a few days, then there would be time to take him. Of course, he would have to interrogate Ransome alone, perhaps at the safehouse. The Americans might lose their taste for Danilov's methods if they saw or heard a real interrogation, with pliers and bolt cutters. And above all, there would be no more fiascos like that idiotic high-speed chase which Ray Nelson had provoked with such childish enthusiasm.

Why had he not ordered Nelson to proceed more carefully? Perhaps it was his own frustration upon hearing Ken Connor's account of the blast at the Paladino place. Had Connor not driven down the road as a sentry while Roberts and Carma broke and entered, the toll might well have been three instead of two. Danilov glanced at his wristwatch. The evening newscasts would probably tell him more; American television was very reliable in this respect.

Now settled on a course of action, Danilov studied the waves of rooftops in South San Jose that slid like an arrested tide across gentle hills. Had he been Paladino, he would have found a hideaway somewhere in this sprawling chaotic maze instead of a bungalow outside a small town. That was a question, one of several, which he hoped to ask Justin Paladino, man to man. There might be time for that. Danilov knew how to extract hope from a helpless man, and then to gain a semblance of camaraderie by giving some of it back.

Not that Paladino would believe in his personal survival; the man was far too wise for that. But he might answer some questions truthfully, especially if Danilov assured him that the boy would not be further harmed. This was a promise that Danilov might even be able to keep, depending on how little the boy knew. As a father of two, Viktor Danilov felt a faint glimmer of warmth about the boy. He had proven himself a survivor; quick of thought, quick to act with intelligence. Those Paladino genes need not all perish with the old man.

Chapter 11

STU Ransome strolled to the far end of school property, crossed Tenth, and walked through two blocks of the housing development to reach the Saab. Men were washing cars; women were calling kids; and kids were trampling new flowerbeds. The contrast between all this domesticity and his own exotic problem lent a touch of the absurd to his walk. *Hi, there, I'm Gilman High's shop teacher and the Mafia is after me, and my friend from Pisa has just blown his house sky-high but we'd like to keep the police out of it, God knows why. Mind if I hide in your closet for a few months?*

He drove through Morganton again, then up the Santa Teresa bypass and cut through an old housing development to Cloud Drive. Karen's garage door was open, her Rabbit parked inside still smelling of diesel fumes. He entered through the garage. Pushing the door open, he held up the bag of trout and said, "Anybody for supper?"

Because the door opened to face the kitchen, he saw Karen at the counter, poised with an unopened fifth of Andre's Demisec champagne over her head, her eyes wild and wet with tears as she wheeled toward him. "Oh Lord, it's you! Thank God," she stammered, setting the bottle down.

His first surmise was that she'd called him at the shop and, because he was a little late, feared for his safety. Then he saw the broom and dustpan, and the thick glass shards she had swept into a pile near the patio door. The glass door panel had burst inward; long splinters still hung in the aluminum frame. His next suspicion was nearer the truth. "Where's Mark?"

She shook her head, bit her underlip, and met him, clasping him like someone drowning. For a moment they stood together, wordless, breathing together as tiny pieces of glass crunched underfoot. Then: "I wish I knew. I've only been home twenty minutes or so, but this is what I found. Come and look."

He dropped the trout on the table and followed her to the back bedroom. The hollow-core door stood half open, its thin plywood face savagely battered near the knob by something that left a hole the size of a cantaloupe and deep gouges near the hole. The bed, which they always made freshly, looked as though someone had been dancing on it. The sliding window was open, the screen and its framing ripped completely away. "Shit-oh-dear," he breathed, and moved to the window, staring at Karen's live bamboo fence. "The glass came inside the kitchen, so somebody wanted in. And from the looks of the screen, someone went out here. Maybe more than one. There are bloody handprints on the windowsill and your bamboo looks like someone ran through it, Kare. I think Mark must've locked the bedroom door and lit out from here."

"Stu, it's past time we called the police." She was still shaking, leaning against the wall.

He nodded. "Damn straight. But I'd like to talk with Wiley before we do. Any hint that this is connected to Justin, and we could be in separate cells. *We don't know everything he may have done.*"

"What have we done, besides help an innocent boy?"

"Nothing. But could we prove it?"

"Goddammit, Stuart Ransome, this is not the Wild West," she burst out. "I called you the minute I walked in, and figured you were at the shop, and when I called *there* I got a message not very well calculated to settle my nerves, and I called the Svensons next door and they're not home, and, and," she began to sob. "God *dammit*, Stu!"

He was holding her then, stroking her hair, kissing her on cheeks and forehead. "I feel the same way, honey. Maybe I should leave my Beretta with you."

"Don't leave me here now!" Her nails dug into his arms.

"I wasn't going to. I meant for later. Right now, I'm wondering about the six o'clock news." His eye caught a dark stain on the shredded plywood of the door, and he disengaged himself gently. "Look," he said, kneeling at the door. "Whoever ruined the door must've reached through to unlock it. And it looks like he was already bleeding. I'll bet it wasn't Mark."

Karen said, between clenched teeth, "I hope he bleeds to death, then. I really do!" Hands holding the sides of her head, she stared at the ravaged door and added softly, "I'd forgotten I could feel this way about another human being. But yes: whoever it is, I hope he dies. That is a terrible feeling, Stu." Her eyes begged him for understanding.

More in consolation than any real conviction, he said, "Mark's quick, and he's resourceful; I think it runs in the family. Ten to one, he'll shag in here pretty soon to ask if dinner's ready." With one arm around her, Stu led the way to the living room and squatted at the VCR, snapping on the big Sony color TV. He watched the VCR's footage rewind, then punched the playback button. He moved back to the futon, which had been knocked awry, and set it right. "You know what I could use? A ciga—oh," he ended lamely, and smiled. They rarely smoked, but Karen was already tearing the wrapper from a pack of Kents.

She sat beside him, lit up, inhaled deeply, and passed the cigarette to Stu as a commercial faded. The anchorman, an improbably handsome gent in blazer and tie, had on his serious face; and Justin Paladino had the lead item. "A late morning tragedy in Gilman, today, took the life of one man and seriously injured another. Lori Matthews has more."

Cut to a striking winsome brunette holding a mike, standing at the Paladino cyclone fence. Some distance behind her, a slicker-clad fellow discharged a foam nozzle into a smoking jumble of beams and wallboard that had been Justin's living room. Somewhere in that mass, Stu thought, lay a modeler's treasure of ancient kits and craftsman's tools—and maybe Justin with it. "Shortly before noon today," the brunette recited, "the small country home of an Italian national, Justin Paladino, was leveled by a blast that shook residents across nearby Gilman, California. One man, reportedly a Caucasian about thirty-five years of age, was killed instantly. Another male Caucasian is in critical condition in Wheeling Memorial Hospital." Stu saw Karen cross her fingers. They said nothing.

Cut to a view from behind Justin's property, evidently with a long telephoto lens. The brunette's voice continued while two men in plain clothes ducked around splintered siding, emerging from Justin's outside basement steps. "Authorities fear that more victims may be found inside, and neither Paladino nor his young son could be reached for comment. Investigators are not certain whether the injured man was in the house, but Deputy Lars Clausen had this to say about the fatality."

A cut like a Cossack's saber, to a rawboned blond wearing a Santa Clara Sheriff's Department patch on his uniform. He did not like facing a camera and kept glancing at the rubble with gestures. "We're guessing the guy had been on the basement stairs when it happened. The, uh, blast wave caught him in the chest and threw him halfway across the back yard, where we found him. The injured man was over near the front steps, we think. He got tossed a ways too, but that cellar opening was like a cannon barrel." His hand described a long arc.

The brunette, offscreen: "Do you have any idea what caused the blast?"

A snort, and a glance past the camera. "No question about it; smell that sweet acrid odor? It stinks of high explosives all over the place. There's a car battery and some other things in the kitchen sink, but for now let's just say it could've been an accident. Takes a while to puzzle through a mess like this; we're working on it."

Another shot of the woman, who faced the camera and ignored the jaundiced gaze of a passing deputy. "The identities of the two victims have not been released, pending notification to their next of kin. No other injuries were reported, though the local telephone exchange was flooded by fears of an earthquake in Gilman. Near Gilman, California, I'm Lori Matthews.''

Another cut to the anchorman, who glanced from his monitor to the camera. ''Authorities now believe the Paladino family may be on vacation. No further victims were found at the scene. In other news tonight, San Jose's Performing Arts Center is putting on the dog for another concert—police dogs, that is. The upcoming . . .''

Karen snapped off the set and sat back, taking a mighty drag from her Kent. Stu withdrew another cigarette, broke off the filter, used Karen's for a light. ''Well, we have it on tape. Whatever the hell good *that* does. At least, if they think Justin's on vacation, he can't be one of the victims. Lordylord. What if those guys were a couple of meter readers?''

''They don't do that in pairs, Stu. Maybe they blew up Mr. Paladino's house and made a botch of it—'' Now her voice raised an octave: ''And Wiley should've called by now. Oh, Stu, he can't dive out of windows and run like a boy, and that damn Okie camper of his couldn't outrun a bicycle! What have we done?''

''Kare, we have hired a professional who knows how to stay in one piece.'' He caught himself, looked away guiltily.

''Uh-huh; uh-*huh*! He's already lost one piece,'' she said.

''That was Vietnam, for God's sake.''

''So is *this*, for God's sake! You want me to play back that tape? If Wiley doesn't call in another ten minutes I am going to call the police and tell them everything. And what about poor Mark?''

Stu recognized that he was her only vent for frustration. To divert her he said, ''Mark is probably hungry. And so am I, and if we're as much in the dark after dinner as we are right now, we'll call the police. Okay?''

She shook a forefinger at him as if to say, ''Don't you

forget it,'' and took the limp bag of trout to the kitchen sink. ''You might finish clearing up all this glass,'' she called.

He was wiping up the fine slivers with a damp paper towel when the telephone rang. Stu reached it in three bounds, Karen standing as if cemented to the floor. ''Stu here. —Well, it's about time; are you okay?'' He waited, miming the name ''Mark'' for Karen's benefit, then let out a long breath. ''Hold it! Your dad thought he shouldn't know where you were, and I'm beginning to think he was right. Don't tell us. Just call us every few hours. I don't know how long it takes to trace a phone call, so I want you to hang up in a minute.''

Another pause. ''He hasn't called, but he was not, repeat *not*, in your house today. Do you have a place to sleep?'' Pause. ''It looked like you took a header out Karen's window. Who was after you? Maybe you should write down every detail while it's fresh.'' He listened, then squinted as if in pain. ''Whatthehell is a boatflake? —Ah; you sure they weren't adults? Some of 'em are pretty small.'' To Karen's double-handed gesture, he could only shrug. ''Okay. Karen sends her love. Call again soon. Very soon.''

He punched the disconnect, replaced the receiver, and took both of Karen's hands in his. It did not occur to him that in his relief, he seemed too carefree for Karen's patience. ''You, my love, are something of a prophet.''

She whisked her hands away, shaking her blonde mane as she returned to her salad makings. Nearby, the microwave oven hummed serenely. ''And you are the most exasperating nerd I ever—is Mark all right?'' To herself she muttered, ''As soon as I get this man stuffed with fish I am going to scream 'cop' just as loud as I can.''

''You want to hear it?''

She spun, glared, spun back. ''You want to tell it?''

He grinned. ''Karen Cavender, I love you.'' Before she could reply he went on: ''Mark got a nice scratch somewhere between your back window and the bamboo, he doesn't know exactly. You said this was Vietnam? Well, two Asiatic kids showed up, one at the front door and one in the patio. He swears they weren't adults.'' Chuckling ruefully, he added,

"The current bigot's phrase is 'boatflakes,' kids that flaked off with the Vietnamese boat people. Must be ten thousand of 'em in the university area. Anyway, Mark ducked down the hall and ignored the doorbell. A minute later, wham, against the back glass. At that point he locked the bedroom door and went out the window. Talk about nerve? He hunkered down and peered back through the bamboo, and evidently they didn't see him. The one that broke the glass had a meat cleaver, and he was bleeding and jabbering as he stood at the window. Mark said Chinese; who knows? But Mark called a friend who picked him up over on Monterey. He'll call again when—wup.''

"My turn," she yelped, and ran toward the ringing telephone. Now it was Stu's turn to fidget and listen. "Oh, have you now? Well, that's nice, that's just wonderful," she said, the words sweet as ant paste. Pause. "No, not at all, everything is just peachy keen. I mean, if you discount two Asiatic thugs trying to murder a boy in my bedroom who is now hiding out somewhere unknown to me, and two men blown to smithereens in Gilman, four more chasing Stu in cars, and let's see—yes, I overcooked the fucking trout amandine.'' Not once had her voice risen above a librarian's honeyed tones, but a terra-cotta statue could have sensed that Karen was fraying around the edges.

She paused again, and then spoke with exaggerated slowness. "Stu thinks it might be nice. Because if you don't, I am going to call 911 and scream—my—head—off. Not necessarily in that order.'' One more brief pause before: "If you stop for a McLardburger you will miss two nice trout. The choice is yours—well, I lied; the trout are perfect.''

She replaced the receiver and chewed her lip, turning her most dangerous gaze on Stu, who sat, holding one hand over his mouth, at the table. He sucked in his lips, biting at his cheeks, and shook his head. "Laugh? Not me,'' was the gist of it.

"You'd better not," she snarled, and marched past him. A moment later, assiduously avoiding his gaze, she said, "Set an extra place at the table. Wiley didn't need three days to find out about your mysterious Mr. Paladino.''

Chapter 12

WILEY owed a modest debt to Karen for being a few minutes late. He paid it by hauling a squat heavy bottle of Drambuie from a brown sack as he walked in. "May have saved you four hundred," he said to Stu. "I'll help you celebrate—uh-oh," he finished, noticing the glassless patio door and a heavy kraft paper bag filled with glass shards.

"Don't give me 'uh-oh,' " Karen said, pulling a heavy platter of trout from the microwave oven. "Sit down and give me one good reason why I shouldn't call the police."

Over a fluffy green salad, Stu described his flight from the four men at Heller Pass, and his use of a second message recorder at the shop. "I figured Justin would know to call me there, and I can call from here to get any messages," he ended, chasing down one last piece of lettuce on his plate.

"You get machines with those damn remote pocket gadgets like Karen's, that she's always losing or feeding fresh batteries?"

Stu shook his head. "I'm a hardware man, Wiley."

"That's what I'm afraid of."

"A *real* hardware man; the fewer subsystems, the better. These use three-digit dial tones. I can erase messages from here, put on new ones, you name it, just with the code digits."

"Pretty sharp; you just might endanger your amateur

standing," Wiley nodded, reaching for a fat ten-inch trout. "But how 'bout the Paladino kid? You said he's hiding out, Karen. Anything to do with that?" He jerked his head toward the patio door.

Karen nodded vigorously, angrily, and recounted her panic upon seeing the bloody mess in her bedroom. "No, don't get up now, it'll keep. Finish your fish before it gets cold," she said.

"Mark called just before you did," Stu said, stripping the long comb of bones from flaky trout fillets. "He's safe, he says. He'll call us later. But the damn Mafia has some Asiatic kids working with 'em." He added the details as Mark had given them.

Wiley, with a forkload of fish halfway to his mouth, paused with a faraway look in his eyes. Then: "Naw," he said, engulfing the bite, talking through it. "Too farfetched." He chewed for a moment as the others watched him; swallowed. "Or maybe not. There's a Chinese Mafia, too; Triads, they're called. But they don't use any round-eyes like the guys who're chasing you, Stu; too clannish. Funny thing is, the real Mafia has no beef with our man Paladino."

"God *damn*," Stu breathed, looking as though he had a bone caught in his throat. "You sure?"

"Pretty sure. I made a few calls around town, and then downed a Chianti with a guy in a back booth at Original Joe's this afternoon."

Karen looked up sharply. "Is that your idea of neutral turf, Wiley?"

"Sure; best food in town. Can they help who eats there? Anyhow, this guy used to be a soldier with the Families, and once you're in, you stay in or pull a Vesco. He's got kids, cousins, the whole nine yards around San Jose so he keeps his nose fairly clean, but he knows what's going down. He owed me a favor—well, never mind. I brought up the demolition job on Paladino's house; told him I'd be much obliged if he could find out why.

"So he goes away to use a phone. Comes back in maybe ten minutes, and now he's wearing a nice relieved smile. He hasn't the foggiest idea why any of his friends might want Paladino hurt, but they knew he was there, all righty. Seems the Families picked up on Justin Paladino right after he moved to Gilman.''

Karen, rigid with suspicion: "What had he done?"

Wiley spread both hands for her. "He had an Italian name and an accent, Karen. Hadn't done anything they knew about, but there are lots of other Italians running wineries in the South Valley and you know how it is; word gets around. So they do a little checking on Paladino. He comes from nowhere, no job, no friends, just a son. Guys happen to bump into him a time or two—just happen to when he's shopping, you know, like a chess game 'just happens.'

"And he's cagey. One guy 'happens' to notice the accent and gives him the old buddy-buddy routine in Italian. And he won't even talk Italian; says he's—I forget—Swiss, Hungarian, something. Naturally this gets some people interested; maybe he was a war criminal, they figure, or somebody hiding from the Families back East. They get some shots of him at a supermarket and mail them back East, just as a friendly gesture. But nobody on the East Coast has any interest, at least not in the connected Families. So they let it drop. Justin Paladino is clean, so far as the Families are concerned.''

Stu put down his fork and leaned back. "You sure know how to take away an appetite. So Mark's been lying, too."

"I dunno. You won't mind if I take this little fella then," Wiley said, helping himself to the last fish.

Karen, toying with remnants in her plate, said, "Mark is almost painfully honest, and he's as American as you are. I don't think his father has told him very much, and we all know he doesn't take his father's word as gospel."

"Besides which, you *want* to believe Mark is straight-arrow," Wiley said through a mouthful. "Hell of it is, we still don't have a clue what the old man is guilty of, or who's after him. Not the Families; not the feds. I guess we'll have to ask him. I'd like to do that before we pull the police in. If that's okay," he added quickly to Karen. "By the way: what'd you come up with at the library?"

Karen got up, found three aperitif glasses, returned, and began to worry the leaden seal of the Drambuie flask with a fingernail. "I've got the notes in my bag. I thought I'd never find anything about La Tuna, but the microfiches of *The New York Times* carried one piece about it. The dateline was El Paso. The map room at San Jose State had USGS charts of . . ."

With great patience, Wiley Reed placed a finger on her wrist as she was hauling on the cork. "You are a dynamite researcher, Karen. The payoff, okay?"

She made a wry face in Stu's direction. "You know what I think? I think you're right about instant gratification and children. Especially grown children. It may be infectious," she sniffed, and began to pour the thick oily liqueur. "La Tuna is about fifteen miles north of El Paso, near a little place called Anthony. The Federal Correctional Facility is only on the old maps. A major geographical feature just east of it is a mountain called Anthony's Nose. A mile or so due west is the Rio Grande and then New Mexico. Now, Wiley Reed, will you please go proposition yourself?"

"Naw, I'm too easy," said Wiley, reaching for a glass. "You know me, I'd hump a light socket if you put a little hair around it."

"That is *gross*," Karen objected, not amused.

"Glad you liked it," Wiley rejoined.

Stu took his own glass and said simultaneously, "Wiley, that's not helping. She's had some rough bumps today."

Wiley, nodding at them both: "Okay, new times aren't like old times. Sorry, Karen. Remember, you used to like gross humor."

"Shut up, Wiley," Karen said, and drank.

Wiley glanced at Stu, who simply shook his head in endorsement. Wiley sighed and drank silently to old times, before the advent of Stuart Ransome, then said, "Right. What else you get on Paladino's background?"

Karen resumed sullenly at first, then grew more animated. "The Army School of Languages did not advertise its faculty in catalogs as other colleges did, but the Boston *Globe* had carried the obituary of Mrs. Rita Teodori Bellini late in January of 1971. Services were held in the Albanian Orthodox Church in Boston. She was survived by her husband and infant son. The cause of death was listed as exposure.''

"Hypothermia," Wiley said. "That checks with his story. Isn't Albania one of the Balkans? It'd be her church where they held the services, so she'd be Albanian. Like Greek Orthodox, I guess."

She went on: "But if you expect him to give you a lot about Pisa, forget it. The place was absolutely leveled in 1944."

Stu, incredulous: "You mean the Leaning Tower and everything?"

"No, that and one big cathedral were left standing. Just about everything else was bombed into rubble. Sorry."

"Hell, that's worth knowing," said Wiley, and paused with his mouth open. "Bombed flat, huh? The city center too, I suppose."

"From what I read," Karen said.

Wiley pushed his empty glass in her direction, the skin tightening over his Amerind cheekbones. From long experience, Karen knew that when Wiley squinted like that, his vision was turning inward, fitting pieces of his puzzle together. "Hit me again, ma'am, I'm getting a glimmer." He watched the glass fill. "If Pisa got creamed that bad, the city's records were probably destroyed. If Paladino knows that—"

Stu cut in: "What better city to claim for a birthplace if you were born somewhere else?"

Wiley aimed a forefinger at him and snapped his thumb forward. "You got it. He could've—holy shit!" He sat up so abruptly that Drambuie slopped from his glass. "He wouldn't speak Italian to other Italians; yeah, goddamn right he wouldn't if he spoke it with a Hungarian accent!"

Karen: "Why Hungarian?"

"Greek, then. Yugoslav; shit, I don't know. Russian, maybe. Listen, we're talkin' about a guy who's been hiding for most of his life. He's a linguist, he's razor-sharp, and the folks after him don't seem to be able to grab him legally."

"Maybe they don't have extradition treaties with us," Stu offered. "That leaves a lot of countries."

Very quietly, almost whispering, Karen said, "Including most of the communist bloc; isn't that right, Wiley?"

"Yeah." He looked down at his drink. "Well, folks, Drambuie has a way of sandbaggin' a feller, and I have just decided not to dull my peawit any more'n I already have. In case you've forgotten, the communist bloc includes most of Southeast Asia, and you say Mark's visitors were Asiatic. We may be missing a better answer, but right now I'm posting some odds."

Karen had seen the tiny price tag on the Drambuie flask. Now she was thriftily pouring the remainder of liqueurs from their glasses back into the bottle. "I don't want to hear about the odds against tomorrow," she warned.

"Five to three, Paladino isn't Italian. Eleven to five, the people he's up against are no friends of NATO. That leaves us with one big puzzler about calling for help."

Karen: "You mean, why we haven't called the FBI?"

Wiley: "Nope. Why *Paladino* didn't. He doesn't want cops of any kind. Jesus! Maybe he *was* a war criminal; it just might fit."

"No, no, nooo." Stu's denial was muffled, his hands cupped over his face as he shook his head. He placed his hands on the table and stared at them as if hoping that some message would appear. "Not Justin. He's not the type."

"They come in all types," Wiley said doggedly.

"Not Justin," Stu repeated, his jaw set, and burst out: "Dammit, I know the man!"

"His own son doesn't know the man," Karen said softly. "Wiley may have hit on the reason why."

"People change," said Stu. "I don't know if there's a statute of limitations on things like that, but for me there is."

"But for a lot of folks, it's the other way around," Wiley said. "They don't give a damn about statutes and they will never quit hunting. I'm not sure I blame 'em."

Stu's fist slammed the table hard enough to rattle dishes. "Maybe I don't either! But I'm sure of one thing: I can't condemn a friend until I know what he's done. And pulling the cops into this may be the same as condemning him. Kare, I'm sorry.'' He stood up, nodding toward the hall. ''Take a look at the back bedroom, Wiley. You said I've got four hundred dollars coming back to me, and that will more than cover the damage here.''

Wiley Reed pushed back from the table, glancing at Karen. In subtle ways, both men made it clear that her decision would be the binding one.

For perhaps half a minute, she sat looking up at Stu, her mouth set in a thin line. At last she said, ''How much longer will you try to protect this fugitive from I-don't-know-what? How many more lies . . . ?''

''One more time. I promise, Kare, if he spins any more yarns or if any of these nameless bastards come after us again, I'll call the police myself.''

''And if you don't, I will,'' she responded. ''Meanwhile, I can't feel safe in my own house and I don't know who's watching me. I feel—dirtied.'' She shuddered, and suddenly she seemed very small. ''Would it be too much to ask if one of you stuck next to me for a few days? I don't want to be alone here.''

The gaze that Wiley shared with Stu was a complex exchange. There had been a time when Wiley Reed shared Karen's life, yet he had accepted her shift of allegiance stoically. Now Stuart Ransome seemed willing to risk that allegiance. Wiley would accept that as well, but made no move to tip the balance.

''Good idea,'' Stu answered. ''You mean a hell of a lot more to me than Paladino does—if you can believe that under the circumstances.''

Her smile lacked conviction. ''I suppose anyone with more than one friend is bound to get his loyalties tangled.'' Then she sighed, stood up, and began to clear the table.

Wiley followed Stu, who snapped on the hall light, then the bedroom's indirect fluorescents. Wiley said little, closely studying the ragged hole in the bedroom door, pulling a long and astonishingly bright pencil flash from his hip pocket as he looked at the blood smears on the off-white window ledge. "Not a decent print in this whole fuckin' mess," he grumbled. "There's enough blood on the door to type it, so leave it that way and keep the door in Karen's garage when you hang a new one; but you might as well scrub it off the sill. It'd only give Karen the willies anyway. But don't wipe off the whole sill. There could be prints I can't see. You gonna change the patio door yourself?"

"Tomorrow," Stu nodded.

"Handle the old one only at top and bottom, and stash the frame with the old door. Hang some plastic over 'em. Forensics boys might get some good prints later, if it works out that way."

Stu did not have to ask the circumstance. It would work out that way only if it worked out badly. It suddenly occurred to him that Wiley Reed was keeping a lot of speculations to himself, possibly because voicing them would do more harm than good. Wiley knelt again at the bedroom threshold, flicking a fingernail at faint dark stains on the carpet. "Wiley?"

"Yeah."

"You've had friends die on you before, I guess."

A slight pause, and a flicker of the Amerind eyes. "Yeah."

"Dumb question. It's just that you take things in stride so easily. It's true that I don't know Justin all that well, but I would never forgive myself if I got him killed. I just don't have a philosophy to cover that."

Wiley started to rise, and accepted Stu's rigid forearm in pulling himself erect. Still looking at the floor he said, "After a while you try to work it out so that whoever it was, killed himself one way or another. Not everybody figures it out my way but it works for me. This way, I figure I'll live forever as long as I don't do something crazy when it's white-knuckle time."

"You think I'm crazy?"

A long glance without expression. Then, with a slowly spreading grin: "Jury's still out, bubba. And I'm posting four to one on us. The little folks who got in here today? One of 'em used a meat cleaver, all right, judging from the wedged gouges. And a cleaver's easy to hide. But it's no good beyond ten paces; what it's best for is scaring the ever-lovin' shit out of people. Makes 'em nice and tractable. For offing somebody close up, give me a snub-nose Ruger Speed-Six anytime.''

"Not an Airweight?"

Wiley shrugged. "Maybe five rounds are enough for Mr. Smith and Mr. Wesson, but when you're as lousy a shot as I am you need all the slugs you can get. But a cleaver, now; it's also handy for going through doors when you don't care about finesse. A real pro could've gotten in here just as fast without all that drama. Stu, these people have had too many chances at you, if all they wanted was to off you. Paladino and the kid, too, for that matter. Man, I want to meet that dago in the worst way!" Now he was chuckling his soft belly-deep laugh, putting away the pencil flash. They both jerked around at the distant ring of Karen's telephone.

They found her settling onto the futon, eyes sparkling as she tucked her skirt under her legs. She was smiling as though she hadn't a care in the world. ". . . But don't worry, we've got it cleaned up. Your dad gave Stu plenty to cover it.''

In the ensuing pause, Stu sat beside her and squeezed her free hand encouragingly. Wiley performed the slight bend-and-twist necessary to lever a prosthetic leg as he sat down facing them. Karen resumed with, "They're both right here, stuffed with good trout and bad jokes. I gather you have a place to sleep tonight. —Well, why not? —Oh. I'm not sure that's a good idea, Mark. —I don't care who else does, they don't have young thugs chasing them with knives. —Su-u-ure they can. Honestly, I'd feel a lot better if you'd avoid being seen in public.''

Stu, with quiet intensity: "What the hell is he up to?"

She waved a frantic hand for silence, but her voice remained calm. "Okay, if you say so. —Well, look: call us first thing in the morning, will you? Stu's having a fit; I guess we've exceeded the two-minute limit or something. —Right; skank a chorus for me. Bye.''

The bright smile was gone by the time she cradled the receiver. "Oh-h-h my. I begin to see why mothers get gray.''

Stu would not show his impatience. "Because?"

"Because Mark is going to a rock concert downtown tonight with his buddies and will be up 'til all hours. He swears, of course, that his friends can take good care of him. God knows what he's told them. He mentioned the Crenna boy and got all flustered, so I'll let Wiley give you the odds on where he is."

"Talk about doing something crazy," Stu grated. "Maybe we ought to find out where he's going and go there ourselves."

"And do what?" Wiley asked.

"Hang out," Stu replied. "Look casual. All right, then, look menacing! You have any ideas, Wiley?"

"Oh, I have an idea he'll be lost in a sea of other clean-cut boys, ever' one of 'em made up like an accident victim or a down-at-the-heels vampire. And there'll be gents in uniform with brass buttons and dogs big enough to toss a saddle on, keeping a very high profile, Stu; count on it."

Stu shook his head in doubt. "Maybe you're right. Hey, Kare: what's a skank?"

"Slam dancing," she said, getting up. "If you have to ask, you're too old to do it."

Wiley lowered his head; looked up at Stu with the devil in his gaze. His voice was slippery with innuendo as he drawled, "You wanta answer that one, or shall I?"

"The smartass who does will get no sherbet," she declaimed, marching into the kitchen.

The men exchanged guilty grins. Stu began, "I wonder if Justin—well, hell!" With this, he reached for the telephone. "Forgot about the damn message retrieval function," he said as he dialed the shop, checking numbers on the back of his Social Security card as he pressed more digits.

Moments after putting the instrument to his ear, Stu glanced at Wiley and nodded. He seemed about to speak, then nodded again to himself, staring out the window. He listened for perhaps a minute before replacing the instrument. "You wanted to meet Justin Paladino? Well, tonight's the night."

Karen appeared as if by magic, her tone outraged. "And leave me alone here?"

"Hold on; let's talk about it," Wiley soothed. "Stu, why not let me hear the message?"

Stu dialed again, then handed the instrument over. Wiley hauled out his little notebook and scribbled as he listened. Then he replaced the handset and leaned back, studying his notes. "I reckon you know what he meant by the place where the bowl was hung in the tree?"

"Bowlus; a model sailplane," Stu explained, smiling at the memory. "Damn thing soared into some trees on a ridge near the practice fields at Gilman High last year. A lot of underbrush along that little ridge, too. It'd be hard to get there after dark without making noise. If I know Justin, he's probably there already."

"One smart dago," Wiley mused, underlining something with his pencil, then glancing at Karen. "He says to come exactly on the hour, any hour after dark. So anybody who comes thrashin' in there at any other time just might be sorry. I like it," he said, grinning.

"You might not, if he has good night vision and sees two of us."

"Three," Karen insisted.

"By God, I coulda used you in Nam," Wiley said to Stu. "Look, I can hang back while you go in and clear me with the guy, and Karen can drive around Gilman and make a pass by the school ever' ten minutes or so. That makes our wheels less vulnerable. How's that sound?" Now he was gazing at Karen.

"Scary," she admitted.

"So go to a movie, or stay home," Wiley suggested.

"I'll drive you in the Rabbit," she said quickly.

"The Saab," Stu corrected.

Karen, who loved her rattling little diesel, came to its defense. "Why not my car?"

"Because," said Wiley, "loaded with all three of us, it couldn't pull a sick chippy off a pisspot. What if somebody in another car decides to nudge you a little, Karen? From here on out, we're gonna take no chances. If I had any goddamn sense, I wouldn't be hauling a pair of"—the word "amateurs" floated unspoken between them—"civilians around on a case, but I've got no choice. It's almost dark now, and we can make it by ten with no sweat. Any problems with that?''

They argued over details as Karen spooned mounds of pineapple sherbet into Melmac bowls. Wiley left a dollop of sherbet and slid the bowl under his chair for Lint, who lapped the bowl spotless. Long shadows softened across the valley as they sat, and Wiley subtly encouraged them to talk their tensions away.

The emollient sundown breezes of South San Jose paid their usual visit, caressing Karen's blonde hair in cross-drafts, and Stu watched as she brushed hair from her forehead. The idea that the three of them would soon be heading for a rendezvous with a fugitive seemed, for the moment, to be nothing more than an evil hallucination, a youth's fantasy. Stu did not consider the possibility that youthful fantasies were already congealing into fact, converging on the center of San Jose.

Chapter 13

KAREN did not flick the Saab's headlights on until she reached Monterey Highway, but the late summer evening dimmed quickly as she drove south through Morganton. On Wiley's advice, Stu wore a dark blue pullover with his running shoes and dark slacks. He showed Karen the Beretta's safety mechanism. "Don't worry; a million to one you won't need it," he said.

From the back seat: "If you ever do, try and aim with both hands," Wiley rumbled. "It's not a woman's piece; has a goodly kick, and it's got more lightnin' bolts than God Almighty."

"So long as it has a bigger kick on the other end," Karen said, and in the dim reflection of the Saab's instrument panel, Stu read determination in the set of her jaw. "I intend to drive around the police station a lot during the next hour."

They were fifteen minutes early, and Stu directed Karen down several nearby streets to familiarize Wiley with the locale. She began a circuit around a wooded area that flanked Gilman High School property, and Stu almost missed seeing a stodgy, high-centered vehicle parked well off the road near covering brush.

He pointed. "See that old Land Cruiser? Justin's. It's a good quarter mile from where we're supposed to meet him."

150

"With good cover all the way," Wiley put in. "He's cased himself a free-fire zone, sure as hell. You want a good laugh?"

Karen, grimly: "You might replenish my supply."

Wiley: "Here I am, thinkin' this is one slick foreign-born fucker I wouldn't want to meet on a dark night, and God *damn* if I'm not doin' it!"

"You don't have to," Stu reminded.

"I know that. Don't get defensive on me, bubba, I wouldn't miss this for a two-week R & R in Tokyo. Well—one week," he amended with a low chuckle.

At five minutes before the hour, Karen turned off Tenth and stopped at a cross-street curb. "This is where I pick you up," she said. "Don't come running out on Tenth waving your arms."

Stu paused before shutting the door. "Why not?"

"Remember what I've got under this seat, and then ask yourself if you really want to make me nervous," she replied, only half in jest.

Wiley watched the Saab squirt away with a whine of its turbocharger. "She'll settle down," he said. "Always does."

They walked across a grassy practice field toward a low ridge looming beyond perimeter fencing, Wiley speaking as if to himself. "Way I figure, he's watching. I'll stop short of the fence and stand where he can see me while you go in. I can't go over a fence with any kind of style anyhow, but he doesn't know that. If I hear any sound I don't like, I'll head for the guy's car."

"Without a weapon?"

"I'm not a fuckin' amateur," Wiley grunted. He stopped at a white-painted, mesh-enclosed soccer goal box a hundred yards from the fence. "I'll try to look like I'm not hidin' behind a hunk of two-inch pipe. Put in a good word for me," he said. It was the nearest to a plaintive note Stu had ever heard from Wiley Reed.

Vaulting the fence, Stu peered at the skyline toward the tallest of the trees—naturally, the trees a good model always sought through built-in cussedness. Funny how you could return in darkness to a tree you'd climbed a year or so before on a trivial errand, without a second's hesitation. And Justin had known he could find it. *No flies on that dago*, Wiley had judged. No; and not just a hell of a lot of concern for anyone but himself and a son who knew better than to trust him. Stu pulled gloves from his hip pockets, moving through high brush, and stopped. "Justin?" No answer, but he had not called loudly. And why not? Surely, *surely* nobody else could possibly know the rendezvous even if they intercepted the message. Well, it might be barely possible if either he or Justin led someone there, but only the shadow of an outside chance. On the other hand, it was probably through his healthy paranoia, refusing to accept shadows of outside chances, that Justin Paladino had lived this long. And with paranoids, you had to play their game or take the consequences. Or maybe both.

Stu recalled Justin's admiration of Respighi's *Feste Romane* and began to whistle its opening bars, taking both the theme of saluting trumpets and the response of the strings. *If only I had some garbage can lids, I could do the goddamn cymbals too*, he thought, desperately forcing humor in the attempt to stifle other emotions which were now crowding in.

He pushed through foliage, stumbling on uneven footing. The high trees were up the ridge a bit, and he began to climb before a shrub caught his pullover. "Dammit! Justin?"

Softly, but not far off: "Are you alone?" The voice of Justin Paladino.

"I've brought somebody to help. He's standing out on the soccer field so you can see him," said Stu, peering around.

"Indeed I can." The sonofabitch had been testing him again. Justin's voice was very near now, and Stu realized with a start that the man was moving without any more commotion than a raccoon. *Uh-huh; ghosting along just this side of the fence in deep shadow, where I should've been.* Justin's voice continued its mild timbre: "Why is he here?"

"Because he's a private investigator I've known for years," Stu replied, his good humor fading, suddenly furious to find that his voice held a tremor. The fury steadied him nicely.

"I've asked him to help me out because other people are chasing Mark now. We think it's time for a war council."

Stu had never heard anything quite like the string of oaths emitted from ten feet away; not Italian. Greek, maybe? The soft outburst ended with, "Is my son safe?"

"He was a half hour ago." Stu felt the fury building and simply let it come, striding down toward the fence with no effort at silence. "And I can do without another second of your goddamned suspicions, and without worrying about whether you're going to shoot me when too many suspicions pile up." He struggled from the brush and reached the fence, and now he could see the bulk of Justin Paladino standing almost within arm's reach. The older man slipped something into a jacket pocket as Stu went on: "You're going to have to trust me, even if you've given me no reason to trust *you*. I could've hot-wired your Land Cruiser parked in the boonies behind the ridge, and I don't need any more of your *shit*, and if you don't want to talk with Wiley and me you can bullshit the cops because I'm one silly millimeter away from spilling my guts to 'em myself, and," his voice rising, "you can save the fucking Cosa Nostra shit! Wiley, you getting this?"

From the practice field, Wiley's wry exaggeration: "The whole town's prob'ly getting it, bubba. Do I walk in, or what?"

Justin had not moved, nor spoken, as Stu bulled his way into the open. Stu leaned against the fence and said more calmly, "Well, does he? He got a fiberglass leg in Vietnam, so he can't shinny over the fence."

Justin's "By all means" was almost courtly. "If we avoid shining any lights, your vision will improve," he added.

"Come to the fence, Wiley," Stu called, and continued, breathing hard, talking rapidly, "Let's get some things straight. Wiley is a professional. From what he's learned, he thinks you're pretty cute, but he's found that the Mafia has known exactly where you are for years; they checked you out a long time ago and they don't give a damn whether you fish or cut bait." Without pausing to consider, suddenly Stu was winging it, taking chances on guesswork as Wiley Reed walked up to the fence. "They say you may be a war criminal, but boys will be boys; you're my friend. They say you aren't even Italian, but I don't give a shit if you're from Mars, you're just my friend. They say the people leaning on you are just as nervous about cops as you are because they aren't all that keen on Americans, period. But whatthehell—"

"I am your friend. Yes. Please, Stuart." Paladino reached over the chest-high fence and, awkwardly, shook hands with Wiley. "Justin Paladino," he said.

"Wiley Reed."

"You do not walk like a man with a handicap," Justin said.

Wiley bent; rapped a tattoo on the hollow member with his knuckles. "You got good eyes, but you don't know much about prosthetics, Mr. Paladino. I walk just fine, and I can play this thing like bongos."

Stu, aggressively: "Stop testing us, Justin. We have no interest in lying to you, but you've been spinning us enough yarns to weave a circus tent. Tell me again how the FBI stuck you in a witness relocation program from the Mafia. That was a beaut."

"The Department of Justice, Stuart," Paladino corrected him. "That is true. The Mafia? Well—" He stopped, perhaps wondering how much they had deduced; perhaps wondering how to fashion a better lie.

"Happens I know a little about La Tuna," Wiley said almost lazily, leaning on the top of the fence. "Tell me the name of the nearest town to it."

"Canutillo," said Justin. "And Anthony; both quite near."

"There's a mountain named for Anthony nearby. What's its name?"

Justin chuckled softly. "Ah; Anthony's Nose? I have seen it too many times. It lacks charm, my friend."

"I ain't your friend," said Wiley, sounding more like a redneck every moment; it was his best tough-guy routine. "Yet. You tend to tell a lot of whoppers to your friends, and I get all whoppered out real quick. Tell us which buildings got flattened in Pisa during the war."

A three-beat pause, broken only by steady breathing. Then, "Too many. Most of them. You cannot expect me to list all of the historic buildings—"

"No, but we can expect you to fake a birth certificate," Stu said. It was a risky gambit.

"Yes," said Justin with a vast weariness, almost whispering. "I have told you much that is true, but some that is not. The less you knew, the better."

Wiley drawled it out, Oklahoma style: "Bu-u-ull sheeit, buddy. We didn't know enough to be leery of Asiatic teenagers. That's who fuckin'-near busted down a house with meat cleavers to get to your kid in broad daylight today." They heard the sharp intake of Justin's breath and a mumble that might have been a prayer. "No thanks to you, they failed. You know how much we better know? Everything! I've met Mark; he's quick as scat, and those little cleaver weasels found nobody home when they got in, and Mark has gone to ground somewheres else. Now I ask you, Mr. whoever the fuck you really are: *who is tryin' to drop a rope around your neck?*"

After a long moment of silence, Justin laughed softly. "You give me no choice."

Whatever Stu began to say was cut off by Wiley, whose Oklahoma diction seemed to have overtaken him by now. "Just lemme tell you somethin' about that, Mr. Paladino," he cut in. "I reckon I've heard that a hundred times in my work, and ever' God-lovin' time it was by somebody who really thought yes, he *did* have some choices but he shore-shit wasn't about to admit it. You got choices; hell, you got lots of choices, startin' with tryin' to bullshit or threaten the only people who are lookin' out for your kid. But I've made some choices too, and you just might not pull that one off even if you *was* goofy enough to try it."

Quietly, from the older man: "I have no intention—"

"Hear me out," Wiley proceeded, as inexorable as nightfall. "Not many folks really and truly drop off the face of the earth like you did, which means you are sharp as a fresh-busted bottle. Shoot, that's why I wanted to meet you. But you been pourin' out lies like shit down a chute, and ol' Stu, here, might be smart to cash you in on some chips he can bet with. In my business you develop a great ear for bullshit and Mr. Paladino, sir, from what I gather you would win prizes in Texas. Yes, we checked on your wife. She was Albanian, right? Happens that I also know about old green cards and new ones. From Stu's description of it, you have one of the old kind; why not a new one? I'll tell you why: because you'd have to fake it, and the new ones have blacklight codes that'd get your ass stuffed in the slammer first time you flashed it on a fed. How'm I doin'?"

"Like a professional," Justin admitted.

"The way I put it all together, you could be one of those collaborator hotshots our gover'ment snuck in here right after the war to teach sneak tactics to us, if they really tried to hide you out in La Tuna. Now Stu, here, don't give a fuck if you're Adolf Hitler: or so he said when I wanted to go to the feds. He just wants the truth, so he can help you. If we don't get it now, we can't help. Not won't, but can't. Count on this, Mr. Paladino: the next teeny little half-truth you tell us, as soon as we find out about it, we take to federal authorities. Same thing happens if either of us fails to get back to my place tonight. Ever'thing we know is on tape."

Stu realized that with this snarling diatribe, Wiley was making himself the rough side of a rough-smooth routine, leaving Stu the smooth role. Perhaps Justin realized it as well. But some gambits retained their impacts even when the opponent knew the strategy. To assume his role, Stu said, "I really can't do anything else, Justin; my lady friend might've been home when those guys broke in with meat cleavers. I don't like thinking about that."

"A *woman*?"

Wiley heaved a long sigh, ending it with "Well, there you go," in disgusted tones that consigned Stu to a loony bin.

"She was taking care of Mark," Stu pressed on. "He's hiding, calling us every few hours. But why are Asiatics trying to grab him, Justin? I notice that every time you lay a big lump of bullshit on me, you do it with a charming grin. Don't. *Who are these people?*"

"I cannot be certain." Justin's voice was leaden with weariness; the voice of a man confessing in court. "I thought at first that they could be elements of the Sigurimi, the accursed Albanian secret police. That is very unlikely. But Asiatics? Albania severed her ties with China long ago—with the Soviets even before that." Now he raised his voice angrily: "If only I can get one of them in my hands! Then we shall know," he muttered, a promise as dark as the looming trees.

Wiley was still using his harshest tones: "So you're from Albania."

A pause, so long that Stu could count the cricket chirps nearby. "Originally, yes. I did live in Trieste for a time. I told you, Stuart, that the men who killed my wife thought I was another Bellini. But the truth is that they were correct: I was the Alessandro Bellini they sought. Of course that was not the name I was christened with, but it was the name I used when I was recruited by your Central Intelligence Agency."

Wiley's tone was skeptical: "Now he's a goddamn CIA spook."

"A field agent, many years ago; the lowest form of life, and terribly expendable," Justin said dully. "I claimed to be a Trieste Italian, to explain my accent. My case officers cared only for success in sending teams into Albania, and God knows I gave them that. I passed through northern Albania easily because I *was* a native, and because I had learned to move alone through the Balkans, especially the mountains." There was a stubborn pride in his added, "The northern Gheg carries the blood of eagles."

"I had a granddad who said the same of the Kiowa," Wiley said. "But goddammit, the guys who bagged your wife must be the ones after you now! Albanian spooks?"

"The man who telephoned me that morning in Boston, to tell me where my wife had been hidden, was a Serb—I know the accent well. I suppose they were trying to force me to return as a favor to the damned Albanian communists, because Albania has few if any foreign agents while Yugoslavia has many. Serbs are Yugoslavs, you know. Your government *did* help me to enter this country, and the only other person who knew my real identity was my wife. Rita was a Gheg like myself; eagles do not mate with sparrows,'' he said loftily. ''Perhaps she relied too much on the *bessa*, because she made a fatal mistake in having our son christened with our original family name. Some Serbian agent must have noticed it.'' He moaned softly. ''I would never have made such a mistake, but Rita—she was very devout. No Albanian would have done violence to a woman or a boy under the age of sixteen, it is forbidden by the *bessa*.''

Stu: ''Who's that?''

''A cultural taboo, Stuart, as compelling as your taboo against incest. More, if you know Albanians. This, one must do; that, one never does. But Serbs and Croats lack these moral principles; they—'' He was breathing heavily, almost choking on the words.

Stu laid a hand on Justin's thick shoulder. ''If you'll just tell me why they would cut you up and then let you go, and why you're still wanted in Albania. Can it be so bad, after all these years?''

Justin's laugh was a dry, humorless croaking. ''You must understand that the blood of eagles runs thick with revenge. An Albanian does not forgive. *Ever*. I was one of a small band of republican partisans who obliterated a German detachment carrying—'' and here he paused again. The next few words seemed forced out of him by external pressure: ''A tremendous fortune in gold. We hid it in a cave. The communists had expected to stop that shipment, and I believe that they captured one of our men afterward. That is the only way, I think, that they would have the correct list of our names. Albania also has learned many cultural lessons from the Turk. And no one is better at torture than the Turk.

''The communists became Albania's new leaders, and they will never stop scheming until they have the fortune that they feel we cheated them of, and me as well. They will pass their pledge of vengeance on when they die.''

Wiley: ''After forty-one years?''

Justin: ''After forty-one generations. It is the Gheg way.''

Stu: "So these Serbs tortured you to get you to tell where you hid the money, so they could tell the Albanians?"

Justin's sighs seemed more from frustration than sadness. "They might, Stuart, but they never got their filthy hands on me. It was Rita they captured, trying to coerce me into returning."

Stu digested this glumly. "So you lied about being cut."

A pause. "Yes. Those scars were from glass exploding across my breast when I was hardly more than a boy. A communist bullet smashed the spyglass I kept under my shirt. I must have flown into the rocks like a rag doll but when I awoke to crawl away, my friend had left me. I have always wondered why; it was not the Gheg way."

"My Gawd, you sure don't ask us to swallow much," Wiley breathed. "But whoever's after you must be tied up with Albania. You really think they want your ass for revenge?"

"Revenge, and ten million dollars," the old man reminded him, his voice swelling. "I will deny them both. I will die rather than lead them to a stinking pit on the Fierze River!" Now he was shouting, facing the billion-star bowl above their heads. Bellowing it to all who might hear: "They will not spill the blood of eagles; Pal Kraga defies them all!"

Chapter 14

FOLLOWING his outburst, the man once known as young Pal Kraga found enough calm to ask for specifics on his own son. Stu recounted most of what Mark had said; he did not mention that, while they talked, Mark was probably raising his own innocent brand of hell in downtown San Jose. It would not have been very fruitful to give that news to a howling Albanian with a gun in his pocket.

Try as he might, Justin could not offer a rational connection between Asiatic youths and the men who had chased Stu. He recovered some of his good humor upon hearing of Stu's escape down a ruined trail. "May I suggest that you avoid sleeping in your own apartment, Stuart? Only until I get my hands on one of these men," Justin added quickly, with a rustling in his pocket. "You will need more money, of course. Here, this should suffice."

Stu took the wad of paper without asking the amount. "You sure aren't strapped for cash, Justin."

"That worries me, Mr. Paladino," said Wiley. "There's been some trouble back East with Albanians running drugs, and the word is that they'd just as soon whack a federal prosecutor as a mosquito."

Justin replied with a hint of truculence, "I would not be surprised. But what has that to do with me?"

160

"No offense, but drug-runners toss a lot of cash around, and when they have a falling-out, lots of funny things happen. If that thought crossed my mind, it might occur to the police."

"To that veiled accusation I can only say damn your suspicious nature. I am no poisoner of children," Justin snarled. "I have invested against a time such as this, taking care that my securities were negotiable."

"When you're suspicious, it's justifiable," said Stu. "When we are, it's not. If you haven't done anything wrong, why can't we go to the authorities?"

Justin shifted, watching a car pass in the distance. "I have told you before: your authorities made wonderful claims, but they utterly failed to provide me with a decent new life. I could have done better, and eventually I did. If I told you how incompetent they were, you would assume I was lying. I can no longer risk that."

"Maybe. Try me anyway," Wiley said.

The breath fairly whistled through Justin's big nose as he considered it. Then: "On their orders, I walked away from my new American car in Boston. I never saw it again. Nor was I reimbursed. My toddler son and I spent over a year in La Tuna, a prison—actually a *prison*—where almost every other inmate was a federal witness who truly belonged behind bars. Enough?"

"I'll tell you when you stray from the rumors in my business," said Wiley. "So far, so good."

"When I was released, my only contact was a federal marshal who got me a day laborer's job in California. I, who speak a half-dozen languages! He thought I should be pleased, the idiot. To refuse any menial job meant expulsion from the relocation program. I had been promised a complete new identity, but after a year in California they had managed only to get me a driver's license. No Social Security card, no passport, no birth certificate, no credit cards; and they had removed all of my Massachusetts records as Bellini. I came to realize that I could do better myself, arranging for false papers in Mexico. They do a brisk business in such things there. Fortunately, I do have a healthy mistrust of governments. I had a nice portfolio of negotiable securities dating from my years in Boston. They bought me an identity as Carlo Lambert that the United States Government was unable or unwilling to provide. Believe me, or do not believe me; I agree that it surpasses belief,'' he said.

"It would if I hadn't heard similar horror stories,'' Wiley answered. "I hear tell that in its early days, the witness relocation program was a real all-American fuckup.''

"Now you ask me to put myself and my son into their hands again,'' Justin said in evident scorn. "How long would it be before Mark was kidnapped through their incompetence? Would I reveal the location of that Albanian cave to save Mark? Yes, though many a Gheg would not. Mark is now sixteen; a man, in Shqiperia.''

Wiley: "Beg pardon?''

Justin: "The Gheg name for Albania. It translates as 'Land of Eagles.' But my son knows nothing of his heritage, and I have grown—American. Many a Gheg would stand fast, let a grown son take his own risks, and then take revenge on those who harmed him.''

"That's inhuman,'' said Stu.

"No, it is simply not your way,'' said Justin implacably.

"Spoken like my grandpa,'' Wiley grunted, now putting aside the rawhide manner. "Look, why don't we get you and Mark together and let you do a fade? You've done it before.''

"It is tempting, but they found me and would find me again—or Mark, which would be worse. I have tried the American way several times. Now it shall be the Gheg way.''

Stu prompted: "Which is?''

"Obliterate them first, and *then* disappear. And to do that, I must know who they are.''

"I was afraid of that,'' said Wiley. "I'm not working for you, Mr. Paladino—thank God. Anybody who does would be a material witness at least, and I'd get my license lifted for keeps. I wouldn't like that a whole lot.''

"I had the impression that you were a private investigator.''

"That's right, and I'd like it to stay that way. Forget all the Mickey Spillane crap; most P.I.'s don't even carry handguns, much less start wars with Albania. I've got a nodding howdy-do with some local cops, but to most federal agencies a P.I. is just so much shit on their shoes.''

"Let me repeat, I have no interest in contacting any federal agency," Justin insisted.

"Well, don't imagine that they're not interested in you. The Alcohol, Tobacco and Firearms people are Treasury agents who also deal in suspicious loud bangs, and if they haven't made three million flat footprints around your house by now I will be some kinda surprised. By the way, we don't really know who booby-trapped your house, and if you did it, I don't want to know. You're starting to leave a trail of bodies already. You knew about your house going up like a tin can, I reckon.''

"I hope the second man lives," said Justin.

"So you can get at him?"

"The thought has crossed my mind. But Stuart—forgive me, Stuart, but it is true: you are the only person who could lead the others to me.''

Wiley snorted. "Why couldn't you lead them?"

"Because a proper trap has hidden teeth. And I will be those teeth. Unless, of course, you would do it for me.''

"Be a Turk? Not my style," said Wiley.

"Exactly. And I have no right to ask this of you, Stuart. Nonetheless I am asking." Justin yawned mightily; sighed. "I have not been idle this day, but I think the preparations are satisfactory with few risks to yourself if you will only help.''

"I'm not up to torture, Justin, or killing people outright. Call me irresponsible," said Stu with dry humor.

"I would not ask that. I would ask only that you drive to the mountains, and then proceed on a backpacking trip. I have the maps.''

Wiley said, in sudden surmise, "You have somebody else working with you?"

"No. But I have put many miles on my old Toyota today. The mountains above Coarsegold are old friends of mine; those without heavy timber are enough like Albania's to make one weep.''

Stu tried to avoid any tone of commitment, but he felt a familiar tingle in his veins. For most Americans, any city would be better turf for such deadly games than California's mountains. But Stu Ransome fancied himself an outdoorsman. He found the prospect weirdly appealing. *All right then, exciting. And it'd take those bastards away from Karen.* "This place have a name?"

"Several. You probably would not . . ."

"Come on, Justin, I've hiked the Muir Trail."

"Then you know Gale Peak? Chain Lakes?"

"Christ in a kayak, that's High Sierra stuff!"

Justin Paladino chuckled. "High enough to bring on altitude sickness for many who press too far during the first day or so."

Wiley injected, "But not you, huh?"

"I have told you what I am," Justin said simply. "The wilder the country, the greater my advantage. I carry too much fat for a self-respecting Gheg, but I am not as old as that Italian birth certificate claims. I can do what I must." Now that their eyes were adapting, they saw his head turn in Stu's direction. "Stuart, there is no shame attached to altitude sickness. How quickly do you acclimatize?"

"Fast," Stu acknowledged. "I rarely smoke, and I run a lot. It helps. Hell, I told you that last year. You don't have to give me an out, Justin. I won't do it if I don't like it—but I'll have to hear more."

Wiley's cavernous chuckle was rich in the dark. "Goddamn, that's cute. He's gonna poison the mawdickers with thin air to start with, bubba. Unless they're Albanians too."

"Even if they are, I shall be waiting," said Justin, and yawned again.

"You've been running your buns off," Stu observed, "but I need to hear more, look at your maps, get Wiley's input. Why don't we go where we can get some coffee and talk it over?"

"I would prefer not to be seen in public," said Justin. His tone was polite enough, but it held a note of absolute prohibition.

"I know a place," Wiley said. "Garza College is just a few miles off. People don't think of it as public."

Stu asked, "You think the coffee shop will be open?"

"The student union was, when I took night courses on police science," Wiley replied. "We'd have to feed machines for coffee, but it's off the beaten path. And there's more'n one road in."

"Very shrewd," Justin said. "Shall we take my car?"

"Better if we swing by in ten minutes or so, and you can follow so we can go our separate ways from there," Stu replied. "Look for my Saab; I saw where you're parked."

"One thing," Wiley said as Stu went over the fence. "We'll have a woman with us."

"Is that necessary?"

"She'll think so. But don't ask her name or anything else about her."

Justin was laughing softly now. "Yes, of course. An interesting irony: the less *I* know, the better—just in case."

Moments later, Justin Paladino had disappeared into the brush while Stu and Wiley hurried across the practice fields. Halfway to Tenth Street, Stu broke the silence. "Well, what do you think?"

"About his story? I think he's peeled the last layer of lies off his personal onion. The witness relocation program is lots better than it used to be, but if I was him I'd move mountains to avoid the feds. I dunno what to think about your chances as bait, Stu. Ask me again when we've heard it all. This Albanian seems quite a guy; one measure of a man is whether he's tough-minded about himself."

"Agreeing the less he knows about Karen, the better?"

"Yeah; especially when she's one of his few links to his own son. Just don't forget: a man who's willing to be tough on himself can be rough as a cob on *you*."

Chapter 15

WHILE city fathers in other regions wondered where their next shovelful of pothole patch was coming from, San Jose built whole new thoroughfares, a convention center, and an imposing new Center for Performing Arts. All of this was benevolent fallout from the unprecedented local boom, brought about by the semiconductor industry. Little wonder that refugees from Southeast Asia swarmed to settle near the center of this action.

They settled by the thousands, and many small restaurants along tacky Santa Clara Street near San Jose State University no longer sold tacos or scallopini. Now their signs were unreadable and unpronounceable to most Occidentals, the fare mysterious and spiced to please the palate of a Vietnamese, a Cambodian, a Thai. Though many of the specialties were authentic, there were glaring omissions; the entrees ran to rice, fish, and chicken not so much because monkey was illegal, but because it was tough, stringy, and hard to get. Many of the customers who frequented these places brought centuries of tradition with them. A fair number of them were determined to become good law-abiding citizens as quickly as possible. Some, however, had kept their cynicism along with their intelligent drive to succeed; the only American laws they memorized were immigration laws.

Between the San Jose State campus and the Bayshore Freeway lay a welter of older structures identified with charming discretion as a modest-rent district. It adjoined Santa Clara Street, and with its large families of boat people it generated jokes to the effect that occupation by more than ten million was dangerous and unlawful.

Among the new cynics were some Asiatic youths, especially those who found rough treatment in public schools. Naturally they banded with their own kind for safety. Inevitably these bands became the petri dishes in which Asiatic criminals could grow their replacements.

Some residents of San Jose spoke of these quietly violent youths as a Chinese Mafia. This was untrue; the Triads of the Chinese Mafia, once called tongs, maintained power as near as Oakland and San Francisco, but the Triads were far too conservative and cautious to enlist these new people in San Jose. Not just yet. Besides, there was no love lost between the subtle capitalist Triads and the communist People's Republic of China, and rumors in Chinatown suggested that the communist consulate on San Francisco's Laguna Street had its own connections among the new people.

Whipcord-slender Willy Thuong was an unlikely connection who had roomed with six other youths on San Fernando, near the San Jose State campus, until Willy read a book about two enterprising young American sweethearts, Daulton Lee and Chris Boyce. In those pages, he first glimpsed his special vision of a ready source of cash. At first, he would have been content to rustle enough money to pay for martial arts practice. Though he had learned necessary street-fighting tricks on the earthen streets of Cao Lanh, Willy had always yearned to develop a sense of style. Now seventeen-year-old Willy had his own room, an unimaginable luxury six years earlier when he had escaped Vietnam with a score of others across the reeking salt mudflats of Rach Gia to a leaky boat.

Thanks to his mother, Willy had picked up passable English and some Chinese as a boy. Thanks to the black American father he never met, Willy's complexion, his hair, and his facial structure made him everywhere a curiosity.

Willy did not like being a curiosity, and so he was cynical about people in general and American fathers in particular. He liked having a lively intelligence, he liked his status as a leader of other youths, and especially he liked improving his martial arts skills. Willy's confidence, intelligence, and cynicism were such that he had followed the forthright policy of Daulton Lee, initially contacting the consulate on Laguna Street, rather than the other way around. It took the consulate staff seven months to ascertain that their great good luck was not some American ploy to play a youthful double agent against them.

The Chinese paid Willy Thuong irregularly but it amounted to six hundred dollars a month, with bonuses for small errands that began with misdemeanors and escalated to felonies in a pattern that cemented Willy's allegiance. Willy could have made twice that much money commanding a floor polishing machine in Sunnyvale, but it was his dream to command his own little army, and generals do not run floor polishers. Taking great care in his selections, Willy Thuong now had three young soldiers: two Vietnamese, one Thai. That a Thai would fit into such a group was a sign of unsettled times.

Sukree Sirikul, the Thai, had begun by challenging Willy in a martial arts class. Sirikul's parents had emigrated with money and pull, and he normally kept a lofty distance from youths like Willy on the few occasions when he met them. But it is hard to be lofty when you are cold meat on a practice mat, staring up at a kinky-haired boatflake half a head shorter than you. Sirikul cultivated Willy to learn his moves, and gradually came to realize that he could never learn Willy's built-in speed. Taller than most Asiatics, handsome and well dressed, ready for any reasonable risk, quick with witticisms—they all spoke the English of the veteran TV-watcher now—Sukree Sirikul could ingratiate himself among the round-eyes where Willy could not. And he could lay his hands on a few glassine envelopes of cocaine whenever Willy needed the stuff for a bribe—the coin of the realm in some parts of Silicon Valley. This was a facet of Willy's work which the folks at the consulate never knew. For Chinese, they were remarkably incurious about Willy's methods so long as they had his allegiance.

Phan Chao and Nguyen Van Trac were Vietnamese boys who needed something to believe in, and had found it hard to believe in crowded apartments when youths like Willy lived alone. Chao, like many Vietnamese, was ethnic Chinese. Small for his sixteen years, Chao had the courage of a Burmese tiger coupled, alas, with the brains of a monkey. His weakness was superstition, and Willy Thuong could play tunes on that weakness as though Chao were a Chinese Wurlitzer. Phan Chao was exactly what Willy was looking for.

Nguyen Van Trac was their eldest at eighteen, a youth of medium height, solidly built, and as obedient as a circus mutt. He had developed the trick of presenting himself to outsiders as a cheerful fool, though Trac was nothing of the kind. Trac could deflect anger or suspicion as a prism deflects light, and he did not mind sandbagging Americans by playing the mystified, stupid heathen Oriental. He did not mind because he knew that, sooner or later, the American would come to realize who, between the two of them, had been mystified and stupid.

To date, Willy's amateur group had been of very modest use to the Chinese People's Republic. Willy imagined that his major coup had been listing the names and addresses of illegal Asiatics who eked out a rough, shadowy existence working in San Jose restaurants. Actually the Chinese had learned more from the boxes of paper that Willy's boys filched from trash bins behind two small firms which dealt in research on machine bubble memories. An engineer's rough notes did not have to be stamped "COMPANY PROPRIETARY" to be useful, if that engineer were fool enough to discard notes in an ordinary trash receptacle instead of a burn barrel. With this small triumph the Chinese verified what they already knew: a professional can be incompetent, and an amateur can be more competent than he knows.

The consulate staff on Laguna Street did not know why their diplomatic pouch from Beijing had included a priority demand for the "recovery" of an Italian-American youth, to be delivered to a certain safehouse in South San Francisco. They did know that two of their loosely attached staff had made arrangements for transshipment of one live body in the hold of a freighter, from San Francisco to Pusan. Only those two staff members knew that Mark Paladino was to be swapped for his own father, and that Justin Paladino might be a useful pawn in serious negotiations for submarine pens on the Adriatic. They suspected also that the Soviet Union might have received the same commission from Albania.

The Soviets kept excellent files on Chinese professional staff, and it was essential that "loosely attached" Chinese trade mission personnel *not* be traced to the vicinity of a Paladino. Beijing only knew what might happen if one of their professionals were caught kidnapping an American youth. Lacking more time to prepare better arrangements, the Chinese elected to rely on what they jokingly called *their* boat people. If Willy Thuong were caught—well, he was easy enough to deny. Who would believe that the Chinese employed a Vietnamese youth who had once risked death to escape communism?

Willy Thuong carefully avoided making the mistakes of his models, Lee and Boyce. None of his soldiers had a drug habit, if one discounted an occasional toke of hash, and none knew that Willy's connections were communist Chinese. Willy's secondhand black Yamaha was registered to Trac, who was eighteen. Sirikul's white BMW coupe was licensed to his parents, and it was Willy's intention to truss Mark Paladino into the Bimmer's trunk for the trip to South San Francisco.

The trouble was that Willy and Trac, on the Yamaha, had only begun to look Mark Paladino over in Gilman, from a safe distance, when they saw him escape from three men in a brown Ford. Willy thought perhaps the consulate people had sent two teams, and was fiercely elated to see the men charge off from Gilman High empty-handed. He decided against calling the South San Francisco number; he would wait until he had the boy safely in the Bimmer. He and Trac waited for hours before they saw Stu Ransome's yellow VW strike out across the practice fields, Mark Paladino riding while a rugged-looking Anglo drove.

Something told Willy Thuong that, if his quarry had spent much of the evening in a high school shop, that shop would be worth watching. He left the obedient Nguyen Van Trac to watch the place, drove the Yamaha aimlessly around Gilman until dark in search of a yellow specially modified VW, then took in a movie at the Valley Theatre. When he returned, Trac was both excited and surly: excited because he had seen a man jog to the Gilman High parking lot around eleven P.M., and while the man sat warming a blue turbo Saab, his face lit dimly by interior lights, Trac saw from the cover of shrubs that the man was almost certainly the same round-eye who had driven the yellow VW. The surliness was because Willy had taken the Yamaha, so that Nguyen Van Trac could not follow and had only a license number. All the way back to San Jose that night, riding behind Trac, Willy wondered how professionals would have pursued the matter.

Willy did not know how to trace a license plate, but he knew that Gilman was small enough to canvass on a Yamaha; and the Saab's driver had jogged in from the north, according to Trac. The next morning, Willy sent Trac and Chao to Gilman in search of a yellow VW or a blue Saab. They found the VW and the Saab both at midmorning, parked in the same driveway.

Because nobody pays much attention to a boy fiddling with his Yamaha or bouncing an old golf ball, it was a simple matter for Trac and Chao to wait from a block away in hopes that Mark Paladino would get into one of those cars. When Stu Ransome emerged with his B-4 bag, Trac followed the Saab alone to the high school. He knew the man on sight by now; spotted him later inside the school quad talking to another man; and recognized the old Land Cruiser parked nearby as identical to the one he had seen when following Mark Paladino from his home. Trac already knew where the Saab's owner lived, so he followed the Land Cruiser this time. He followed it some distance out of town on the highway toward Los Banos and the High Sierra range over the eastern horizon before returning to Chao, who was still loitering within a block of the parked VW and waiting for Mark to appear.

When Stu Ransome made repairs to his VW's upholstery, the youths were watching. Trac was quietly furious with himself because it was that numbnuts Chao who thought to ask where the Saab might be. Trac found it parked two blocks away and knew, with mounting excitement, that this husky Anglo was playing some sort of serious game. Both boys settled down to wait within sight of the Saab, pretending to work on the Yamaha. Chao would have taken to his heels when this Anglo suddenly appeared from an alleyway, but Trac gripped his sleeve and forced him to hunker down as though inspecting the engine casting. The moment passed, and so did Stuart Ransome. When Stu heard a distant explosion and hurried to drive the Saab past the Paladino home, he was too intent on watching for smoke on the skyline to see that the Yamaha was no longer an immovable object.

Trac and Chao had stayed well back, keeping the Saab in sight easily because traffic was light. Trac had no difficulty trailing the Saab up the freeway, and felt only a moment's panic on Coyote Road before Chao leaned forward, his arm pointing toward the Saab as it circled up toward Cloud Drive. The boys could not know that Mark Paladino was very near, but they saw where the Saab was parked, in the driveway near a limp-springed GMC camper. It seemed likely to Trac that the place might be full of people. Because the boys were within fifteen easy minutes of Willy Thuong's place, they made it there in twelve. Chao's account was chaotic; Trac's too optimistic. Willy felt that the chances were very small that the house on Cloud Drive would yield Mark Paladino, but certainly the place was worth a dry run. Sukree Sirikul's little BMW coupe was buzzing up the hill toward Karen Cavender's house an hour and a half later with four occupants. With great luck, it might soon hold five—a spare, so to speak, in the trunk.

Trac had spoken of cars, but none were visible in the driveway. Trac and Sirikul drove around the hilltop neighborhood as they had seen gangsters do on TV. Willy himself went to Karen's front door, armed only with his skills and confidence, while Phan Chao climbed around to the patio with a weapon he had always fancied. It was Chao who became overeager, smashing the glass and cutting himself badly, after he saw and heard movement in the house but no response to Willy's ringing.

Willy was seconds too slow to see Mark Paladino diving through the bamboo hedge, but very quick to realize that any alert neighbor might have squad cars converging within minutes. He might have saved himself the worry: Cloud Drive was home mostly to two-income families and the neighboring houses were empty. Willy helped Phan Chao stanch the blood from two deep gashes on Chao's right forearm and bundled him into the BMW, calling for Trac's long-sleeved shirt. Sirikul drove with more spirit than good sense, but the Bimmer was forgiving—more forgiving than his old man would be, if any of Chao's blood soaked into the rear seat.

Hours later, passing a small joint around in Willy's apartment, they all agreed that Phan Chao's arm had bled through the bandages as much as it was going to. It was equally obvious that Chao was not up to any further escapades for a while. "We can't set up a watch around that house now," Willy complained. "Chao told the whole hilltop that we are Asians."

"I forgot," Phan Chao muttered, crestfallen about his loud calls in Vietnamese. "Anyone might have. I swear, when I reached that glass, I saw a round-eye boy run into the hall."

"He runs too well," Willy said, accepted the butt, and inhaled deeply. For a moment there was silence. Then, passing the pungent butt to Trac, he slowly exhaled. "At least we know that Mark Paladino cannot sleep in his own house. Sirikul, you might drive down tomorrow. Ask around at video arcades in Gilman for your old friend Mark."

Sirikul, accepting the butt from Trac: "And say what?"

"You are very worried about him. Did he really take a vacation as the TV says?"

"But first I get a Mohawk haircut and tear my clothes,"

Sirikul replied with sarcasm. "The only Asians who could make that work are without accents." He inhaled; held it.

"And most of those will be at the rock concert tonight," said Nguyen Van Trac.

Willy brightened. "In Gilman?"

"Right here," Trac said, nodding with his chin toward the west. "Performing Arts Center. Along with every round-eye punker in town."

Willy grunted and waited for the smoldering marijuana roach. Sirikul said glumly, "If *every* one of them went, we would know where to find Mark Paladino."

Trac smiled, and Phan Chao returned it. It was Willy who suddenly exclaimed, "Why not?" Chao, fumbling left-handed, dropped the butt and watched silently as Willy Thuong crushed it with his heel. "We will need clear heads tonight," Willy said.

Sirikul: "You think he would show himself in public after all that has happened?"

Willy: "I think we would be stupid to decide either way, without seeing for ourselves."

Trac: "And he is stupid if he does."

"We will know tonight whether he is stupid," Willy said, glancing at his wristwatch. "Hand me the *Mercury News*. It will have something in the entertainment section, and I can see the price of tickets."

Sirikul lay down on the butt-sprung couch and stretched. "You won't need tickets," he predicted. "Just wait until the main thrash takes a break, and watch the punkers as they flock outside for a quick pop."

Trac was amused by Sirikul's aping of round-eye jargon and laughed as Willy scanned the entertainment pages of the San Jose newspaper. "We would give the Paladino scum a pop, at that," Trac said.

"One extra, for this," said Chao, lifting the arm with its darkly crusted bandage, and Willy grunted assent.

Studying the *Mercury News* ad, Willy noted that they had only an hour to camouflage themselves as punkers before the festivities began. He was canny enough to listen as Sirikul explained a few facts about rock concerts. A local group calling themselves the Jerk Coughs would perform as an opening act, and the featured Immune Deficients would not begin pumping out their throbbing punk rock rhythms until around ten o'clock. At eleven or thereabouts, the real intermission would send hundreds of young people spilling into the open arcade bordered by Almaden Avenue.

Further, the neatly dressed Sirikul insisted, there was no crying need to wear punk trappings: a rock fan could dress as preppie as he liked in accord with the punk creed, "Be yourself." The real problem was getting the Paladino kid isolated if they *did* find him. Fortunately a multilevel parking structure squatted directly across from the Center for Performing Arts. If he was to find parking for the BMW there, Sirikul would have to hurry.

Willy Thuong and Nguyen Van Trac did the best they could on short notice, dressing in the black buckle boots, jeans, and leather jackets favored by the motorcycle set. Willy would have preferred sneakers for agility, but there was something to be said for the heavy steel toes of cycle boots. Willy furnished Trac with a small canister of Mace and a bike chain, pocketing extra canisters for himself and Sirikul. Both Willy and Sirikul could use their bodies as weapons, while the spray canisters should render their intended victim as malleable as mud until they could get him into the car.

Willy's plan would have sent fever and chills down the spine of a professional, for he intended to render Mark Paladino helpless in a crowd if he could not maneuver him away from it. If necessary, he would claim that the victim had popped too many pills, while carrying him bodily to the BMW. The plan, along with the behavior of some youths, was just bizarre enough that it might work. The ugly little short-barreled .22-caliber revolver went into Willy's jacket pocket more to be flourished than fired, since Willy had found that the damned thing did not always fire when he squeezed its trigger.

Mark Paladino tapped impatient fingers on the windowsill of Mel Crenna's ten-year-old Chevy pickup as Mel turned on

West San Carlos in downtown San Jose. "We'll never find parking now. Thanks, Adele." Adele Nichols, crammed between Mel and Mark, said nothing; they were late partly because the girl had insisted on teasing Mark's black hair into raised spikes like Mel's and her own, using Knox gelatin.

Neither Mark nor his friends realized the irony of his nickname. "Hang loose, Pal," the Crenna youth said, pulling over past the Almaden intersection. To their left, a round-edged, sand-colored building loomed in the dusk like some great snail shell into which other young people streamed like so many foraging ants. "I'm dropping you two here; my old man's parking permit will get the Li'l Tchebby into the faculty lot."

Mark hopped out, letting Adele fend for herself. She slid out and shook her head, spikes of her hair leaning back and forth in a pageant of blond, green, and crimson. "It's a ten-minute walk, Mel," she said doubtfully.

Mel Crenna's status could be inferred from the fact that he gave nicknames but refused to accept one; or from his use of a vehicle bashed into a punker's ideal, which Mel named "Li'l Tchebby Peekop" because it looked like something abandoned by a Mexican laborer. Mel understood Adele's worry, and discounted it. "Get real, Nookie; nobody hassles you downtown on thrash night. Besides, I got these." He lifted one foot and waggled its high-laced old paratrooper boot.

Adele sighed and slammed the door, the only way it would close. "We'll wait outside," she called.

Mark and Adele walked across a broad esplanade toward the front of the building with studied nonchalance. Mark's borrowed combat boots fairly flopped on his feet, Mel's tightly pegged pants stuffed into the high tops, bagging on Mark because Mel was much taller. Mel's tee-shirt fitted Mark better; it was almost identical to the one Viktor Danilov had torn, complete with the black death's head and "Society Threat" scrawled on the back. Mark wore black leather bracelets to complete his outfit, with dull metal spikes protruding a half inch like those on a dog collar. Sharp spikes would get you stopped at the door; but the security people rarely seemed to notice the nails driven upward through the edges of boot soles so that they protruded a quarter inch around the toes. It was the kind of equipment that let you skank like a seizure victim in a sloping aisle because others tended to give you all the room you needed. Mark owned no footgear of this sort, but he had been glad to borrow Mel's.

Adele wore stylish high-heeled booties with a torn body stocking, and wore her own studded bracelets on her ankles. Her long-sleeved coat buttoned down the front and ended at her thighs, revealing long expanses of good leg and providing some padding over her upper body. Nookie Nichols had the courage to skank in close quarters, but knew better than to do it without some protection. Besides, the lining of that coat hid the short marijuana roach Mel always enjoyed between sets.

Mark and Adele would have denied that each was jealous of the other's friendship with Mel Crenna; they endured one another as two household cats might, giving each other room, spitting only as necessary. Adele found the ticket line. Mark ignored her and found two youths, close friends of Mel, warming only momentarily to their interest. Yes, a pair of boatflakes had broken into the house where he was crashing. No—a lie—he had no idea what had caused the explosion in his own home. Yeah, Mel would be along soon.

The youths leaned on a low stone retaining wall, shared a Winston, and listened to the catastrophic whangs of the Jerk Cough guitars from inside, and to the snarled lyrics at a deafening volume. It sounded, one youth said, like a slow train wreck. Mark smiled agreement, but the smile faded quickly. He was beginning to wonder how many other youths Mel Crenna had called in the past few hours. He understood the reason: the story of Mark's troubles lent Mel the charisma of a TV commentator. Mel had a half-dozen ways to hold the spotlight, not to mention his soccer prowess and the good looks that had swept Nookie Nichols away. Damned shame, thought Mark Paladino, that Mel couldn't keep a secret. It did not occur to Mark that the way he ordinarily dressed made his recreations no secret.

Chapter 16

MARK Paladino's major oversight was not in telling Mel Crenna of his fugitive status, for Mel's friends included a few asskick specialists who happened to dress punk. Nor was Mark particularly stupid to attend the rock event: punkers in fantastic garb and Gene Simmons makeup could parade in front of their own mothers without being recognized. Mark's single great mistake was in wearing Mel's Society Threat tee-shirt, which Mark had copied to begin with.

Sukree Sirikul, smug over his good luck in finding a slot in the parking structure just across Almaden, had already wandered into the performance center to check out the exits, which were manned too well for his liking. He felt the chance was remote that the Paladino boy would show up but just in case, he must remember to tell Willy not to even think about grabbing the kid inside. Sirikul accepted a stamp on the back of his hand and ambled out the main entrance, giving his ears a rest and waiting for Willy and Trac. He watched the girl with the red and green hair spikes, the booties, and the good legs as she strode past clots of other youths, and saw her greet the Society Threat boy with a notable lack of enthusiasm. But Sirikul had never seen Mark Paladino, with or without that shirt. The girl and her friends seemed to be waiting, just as he and others were waiting. Sirikul forgot them, leaned against a stone planter box as high as his waist, and smoked a Camel.

Mel Crenna left Paseo de San Antonio and crossed Almaden to the Performing Arts Center at the moment when Willy and Trac entered the Paseo three blocks back. Mel greeted his friends near the front entrance and stood talking with them for a moment; Sirikul heard the names Nookie, Thrasher, Pal, and Fuzz, and turned his attention away as the quintet hurried inside to risk their hearing. The top of Mark's spiked hair was still visible over Mel's shoulder as Willy and Trac strode across Almaden, but that tee-shirt was not visible from Willy's viewpoint. Sirikul spotted his leader and walked into the dusk to make his report.

Willy heard Sirikul out and agreed that even if their prey were inside, they would wait until he came out. Willy's chief reason was not the exit problem; though unwilling to admit it in front of Sirikul, he simply did not want to pay for two twelve-dollar tickets. Leaving Trac with the half pack of Camels because Trac knew Mark Paladino on sight, Sirikul took Willy Thuong across the street and climbed the exposed zigzag stairway of the parking structure to the second level. The squat BMW coupe was well placed, Willy decided. He took the stairway to the third level and there, with Sirikul at his side, he gazed across Almaden at the great sandy snail of a building outlined with softly glowing globes of light in near darkness.

"I could spot him from here," Willy said, "but not in full dark."

"And not very well among a thousand other round-eyes," Sirikul reminded him. "With all those blue faces and dinosaur haircuts, you might see him and not know it."

"I will know him," Willy muttered savagely, angry because he knew that Sirikul was right. At the moment, he did not much believe that Mark Paladino was within ten miles of that monstrous din with which the Jerk Coughs insulted the summer night.

Then Willy saw Nguyen Van Trac skulk near the entrance, interested in a latecomer, only to move back again.

"Trac is too obvious," Willy said, leading Sirikul down the stairway and back across the street.

Now the darkness was nearly complete, mitigated by globes lighting the esplanade. Willy noticed a uniformed policeman just outside one exit, talking idly with a rent-a-cop security guard. He saw another, accompanied by a large and wonderfully obedient Airedale, wheel and come to something like unconscious attention as he spoke with a big man in a dark suit. "The man in the suit will be a plainclothes cop," said Willy as he strolled around the building with his two soldiers. "See who else he speaks to; we must avoid them."

Trac laughed. "My uncle used to say he could smell the beef eaters across a rice paddy," he said, and ingratiated himself further to Willy by adding, "But you can smell a badge."

"But I can't smell an Italian," Sirikul said. "One of you must point him out to me. Then I could offer him a very special deal on something I have in the car."

"What do you mean?" Willy asked.

Sirikul made a very American shrug. "Whatever he wants, from nose candy to a suck job. He isn't going to get it anyway."

"Remember, I'm supposed to deliver him in one piece."

Sirikul always knew he was taking a chance when he hinted for Willy's secrets. He took one now: "To other Italians, I suppose."

Willy Thuong favored him with a smile, something Willy did not do very often. "I'll tell you when the time comes." That time would come only if, and when, Willy needed to scare Sirikul's almond eyes round as saucers. If ever the time came when Sirikul balked at Willy's demands, Willy could simply tell Sirikul that the name Sukree Sirikul was on a list kept by the Chinese People's Republic. Then Sirikul would shit gruel—and would eat it if Willy told him to.

The three completed their tour of the building and Willy staked Trac out near one side of the building, warning him to do a few hops and skips now and then as if transported by the cacophony from inside. If either Trac or Willy spotted their quarry, the signal would be the lighting of an entire pack of paper matches as though by mistake; a flare that could be seen across the esplanade, yet was perfectly legal. Sirikul and Willy strolled again to the Bimmer coupe. When the set ended, everyone in downtown San Jose would know it.

Inside, Mark Paladino tasted the curiously thick sweat that ran down from his forehead to the corner of his mouth. Next time he'd suggest they mix in a little Jello-O with the Knox stuff that kept their hair spikes rigid; that would tickle Mel. He saw people he knew, and people he thought he knew but couldn't be sure. Nookie and Mel skanked through a chorus of "Ronnie and Bonzo," and Mark saw one Mohawked youth wearing high boots with four-inch platform soles dive from the edge of the stage into the sea of bodies undulating in the aisles below. He could see laughter from those he bore down with him as they got up, though he could not hear anything over the 110-decibel screech from the speakers.

Then Mark saw something from the edge of his vision that sent a wave of sick fear through his body. A slender swarthy youth of roughly his own size gyrated to the rhythm, looking in Mark's general direction. The youth's hair was black, in tight, almost kinky ringlets, and his eyes were impossibly long and narrow. Then Mark saw that the Oriental effect was merely black greasepaint; part of the youth's hair was spray-painted black but in back it was natural blond. Mark had not realized until that instant that he could recognize either of those youths who had tried to take him from Karen Cavender's house. He had only glimpsed the boy as he passed by the front windows, but yes, the boy's hair had been kinky; not the straight black mane of most Asiatics.

Stu had told him to make notes before he forgot the details. Damn if he wouldn't, first thing in the morning. Right now he was going to let the music unfreeze his blood, enjoy the moment, and stay until the Immune Deficients had played their last encore. Unless Mel had other ideas. When you made a gig with Mel, you left when Mel left.

Punkers are always rough and ready critics, and catcalls from the crowd made it clear that they were growing impatient for the feature band. The Jerk Coughs played no encores. Most of the audience spilled outside while audio equipment was trundled away and other equipment was hauled to the stage. The Immune Deficients, five young men who thought of themselves as a quintet and had the adulation to support the idea, busied themselves with an equipment sound check. This part of the process always intrigued Mark, who had manned a soldering iron when his father built their home hi-fi system two years before. Well, it was blown to hell now, he thought. And no matter what his father had done, he would like to blow his enemies to hell, too. Mark stood by and listened while several other youths asked a sound technician the kind of questions that might be expected from the sons of electronics engineers. It was too high-tech for Mark, but he would have bet that Handsome Ransome would understand it all. It was easy to criticize Stu Ransome, even to his face, but at least you could talk to the guy, unlike most of those assholes who gave lousy classroom lectures and whose glances said you were The Enemy.

Caught up with his own thoughts, Mark Paladino spent twenty-five minutes inside during the setup for the Immune Deficients. He went outside only to find himself fighting a tide of returning punkers, and edged to the side of that undertow. He wouldn't be surprised to find that Mel had taken Adele to the Tchebby Peekop just to coax a little nookie from Nookie. But then he saw Mel waving and fell in beside his friend. He did not see Sukree Sirikul or Willy Thuong, who were crossing against the current in Trac's direction; and because Willy had been studying costumed round-eyes for a half hour without success, Willy was so intent on Nguyen Van Trac that he did not notice the high-contrast lettering of Society Threat as Mark turned his back.

The Immune Deficients performed up to expectation, and needed those big amplifiers to be heard over the audience. Mark knew by now that Mel had called Fuzz Stacey and Thrasher Belton earlier because both knew Pal Paladino slightly, and because Mel delighted in the power to provide bodyguards for a friend in need. Mark watched Thrasher and Fuzz skank like dervishes, admiring the surges of the Stacey youth, who affected the kind of spastic grace that drew an audience. Fuzz, a borderline punker who wrestled at 159 pounds, had sprayed his cheeks, muscular arms, and tee-shirt over paper doilies so that his upper body seemed covered by huge glittering snow-flakes. Thrasher performed moves he had learned as a Los Altos soccer goalie, the long arms sweeping a huge volume of space, his studded black bracelets seeming to throb with the flicker of stage lighting. Thrasher knew that, while girls like Adele Nichols claimed to despise violence, they were mightily impressed by a youth who seemed *capable* of it. And while Thrasher liked Mel Crenna, he longed for the time when he might be the one to call Adele by that nickname. Thrasher and Fuzz knocked each other down twice as they flailed in the aisle perilously near plush seats, howling with ferocious glee.

Streaming sweat from hot lights and their own stage gymnastics, the Immune Deficients walloped out rhythms and snarled the lyrics of protest for nearly an hour before the end of their first set. Most of the audience stood, then leaped in ragged unison with the band as the last chords slammed through enormous speakers, and then thirteen hundred young people poured into the summer night for cooler air.

Lighters flicked like fireflies across the esplanade; some kindling tobacco, some igniting other substances. The few police ignored it all, moving in on the brief flares of violence among youths before anything could escalate into a riot. It was Mel's idea to share the roach from Adele's coat lining five ways; Adele's idea to do it in a quieter spot.

A half block away, across Almaden and past the parking structure, lay the San Jose Convention Center with stacked fountains and undulating grassy knolls that formed a tiny park in the shadow of the building. Adele had been busted once for possession and once-busted, twice shy. She led the way with Mel; Mark, Fuzz, and Thrasher followed, turning their backs on the esplanade.

Thrasher laughed, seeing a youth near the street toss a furiously burning pack of paper matches onto the pavement. "Some of these dudes are already waaasted." He drawled the last word comically. "Shit, so am I, Fuzz, I feel like I been defending against Pele."

"You caught me with that fuckin' bracelet, man, I'll have a mat rash for a week," Fuzz replied, rubbing his forearm. "Pal, you pick up any bruises?"

Mark was better on a skateboard than a skank, and said so as they neared the tiny park with its canopy of small trees. The artificial slope of grassy turf fell away toward the murmur of water from the top tier of pools over stone parapets. Perhaps a dozen other youths were congregating in dark clumps, some choosing the dark scooped-out grassy hollow near the lowest pool. Closing quickly behind Mark were Willy Thuong and Sukree Sirikul, as Nguyen Van Trac trotted to catch up. Willy had almost missed the Society Threat tee-shirt again, but by now he was ninety percent certain of his quarry. It was up to Sirikul, with his near-perfect use of punker English, to make certain.

Adele produced her roach and Mel lit it, inhaled, then passed it to Mark, who handed it on to Adele immediately. She took a drag. Mark noticed that she did not hold it, and decided that Nookie Nichols was smarter than he had thought.

"Hey, Pal, you're not tokin'," Fuzz accused.

"Nah. Don't feel like it." Mark avoided the admission that he had never felt much like it, but took a step back as if to cement his decision. Three strangers, moving quietly, had now stepped within arm's reach of Mark but stopped, heads together, to light a cigarette. Mark imagined that they were sharing a toke instead of Trac's Camels.

Softly, from a tall youth in preppie dress: "I got heavier stuff, if you want it," said Sirikul. In the darkness, his features were anonymous.

"I'm already fucked up; thanks anyway," Mark lied to the stranger, while Mark's friends attended to their own toking.

Sirikul recited his next sally in his head to be sure his phrasing would avoid any hint of the kow-ow accents of a Thai. Then, "Hey, I see you in Gilman High?"

Mark wondered if it was the gloom that kept him from

recognizing one of Gilman High's lofty seniors. "Yeah, but I don't—"

"Paladino, right?"

"Yeah." In that instant, Mark sensed that he had made a terrible mistake. He did not see the bike chain that swung at Trac's side as the Vietnamese youth stepped between Mark and Fuzz, but he saw Willy Thuong's face around the glow of Willy's cigarette, and his knees became puddles of Knox gelatin.

Mark tried to speak, and then he saw quick movement from all three youths as Willy dropped the Camel and said, quietly as though to no one in particular, "Now."

Because he could see hands rising around him, Mark went the other way by sheer instinct, squatting as if grabbing bio-air on a skateboard, then rolling away on sloping grass. The little spray canisters emitted not a diffuse spray but thin streams aimed where Mark had been a second before, then redirected to follow Mark's progress.

Willy's spray caught Fuzz Stacey, six feet away, on the back of his neck and angled downward across his tee-shirt. Sirikul's spray splattered against Adele's body stocking at knee height. Trac's caught Willy Thuong full on the breast of his tight leather jacket. Mark felt an itching, burning sensation across his calves as he sprang to his feet.

Fuzz had bolted forward into Mel as he reached up to wipe the liquid sting from his neck. Willy uttered a short phrase in Vietnamese, staggering back, turning his head away from an acrid eye-watering tang that rose from his jacket as he slapped at it. Adele squealed and jumped, slapping at her legs, stumbling against Thrasher, who could not understand why a half-dozen people were suddenly snorting and slapping. Thrasher Belton had never seriously entertained the notion that Pal Paladino would need bodyguards this night.

Trac dropped the tiny canister and swung the bike chain high, catching Mel across the bridge of the nose, the chain wrapping halfway around his head and ripping as Trac jerked. Mel went down with a wordless cry but Fuzz Stacey, blinking furiously with wet stinging hands, saw the dim glitter of the chain and engaged Trac's right arm in an armlock, pitching the smaller Trac to the grass. Fuzz smeared his hands across the face of the little Vietnamese, then grunted with the impact of Sirikul's shoe in his ribs, rolling with it. Adele Nichols writhed on the grass, sobbing, and at last Thrasher realized that this was really happening, and moved on the tall Thai with a looping right just as Sirikul lashed Fuzz in the ribs with the side of his shoe.

It was not so dark that Sirikul could miss that long slow punch, and Sirikul went in under it, twisting, knuckles like a splitting maul as he slammed twice beneath Thrasher's breastbone, then levering the big goalie up and over. Sirikul did not intend to go to the mat with this round-eye, and he knew that the youth on hands and knees beside him was Nguyen Van Trac. "Get up, get up," Sirikul barked in English, seeing Willy Thuong fling his jacket as Mark Paladino charged a shape he knew, and remembered, and feared.

But somehow these youths were tied in with his father's fear, and the destruction of his home, and Mark Paladino forgot about meat cleavers as he ran at the frizz-headed little boatflake who was tearing off a jacket while others went hand-to-hand in semidarkness. Mark deflected the jacket with a slash of one arm; saw Willy spin, saw a slender leg rise with that spin. Mark did not know martial arts, but he had played baseball with Stu Ransome. He slid in sidelong on his left side, right leg kicking low as Willy's vicious kick arced overhead.

Willy had not bothered to look closely at the footgear of the youths he followed, but now he gave full attention to the tearing agony against his calf as a half-dozen nail points on Mark's borrowed boot tore across his leg just above his own cycle boot. Bouncing to his other leg after his foot-sweep, Willy hacked swiftly at Mark's collarbone with the barrel of his little revolver but caught him across the skull instead. Willy's eyes were not working all that well, thanks to Trac's errant Mace spray. Mark grunted, head down, on hands and knees, as Willy grabbed for his stiffly spiked hair with his free hand.

Mel Crenna swayed to his feet holding his head in both hands, and kicked hard at the tall figure who was urging someone to get up. Sirikul caught Mel's trouser leg with his left hand, gripped hard at the boot toe with his right, and wrenched hard as he spun. Mel screamed and twisted in midair; Sirikul snatched his hand away, feeling the multiple punctures of nail points in his fingers. He bent to grasp Trac's jacket as Trac gasped for air with a faceful of the fiery stuff Fuzz had smeared there, and Fuzz Stacey, breathing through two broken ribs, caught the tall Thai off-balance. Fuzz forgot his streaming eyes, the tightness in his chest, and the rules of wrestling. He remembered the great strength of his arms and shoulders, pinning Sirikul's arms with his own, wrapping his legs around Sirikul's and butting as they went down together. And as many a coach will attest, wrestlers have notoriously thick skulls.

Trac scrambled to his feet in time to hear the *crunk* of a cranium against a nose, the bike chain again swinging though he could not see very well to slash anything with it. He could see bodies on the grass, could hear them crying out, but now he heard an older, familiar tongue.

"Come to me, I have him," Willy singsonged in Vietnamese. In English he said, "I will shoot anyone that moves." He tugged hard at the groggy head of Mark Paladino, waving the short-barreled weapon so that it could be seen. Mark staggered up with a moan, and Thrasher Belton's paralyzed diaphragm began to let him breathe again in the same moment. Thrasher did not hear Willy's words through his own gasping, and he could not see around Trac's small bulk to spot the pistol. Thrasher stood up, yelled, "I'llgetyousonsabitches," and caught the bike chain around his bare arm, hauling Trac in like the weight on a flail.

Willy Thuong fired twice, the little .22 rounds making no more noise than small firecrackers. The first round caught Thrasher Belton a hand'sbreadth to the right of his navel. The second would have struck Thrasher just under the heart, but Trac's head had snapped back as Thrasher pulled him in, and the tiny slug entered roughly one inch into the base of Trac's skull. Grazing the cerebellum, it mushroomed into that bundle of fibers of the medulla oblongata which control heart rate and breathing as well—functions so automatic that Trac had never given them much thought. He would never give them any thought again; Nguyen Van Trac had enjoyed his last breath, his final heartbeat.

Willy would have sent more rounds after those, but his Saturday night special misfired on the third trigger pull and Mark Paladino, already rising with Willy's hand in his hair, felt panic at the flashes just above his head. Mark came up like a broaching whale, his hands locked together, the dull spikes of his bracelets carrying away three of Willy's teeth and tearing Willy's lower lip so badly that it sagged away from his lower jaw. Willy, flung sideways by the impact, turned the pistol on Mark. It was at that precise instant that Adele Nichols, having come upon Willy from behind, swung the spike-heeled bootie in her hand with all her force as if batting one-handed.

Nookie's weapon punched a hole the diameter of a pencil through Willy's cheekbone without knocking him down. He staggered, unable to keep Mark from wrenching the pistol away, now in agony as he tried to remember defensive moves during a retreat. Willy flung himself forward, away from the girl's nails that raked at his throat; hit, rolled, leaped to his feet, and ran forward into deeper shadow. He knew that the pistol was in enemy hands; could hear the raging Mark Paladino at his heels. Already half blind from the Mace, in shock from a puncture of his cheekbone, Willy essayed a fall that would place him on his back, ready to dispatch Mark with a kick-throw.

But Willy had reached the verge of the upper pool at the Convention Center fountains. Instead of finding grass as he splayed his hands, he found the edge of cruel stones. Willy Thuong crashed onto his back, his head dipping into water, and Mark's stupefying backhand with the spiked bracelet across his face sent him spinning over the stone lip to the next pond several feet below. Willy came to his feet somehow, missed his first step, and fell headlong into the lowest pond in only a foot of water. Had it not been for Mark, who scrambled down in the savage hope of feeding him more bracelets, Willy Thuong's last breaths would have been lungfuls of dirty water.

It was Thrasher Belton who ran shouting across Almaden for the police while Mark sat on Willy Thuong, ready to bat his head against cold stone if the bastard happened to wake up. Fuzz kept Sirikul in a sleeper hold that allowed little air while Adele Nichols ministered to Mel, who could not stand with torn knee cartilage. And it was another ten minutes before Thrasher, the anesthetic of excitement wearing off, noticed that the sticky mess on his abdomen was his own blood.

Chapter 17

KAREN had shown more curiosity than fear, listening to the men make their plans at Garza College. On the way home with Stu and Wiley she fell silent, and then refused to enter her own house until Wiley pronounced it safe. Fifteen minutes later, sitting with her companions at her dining table, she stayed out of the conversation and chased crumbs of last week's carrot cake across her plate with a fork.

Stu yawned, watching her. "So it's a go," he said. "I still haven't heard what either of you guys thinks of Justin."

"He scares the shit outa me," Wiley replied softly. "Reminds me of those spook inserts in Nam who used to come out of the bush in civvies with Swede weapons. You watch him sitting across from you mild and sweet as sugar cookies, drinking bad coffee with his pinkie held out and treating Karen like a duchess, acting like your goddamn broker or somebody, and all the time he's working out ways to trap a professional hit team."

"I thought he was charming," Karen admitted. "It was hard for me to sit there next to him, and think of him as an old-time Albanian."

"Albanians are just people," said Stu. "Every minority feels special. The old buzzard thinks he's an eagle."

"The old buzzard is right," Karen insisted. "When Enver Hoxha died this spring, I helped a bunch of poly-sci students research the guy in the library." She shook her head at the memory. "Did you know that many traditional homes in Albania have no windows on the first floor?"

Stu frowned. "So?"

"So before the war, according to the files, roughly a fourth of all male Albanians were murdered in blood feuds. *Now* you know why they build their houses like forts," she persisted.

Wiley squinted hard. "A fourth? As in twenty-five out of every hundred? Hard to believe; sounds like the Hatfield-McCoy feud."

"Nationwide. Here's another tidbit," she said as if daring him to demand her sources. "The Basques are supposed to be great mountain fighters, but guess who they imported to help during the Spanish Civil War."

"You're kidding," said Stu.

"Albanians. Including their top cop, Shehu. I still think you're both crazy," she said, rising to deposit dishes in the sink. "And I bet you'll agree tomorrow morning—this morning, I mean," she said, glancing at the wall clock.

"Jesus, it's after midnight," Stu moaned, pushing his coffee cup away. "I'm sure not going to stuff my backpack until after I've had some sleep."

"I thought you said your backpack gear was at home," Wiley said. "You've gotta hang around there in the morning anyway, 'til we know you've picked up your tail."

"You're right. I'm too tired to think straight."

Wiley clucked his tongue. "And while we're crapped out watching the insides of our eyelids, Justin Paladino will be heading for tall timber. Beats me where the ol' fucker gets his stamina, but—" The telephone cut him off.

"I'll get it." Karen swiveled through the space between Stu's chair and the wall, hurrying across the living room. She answered brightly enough, greeted Mark, and then sat down abruptly on the futon. Stu watched the color drain from her cheeks; moved quickly to sit beside her.

She began to feel her cheeks and forehead as though checking herself for fever, her eyes blinking rapidly. The men exchanged glances; it was not the best of signs.

"Of course we will," she said. "We wouldn't leave you there alone. Who did you say was shot?"

Wiley stood up slowly. "Shit-oh-dear-oh-shit," he said to no one in particular; "it is now well and truly in the fan, folks. Karen, can I talk to the kid?"

Karen ignored all but the telephone. "Ohmygod, Mark. And how is your friend? —Oh wow, which hospital?"

Wiley, standing before her: "Karen, can I please talk to him?"

Karen: "Crenna? Spell it, Mark. Have the others called their parents yet?"

Wiley, gritting it out: *"Karen, will you for Christ's sake let me talk to him?"*

She moved swiftly from the futon and handed over the instrument. "I've just got to get a pencil," she explained calmly, as if discussing a shopping list.

Stu, mildly, as she searched the telephone shelf: "Have you two thought of taking this act on the road?"

Karen replied infuriatingly, "Just leave this to us professionals, hon," and returned to the futon.

Wiley remained standing. His questions were short and pointed. What were the charges? Had the police connected Mark with the explosion in Gilman? Had the parents of his friends shown up with an attorney? And finally, were all of the attackers in custody? He nodded to himself, then held his hand over the mouthpiece instead of returning the instrument to Karen. "We have a choice," he said to the others. "We can probably get the kid released in your custody, Stu. Only it'll be Karen who has to ride herd on him alone. We don't know who else might try to grab Mark, and he's probably safe in police custody as long as they don't stick him in a cell with chronic offenders."

Karen, astonished: "What are you saying?"

Wiley: "Leave him in custody for a couple of days. You can't keep him safe here, and you know it. And he nearly got zapped tonight trying to take care of himself. I can make a call or two and make sure Mark isn't locked up with the wrong element." With that, he handed the telephone back to Karen.

Staring at Wiley as though he had done her some terrible wrong, Karen forced the smile in her voice. "Okay, Mark; give me the names of your friends' parents. Telephone numbers, if you have 'em." She began to scribble on the back of an envelope.

"Justin won't like letting the police look after Mark," said Stu.

"It's not his decision," Wiley said simply. "He's already told us in so many words that he's become a goddamn Albanian again. Look, I know a couple of guys on the force; they aren't all heartless boobs, you know. I can pass the word that Mark is an innocent kid who needs protection. Trust me on this, bubba."

Stu saw that Karen was paying attention to the interchange and, after a moment, he nodded without enthusiasm. As Karen continued talking, she wiped angrily at the single tear moving down her cheek. "Mark, you aren't going to like this, but something has just come up. —No, your father is fine, I met him earlier tonight. It's just that we won't be able to come and get you tonight after all. —No! The truth is, you'll be safer where you are. —No, I'm just catching a cold," she added, sniffling as she inhaled. "Yes, Stu and Wiley both agree. Mark, dear, we aren't forgetting you, and we will get you out. You'll just have to trust us," she said, looking daggers at Wiley Reed.

When Karen broke the connection, it seemed to breach her last defenses. She handed Stu the telephone, hugged her knees, and wept. "Poor little guy," she said, her voice muffled through her hands. "He was so sure we'd take care of him."

"We are," Stu grumbled, as Karen shook his hand from her shoulder. "We're planning for the worst, which he sure as hell didn't do. The tragedy of kids is, they don't plan for failure."

"You can chisel that in granite," was Wiley's endorsement, "so we won't make the same mistake. For a start, why don't you get some sleep while I make a call or two? There's been one DOA by gunshot and Mark could be lookin' at some heavy charges, depending on how all the stories check out. Uh, who's that lawyer Paladino contacted in Gilman?"

Stu told him, offering his hand to Karen as she arose.

"It helps to have a name to toss around," Wiley said, and raised his voice to carry down the hall. "Look on the bright side: Mark's in one piece, and those Asiatic scufflers are out of commission. You wanted the police in on this? Well, you got 'em."

He heard the splintered bedroom door creak into its facing, shrugged, and then dialed a number from memory. One o'clock in the morning by Karen's clock; it was shaping up like a three-week headbanger of a day.

Chapter 18

JUSTIN Paladino reached Coarsegold two hours before dawn, and in the room he had already taken at the Halfdome Lodge, found that sleep met him halfway. Three hours later he was blinking away sleep, tying the laces on his scuffed old high-top Herman Survivors, tucking khaki trouser ends neatly into his boot tops with wool socks to prevent chafing; the Gheg way. He knew that those boots were far heavier than Nike's new lightweight models, and that the Nikes would accept Sherpa snowshoes almost as well. Justin did not give a damn. His ankles were fifty-six years old and they needed all the support they could get.

By seven o'clock Justin had fortified the inner man at a cafe in tiny Oakhurst, wolfing two eggs over easy with sausage on the side and strong coffee, coffee sugared as a Turk would sugar it. Coffee to goad a man on the far side of middle age into the Sierra, past Bass Lake to Beasore Road, and then to the end of rutted trails identified by four-digit numbers: 8023, then its offshoot, 8026. The morning sky was tinted the deep hue of a high volcanic lake, cloudless, with a haze that thinned as the old Land Cruiser gnashed its way above six-thousand-foot elevation north of Bass Lake following the treadmarks he had laid down the day before. As he had reminded Stu Ransome at Garza College, one must never

195

make assumptions about the Sierra in June. The pounding of the Toyota's stiff suspension through his ample rump and thence to his joints reminded Justin again of his arthritis, each jounce a savage ache in the crisp, near-freezing air. His face betrayed no pain, but he snapped on the exposed heater that Mark derided as freeze-me, boil-you.

The twist of road yielded occasional glimpses of peaks to the north, vast white fangs that snarled defiance at the sun. The snow load on some of those peaks was still a full twenty feet deep in June. The mighty Sierra range soared eleven, twelve, occasionally over thirteen thousand feet beyond the eastern, wild boundary of Yosemite Park. This was country familiar only to those who challenged it afoot or by saddle mule, and mules were helpless in deep snow. Red Peak, eleven thousand seven hundred; Mount Lyell and Maclure, each over thirteen thousand. Even the passes up there were two miles high. If Justin's enemies followed Stuart Ransome far enough, they would soon have a cold taste of those heights.

Rotting snow lay several inches deep along the north sides of granite outcrops at the trailhead, which boasted a weathered old wooden marker: CHAIN LAKE TRAIL. Justin backed the Land Cruiser up a slope at the turnaround, knowing that car batteries gave poor starts after a day or so in such cold. He exchanged his leather gloves for mittens, zipped up the white nylon coverall for an extra layer of insulation, and strode away exhaling little vapor puffs, carefully avoiding telltale prints in snow areas. Presently he found what he sought, an outcrop of stone with a foot-thick overburden of humus that was mostly pine needles matted like a blanket. He returned to the truck, raised the hood, and deftly removed the distributor cap, placing it in a Baggie. Now the vehicle might be towed, but never driven. And why would they bother? Well, he expected them to vandalize him in other ways. He patted the heavy-gauge steel of the hood with something like affection, then detached the dented five-gallon jerrycan from its massive bracket bolted to the vehicle's side panel. There were several ways to drain the fuel tanks under the seats, but five extra gallons would get a Land Cruiser to civilization again.

He lugged the heavy fuel can and the Baggie to the bank of humus, separating its upper few inches with care, and scooped out a hollow large enough to hide both. He carried the scooped-out material some distance away, scattering it on virgin humus. A moment later the top layer of that organic blanket lay flat again.

Justin was perspiring more than he had expected. He swung into the passenger seat, communing with his body's complaints. Was he already light-headed, at only seven thousand feet? Perhaps a little; even a Gheg required a bit of pacing on the first day. The mittens removed, he began loosening the tiedowns from equipment in the cargo bay behind the seats. The first item was to get his yellow Marmot tent half rigged, so that it would appear that he had been interrupted while making camp. This took only minutes before he pushed the second stiffener hoop into place, leaving the third hoop rod lying across the ripstop nylon, tent pegs scattered about.

He found his compact little monocular spotting scope and decided to study the condition of the snow nearby. He might find corrugated crust or virgin powder at higher elevations— always assuming he would get that far—but either way, he must determine whether the first mile would be smooth going or full of treacherous pockets of depth hoar. It was best to know these things before shouldering a heavy pack. He strung the monocular's thong over his neck and checked the staunch old Timex on his wrist. Nearly nine A.M.; with luck, the hunters might already be pursuing Stuart Ransome out of Gilman.

Very few KGB agents enjoyed much freedom of decision, and Viktor Danilov was not one of those few. His report, to *rezident* Stefan Rozhin in the safehouse off Alum Rock Avenue, had not gone well the night before. Rozhin's questions left little doubt that he considered the explosion at the Paladino house a mark against Viktor himself.

At least Rozhin set Viktor's mind at rest on one count: their mole in the new Sunnyvale office of the Federal Bureau

of Investigation had made a negative report on Stuart Ransome.
If Ransome had not gone to his own authorities yet, Viktor's
own ragtag team was still running clean. On the other hand,
Rozhin had denied Viktor's request to hire a legitimate private
investigator. They had the essentials from Ransome's VW
registration, they had his address and telephone number. They
still had that little transmitter affixed to his car, and while
Rozhin denied permission for a telephone tap—too easily de-
tected, he said—the *rezident* offered something better.

The device he gave Viktor was, from external appearance, a cheap ballpoint pen. Placed within ten feet of a telephone, it would transmit Ransome's end of a conversation
with fair fidelity for almost a kilometer. The slender post atop
the device needed only to be tuned to an uncluttered frequency in the FM band, and anyone could do that in Gilman.
Stefan Rozhin had agreed that Ransome was their most likely
connection to the Paladinos, father and son. If Ransome left
the region, Rozhin would—reluctantly, because of internal
rivalry—turn the matter over to the GRU, the KGB's military
arm. For the present, Ransome was still the problem of Viktor
Danilov. Viktor and his *rezident* shared two glasses of
Stolichnaya, drinking to success, before retiring to their rooms
in the safehouse for the night.

Now, at nine o'clock on a bright summer morning, Viktor
waited in Ray Nelson's motel room, willing the telephone to
ring. One ring would mean trouble. Two rings would mean
that the transmitter was in place in Ransome's apartment. He
would reach for the instrument only if it continued to ring.
Viktor Danilov lit his third unfiltered Camel and prayed for
two rings.

He got three before he lifted the receiver. "Yes," he said
without optimism, and waited. Then, with rising excitement:
"How do you know this?" A longer wait. "Good. Ken must
stay in place, but transmitting only when necessary. Tell him
that now." Viktor heard, as if from a great distance, Ray
Nelson with his little CB unit talking inside a Gilman telephone booth. Finally, "If he leaves, you must all follow.
Ransome may be running only to hide after Carma's stupid

vandalism on his car, but we must hope he will link with the Paladinos.''

He gnawed his lip, frowning at the reply, and cut it off: "Listen carefully: go back to that truck of yours. Since you have bought only one fresh vehicle so far, two of you must stay low in it. Leave that damned black thing; he would spot it immediately. Make sure you have a pocketful of coins. If he is going far, you must telephone me here every half hour. If necessary to keep the man in sight, drop Ken off to make the call; you get off second, leaving Allen to continue. —Of course, I will pick you both up later.'' He had almost said "we"; he knew that Stefan Rozhin would be calling for GRU backup now. And the GRU tended to bring victims back in plastic bags.

Viktor punched another number carefully because his fingertip tended to span more than one button. He was anxious for an answer to his first question: would the *rezident* still be lounging around at the safehouse? He was. "Danny here," said Viktor, heard a grudging reply from "Steve," and continued: "My sons tell me that their friend is at home, packing his car for a camping trip. —Yes, I have allowed them to go, provided they call me often. It will be vital for someone to remain here to take those calls. —Their phrase was 'a backpack trip.' I have no way of knowing where they will camp, Steve.''

An instant later he was listening to a dial tone. He cradled the receiver with a sigh; no point now in bugging the man's apartment. If Ransome was running a long way, the job would be turned over to others. But his flight would be laid at Viktor's feet. If Ransome ran only a short distance, there was still a chance for commendations in Viktor's file. But almost certainly, in any case, Viktor would soon be seconding one of those GRU bastards who swaggered around the consulate like so many little commissars. So long as it wasn't the one they called *sretsvah*, the remedy. The wolf and the Greek were almost as bad; poor companions at best. It might depend on which one happened to be nearest.

At ten minutes before ten, Viktor saw a gray Dodge Lancer pull up with two men. He did not recognize the driver, but there was no mistaking the sturdy specimen they called Grichanka, the Greek, with his triangular face, close-cropped dark hair, and economy of motion. Viktor opened the door for them.

The Greek assumed command easily, coolly. Despite his nickname, Grichanka had been raised as a Soviet subminister's son in Ottawa and his command of the American idiom was as flawless as that of Soviet commentator Vladimir Posner. Standing in bell-bottom jeans with his Vasque hiking boots, he folded his arms and looked Viktor up and down, as a schoolmaster might survey a slow learner. "I hope you have heavier shoes than that, Viktor. The coast range is rugged and wet."

"You know very well my room is in San Francisco," said Viktor.

"Has your team called again?"

"No, but I will remain here to—"

"Get in the car. I may need your muscle. Lev will take the calls, and you can brief me on the way. There's a two-way phone in the Lancer."

Viktor thought hard for five seconds. "My team thinks that we are Italians. They will be suspicious of—"

Lev spoke for the first time, and in fair English. "I have been briefed. I use the language as well as you, and we have their names. Do as you are told, Viktor Grigorovich."

Yes, with a radiotelephone in that Dodge, they would have all the information they needed so long as they stayed within range of the base transceiver. Viktor did not fancy slogging around some coastal hillside in low-top brogans, but he had not risen this far by disobeying orders. Nor had he botched a job this badly in years. He swept his expensive black leather coat off the back of a chair, shrugged, and followed Grichanka to the car wondering whether his Americans were stupid enough to accept still another Italian with a distinctly un-Italian accent.

As Grichanka veered up the on-ramp heading south on the freeway, Viktor smiled to himself. "For all we know, they may pass us going north."

"Look at the maps," Grichanka said, nodding toward an

accordion file in the passenger footwell. "The chances are four to one against his going north, and Gilman is an access to roads in the other directions."

Pleased to correct this stolid GRU assassin in even a small detail, Viktor said, "Then the chances are three to one."

"Four," said Grichanka in tones that implied *gotcha*. "He could be pulling your leg, Viktor. There's a good chance he's trying to draw your team of *nyekulturniy* dimwits into trouble, in which case he won't go far."

Reid-Hillview Airport, within two miles of the KGB safehouse in San Jose, offered a few options in aircraft rentals. Wiley would have preferred the reconditioned taildragger Piper because it was dead slow and cheap as well. The blue Cessna Skyhawk would fall right out of the sky if you tried to loaf at sixty knots behind a car, but the toe brakes of the Cessna 172 were much easier to operate with a prosthetic leg. He would simply have to stay high, say seventy-five hundred on the eastern leg, and weave broad esses or luck into a headwind.

Wiley flashed his license and his third class medical in the office, but they had to look him up in the office log because, the way business was these days, Wiley Reed logged only a few hours a month. The Skyhawk rented at forty-five dollars an hour.

He made a quick walkaround inspection and saw to the Cessna's fuel, pleased that its Lycoming engine had only thirty hours since overhaul, noting that the sectional charts were recent. He did not file a flight plan, finishing his paperwork before he pulled the little flight bag into the phone booth with him and dug for quarters.

A few minutes past ten, the telephone rang in Stu's apartment. He answered immediately. "Yeah," he said after a moment, "fifteen minutes is fine. No problems? —Hey, there's forty different places I can meet you, if you get my drift. I'll meet you on milady's next birthday." He replaced the receiver and checked his watch. He had already tossed his bulging old Himalaya pack into the back seat with his faded blue Levi's jacket, but any idiot passing by could see the big Coleman stove and the two-man tent he had placed outside near the Baja Bug, and could draw the obvious conclusion. In some parts of San Jose that would have earned him a burglary, but Gilman wasn't the big city just yet. A dozen cars had passed in the half hour since he had set out these telltales. He would simply have to hope the bait wasn't too obvious.

Justin had said it would be winter up there. And he did tend to get windburn, so— He grinned and went to the bathroom, pawing through tubes of half-forgotten gunk until he found the zinc ointment. That was one detail even Justin might have overlooked: a paste that would turn a tanned face dead white. Now that he thought of it, his frayed old zippered goatskin jacket would be just as warm as Levi Strauss's, and the leather was still white. Or almost white. Whatthehell: take them both. Plenty of room in the back seat.

He stuffed the leather jacket into a Safeway sack, changed to a white turtleneck with push-up sleeves, and mentally reviewed the stuff he had collected in the backpack. The tiny Primus stove and fuel; his ancient scout cook kit; foil bags of freeze-dried stroganoff, ham and eggs, chili, and soup mix; instant coffee, sugar, hard candy, olive oil, and popcorn for its roughage; a tin of instant biscuits; his repair and medicine kits; spool of forty-pound-test monofilament nylon and heavy parachute cordage; extra socks and gloves in a side pocket with mosquito repellent; ten-mil clear polyethylene dropcloth folded flat; spray-protected maps of the Yosemite region in the back pocket, protecting his orange Suntiger ice-climber glasses; and separated from the four highway flares, beeswaxed matches with toilet paper in one side pocket, the Baggieful of nine-millimeter ammunition stuffed into another pocket with the rolled-up mosquito hoods. His little down-filled Thaw mummy bag was in its stuff sack, lashed to the pack frame. His fishing knife was already in his pants pocket, the Beretta in the VW. If he wasn't ready now, he wasn't likely to *get* ready; and it was time to go before he had time to reconsider this madness.

Pit stop to empty his bladder, quick check of doors and windows: all secure. He inhaled as though leaping into deep water and pulled the side door shut as he stepped outside, trying to avoid peering up the street, his shoulders itching with tension as he flung the stowed tent into the back seat atop a Coleman stove he hadn't used in years. He let the Corvair engine warm up for thirty seconds before backing out, then drove east under the freeway on Highway 152. He kept an eye on the rearview but saw nothing behind him that resembled the Mustang or the Camaro as he got up to highway speed. Christ, was this all for nothing? Then he remembered who could tell him one way or another, and flicked on the CB unit beneath the dashboard.

At Karen's next birthday she'd be twenty-five. He switched to channel two five and instantly heard, over the drone of a Lycoming, "Rig to Highballer, come on? Lint got your tongue, bubba?" Wiley had been right: with his little hand-held Radio Shack CB and seven thousand feet of air, he might have been in the passenger seat beside Stu. Except, of course, for that hellacious background racket.

Jungle experience had made Wiley cautious about open transmissions; anyone monitoring Channel 25 would hear two truckers relieving the long miles across central California. But Wiley had forgotten how loud the engine of a light aircraft would be. Using the bored monotone of the jargon, Stu replied. "Highballer to Okie Rig, had my brain on automatic. Mercy sakes, but your background weighs a ton, good buddy. Pickin' your teeth with a chain saw, come on?"

A moment's pause before Wiley's reply: "You never hauled a reefer before, Highballer? That cooler unit's leanin' on my cab; sorry."

"Negative perspiration, Okie Rig. Just thought you oughta know," said Stu. "Is there anything I oughta know?"

"Possible ten four. Ah, would you believe something like my other Pete with a suicide box, come on?"

Stu thought about that for a few seconds. Wiley's other vehicle was that spavined old pickup. A Peterbilt? Okay, a truck the size of a pickup; but with its own sleeper attached to the cab. The rearview showed only a red MG roadster and, so far back that the slight vibration of his rearview obliterated all detail, a squarish chocolate-toned high-center carryall; a Sierra, or a Chevy Blazer perhaps. That had to be Wiley's suicide box. "Eyeballing the Pete now. The more the merrier, Okie Rig, come on?"

"Uh, I'll be swillin' some thirty-weight at the next waterhole. Wouldn't hurt you none, Highballer."

Stu smiled briefly. Listening to that southwestern twang, he could have half convinced himself that he was really setting up a meeting with some Tulsa-based trucker. The confluence of two state highways a few miles ahead was a well-known rest stop for all kinds of traffic. Stu did not need coffee, but if he stopped, Wiley could tell him whether that carryall did anything suspicious. "Ten four, Okie Rig. Highballer down."

Stu eased off the highway a few minutes later at the Y, passing up several roadside booths, and parked next to a fruit stand. He bought a pint of chilled apricot juice, letting his eyes rove as he tilted the bottle to his lips. The little MG had passed, but that carryall had simply disappeared while he was parking. The silver wink of a Cessna with tricycle gear and blue trim flashed far off as the aircraft banked away behind the hills to the west. Stu slid into the VW, turned its key, lifted the mike as far as his breast while holding his arm against his side, watching the rearview. He saw nothing worrisome, but worrisome people could be watching him. "Breaker two five, Highballer to Okie Rig, come on?"

Again the droning buzz under Wiley's reply. "Okie Rig up, Highballer." A double entendre there. "Bring it on, I'm peelin' eyeballs just for you." Wiley's mythical trucker might be watching for his good buddy, but for Stu the message was an invitation to move on while Wiley watched.

Stu sipped more juice for a long minute, then locked his safety harness and drove obediently onto the highway that snaked up toward Pacheco Pass and, beyond that, the valley town of Los Banos. Two minutes later, Wiley's voice issued again from the speaker as if half asleep: "Okie Rig to Highballer, I do believe I've got some company for you, come on?"

"Highballer up, Okie Rig. Nice to know I'm appreciated." It was far from nice; it was frightening. He had seen the brown carryall storm onto the highway ahead of a dustcloud, grow from a tiny dot to a discernible vehicle, then drop back again. At least Wiley, from his perch in the Cessna, could see for miles up the grade toward Los Banos. "You notice if bears are thick ahead, come on?"

"Ah, negatory. Play dead, Highballer." Stu waited while two minutes passed, keeping the speedometer a shade above sixty, before Wiley responded: "Okie Rig to Highballer, you're a clean machine."

"Roger, you can saucer me some thirty-weight shortly. Down and out south of the waterhole, Okie Rig."

"Ten four, Okie Rig down."

Stu waited another minute, then gradually increased his speed, adjusting his external rearview. On the open road his powerful little hybrid could almost certainly outrun the heavy brown Blazer that followed him more than a mile back, but the point was *not* to. There was still a chance that Wiley was wrong. Another stop to stretch at Pacheco Pass? No, that might look suspicious. Fuel at Los Banos? Not so suspicious. If he was followed beyond the cutoff at Madera, then there would be absolutely no reasonable doubt. And, unless he got a sudden attack of good sense and broadcast a Mayday on Channel 9, he would find no help short of the Chain Lakes trailhead.

Chapter 19

GRICHANKA wasn't worried; the range of his Lancer's old radiotelephone went beyond Gilman. In any event, he could always call Lev from a pay phone. He was within sight of Gilman when the instrument buzzed, and he was much quicker than Viktor in reaching for it. Viktor saw from the smile that Grichanka's odds were paying off. "It's hard to believe they did something right," he said into the mouthpiece. "Call Connor back. Tell him to pass the word not to drop the second man off, because we'll be along soon; describe this car to him. —No need for you to stay there since Connor had the sense to keep a radio."

He replaced the instrument and slowed a bit as he turned to Viktor. "Give me the south valley map. Quickly," he snapped. Viktor fumbled among the folded maps, and sighed as Grichanka snatched the correct chart before Viktor could grasp it. Deftly shaking it open, talking as he divided his gaze between the freeway and the chart: "Ken Connor is waiting at the intersection of Highways 152 and 156. I'd say they're twenty minutes east of us, possibly less. Fold this for the intersection," he added, thrusting the open map into Viktor's face.

Viktor did as he was told, noting that the map did not extend much past that highway confluence. He rummaged again, finding a spiral-bound California road atlas, consulting it at some length. Viktor found the correct pages, checking everything twice, feeling the silent scorn of the Greek. To Viktor, slow progress meant great care. He knew that to Grichanka, slow progress meant stupidity. The Greek took the turnoff with a swerve that slid Viktor half out of his seat. "There is a boating and recreation area around a reservoir to the east," said Viktor. "Kraga may be waiting there."

"Never use that name," said Grichanka. "It's a bad habit that can pop up at the worst time. By the way, your man Ken Connor is in contact with the others using his walkie-talkie."

"A pity this car is not equipped for those channels," said Viktor.

"Save your criticisms. By the time we're out of range for my radiotelephone, we'll be picking up your man. Oh, and Viktor: introduce me as John Smith, your American supervisor in Italian affairs. If these morons think I'm a U.S. official in some unidentified agency, so much the better."

"Do not underestimate their intelligence," Viktor said morosely.

"That will be the day," said the Greek, gunning around a rattletrap stake-bed truck, judging his opportunity too closely for Viktor's comfort.

The trouble with these *boyevaya* combat types, thought Viktor, was that in violation of all rules of tradecraft, they enjoyed taking chances and some of them were too damned good at it. It was worse, somehow, when they were thoroughly Americanized. Viktor asked himself why, and realized that it was because they managed to convey the idea that the American way was infinitely superior to the Soviet way. He would bring that up at the debriefing in San Francisco, after all this was over. It was the sort of wedge Stefan Rozhin could use to force a little humility into these arrogant GRU troubleshooters.

Ken Connor hung up the phone and walked out of the cafe, seeking the shade of orchard trees that skirted the gravel parking area. Now *this* was a curious load of shit: another guy with a funny accent, calling him back to say the Big Wop would be along in a gray Lancer. But was it really a pal of Danilov? Or maybe the cops trying to snooker him? Best if he lay low nearby in the showy little orchard, waiting to see whether it would be Danilov in that sedan. He toggled his hand-held CB on Channel 7, as agreed. Ken did not understand CB jargon or its traditions very well and did not give a good shit; it was a tool, like the .45 stuck beneath his belt under his jacket in the small of his back, or the switchblade in his pocket. "Breaker seven, hello Al, hello Al," he said, watching traffic slide up Route 152.

"Al to Ken, go ahead," over the background throb of a Chevy 350.

"Fellow says Vic will be picking me up right away. He says tell you not to let Ray off; just hang with it until Vic gets here. I don't like this; I feel bare-butt naked. If a gray Dodge Lancer comes in here and it ain't Vic, I'll haul ass on foot. Listen, you know this guy has a CB in that fuckin' Bug? I wonder about that."

Another voice, a deep basso Ken had never heard before: "Two-belly up for Mr. Ken. Gracious me, Ken, it's potty-mouths like you that give us a bad name. You wanta clean it up, over?"

Then his brother's voice: "Al to Ken, do like the man says. But you monitor from twenty on down and we'll do it from twenty-one up. Back to you in, uh, five minutes."

His ears burning as though he had been publicly humiliated by a stranger—which was true, in a way—Ken Connor began to turn the channel selector knob, listening a few moments on Channel 20, then on 19. If a gray Lancer came swinging in and he didn't see Viktor's bulk filling it, he would head for the nearest creek without looking back.

He was monitoring Channel 3 when he saw a gray sedan pass two cars at once, whipping back into place as it approached. The way that sumbitch was coming on, either he didn't intend to stop or he just plain liked tempting fate. Ken Connor knelt in perimeter weeds as the gray Lancer nosed off the highway toward the parking area, its brakes keening as it passed him.

He did not begin to run until he saw, peering from the front passenger seat, the big square face of Viktor Danilov.

Sweeping down the long incline toward the San Joaquin Valley, Allen Connor revised his guess about the destination of that tiny yellow dot two miles ahead. Unconsciously, sharing the error of many men who liked big vehicles, he equated the size of the machine with the driver. "I bet you the little asshole heads up I-5," he said to Ray Nelson, who had stopped monitoring alternate channels soon after hearing Viktor's familiar voice on Channel 7. "Gimme that thing."

In the great expanse of open country, even a four-watt CB will carry great distances. "Al to Vic, over."

"Vic to Al, over."

"Passing Highway 33 junction, Vic. I'm pulling in closer in case we have to turn on I-5. It's not far. Over."

A brief pause, then Viktor's voice: "We will be in sight of you soon. Be careful, and let us know which way you go. Out."

Allen handed the unit back to Ray Nelson without bothering with a proper sign-off. Ray held Viktor's directional receiver, tuned to the tiny transmitter hidden below the Volkswagen, so that he could see the dial pointer. There was little use in it, so long as they could see the yellow VW anyway, but at least it gave Ray something to do. Checking his gauges, Allen said, "This fuckin' Blazer really hogs the gas, but she don't hang back." He patted the short tunnel-mounted lever to the right of the transmission lever. "Can I engage four-wheel drive while we're rollin'?"

"Don't!" Ray snatched the hand away, then laughed nervously. "You could blow the whole tranny out of this thing. No, first you pull onto soft stuff and stop. Then put 'er in four-wheel. It don't look like we're gonna have to worry about it anyway, we're clean the fuck and gone from the mountains."

"Yeah?" Allen pointed over the broad metallic chocolate of the Blazer's hood. At seventy miles an hour, he spoke loudly over the whine of big tires and the huge V-8 propelling them. The yellow dot was now clearly a car, and just as clearly it was not slowing at the overpass of Interstate 5. "Look on your horizon, Ray. Those big piss-rippers are fifty miles away but if they ain't mountains I'll kiss your ass. Gimme that CB again and keep your fingers crossed. Maybe he's headin' south on I-5."

Stu could not know the relief he afforded to others when, after passing the I-5 interchange, he turned south on Highway 99 toward Fresno. But that relief was short-lived. He turned off again at the little town of Madera and pulled in to a gas station, first alerting Wiley by referring to a "nap trap"—a rest stop.

He took roughly four gallons and a Pepsi Light, oblivious to the gray sedan that passed and turned down a side street as he reseated his gas cap, unaware that a brown Chevy Blazer was taking twelve gallons some blocks away at a Union station where the prices discouraged most motorists and ensured fast service. Stu resisted the temptation to wave toward the Cessna that circled lazily to the south, asked directions to refresh his memory, then picked up State Route 145 at a leisurely pace, heading northeast from Madera through the first rolling hills at the foot of the Sierra chain.

Moments later, on Channel 25, Okie Rig had disturbing news for Highballer. "—And the Pete is running a clan the color of a cat. You know my cat, come on?"

Stu could not see any evidence of that, at the moment. He had recognized the brown carryall as a Chevy Blazer when, briefly, it had grown in his rearview near Interstate 5. But now, according to Wiley, it had picked up a gray convoy—a clan, in trucker parlance. And convoys did not assemble without some discussion. "What your cat has is all torn up, Okie Rig. The Pete may have good ones if he's found a clan, come on?"

Lint's ripped ear was among his outstanding features. Wiley, throttled back at seventy-five hundred feet with Madera Lake shining ahead in the near distance, made the connection. Stu had avoided the word "ears" because CB users knew that the term referred to the radio unit. If they were being monitored from that brown Blazer, they would have to be very picky about their phrasing. And very deceptive. "You're cookin', Highballer. You gonna catch some z's in Fresno town, come on?"

"Affirmative, Okie Rig." They were getting farther from Fresno by the second. "How's your go-juice?"

Wiley, running with a lean mixture and throttled down to minimum cruise for the entire trip, had no fuel problem. "Topped off in Frisco and I'm coolin' it to ole Merced town, come on?"

"Won't modulate with you for a while, then, ah, I'll be pullin' the plug for a while. Highballer down."

"Eyeball you on *your* birthday, Highballer. Okie Rig down."

Stu reached over and adjusted the channel selector upward, wondering how Wiley Reed would have specified a channel change if he hadn't known Stu's age. There was a bit of traffic on the new channel, none of it from Wiley. Stu turned at Route 41 toward Coarsegold and loitered long enough to see, far behind, the brown Blazer follow him through the turn. A half mile behind the Blazer, too far for Stu to identify its type, a gray sedan turned its nose in the same direction. Right; a Lint-colored vehicle. Stu began to switch channels, monitoring each for a few moments before switching back in case Wiley was trying to raise him.

Now the road swept upward, above two-thousand-foot altitude. Some miles farther on, Stu noted the Halfdome Lodge on his left as he drove through Coarsegold. Justin had told him to stop and use the extra room key only if arriving in Coarsegold after four P.M., but it was only a bit after one. In less than two hours he would be at the Chain Lakes trailhead, if Justin's judgment could be trusted.

And if Justin's judgment could *not* be trusted, Stu was driving farther into deep trouble as he rolled past Oakhurst, then eastward along the sudden congestion bordering Bass Lake. *Better slow it down, we don't want to lose our tails in all this vacation traffic, do we?* The population density around

Bass Lake was as great as in many small towns, and Stu braked for swimsuited kids flipping towels at each other. He turned back to the prearranged channel and heard, over a now-familiar background noise that identified Wiley only too well, "—for Wiley's Coyote, come back. Pegleg for Wiley's Coyote, got your ears on? Come back." Whoa; it was Wiley again with new handles for them both.

"Go ahead, Pegleg, you got Wiley's Coyote and a bucket of background from that reefer." If Stu's voice wasn't enough of an identifier, reference to the Lycoming's snarl should do it.

"Coyote, take it down to seven just for fun, but stay on the side. I'll be on the bye here, over."

"Ten four," said Stu, and switched to Channel 7.

"—Cannot lose him if your equipment is working, Ray. Allen must take no stupid chances." Somewhere, thought Stu, he had heard that accented deep voice before. He saw the Beasore Road sign and turned upward, passing among sturdy summer cabins north of the lakeshore.

"I hope you're right," someone said in slightly countrified tones. "Hey, the needle's swingin'. I still don't see him." The hair on Stu's nape crawled with the next transmission: "He musta turned left, just a minute. —Beasore Road. You still see us?"

"Yes. Proceed carefully." That bass voice again; Stu was increasingly sure that it belonged to that hairy ape he had seen twice before.

Stu turned the channel selector again. "Wiley's Coyote up for Pegleg, come on?"

"Pegleg up, Coyote, you got it."

"That's a big ten four, Pegleg. I got a turkey I recognize, sounds like you do when you laugh, and looks like Mongo, come ahead."

"I'll stay right here, Coyote, you may want to hang out with him awhile, come back."

"Yo, pegleg. You might head for our M-twenty. If I don't have my rubbernecker I wanta know it, come back."

"You got a lot of confidence in my X-ray vision, Coyote. I'll work on that M-twenty. Pegleg down on the side."

Scanning the hundred-foot conifers that almost hid the twists of Beasore Road, Stu realized that he had asked a lot of Wiley. From the Cessna it would be no easy task to follow that road to their "M-twenty," the meeting place, which Justin had designated. In the increasingly rarefied air Wiley needed more altitude, and all turnarounds probably looked much the same from aloft. But not all of them would contain an old Toyota Land Cruiser. Stu prayed that his private bear in the air would locate Justin, set his selector on Channel 7, and reminded himself that the incompetent bucketmouths chasing him might become highly competent when they weren't using a CB rig.

Monitoring his pursuers, Stu took some comfort from their dismay as the roads developed deeper ruts, steeper inclines. Evidently the men in the lead Blazer were now wishing they had dressed for the high country. For a time, Stu suspected that their frequent transmissions were intended to be overheard, but if so, they were all natural actors.

And they gave away a lot of information. After listening for twenty minutes Stu decided that they were using a directional receiver to check his progress. That explained a lot; no wonder they'd followed him when they couldn't see him. It was nearly a half hour after Wiley's last transmission, and Stu had once barely glimpsed his pursuers turning onto a numbered dirt road far behind him, when a brief transmission interrupted that accented voice on Channel 7. The fresh voice might have been anyone's—but not to Stu Ransome. "Breaker, breaker, seven. Pegleg for Coyote. Bring it to me." The interruption ceased; it had been little different from many another.

Stu immediately found their own channel. "Wiley's Coyote up, you got it, Pegleg."

"Your rubberneck's standing by, Coyote. Man, it's easy to spin a brodie in these parts, an' there's no such thing as a fender bender around here, come ahead."

So Wiley had spotted Justin! Or the Toyota, at any rate. It could not have been a smooth passage between those peaks, fighting vicious downdrafts in a region where propellers and

wings clawed hard for air. "I copy, Pegleg, and thanks a
bunch. You headin' her for the barn now?"

"Ten four, bubba, for fresh skivvies. Come ahead."

"Threes to you, Pegleg, and eights to milady. Wiley's
Coyote down," said Stu. *Regards to you, and kisses for
Karen.*

The reply was gruff, good-humored: "Pegleg durn near
down, fer sure. I'm pullin' the plug, Coyote."

Somewhere to the south, Wiley Reed was returning to
smoother air, flatter country; and from the sound of it, with
clammy hands. Somewhere to the north, Justin was waiting; or
had damned well better be. Stu checked his notes and saw that
the next turnoff would be the last. He could drive as hard as he
liked, raising a cloud of dust no one could miss, once on that
horrendously crevassed trail. After that, every few yards he
extended his lead would mean precious seconds, improving his
odds. Above all, he could not afford to let those determined
sons of bitches catch him halfway out of his car at a trailhead
he had never seen, seven thousand feet up in the High Sierra,
with only Justin Paladino for a backup. The thought came
unbidden: *And when was the last time Justin proved himself
dependable?*

Chapter 20

FROM the moment when the Corvair engine flung him up that first set of steep switchbacks on the final leg of his run, Stu could see no pursuers in the rearview, but big trees and ravines limited his view and he made no assumptions. Four-wheel drive and a whopping V-8 could push a well-driven Blazer into stiff competition with a Baja Bug. For all he knew it might be closing on him despite the almost constant twists of the trail with occasional patches of snow. For fully half of the remaining distance to the trailhead, the Baja Bug was pointed in one direction but going in another, rear wheels hung out, their rims battering against roots and boulders, gouts of red earth and stones flying in the wake.

Then the broad turnaround area lay before him as the yellow VW crested a rise, clearing the trail with all four wheels in the air for one instant. He spotted the old Land Cruiser backed up on a nearby slope; sawed at the steering wheel and blipped his throttle to help the ZF differential power him through a sliding U-turn. He was out of the car, the Beretta stuffed under his white pullover, snatching for his backpack before he saw Justin Paladino shuffling toward him in a shambling trot. There was something in the set of the Paladino features that Stu had seen before: the emotionless intensity of a man studying a familiar but complicated set of plans.

"How much time?" Justin, encumbered with a huge canvas backpack and his old scoped rifle, wasted no words. He reached the VW in time to hold Stu's pack as Stu tore his white leather jacket from the Safeway bag and shrugged into it.

"Minute or two at most," Stu replied, slamming the door with his foot, thrusting his arms through the pack's shoulder straps as Justin held them.

"Follow my footsteps exactly," Justin cautioned, setting off not up the foot trail with its patches of snow but through the brush twenty yards from it. Near the foot trail, a yellow two-man tent was spread out, half erected. "Remember the altitude," Justin flung over his shoulder as he led the way, walking quickly.

Stu managed to tighten his pack's bellyband, shrugging the load higher on his back as he walked, and now its weight seemed to drop by half as the bellyband settled much of the load over his hips. Justin picked his way across bare outcrops of granite where possible, stepping on dry humus when necessary, the length of each pace gauged to place his next foot where it would leave no scuffmark.

Faintly, as though miles away, the thundering chop of a laboring V-8 floated to them in the thin air. "They're in a brown Chevy Blazer and a gray sedan," said Stu, panting already and damning himself for it.

"*Two* cars? How many men?" Justin stopped and turned, consternation on his face.

Breathing heavily, Stu halted as well. Now, intermittently, they could hear the whine and axle-tramp of a heavy vehicle forcing its way up the rutted trail. "Couldn't be sure from that distance. A half dozen," Stu hazarded.

Justin blinked several times rapidly, revising plans, shaking his head. "Too many. Go back down the mountain afoot," he snapped. "Follow the creek. You have done all I could ask, my friend. They will see the Toyota, and will soon find the tracks I left for them.'' With that he set off again as if the matter were closed, moving more quickly now, galvanized by the continuous crashing roar of the Blazer.

Stu remained still for the span of time it took him to realize the sentence Justin Paladino had just pronounced on himself. If he had deliberately left another trail, then the half-erected tent was probably a ruse as well. Justin was, in the ultimate white-knuckle crunch, a dependable friend; and now he had released Stu Ransome from further risk. "Horseshit," Stu puffed, "just don't go too fast."

"I must not stop to argue," Justin barked softly, not slowing at all, speaking between deep breaths. "They will leave one—hidden near the cars. Five good men—can cover enough ground—to pick us up quickly. I have no option now—but to reduce their number. Go, Stuart!"

Blinking at the tiny spots in his field of vision, Stu forced himself to breathe more deeply. All he said was, "Screw you."

Justin moved past a mound and stopped, his barrel chest heaving, face florid as he glared at the man following him. The Blazer's progress was now echoing from nearby outcrops. "God *damn* it, Stuart! With me you must kill—without hesitation—or be killed. You are not even armed."

Saving his breath, Stu lifted the edge of his shirt so that Justin could see the Beretta's thick butt. He kept walking. And blinking.

"Spots before your eyes? Headache and nausea?" Justin turned away, striding off, momentarily downhill.

"I'm okay. Gimme a break, Justin."

"I am trying," was the angry response. "You are no—killer of men, Stu. It will be necessary—against so many."

Stu, light-headed already, grinned as he realized that Justin himself must be very short on oxygen if he was saying "Stu" instead of "Stuart." *Formality is only a matter of having surplus oxygen*, he thought idiotically. Pausing a moment to lean against a huge fir, he said, "I'll shoot back; depend on it."

"You will have to shoot *first*." Justin, too, leaned against a tree, meeting Stu's gaze as they heard a mighty *slamm* and a

squeal of brakes in the distance. They were only a quarter mile
from the trailhead. Justin said something in a tongue Stu did
not recognize, added, "Stay here," and used his hands to pull
himself up a nearby boulder. Secured to D-rings on the outside
of his big canvas backpack were two sets of short snowshoes
with aluminum frames and neoprene webs. They protruded
from the pack almost as high as Justin's head.

Stu kept his bellows pumping; sensed that the tingle in his
fingertips was now diminishing. With a one-minute break in
every four, he just might stay conscious at this elevation. He
identified distant sounds as the second vehicle bottoming on
that last crest; doors slamming; a man calling excitedly; another answering.

Justin eased himself back down, let his gaze sweep the
slopes ahead, then set off again with Stu two paces behind,
using stands of fir and the jumbled terrain to mask their
escape. "Five men," he said, moving up the backside of a
rocky slope. "At least two with automatic weapons."

Stu slipped, struck on his hip, cursed softly, and regained
his feet. He saw the scar his boot had made in the humus, then
noticed Justin watching him without expression. He waved the
older man on with a flick of his gloved hand, now taking more
care where he placed each foot.

They had gained another three hundred yards of distance,
perhaps two hundred feet in altitude, when Stu leaned against
a boulder, eyes closed. "Hold it," he gasped.

"A few more paces," Justin replied softly, moving up a
steep rocky escarpment on hands and knees. "You will see."
He unslung his scoped rifle near the top, shrugged out of his
pack straps. For the first time it occurred to Stu that Justin's
ancient pack did not even have a bellyband; its full weight
would rest on Justin's shoulders, but he could shuck it in a
hurry.

Stu forced himself to crawl the last ten yards, then eased
his head up near Justin's. He saw tiny figures, men darting
through underbrush near the trailhead, heard voices straining
with urgency but could not make out the words. Beside him,

breathing deeply and regularly in forced rhythm, Justin Paladino sighted through a powerful little spotting scope, his rifle leaning on granite between them. The long-barreled weapon, a bolt action with scarred wooden stock and telescopic sight, carried a wedge-shaped ammunition magazine protruding just ahead of the trigger guard. It had seen a lot of service somewhere. Stu judged that it was older than he was.

Justin moved his head slowly around and saw what Stu was looking at. "British 303 Lee-Enfield Number 4," he said softly, smiling. "Highly prized in Albania, perhaps even today."

Stu had enough breath now to waste some of it as he turned his attention to the trailhead. "A museum piece against burp guns?"

"Few burp guns are accurate at six hundred yards," Justin murmured, squinting through the little monocular again.

Stu glanced at the scarred old Enfield with awe. "Good God. Sniper rifle? You could pick 'em off from here."

"If I knew whom to expend," Justin said, studying the scene below. "Take the Enfield. Use the eyepiece, not the trigger. The man who gives orders is the one I must have alive."

"You're a fool, Viktor Grigorovitch," said Grichanka, watching Ken Connor dart among clumps of manzanita carrying a .45 Colt automatic. He spoke in an undertone as he and Viktor inspected Justin's tent. "These hoodlums must hear from you that you're all under my orders now. Or do I have to make a point of it myself?"

"You heard me tell them," Viktor rumbled softly. "Two of them have seen you face-to-face for the first time in the past two minutes. Give them time to adjust; they are not disciplined soldiers, Grichanka, and they have good reason to hate American authorities. It was you who wanted to take that role. Do you want me to put new questions in their empty heads now? I shall, if you insist." He flicked the blunt nose of his Ingram submachine gun against a tent peg. "I believe we surprised Krag—Paladino," he corrected himself quickly, "setting up camp here. They cannot be far away."

"But they can be armed," Grichanka said, and returned to the previous topic as he dumped canned goods from a heavy plastic bag which Justin had placed nearby. "I intend to report your foolishness. You can at least defer to my decisions without argument. Make it clear who's running this operation."

"Then run it. Tell me what to say," Viktor muttered, swinging the Ingram's muzzle to indicate the armed men who coursed around the trailhead like hounds. The big man shuddered, stamped his feet, and stepped from shade into a patch of direct sunlight.

Grichanka's smile was like the shade. "If I were the Albanian, I would be heading down the mountain afoot, or waiting in ambush. Send your best man back to that bridge we crossed; have him work his way up the creek slowly, well above the creek level. He just might catch our rabbits. Be sure he knows that if the Albanian dies, no one gets paid."

Viktor had turned, cupping a hand at his mouth, but paused. "Ransome is expendable now?"

"Of course. The only hostage that Albanian would care about is his own son. The boy may be here with them, you know."

Viktor called the men in. Allen Connor strode in last, holding his own Ingram as though it weighed fifty pounds, sitting down heavily. He was unable to speak for the moment.

"It's the air," Grichanka told him. "Don't try to do too much."

"Found snowshoe tracks," Allen said, grimacing, and pointed away from the trailhead. "In snow. Headed up."

Viktor darted a glance at Grichanka, who shrugged and said, "You'll still have to cover the creek to make sure. We may as well leave these radios in the cars. Notice how the signal faded every time a piece of mountain got between us? It's better not to depend on them."

While Grichanka locked the CB units in the Lancer, Viktor explained the strategy. His steadiest man was Allen Connor, who had obviously overtaxed himself. "Leave your truck on the bridge. We will control the traffic," he told Allen, and turned to Grichanka. "What else, Mr. Smith?"

"Take your time, Connor. If we're gone when you get back up here, watch the vehicles and stay out of sight. It's obvious they know we're at their heels now," Grichanka added, waving a hand at the abandoned yellow tent and food.

Allen Connor stood up, glancing from Viktor to Grichanka. "You're a fed," he said, licking his lips. "Why don't we just call for help with the CB?"

Grichanka stared steadily back at the balding American, very much aware that the others were waiting for his answer, refusing to break eye contact. "The FBI doesn't know my agency exists, Connor. And Uncle doesn't issue us badges for U.N. work," he went on, temporizing to head off difficult questions. He jerked a thumb at Viktor. "The Italians called me in to supervise. If *I* have to call for help, my cover is gone and I might not have a job tomorrow. Where'd you think Viktor got your names?" His lopsided smile was quite convincing. "I picked you from your files because I thought you could do this."

Allen Connor grunted, with a sideways nod toward Viktor. "I told him, and I'm tellin' you: I won't shoot the kid."

"He probably isn't up here," said Grichanka, moving to the sedan, "and we're wasting time. If we hear shots, we'll head down the creek toward you. Otherwise we'll meet you back here before dark."

Allen Connor fired up the Blazer with mixed emotions. He disliked being separated so frequently from a brother who always looked to him for guidance and usually operated three rounds shy of a full clip. On the other hand, he didn't want these hotshots to know he felt like shit: cold sweat, headache, and a belly that didn't want to keep its breakfast. He waved to the silent Ken, who looked like he might puke himself a puddle, then drove over the nearby crest and out of sight.

"Now, let's check out those prints in the snow," said Grichanka, withdrawing a bulky felt-wrapped object from the Lancer's trunk. He folded the cloth back with the care of a surgeon, slipping two long banana clip magazines into his coat pockets.

"What the fuck is that?" said Ray Nelson, goggling at the folding skeleton stock and scope sight.

"A light machine gun from our friends in Israel," said Grichanka, with the faint smile of a private joke, thrusting the weapon into his armpit inside his coat with the stock still folded. "Let's go."

There was simply no point, Justin had said, in firing a handgun from a hundred yards except for its threat value. Stu would be of more use farther up, on the way to the Chain Lakes, which lay some two miles distant at an altitude of nine thousand feet. There was no sign that the trail had been traversed since the previous summer. Justin's false track across an open snowfield had doubled back to the trail, and by setting out alone to intersect that trail at a higher elevation, Stu would arrive first at the upper creek crossing. That crossing, Justin had warned, might be impassable without a footlog during the spring snowmelt.

Stu husbanded his strength, stopping frequently to stoke his lungs, no longer trying to avoid prints in the snow that lay ever deeper on the trail. He heard the hissing roar long before he spied the creek, and for long moments he stood irresolute, scanning up and down the narrow ravine. A creek? No, a cataract; a thundering juggernaut of white water carrying snowmelt to the San Joaquin Valley—and boulders with it, judging from the heavy concussive thuds within the torrent. In late summer a man might leap across, or wade. Today he would have to leap thirty feet, over white water ten feet deep. Stu had never braved frozen heights such as these so early in the year, and had never imagined the creeks could boil with such white-water fury. He raised his estimate of Justin's mountain expertise another notch.

Stu found a dead fir spanning the ravine fifty yards up, but it had been swept partly aside when the creek was even higher and its battered end was lodged in boulders beneath the swirl across the torrent. It would have been suicide to negotiate the last ten feet.

Stu slipped from his pack harness and withdrew the collapsible Svensaw Justin had hauled from his own canvas pack. The tree he chose was only a foot thick, but its lower branches began near the ground. He assembled the saw and made his undercut on the side facing the creek, clammy with sweat despite the chill air, near unconsciousness as he completed the slanting downward part of the undercut. At last the wedge of fragrant sap-filled wood lay before him, and his head spun from momentary exhaustion.

The main cut was tougher, a vagrant breeze blowing the treetop just enough to bind the blade so severely that, once, Stu feared the saw blade was hopelessly bound. He worked the blade loose then and made a dangerous decision, beginning a fresh and almost horizontal cut through the raw wound where he had removed the wedge of treetrunk.

He made several passes, kneeling sideways, so dizzy with fatigue that he could only fall to one side when the tree cracked like a gunshot. A series of grinding pops, and then the fir crashed across the ravine, its tip twenty feet beyond the lip of the ravine. The fir did not lie still; with its lower branches in white water, it shuddered and rocked with the flow.

Somebody had to shinny out there and cut those branches from the underside. Stu sat panting near the stump and studied the handholds. And cursed.

Viktor shaded his eyes, watching Ken Connor's sweeping gestures from above the snowfield. "Those tracks cut back to the west," he said.

In the midafternoon sun, shadows were deep, their edges knife-sharp. Grichanka stood in the shadow of a great fir, using the scope of his weapon to study the region to which Connor pointed. "Have him stop for the moment," he said calmly. As Viktor made broad two-handed pushing motions to the man far above, Grichanka himself replaced the scope's protective covers and called up the trail. "Nelson! Nelson! Wait!"

Following the GRU man, his great bulk now a great

disadvantage, Viktor wasted too much breath in talking. "Paladino went back to the trail. He made a mistake, wasting his time on that open snow," he said.

A snort of derision from ahead. "Wasting *our* time. We must advance together. Nelson on the trail, Connor following tracks, you and I from there," he ended, his hand describing an arc west of the trail.

Ray Nelson stood, shuffling his feet in two inches of snow, waiting for the others as he tried to catch his breath. Grichanka, breathing heavily but without the difficulty of Viktor, smiled at the little man. "Trouble breathing?" Ray Nelson only nodded. "The trail will be easiest on you. But look ahead carefully at every turn. We'll have to make our own trail, the hard way," he said, and moved up the slope gesturing for Viktor to follow. Grichanka was secretly relieved to find that these altitudes bothered him so little; his previous hunts in snow had been with his father many years before in Manitoba, and no point in all Manitoba reached over twenty-eight hundred feet above sea level.

Ray Nelson watched them scuff through humus and snow, not moving for many seconds, and then began to walk up the trail, hands hanging listlessly at his sides.

Grichanka did not seem to be watching Nelson. A hundred yards west of Nelson, he turned north and began to parallel the man's path. Nelson kept glancing up to his left, assuring himself that he was still near the protection of Mr. Smith's fearsome-looking weapon, stopping several times to catch his breath. Whenever Nelson stopped, the others stopped. Viktor thanked a God he was not supposed to believe in because, each time, Nelson needed to stop a few paces before Viktor himself would have fallen on his broad face. They had progressed almost to the elevation where those snowshoe tracks veered toward Nelson when Viktor, walking between the others, turned so that his voice would be heard only by Grichanka. "These Americans are your tripwires, then."

"*Our* tripwires," said Grichanka amiably. "But our Albanian must be putting more distance behind him at the moment."

"How do you know?"

"That fool Connor?" Grichanka pointed through the trees where Ken Connor stood, still dutifully waiting, near the treeline above the snowfield. "A perfect target, following tracks of a decoy. No, Paladino has bought time to—"

The painfully sharp crack of a medium-caliber rifle sent echoes chasing across the mountainside. Viktor sprawled on his belly, the Ingram held in both hands, as Grichanka slipped behind the trunk of a ponderosa pine. Grichanka made a palm-down slapping motion in Ray Nelson's direction, risked a look up the trail from between heavy scales of ponderosa bark, then glanced again to see what Nelson was doing.

Ray Nelson was doing the only thing he could do under the circumstances, lying on his back and twitching, a red stain spreading on the snow in the trail beneath his head. From Grichanka's view a hundred feet higher, it looked as if there was no longer a top on Nelson's head.

Another crack, its echoes chattering away, and now they could see glimpses of Ken Connor tumbling down that snowfield, glissading on patches of tree-shaded ice, scrambling like a hyperactive child at play toward a large stone outcrop.

"He has bought a man, and cheaply," Viktor said, glaring at the GRU assassin.

Grichanka fired three rounds up the trail. "But we know they are near. Fire short bursts," he called, "to keep them down." Then, as Viktor fired blindly at nothing, Grichanka began to flit low, working his way up the ridge using treetrunks for cover.

No man's voice could have carried over the roar of water, but Stu held his backpack in one hand, pantomiming his own passage across the felled tree. Justin nodded, shucking his long canvas pack, gripping its straps in the crook of one arm. If a man fell into that gushing torrent unencumbered, he might have a ghost of a chance; with that pack, no chance whatever.

The tree swayed lower under the load, but with two of its lower branches sawed free it did not threaten to roll as it had with Stu himself for one sickening moment. Justin moved across the spume-slick bark, freeing the rifle muzzle from a protruding branch with a deep shrug, choosing his handholds with the deliberation of a man in no hurry to die, pausing to catch his balance once, twice; and his grip on Stu's, finally, was like chilled steel.

Stu cupped his hand to Justin's ear. "I could cut almost through the trunk at this end," he shouted. His hand mimed something crashing into the cataract.

Justin smiled but shook his head, shouldering his pack, setting off again with Stu in arrears. Not until the rushing maelstrom was a distant murmur did Justin pause for a breather. "We want them up here," he said, gazing around him with a smile. "They must advance slowly now."

Jesus Christ, he likes it! This is his turf, thought Stu. Hitching his pack higher to rest against a tree, he said, "Are they near?"

Justin shook his head and made a hand-waggle of doubt in the air. "There are only three now. You heard the shots?"

"Not standing guard at Niagara Falls. What happened?"

A shrug. "I missed the second man—from seven hundred yards. Not the first. Does that upset you?" He waited, got a grimace that suggested it was bearable, and went on: "Due west, only a few miles—is a ranger station. The first trail you cut—turn downhill toward it."

"Why keep trying to dump me—now that the odds are better?"

"One young blond man—has a pistol. Your big man, a machine pistol. He gives orders. I want him. The third could mean—the end of us. I watched him, he moves well." Justin's headshake was like a death sentence: "I think he carries—a Galil machine rifle."

Cold tendrils slid down from Stu's hairline along his arms, his back, his thighs. "Is that bad?"

"Scoped automatic, flat trajectory, huge magazine. I might be his equal—at a half mile. Go back, Stuart. You will only impede me now."

Stu's smile was bleak. "You're lying about that."

"And I swore no more lies. Well—" He raised one hand; let it drop.

Stu inclined his chin up the trail. "Let's see what's up there," he said, his gloved hand out, palm up.

Justin's smile was brilliant in the deep shade of snow-clad firs, and his gentle slap against Stu's hand was somehow very American. "Three lakes not far ahead, with clearings," he said.

Chapter 21

PLODDING toward the heights north of icebound Lower Chain Lake, Justin stopped in sight of the second lake, which spread beyond encircling trees like a broad snow-covered plain. He chose what seemed a poor spot among snow-clad boulders for donning snowshoes and, when he had his breath, Stu asked why.

"It commands the trail and gives us cover. The Galil man is a shrewd hunter," said Justin, unlashing the western snowshoes from his pack. "If we abandon the trail to gain these heights, he must follow similar contours or provide an easy target. They do not have these," he added, toeing one boot into a cat's cradle of nylon straps, "and from here on, they will be slower than we. How do you feel?"

"Better; getting used to it, I guess."

"Finding your pace is half the battle," said Justin, passing a pair of snowshoes over. "Have you any experience with these?"

"Not a damn bit."

"It is quickly learned. Like this," Justin said, tightening the forward bindings, then slipping a rear binding behind his boot heel. He stood on it, flexing one knee so that his boot pivoted, heel up, its toe dipping through the broad hole in the neoprene membrane. "Your boot must not catch as your toes dip through," he said, and bent to attach his other snowshoe.

Stu copied the rigamarole poorly at first, readjusting the forward bindings so that the toe of his hiking boot did not engage the neoprene. He tried it, noting that the shin-deep snow supported his tentative steps, and grinned. "Aren't these a little high-tech for your taste?"

"I have come to terms with them," Justin said a bit sadly. "Much more maneuverable than traditional snowshoes in country like this. Now I wish I had bought ice cleats," he murmured, scanning a vast tooth of white that soared thousands of feet above them, perhaps two miles distant, against a sky the color of turquoise.

Without warning, a heavy concussive report boomed across the lake. Stu ducked, glancing quickly at his companion. "They've spotted us!"

"Not gunfire," said Justin. "But I trust they will react as you did."

"What the hell else could it be?"

"The sun weakens ice on the lake. In the afternoons, whole sections of ice split, to refreeze later. The report is more like a cannon than small arms."

Stu listened to the aching stillness that ensued, following Justin's gaze, sensing for the first time what motivated otherwise sensible folk to strike out across God's personal deep-freeze for, of all things, *fun*. "That mountain have a name?"

"Gale Peak. Upper Chain Lake lies in its lap. I want you to skirt Middle Chain Lake at this elevation, and stop at the outflow of Upper Chain. I will follow your tracks there. You may find old campsites under the snow. Start an open fire if you can; a big smoky one," he said, smiling.

"Wanta tell me why?"

"You need practice kick-stepping the upper edge of your frames into snow when crossing slopes, and in keeping those upturned tips clear of snow, Stu. This may be the only time we can spare; I can catch up quickly enough. We have been stepping through depth hoar under the surface snow, and it will get worse. It is porous, spongy. Now, this is important:

with each step, first put part of your weight on the forward foot, wait a half second, then your full weight. And so on.''

"I don't get it.''

"I cannot explain. In the Dinarics, Albanians say one must ask the snow's permission with each step.''

Stu felt resistance in his numbed cheeks as he smiled. "Age hardening! Compress snow crystals for a split second and they'll resist a heavier shear force.''

"Engineering talk," said Justin with a wave of his hand. "Just ask the snow's permission.''

Stu slid into his pack harness, tightened his bellyband, and took a few steps between boulders bearing caps of snow. Justin peered back the way they had come, the Enfield in the crook of his arm. "You're gonna kill another one and you don't want me around," said Stu. It could almost have been a question.

"I am going to try," said Justin, his face again devoid of expression. "But they may be quicker than I think. Do you want a head start, or do you not?''

"If they see smoke they could cut up and across toward it.''

"I hope so," said Justin, and winked.

Grichanka motioned for the others as soon as he saw the clearing ahead, near the lowest of the lakes. There was no mistaking the two sets of tracks, made by different caulked patterns, that left the trail angling up a steep slope at the beginning of the clearing. "I'll go around the west side of that ridge," he said. "Viktor, use all the cover you can find for your fat Italian butt, and go up parallel to those tracks. Ken, you can stick to the trail east of the ridge.''

"The hell I can." Ken Connor shivered, his K-Mart jogging shoes hidden in a foot of snow, chest heaving beneath his light nylon jacket and mutiny in his face. "I got icicles packed in my ass—from dodgin' bullets. I went across that fuckin' log first—fightin' dry heaves. But Mr.—high and mighty Smith—if you want me in the open—for bait, switch guns with me.''

"You don't send your heavy weapons out front like that," said Grichanka.

Connor licked dry lips; packed a tiny ball of snow in a reddened hand; put it in his mouth, glancing through the trees toward the outcrop far ahead and to their left. At its top, boulders protruded from rounded caps of snow. "You figger they're sitting right up there," he said, mush-mouthed.

"You shouldn't eat so much snow either. It'll make you sick," Grichanka said as though commenting on a matter of no importance. "No, I think they want us to figure that way, to make us slow and cautious while they take off as fast as they can go."

In Russian, Viktor said quickly, "We are only three, Greek. We may need him."

Ken Connor blew on his hands. "Talk American, okay?"

Grichanka sighed; shifted the Galil to his other armpit. It was galling to admit that, for once, Viktor Danilov was probably right. And even Connor had limits to his stupidity. "No more Italian, Vic. And I disagree; Ken has shown a lot of guts." He gazed blandly back at Viktor's hard stare. "All right, then: Ken, you follow above the tracks, and Vic can circle around ahead of me. If you see them, fire once. If you see tracks leading a long way off, two spaced shots."

Grichanka watched Connor slogging up the incline and followed the wallowing progress of Viktor as long as he could stand the slow pace of the big man, then moved around Viktor and broke trail himself. He and Viktor snarled to each other in Russian, louder than was necessary: mutual promises of official complaints one day very, very soon.

Upper Chain Lake stretched for half a mile under the brow of Gale Peak, wind-driven drifts of snow lying like frozen wavelets on its surface of solid ice. Two open campsites were identifiable by regular lumps of white surrounding a circle of smaller lumps: stone seats around the stones of old campfires. Stu shucked his pack on the dry slanting face of a sun-warmed boulder, not far from the muted roar of the lake's outflow. His thin leather gloves were oozing moisture by the time he cleared one ashpit, but in hard sunlight he was not unpleasantly cold. Presently he spied brown ponderosa needles peeking from a pile of debris near the mouth of the lake's outflow, and dragged a dead pine branch the thickness of his wrist from its natural igloo. He had never realized how thoroughly repeated snowfalls could bridge gaps in foliage, to create a dry enclosure.

Far away, spaced a few seconds apart, two thin reports sent echoes ricocheting from the mountainside. Stu could not decide whether they were gunshots or the cracking of lake ice, and he hurried with his work.

By now he had learned the slightly bowlegged stride that avoided placing one snowshoe frame atop the other, but he could not wear them while building a campfire. Stu leaned the devices near his pack and fished in a zippered side pocket for wax-coated wooden matches. He knew that the secret of a fire in these conditions lay in careful preparation, and began by crumbling dry pine needles for a foundation. Bark would not burn as readily as the wood inside, and he stripped bark from twigs before arranging them, tepee fashion, above tinder-dry needles. This tiny assemblage would flare quickly, and die just as quickly, unless he bridged the tepee with larger dry twigs. He set about stripping the bark from these larger pieces. His gloves were too wet, and he pulled them off. Had his hands not been shaking, he might have managed a fire in five minutes.

The faint dry crunch of footfalls on snow did not reach him until they were very near, and Stu whirled up from the ashpit still holding one sopping glove in his teeth, the Beretta in both hands.

Justin came into view puffing from exertion, placing his snowshoes exactly in the prints Stu had made. He managed a smile before leaning back on a boulder, eyes closed as he faced the afternoon sun. "You cannot be that hungry," he said at last.

Stu removed the glove from his mouth, took both gloves and wrung a spatter of water from them. In another minute he would have been ready to strike a match. "Very funny. Still want that fire?"

"No time." After a few more breaths: "We must go now. They flanked me too well for a shot."

"Thought I heard shots," Stu replied, donning the gloves and hurrying toward his gear.

"They may have seen me. Either they missed, or they were signaling. We have snowshoes, they carry no packs. In sum, no great advantage either way. Yet."

Stu bent to don the snowshoes. "What next?"

Justin was shading his eyes as he gazed toward the great sweep of Gale Peak with its huge snowfields sloping toward the lake, broken by occasional snow-laden trees and outcrops of stone. "You may have to kill soon," he said, breathing more easily now. "We must stay out of sight en route to higher elevations."

"Why not double back on 'em?"

"The country is too open up here," said Justin. "I admit I had forgotten that." He studied the distant snowfields across the lake, then pointed. "Those trees sticking up from the snow are our goal. I go first; you must place your feet exactly in my tracks. It will prove useful, I hope."

Moving on level snow, Stu made fairly good time near the lake's edge. Pockets of clear water showed here and there at the shoreline, revealing waterlogged debris in blue depths. He picked his way through brush, following what seemed to be an old trail, for over a quarter mile before stopping to rest. For the next several hundred yards, towering outcrops of stone rimmed the shore. Above them lay only a blinding expanse of white, broken by occasional trees and, slightly nearer and higher, one enormous stone outcrop.

Justin finished scanning the region they had left; turned the little monocular to study the heights ahead; stuffed the monocular beneath his shirt again. He pointed upward.

"We'll be in the open, Justin."

"I will explain." As Stu kick-stepped sideways and forward, fumbling for handholds in brush beneath the surface snow as he sidled up the slope, Justin spoke with great economy. "They will see tracks—ending in trees. They must flank those trees—above and below. At least one should pass you near enough—for that handgun of yours. Whichever one it is—kill him."

Stu found himself atop a jumble of boulders the size of two-story houses that stretched for perhaps a fifth of the circumference of the lake. One slip now, and he would be splattering through thin ice below. At least some of those boulders rose high enough to hide them as Stu moved in sight of the group of trees that shouldered their way above knee-deep snow.

Then, after a delay of too many seconds, Justin's words triggered an implication. "Near *me*? Where will you be?"

"Deceiving them. The snow is a—wonderful liar, Stu."

"It's got nothing on—you, Justin. Why don't you care anymore—if I nail the bigshot?"

"Because he is not our only Soviet. When I—heard them arguing in Russian—I knew for a moment—what men mean by despair. Theirs is the world's—largest network of agents. But I must know more—and I will if we take one—of the three alive. Start working your way up now," Justin said. "They may see us at any time. We must not rest—until we can stand behind—that last single tree."

Had Grichanka known where to look, he might have spotted two tiny dots inching up the snowfield beneath the great sloping shoulder of Gale Peak. Instead, he divided his attention between studying possible ambush cover at the lake's edge and picking the easiest route through shin-deep snow. Snow melted faster between sloping reflective faces of granite, and the trickle of water also tended to melt snow from beneath. The unpleasant side of it was that you walked in freezing slush.

Grichanka knew better than to walk in the slight depressions made by snowshoes, as Ken Connor was now doing. After all that mutinous complaining, the man seemed to have thrown caution to the winds after having heaved up his last meal in the snow. So much the better: the KGB had one tripwire still functioning.

Viktor brought up the rear, shambling along in low-quarter shoes and that black leather coat, an obvious target against the glare of a white world. He had called to Grichanka, warning him that two sets of snowshoe prints had blended into one, and now neither of the men gave a damn whether Ken Connor heard them speak in Russian.

And then Connor blundered straight to a recently abandoned campsite, too sick to care much, fumbling with his cigarette lighter before a ready-made pyre of sticks. He sat back on his haunches and cursed as Grichanka, taking in the scene instantly, crushed out the wisp of flame with his hiking shoe. "Whatthefuck, man? What the *fuck!*"

"They left that for us," Grichanka spat, making a poor guess. "To slow us, maybe. They're not your friends, Connor; use your head."

Doggedly, Connor came to his knees, slapping Grichanka's leg away from the smear of twigs. "I am. My feet are fuckin' *froze*; my hands too." Trembling, clearly beyond taking orders for the moment, he set about assembling the pyre. As Viktor came puffing up, Ken Connor muttered, "I gotta get warm," and began to sob as he watched his lighter kindle the pine needles.

Viktor dropped to his knees and thrust his big hands over the wisp of smoke, breathing through his mouth with the sounds of a man snoring lightly. Grichanka, wearing good leather gloves, shrugged and began to scan the area. It was obvious that this spot had not been chosen for an ambush, else bullets would already be searching around them. Kneeling near the shoreline, trying to ignore the dull ache in his feet, he looked closely at the long scuffing prints of snowshoes. Yes, they were still trying to leave only one set of prints; a cunning effort, but a failure. One in every five or six prints showed a slight overlap. He stood up, letting his eyes rove around the lake's perimeter, and then slipped the covers from the Galil's scope. Cold as he was, Grichanka stood absolutely still, denying the shake of skeletal muscles long enough to traverse distant slopes with the scope. The glare was ferocious but finally he saw what he had hoped to see.

He strode back to the little fire that crackled and spat as Connor heaped fresh twigs on it, bark and all. Brushing snow from a nearby stone, he extended the soles of his shoes toward heat he could feel on his face. "Our rabbits have dived for a hole," he said with satisfaction.

Connor ignored him, moaning as he toasted pink hands in the sorry little blaze. Viktor, with an effort at professional intensity: "Nearby?"

"In plain sight," Grichanka replied, nodding across the lake, "in those trees halfway up the mountain. The tracks lead there and stop. He thinks we'll worry about—where the second man went, but the second man is with him. He expects one or two of us—to come marching in and give him a good shot, but—he should have picked a place with an exit."

"The rabbit is not in your bag yet," Viktor muttered.

"But I can flush him out," said Grichanka, patting the receiver of the Galil. Excitedly now, with impatience: "Don't you see it? Finally, he has made a mistake! We can surround them. That upper slope is—too steep to climb, and he can't—double back without showing himself while he does it."

Connor looked up with tear-stained cheeks, glancing to the west. "They might wait until dark," he said.

"If we let them. These are the longest days of the year. We have four hours, but—we must not waste them. Go ahead, toast yourselves," Grichanka said expansively. Despite his excellent conditioning, the mere act of talking was now an effort. For a middle-aged man softened by decades of the American life, it would be far worse. Grichanka permitted himself a smile. "We can rest for a few minutes—while they freeze up there in deep shade."

Chapter 22

GRICHANKA'S war council, at the spot where Stu had begun to climb lakeside boulders, did not take long. It was remarkable, he thought, how a fifteen-minute rest and warm feet could instill new determination in the disheartened. The prints of their quarry could not be mistaken, winding up to take advantage of solitary trees on the way to a solitary stand of firs. But that group of trees was now only six or seven hundred yards away. Ray Nelson had been shot from nearly that distance, so at least one of the two men would be deadly to anyone who showed himself from this point onward. Connor's Colt automatic would be useful only if the quarry broke into the open—and only a madman would break uphill on such a slope. Connor, then, was dispatched among the lakeside boulders where he would work his way upward as far as cover could be found.

Viktor's stubby Ingram carried tremendous firepower in its thirty-two-round magazine, but could not be relied upon at distances much over a hundred yards. Therefore it was Viktor who drew the job of angling upward parallel to the tracks, keeping out of the line of sight of those trees where the tracks stopped, drawing as near as possible behind the cover of snow-laden trees. In all probability, because of his nearness, it would be Viktor who would set terms for the surrender. For

237

much of the distance he would be in the open, floundering through deep snow. That did not matter, Grichanka pointed out, because neither of those men could possibly be anywhere but where the tracks led. Viktor need not fear fire from his back because only Grichanka would be above and behind him. What he must do, at all cost, was draw near enough to offer terms to Kraga, using available cover just as Connor was doing.

Grichanka's was the most physically demanding job, and he was pleased to find that he could do it where most men would have collapsed in exhaustion. The great stone outcrop stood higher than the trees where their quarry lay, but from that height Grichanka's Galil was within easy range—perhaps a bit under five hundred yards. The damned Galil grew increasingly heavy as Grichanka fought his way through covering brush, but with it he could pour a withering fire into those trees, depressing his aim a bit with every burst. The impact of slugs in treetrunks would probably bring snow cascading down on the men hiding in there. Time enough, after that, to offer Pal Kraga a bargain he could not refuse.

Grichanka peered around a projecting ledge and saw Connor fighting his way between boulders almost below that copse of trees. Poor Viktor Grigorovitch made a comical sight below, staggering along above those snowshoe prints, weaving like a drunk as he kept solitary trees between himself and the quarry. His own spoor was broad enough for two men but give the hefty devil his due: Viktor was a good soldier who would obey until he dropped.

Grichanka had reached the swell of bare stone rising the height of a ten-story building and was resting halfway up the slope behind it when he heard the thin, snapping crack of a long-barreled weapon with its attendant echoes.

Justin had seen only momentary glimpses of the big man in the glistening black leather coat, and knew that with such a short barrel the ugly little Ingram submachine gun would not reach across the last two hundred yards with any accuracy. But a spray of bullets might make up for that. Justin felt that they still wanted him alive, but their motive just might be pure revenge stretching across forty years. It was a motive any Albanian could easily believe, and if it were true they only wanted to bury him.

He had counted the trees, none of them over sixteen inches at the base, that crowded together giving him a damp humus crawl space the area of a large blanket. There were nine of those trees, their lower branches overlapping, and his own movements while opening his pack had dislodged too much snow. He paid no attention now to what Stu Ransome was doing but brushed snow aside with cold hands, his joints stiff in this cavelike shade, and spread his plastic ground cover so that he could lie prone without getting more damp than perspiration had already made him.

He eased up to his knees, peering down the slope crusted with glare ice, and saw what might have been bobbing movement of a snow hummock far below. The Enfield's scope gave him a better view with less glare. Yes, someone was disturbing the low snowcapped brush near those boulders that circled the near lakeshore. If it was the Galil man, soon he could easily pour accurate fire upward, into Pal Kraga's position. Two generations of deep cover had gradually been torn from his shoulders, and now the man who leaned his elbow on his knee was flooded with the deadly teachings of Elbas Hamid as though his training had been only yesterday. "I aim beneath the brushtops, uncle," he murmured in Albanian, and waited for another mound of snow to move.

His field of view in the scope was very limited, but also very sharp in such brilliant lighting. He saw a snowcap collapse into a leafless shrub, swung the Enfield's muzzle a hair, and squeezed the trigger. The Enfield's old wooden stock nudged him and he worked the bolt quickly, steadying the scope again, wondering if he had allowed for too much drop when firing downward. Another movement in the brush, and Kraga fired again, slightly lower. Amid the echoes, the song of a hornet *zizzed* into silence. The Enfield's slug had struck something hard enough for a ricochet, and Kraga concluded that the manzanita shrubs did not rise more than a foot above those granite boulders.

Then, at the edge of the scope view and with the sudden jerk of a marionette from a box, a head and arm bobbed into view. The man fired twice with a large-caliber handgun, so rapidly that he could not have aimed with precision, then bobbed back from sight.

Kraga knew that this man was the least of his enemies, but he could move back and forth for many yards without being seen. Problem: to remove an enemy who hid in a line of boulders below a snowfield, when that enemy might be potential trouble later. Solution: sweep those boulders clean.

Kraga had thirty rounds of ammunition, plenty for any but the most cross-eyed Gheg sniper, but no amount of .30-caliber ammunition could punch through boulders. In late summer, he recalled, this slope was covered with scree, loose rock; dangerous to cross when a misstep could start a rockslide. He smiled then, and laid the Enfield on the plastic tarp, rummaging into that big canvas pack.

The silver duct tape was not its usual sticky self in such cold. He tore loose an eighteen-inch piece, holding it in his teeth, and thrust his arm deep into the pack, feeling for wax-coated cylinders he had taken from the hoard in his basement to be reworked in the motel at Coarsegold. He pulled out the ten sticks of dynamite one by one, each with a foot of orange fuse the thickness of a pencil protruding from the waxed cylinder. The copper-shrouded blasting caps had already been crimped with loving care around the fuses, thrust deep into the oily blasting compound.

He estimated that two sticks of "eighty percent" would create the shock he wanted, and wrapped them with the tape, pulling one fuse and its cap carefully out. He might need that cap later, and one blasting cap per explosion was quite enough. He made up a second two-stick bundle, and this time he pawed through humus to find shards of stone, wrapping them against the dynamite with more tape. He stuffed this second device, once known in some parts as an Albanian grenade, into his shirt.

The little disposable lighter needed adjustment but its long flame soon had its effect as a fierce pinkish blaze responded from the frayed end of the fuse. A foot of dynamite fuse gave him perhaps forty seconds. He counted to himself, holding the sticks in his teeth as he crawled into the open, on the side opposite his pursuers. Kraga did not even think about carrying fused, lit dynamite in his teeth because he knew how much time he had. Hamid had done it, Kosovo and Murra had done it. It was simply a thing one did with confidence—if one could count.

At the count of thirty, Kraga shouldered his way up through fir branches and, on hands and knees, hurled the little bundle out as far as he could. He saw that its arc was too shallow, for instead of penetrating the snow crust, it bounced, creating a pinwheel trail of smoke from the fuse, glissading downward. Well, at least the angle was such that the results would not extend back to his location.

Probably not, anyway. That was what trees were for: to secure a snow load. A load only knee-deep was, in any case, not all that critical.

Usually.

The explosion was louder than most because the dynamite was still spinning lazily downslope atop the crust when the cap sent its miles-per-second detonation wave racing through the blasting compound. By that time Kraga had already hurled his second package, the Albanian grenade, and he knew that whatever else happened they would try to punish him for his cleverness. He tossed it in a high arc five seconds before the first explosion, leaping with the throw, scrambling back to safety between the firs.

The shock of that first explosion slapped Kraga's chest gently even through soft humus and covered him with six inches of snow that filtered down through the firs. He offered an apology to the shade of Elbas Hamid for having forgotten that would happen. *But what choice did I have, uncle?* He heard a soft, almost surreptitious rumble and burrowed against the base of a tree, blinded by snow, half expecting to be covered by an avalanche much larger than the local slide he had intended.

He heard the passage of several high-velocity slugs that toured the trees overhead, some thudding deep into wood, and in almost the same instant a rattling burst of fire; the Galil's little rounds had reached him before the sound of firing.

Then the resounding report of his Albanian grenade, loud as a heavy mortar round, and another muted punch against his breast. Perhaps the grenade had dropped through crusted snow, or perhaps those stones taped in place had redirected the shock wave: in any case, the result was a loosening of countless tons of snow from its fragile balance on scree.

Pal Kraga scrambled to his knees, peering down the slope where billions of tiny ice crystals sparkled in hard sunlight, a low-lying fog that paced the avalanche. He felt confident that the Galil man would be watching the snowslide for the moment, and not peering through his scope.

But Kraga's confidence was misplaced. Grichanka did not care greatly whether Ken Connor lived through that avalanche or not, but he fired three times into the stand of firs because whatever Kraga was using for grenades, his next effort might be in Viktor's direction, and Grichanka still needed the big man. Kraga felt little pain as the last round struck him, but knew he was hit as it flung him around.

Viktor Danilov was crouched just beyond the lower branches of a solitary fir, wondering how he might make his way across open snow to the last lone tree, when the first explosion *whoommmed* across the slopes; and instinctively he knew that this might be the only diversion he could expect. The last tree lay two hundred yards from the firs where those tracks led; perhaps only a hundred from where he stood; but by floundering straight up the slope for ten yards, he could approach that tree while keeping it between himself and the line of sight to Kraga and Ransome. His thigh muscles ached so damnably from high-stepping that he wanted to scream aloud, but Viktor clenched his teeth and struggled into the open, up the slope, fearing a bullet even while he heard the sluggish displacement of part of that snow toward Connor.

No shots from those firs, but a short burst from Grichanka far above. Viktor hoped Grichanka would avoid killing Kraga outright, but cursed the GRU anyhow on general principles. Still a hundred yards from that nearest fir now, but on a level with it, Viktor hurried forward. At the second explosion he fell forward, still fifty yards from the cover of that tree. He felt the faint rumble of the avalanche shudder across the slope beneath him and feared that somehow, invoking one too many primitive tricks of the mountain Gheg, Kraga had triggered the disaster that would kill them all. *How like a Gheg*, he thought bitterly.

Viktor spat snow as he stood erect, watching horrified as a broad inverted V of snow, a hundred feet wide at its base, slid toward Connor. *A cold, hideous death even for such a fool as he*, thought Viktor, as more snow began to detach itself higher up the slope, the upper point of the V broadening. Viktor realized that the entire mountainside could go like dominoes in a series of slides, and that he would go with it. He started back on trembling thigh muscles; fell again. His head was pounding as he rolled to his knees. Viktor had never been so near the absolute end of his stamina as he swayed, trying to stand erect.

With a soft rattling rumble, the last of the avalanche battered itself into a sparkling cloud of fury against boulders below. Silence for perhaps three seconds, and then a series of falsetto screams in the near distance.

It was Ken Connor, flailing, scrambling into Viktor's sight back across the boulders, covered like a wedding-cake groom in white icing. As he fled, he thrust the Colt above his head and fired at the sky. "Fuck it," he screamed, and followed it with a wordless howl. "Fuck it all!" More blubbering cries paced his retreat.

Viktor cupped a hand to his mouth and got as far as "Connor, get back to your" before he saw Connor let fly with the Colt in his general direction.

"Forget it! Fuck this mountain, fuck the money! I'm

goin' home, I'm not gonna fuckin' *die* up here!'' With that, Ken Connor slipped. His progress could only be guessed from the noise, but it ended for a moment with a distant splash. Viktor looked up toward Grichanka and mimed a shrug that would have done credit to any Frenchman. He began plodding toward that tree again, pausing only when he heard Connor's despairing shrieks and turned to see the little man, now glistening with water to his waist, retrace their path back toward the fire at panic's pace.

In the sunlit glare, Viktor could not see the near edge of the exposed scree but clearly the slippage had not reached the men he sought. He followed the sets of tracks which led around the last lone fir, smiling because Kraga had hoped to dupe him by making two sets of tracks seem as one. With his last energy he floundered almost into the lower snow-laden branches of the fir and then went down on hands and knees, gasping with the effort.

Viktor knew that he would faint without a rest; saw through the glare under his nose that deep within those branches near the trunk lay a dark cavelike hiding place. His breath whistled painfully in his throat as he crawled forward, and then he was blinking into the nine-millimeter eye of a Beretta automatic thrust within inches of his face. Behind it was a face smeared unnaturally white, a mask of deadly intent.

"Just any old excuse will do," said Stu Ransome softly from the darkness. "Yell, or run—whatever. I was supposed to blow your head off anyway."

Viktor Grigorovitch Danilov closed his eyes. *Why make two sets of tracks seem as one? So that it would be easier to make one set seem as two! Duped by Albanians again . . .* When he found himself still alive after five seconds, he opened his eyes, fighting for breath and consciousness. The Beretta's muzzle shook slightly, as if the user were trembling with cold, or with fear. Either way, it might make a trigger finger tremble too much. "Tell me—what—to do," Viktor wheezed.

"Take that gun by the barrel and give it to me. Move too fast and you'll never know it."

A groaning effort to lift the Ingram from snow, before: "I

cannot—lift it.'' Viktor hung his head, his belly convulsing him with shudders.

Stu realized that the third man might be watching. "Crawl in here without it then. Lie on your face upslope of the treetrunk.'' As Viktor complied, wheezing and retching, Stu moved back in the six-foot-wide circle cleared to bare humus. "You know how many rounds this thing has? Give me one good reason and you'll get a dozen enemas.''

Viktor coughed; spat. The trouble with gifted amateurs, he knew, was that they had no tradecraft. Ransome might do anything at all. Wheezing: "I believe you. I am—your prisoner.''

Stu, on his knees, patted the man up and down in a futile search for other weapons. Then he glanced back through the broad groove of snow and gnawed at his lip. The goddamn little burp gun was barely visible in the snow, but to reach it he would have to slide into the open. It had been rough to dive sidelong and headfirst, on Justin's command, into this hideyhole from the back side of the tree without knowing whether he would coldcock himself in the process. By whacking at branches he had caused enough snowfall to erase his entry sitzmark, just as Justin had said he could, and so far so good. But if that other guy had a scope, he might see a man in a white jacket reaching for the gun, and that would be all she wrote.

But if the big man reached back for it, he might somehow make a signal, or try to use the weapon. Well, Stu knew one solution, if he was quick about it. "Shuck that coat off. Move!''

Viktor sat up, rolling from side to side, snow dribbling onto his head and shoulders as he wrenched at the sodden leather. "I will freeze.''

Stu hauled on the coat with one hand, pulling it toward himself. "Lie on your face; hands behind you.''

Stu, shifting the Beretta from hand to hand, had little difficulty getting into the coat; it might have been a circus tent. He paused, the collar turned high to hide his face, realizing that the big man would suspect what he was about to do. "This is when you get cute, buddy. You'll think you can get up, or crawl around to grab me. There is no way in God's earth you can do it in two seconds flat but you're welcome to die trying.''

Muffled, between coughs: ''I am—your prisoner.''

''Or my target. Suit yourself,'' said Stu, and crawled into the open, now with only his legs hidden. He grasped the weapon, tugging hard to free it, then rolled on his side back to safety. Blinking from the momentary glare, he saw that the big man had not moved.

His prisoner was having trouble just breathing, spitting bitter vomit. Stu shrugged his way out of a half acre of leather; felt a small rodlike something in the lining; hauled out his fishing knife and slit the chamois cloth lining. He palmed the slender tube, thrust the coat near Viktor's head. ''What's hidden on your body?''

Pause. Then, ''Nothing.''

''In your clothes?''

Longer pause. ''Identification—and a death needle.''

''Damn. I was hoping you'd give me a reason. Justin was right, buddy, I couldn't blow you away without an immediate reason. That's okay, you'll give me one sooner or later. Put your coat on; if you shake any harder you'll start another slide.''

Stu's backpack lay near the lower edge of the space and, as Viktor struggled into his coat, Stu rummaged one-handed in a zippered pocket for parachute cord. At Stu's command, the big man thrust his arms behind his back. So great was his bulk that his hands barely reached each other, but Stu bound them well. ''Nylon stretches,'' he muttered, breathing heavily again from his exertion. ''So go ahead and fight this cord if you want gangrene in both hands.''

Viktor cleared his throat, kneeling, his breathing steadier. ''Please understand—I am not a madman. I choose custody— not death.''

''Hold that thought,'' Stu replied, working his way around the treetrunk. With time on his hands and a need to keep warm in this natural refrigerator, he had cut through two of the lower branches with a wiresaw to gain freedom of movement. He moved within sight of Justin's lair. ''Justin! Got him,'' he called, hoping his voice would not carry as far as that high rocky promontory. "Justin?"

Floating disembodied across the slope, Justin's voice: "Without gunfire?"

"Sorry 'bout that. He's tied. Got his weapon." He got no response and after long moments, called Justin's name again.

The reply was spoken slowly and not very loud. "Take him back to better cover. Leave your pack and snowshoes. Dead or alive, he will be your shield." A sputtering burst of gunfire from the middle distance, and bits of snow cascaded around Justin's bower. "Perhaps your weapons will reach the rocks above," Justin finished when the echoes had subsided.

From nearby, Viktor spoke: "He will kill me, then you."

"Then make it look like *you* have *me*," Stu replied. He called softly across the slope: "Can do. He's alone up there."

No reply.

"Justin? You okay?"

"Well enough. Go quickly," Justin called.

"Okay, buddy," Stu grunted, moving with difficulty while holding both weapons. "Tell me how to remove the clip from this damn greasegun, and the round out of the chamber. Carry it for show, holding me by the collar. Just stay upslope, and remember why my hand will be inside my jacket."

Chapter 23

STUMBLING back on Viktor's tracks, Stu realized why he had been advised to leave his snowshoes behind: he would have stood taller than the big man, more vulnerable to the sniper above. He was vulnerable enough as it was with one hand thrust into his jacket, falling once as the treacherous depth hoar gave way beneath his feet. He never took his eyes from Viktor, knowing that the stubby weapon could be used as a club.

Viktor actually kept him from sprawling with that ham-handed grip on his coat collar. The big man only muttered, "He will shoot us both. I feel it," and waved toward the heights with the stubby Ingram.

"Fooling him is your problem. Solve it," Stu husked, regaining his feet, glancing to the outcrop where he knew a man lay with an automatic weapon, perhaps watching through a very good scope.

From the outcrop far above came a shouted message. At such a distance, in this enormous reflective natural bowl where echoes collided, Stu could not even identify the language. Viktor squinted upward, waved his empty weapon again, and kept walking.

Stu: "What did he say?"

Viktor: "Who knows? Be glad he is talking, not shooting."

248

Stu: "Some pals you've got, buddy."

Viktor: "My choices were limited." He paused, gasping, and Stu could see the big man's facial muscles sag below bloodshot eyes as he fought for breath. They leaned together then, almost companionably, recovering from their efforts.

Presently Viktor tugged at Stu's collar and they lurched forward again. Fifty yards away, low twisted branches of manzanita without snowcaps revealed where they had crept upward between boulders. "I go first," Stu warned. "If you don't follow me—well, you're too damn big to miss."

As they neared the declivity, a brief burst of gunfire searched Justin's stand of firs again with a soft rain of snow from the branches. Stu's mind flashed with the sudden image of a man dividing his time between targets. He had kept his courage enough to stagger slowly across an open snowfield with an enemy who dwarfed him, but for this instant he felt certain that he was not centered in a sniper's crosshairs. Stu Ransome tore from the bigger man's grasp and fled, tumbling between rounded granite boulders to safety, the Beretta flopping in his half-open jacket.

Seconds later, before Viktor could lever his great bulk between the rocks, a series of sharp reports sent metal fragments spanging from nearby boulders. Viktor dived headlong, the Ingram skating on snow crust, and rolled to a stop near Stu, who wiped a sleeve across his face as he retrieved the weapon. For the moment, at least, they were safe.

Viktor struggled to his feet, his face a study in utter weariness and disgust.

"Couldn't hack it another second. Sorry," Stu mumbled.

"Amateurs," Viktor said with scorn. "I told you he would shoot."

Pulling the long clip from his side pocket, fitting it into the Ingram's handgrip, Stu nodded. "Well, he missed. How d'you work a round into the chamber of this thing?"

Viktor said nothing, but the curl of his lip was eloquent. He spat, watching the American's face from a distance of ten feet, and then his eyes widened as Stu, with deliberate calm, pulled the Beretta from his jacket with his free hand and fired slightly to the left of Viktor's ample middle.

Stu waved the Beretta's muzzle up and down the big man's frame. Cheeks stiff with cold, he said, "I've got my guts back, buddy; it's easy when I have this. Even for an amateur." He stopped to breathe a moment, then went on: "Down on your belly. You're getting too feisty to have your hands free."

Viktor licked cracked lips as he locked his gaze to Stu's, but he saw no indecision there, and no pity. He turned, grunting as he lay across a domed rock, and thrust his hands behind him. Perhaps a bit too readily.

For a moment, Stu remained still. "I watched you awhile, buddy," he said. "You're strong, but I'm lots quicker and I'm mad as hell, thanks to you. Remember that while you think about jumping me." Pulling the parachute cord from his jacket pocket, Stu used its end loop to make a noose, then cursed to himself and took a calculated risk. "Feel this? It's a Beretta muzzle jammed under the back of your belt. How fast can I grab it and fire up your spine? Ask yourself if you really want to find out."

Stu worked with feverish haste, drawing the cord tighter until Viktor hissed with pain. "You can get up now. Just remember that this lousy amateur bagged your fat ass. If I don't get this burp gun working right, a friend of mine may be killed. If that happens, you die—at the hand of an amateur. That's a promise."

Viktor, his face now mirroring a certain amount of self-disgust, described the cocking handle and the loading operation. Then he lay back against a sloping boulder and let his face be bathed in sunshine as Stu wormed his way to a better view of the heights. Viktor was too tired even to jump when Stu Ransome began to fire the Ingram toward the outcrop.

Settled nicely in a crevice between rounded stones, Grichanka had been wadding his own coat as a bench rest for the Galil when Viktor disappeared beneath that last single fir. There was no point in firing on the fleeing Connor, though it was a real temptation. The Connor brothers might hot-wire the Lancer, but other vehicles would be available; Grichanka might need every last round to flush the Albanian. Ken Connor survived to flee back down to the trailhead because he was literally not worth a cartridge in this high-stakes game.

When tentative bursts of fire drew no reply from Kraga, he considered the possibility that he had already killed the man. How to find out? An interesting problem.

Grichanka was reasonably snug up here, with stones blocking the wind and a warm sun on his back. His sense of well-being grew when he reflected that, if worst came to worst, he had the sanction to kill Kraga. For Soviet purposes, anything was better than to have him running loose and available to the Chinese.

No telling how the man had caused those explosions, but judging from the booby-trapping of his own home, Kraga knew his way around detonators. Grichanka's thoughts jerked to the present when he saw Viktor emerge from beneath his covering fir with the Ingram in one hand, tugging on something with the other. He moved the Galil, turning it toward this mystery over a quarter mile distant. By the time he had the four-power scope trained, Viktor was making his way back across an open stretch.

The apparent distance was still over a hundred yards, but obviously Viktor had captured a man hiding where none had been suspected. He was leaving the field of battle; could the captive be Kraga himself? No; though mostly obscured by Viktor's own bulk, this man lacked Kraga's thick torso and seemed to be cradling one arm. The captive had to be Ransome. The captive stumbled or tried to escape, but Viktor held him and waved as he urged the man onward. Grichanka failed to notice that the Ingram was missing its long clip, but with sudden clarity, he saw how he might learn whether Kraga was still dangerous. Now, despite their extra weight, he wished for those radios he had left in the Lancer. Cupping his hand, he called in Russian, "Viktor! Give him your coat and force him forward!" If Kraga did not fire on this tempting target, Grichanka himself would shoot the man before he reached Kraga. Even an Albanian might lose heart when his confederate lay bleeding on a snowfield.

Viktor waved the Ingram but did not reply. The great lard-ass seemed on the edge of collapse. Furious at this failure of a good plan, Grichanka turned the Galil toward Kraga's lair and sent three rounds a bit lower into the branches.

From the tail of his eye, Grichanka saw sudden movement in Viktor's direction and hauled the rifle around fast. The white-jacketed prisoner was escaping! To stop him from bursting out of the boulders where he might outdistance Viktor, Grichanka poured several rounds into the region where the man would probably emerge, and saw Viktor tumble headfirst from sight.

Grichanka waited for a long minute, without success, for that man to come into view, then heard a single report and assumed that Viktor Danilov had meted out final punishment to the American. Just as well: Grichanka had slated the man for termination once he had led them to the Albanian. How many rounds were left in his own deep magazine? Perhaps twenty; he exchanged it for a new magazine, refilling the first one expertly without looking as he turned his attention toward that stand of trees. If he kept depressing his sights, sooner or later he would kill Kraga or drive him out.

Pal Kraga vented Gheg curses at his inability to see his friend's progress through that intervening tree. He knew where the sniper had to be within a three-meter radius, yet that was little help to him while he was pinned down in these trees. But was he? Now that he faced only one weapon, Kraga could leave the trees, using them as a blind. His path would take him downslope to the almost bare scree from which he had blasted most of the snow burden. And while the glare robbed him of most detail, he knew that the severed edge of the remaining snow might be almost as steep as a low wall. Leaving the remaining sticks of dynamite ranked neatly, he chose two sticks and thrust them with the duct tape into cavernous pockets before he moved out with the Enfield over his shoulder, scanning and squinting, onto the open snowfield keeping the trees between himself and the outcrop above. If he misjudged the sniper's elevation, he might soon be a perfect target.

By some trick of the wind, standing in the open, Kraga heard every word shouted in Russian by the sniper. He could not be certain what it implied; perhaps his friend's capture. The single shot from below might mean a struggle. This was not the time to dwell on that, nor on his own wound, nor on the burst of gunfire from the towering outcrop across the slope.

The stutter of a heavier automatic weapon, much too fast for a Beretta, clamored across the mountain presently. That meant—he *hoped* it meant—his American friend was trying to gain the sniper's attention. At such a range, a short-barreled submachine gun had a trajectory like a lobbed snowball. But if Stuart Ransome could see where his slugs were landing, he might just lob a few very hard balls up there on the heights. Kraga, without snowshoes, crunched his way downslope, glancing back often to keep his bearings. Over a kilometer away, he saw a tiny figure stumbling past the smoldering fire on his way down the mountain. He grunted with satisfaction: the avalanche had driven one man to sustained panic.

The edge of a snowfield split by avalanche is not the most stable platform; it can follow the avalanche for the slightest reason. Kraga stepped slowly on his thirty-yard traverse, trying to give it no reason. Now he could see the lip of the snowfield, bare scree mixed with crusted snow lying beyond. He was only ten short paces away from it when he felt the shudder of snowburden, and on snowshoes a man might have danced lightly the rest of the way during the first second or so when a surface began to slide under him. But without snowshoes, Kraga did not have this option. He stood still, invoking his Orthodox God, and waited. The soft growl under his feet ceased. He continued doggedly, refusing to look at the small crevasse that had opened above him. Five child's paces, with a glance behind; then two. When he eased his way down onto hard clattering flakes of stone, Pal Kraga knelt and studied his field of fire. Like it or not, he must crawl on his belly with a hole through his left triceps muscle, toward the upper limit of bared slope. There the slope was even steeper, the danger of another avalanche more extreme.

And there, he found, was the reason why the avalanche had not worked its way up, domino-fashion, any further: a low stratum of bare granite, projecting slightly like worn and rounded teeth above the scree, anchored the upper burden. He unslung the Enfield, rising with his knees on scree, leaning carefully into the edge of deep snow. Another distant rattle of gunfire from Stuart Ransome's direction, and faint hums of slug fragments from granite in the distance. He felt more certain now that Stu was manning that weapon.

Pal Kraga saw the faintest of movements from the outcrop, still hundreds of yards distant but now not much higher than he, and put a 303 slug where it might do the most good. In bright sunlight, he might fire several rounds before the sniper found his new location. But that was the stupid way; the Gheg way was to bide his time, and to kill with every shot.

The return fire came in two bursts. The first was a brief series of winks that Kraga saw clearly, from a muzzle that was tantalizingly hidden behind bare stone. Evidently, by punishing the fir copse, the sniper thought Kraga was still inside it. The second burst was longer, with a result no one wanted. Pal Kraga might have fired back hoping for a ricochet wound, but he never got the chance.

The stand of firs erupted from within, the blast ripping green branches and snow into a deadly flower that spread across the snowfield, a field already beginning to shift again even before two of the trees began to topple. Kraga moved backward, hugging a tooth of granite that projected from the scree, feeling and hearing the thunder reverberate. *Idiot! Leaving those caps and dynamite atop my pack. Fool!* Well, it could have been worse; he might have been down there with it.

Only a few heavy chunks of crusted snow, some the size of manhole covers, pinwheeled from above him, breaking into debris as they fell. Kraga waited for ten seconds before scrambling back to the near lip of snow. He knelt on one knee as he saw what he had never really hoped to see, took a breath, released it. It was essential that he ignore the agony through the arm that supported the Enfield's forestock. His target was the man who stood overconfidently with bent knees, surveying the destruction he had wreaked by firing blindly into a dynamite cap. He stood hidden from below but, from Kraga's position, etched against a stark white background with a Galil in his hands. Kraga heard the man, shouting in Russian, as he squeezed the Enfield's trigger. The shouts ceased a heartbeat after the stock jumped against Kraga's shoulder, but Kraga worked the bolt and fired again as soon as the target lay sprawled in his crosshairs.

Without rising, he gazed below at the ruin of the fir trees on a slope now half cleared of snow. "You may use my canvas pack in heaven, uncle," he said to the shade of Elbas Hamid, and smiled.

"Oh, Jesus," Stu gasped, watching a fog of green and white spread across the slopes as echoes of the blast caromed across the lake. He slid down from his perch, teeth bared, and swung the Ingram toward the big man with the frightened eyes. Face flushed, hot tears brimming: "I didn't think I could do it, but I can."

Viktor, resting below the boulders, had not seen where the explosion occurred. "I do not understand," he stammered, though he was beginning to.

"It doesn't matter," Stu gritted, then cocked his head as a voice floated down from the heights. "What's he saying?"

"I could not hear. I can ask him to repeat it," said Viktor, playing desperately for seconds.

A single emphatic crack pierced Viktor's words. Without giving it much thought, Stu identified the difference between the small-caliber Galil and the solitary report of the stalwart old bolt-action Enfield. He heard another single report and lowered the barrel of the Ingram, grinning as broadly as numbed cheeks would permit. "Never mind," he murmured. "You lucked out."

Far across the open slopes, a familiar voice bawled, the

words spaced widely to minimize echo. "Stuart! Are—you—all—right?"

Stu wormed his way up the boulders, ready to continue his probing of the heights. "Yes," he shouted. "I—have—my—man!"

"So—do—I," was the slow reply, and Viktor began to curse in a low monotone.

It took five minutes for Stu to get his prisoner down to the lakeside path, where he re-bound Viktor's hands around a slender fir so that the captive, with his thick bull neck, could not twist to see just how far they would be separated. He ignored the big man's complaints and stalked back to the slope, operating on reserves that elation provided. Returning across well-used tracks for his equipment, he saw his friend staggering down steep slopes toward him, dragging an inert body by the collar.

They met as Stu was securing the bellyband of his pack, and they pummeled each other. "Careful; he put a round through the flesh here," said the Albanian, nodding at the sodden dark patch high on his left arm.

"My God, Justin, you look like Pancho Villa," Stu laughed, eyeing the two rifles slung over the man's shoulders, then glancing lower. Sobering: "Is he alive?"

The Albanian shook his head, clearly near the end of his strength. "Is yours?"

"Yep; tied to a tree."

"Then we will claim—this one is wounded," the Albanian said, chest heaving. "Can you—roll him under—that tree?"

Stu handed over the Ingram and pulled the dead weight under the fir's branches, trying to ignore delicate pink traceries of blood in snow. He told himself that this was only a weight, a thing, and not a man. His churning stomach would not accept the lie; minutes before, this object had been trying to kill him. *It was you or us*, he thought, and swallowed hard.

The dead man's hair was matted with blood, and trails of crimson runneled from his nose and one ear. His face was contorted in the rictus of a scream, or a yawn. *This is what you wanted to do to me.* And with his flash of anger, Stu's knotted belly relaxed.

As the two men walked back together, they exchanged accounts of the past half hour. They had over two hours of sunlight left, but a cheery blaze and a change of socks from Stu's pack would not have to wait. In any case, the time was here and now for a Gheg lie detector.

Viktor Danilov had never heard of a Gheg lie detector, but in principle it was hideously simple. As Stu Ransome cleared an old firepit not far from the tree where the big man sagged on rubbery legs, the Albanian captor explained. "We have you separated, and we ask you both the same questions. The first time your answers do not agree, we shoot you both through the hand. The second time, a foot. And so on."

Viktor's mouth sagged open. This was not how things were done in the West—but Kraga was of another tradition. "As your prisoner, I demand humane treatment," he said stiffly.

"This is the humane way," Kraga purred. "My uncles severed fingers. Your companion already knows this, and claims to fear death by freezing more than he fears the truth." He spoke in Russian now, with faintly rolled *r*'s on the words *smiert* and *pravda*. It pleased him to see the big man's eyes widen.

"They did not tell me you speak the mother tongue," Viktor replied, also in Russian.

"Well enough," said the Albanian, proving it. "Your name and your agency first."

Viktor told him the truth. This was terrorism, he reminded himself piously, and a KGB agent was not really expected to hold out in such cases.

The questions proceeded. Viktor Grigorovitch Danilov writhed inside, trembled outside, as he gave grudging answers. This double jeopardy put both him and the Greek under maximum pressure to peel back their layers of cover, and this damned Albanian plainly enjoyed the process. Worse, he knew the ways of tradecraft, though his terms were many years out of date. Viktor moaned as he gave the name of his *rezident* station leader, but he gave it. If Grichanka gave a different name, they would both suffer horribly.

The Albanian asked for paper and pencil, and the American found both in his pack. It was little comfort to Viktor that Kraga's hands shook so that he could hardly write down the data. Viktor explained his team briefly; gave their names. "Amateurs and ignoramuses," he volunteered sadly. "I forbade them to harm your son."

"I will note that when I carry out your sentence," said his interrogator. Kraga's demands for more detail included the crucial one; the one which Grichanka might not divulge no matter what the threat. Viktor sighed and gave up his last hope of salvaging anything from this debacle. "Let me near that fire and I will tell you about the attempts on your son," he begged, sagging as the bark bit into his numbed hands.

Kraga agreed, wrapping duct tape around the man's ankles as he sat by the growing blaze. Many years before, a man named Fred Taylor had taught him how each small loss of freedom deepened a captive's despair and loosened his tongue. As the big man shuddered and tried clumsily to rub life into his hands at the fire, he talked.

"He speaks good English," Stu called, erecting his small pyre of dry debris. "Why not let me in on this, Justin?"

"His name is Pal Kraga," called Viktor angrily; "a defector from Albania."

"I know," Stu replied, and made himself cheerfully callous. "He's also the toughest, most devious sonofabitch I ever met, I'm happy to say." Stu's voice and hands trembled with cold, but he was smiling as he worked.

"In English, then," said the Albanian.

Viktor complied. Kraga's odyssey, he said, had been pieced together only recently by the KGB, after the death of dictator Enver Hoxha in April. Hoxha's successor in Albania, Ramiz Alia, was a man capable of reason, but he had inherited Hoxha's files. He had, therefore, inherited all of Hoxha's rights to revenge. And revenge, in Tirana, was still viewed as a pleasure; failure to exercise it might even be seen as weakness in the new leader. Alia acted quickly; he might make some important concessions to Moscow if, and only if, the Soviets performed certain small favors first.

To many people in the West, Alia's bargain might seem ridiculous; it *was* ridiculous, said Viktor, but it made sense if you understood the lengths to which bruised pride and revenge would drive an Albanian. Mehmet Shehu had been such a man, said Viktor; and so had Enver Hoxha.

"And so am I," said Kraga. "Go on before your assassin freezes."

Mehmet Shehu, said Viktor, had known since 1944 that a ragtag band of republicans had hidden a great fortune in gold, which Shehu regarded as his own, somewhere in the Dinarics. During his rise to the top of Albania's pitiless, unforgiving Sigurimi secret police, Shehu had maintained his personal file on this matter, refusing to share it with the one man he feared, Enver Hoxha.

Eventually, only two of the BK republicans remained unaccounted for: their leader, one Elbas Hamid, and a youth, Pal Kraga. During the period of good feeling between Albania and the Soviet Union, the Soviets began building submarine pens on the Albanian coast; and this was when Shehu forwarded his requests for tracers on many Albanian defectors, including Hamid and Kraga. Soviet agents in Trieste, as a matter of standard practice, studied suspected enemy agents including those who worshipped or spoke as Albanians. They passed photographs back, some of which eventually reached Shehu. One photograph, identified by a young courier who had met many republicans early in the war, went into Shehu's secret revenge file: Pal Kraga was probably operating under CIA funds out of Trieste as one of their Italians, cover name unknown. Before Shehu could arrange a capture in Trieste, Kraga dropped off the face of the earth.

Elbas Hamid had died on Albanian soil, to Shehu's intense rage, without giving Shehu a chance to interrogate him privately for the location of that gold. In due time, Albania repudiated her links to Moscow and kept those submarine pens, creating enormous frustration among the Soviets, who still, in 1985, lacked a naval base with free access to the Mediterranean.

Years passed. Albania began cautious dealings with neighboring Yugoslavia. Without a global spy network of his own, Shehu requested tracers from Belgrade on several Albanian "defectors," and included photographs. In 1970, by sheer happenstance, a Yugoslav informant who kept tabs on Albanian communities in the United States passed on a list of recent christenings in the Albanian Orthodox Church in Boston, Massachusetts. In Belgrade, analysts saw the name "Kraga" and tagged the event to one of their inactive files. At the moment, Tirana was making particularly scurrilous remarks about Belgrade, and Shehu did not learn of the discovery in Boston.

But the Yugoslavs, who understood the swiftness of Balkan changes as well as anyone, thought that Albanian relations might soon improve. Their agents in Boston found that the recently christened Kraga infant was the son of one Alessandro Bellini, whose features were a perfect match—allowing for a few years—with the photograph of Pal Kraga. "They hoped to take you back, but their tradecraft was poor," Viktor sighed. "They fumbled it completely. Your Belgrade file included a report that you probably would never surface again."

"They let my wife freeze to death," Kraga said in a voice that could have come from a frozen body.

"I am sure you will make them pay," said Viktor.

"I did, years ago," said Kraga. "Furtive Serbs on trade missions became a specialty of mine."

"Jesus Christ, Justin," Stu murmured, adding dead limbs to the fire. "You never told me that."

"No. Ten for one; Rita is avenged." He turned back to the KGB man. "It was another Serb who recognized me a few years ago, in a California restaurant. I knew him slightly in Boston. An agent?"

Viktor nodded. The Yugoslavs, he said, actually paid a private investigator in Monterey to trace a man well known to the restaurant as Carlo Lambert. Lambert had disappeared, but Lambert's attorney began to forward financial materials to a

Mr. Justin Paladino, General Delivery, Gilman. The rest was easy even for a Serb, said Viktor.

"Then in Belgrade they have known my location for years," said the Albanian in wonderment.

"Yes. They simply had no immediate use for the information because the Balkan situation had changed. It was only after Hoxha's death that Tirana and Belgrade began to share those old files," said Viktor.

"You said Shehu had kept my file to himself," Kraga injected quickly.

"True; it killed him," said Viktor Danilov. "In the fall of 1982, one of Hoxha's private cadre found Shehu's revenge file and passed it on. You may remember that after Shehu's so-called suicide in 1982, Hoxha publicly denounced his friend of forty years as a collaborator with us, and with the Yugoslavs. You, Pal Kraga, were what that collaboration was all about. Shehu had merely kept a few small things from official files all those years, but Hoxha was a madman about that. Also about gold; and to a small country, a treasure in gold exacts heavy revenge. I am sure that Hoxha's men wrung poor old Shehu quite dry before they killed him."

Something was shining in the Albanian's eyes. "Then I caused the beheading of the Sigurimi," he said, and wiped a tear from his cheek.

"You are sorry?"

A smile, and a shuddering breath filled with emotion. "Proud, you fool. Proud to have been the instrument." He smiled toward Stuart Ransome, whose returning smile was a very poor construction. "Very well. I know that Hoxha never made final peace with Belgrade, but after his death this spring, Ramiz Alia traded information with them. And I was a piece of that trade."

"A piece the Yugoslavs would never have traded so cheaply had they known its value to Alia," Viktor said, nodding. "Alia's new Sigurimi deputy was very forthright about the whole matter, and would hardly trust an operation to Serbs again. He asked us last month to see to your return. We pieced your file together and realized that only your son would—um. Well, actually, it was the Sigurimi man who wrote it: Pal Kraga's only vulnerability will be his son. I am sure he said it to others as well. The rest you know.''

''Not quite. I know you were running the American hoodlums, but who was running those Orientals? I shall ask your friend the same question.''

''Ah,'' said Viktor, smiling for the first time to feel some circulation in his hands again. ''That problem, you can never overcome. Comrade Alia gave the sanction to us, *and to the Chinese*. They would very much like to use those submarine pens at Vlore, and to deny them to us. You must know how that works, with all your background in CIA tradecraft.''

''You knew about me in Trieste,'' Kraga said with a shrug. ''I retired from clandestine work before coming to this country.''

''Your entire life has been clandestine,'' Viktor said, with the faint bow of one offering a compliment. ''In any case, whatever happens to me or the Greek, you and your son will be hunted for the rest of your lives.'' Now his deep voice became smoothly coaxing. ''The boy has only one chance for a normal life, Kraga. Surely you see that.''

''You mean give myself up,'' said the Albanian.

Viktor said nothing, but his faint smile and open-handed shrug endorsed the notion.

Chapter 24

"WHEN dealing with a horse trader, Danilov, make sure you are not the horse," said Kraga coolly. "My son *will* have a normal life, because you will report that I am dead."

"I cannot imagine why I would do that," said Viktor, straining to massage a naked foot while his ankles were taped, stretching his feet near the little blaze Stu was tending. His bearing was now that of a man who felt that he might have something to trade, yet did not know precisely what it was.

"Then I shall tell you. You will do it because your masters cannot have changed all that much. Even if you escaped, you would be punished severely for a failure as complete as this. Your GRU assassin wounded, another of your men dead, your weapons taken, your mission in ruins—oh yes, you may kiss your career goodbye. But I can turn your abysmal failure into success," Kraga said.

Viktor, acidly: "Then you are a magician. Why do I doubt you, I wonder?"

"Because you lack imagination. Tirana wants the location of that gold, and wants me dead. Let us say that you ambushed me, well-trained agent that you are. You forced me under torture to draw a map. I can do that, Danilov; I can describe its location exactly.

"And Alia will have a fortune in gold, with your word

263

that I died. You may claim that you killed me, or that I tried to escape across the lake ice and drowned; anything you like, so long as no one expects to find my body.''

''You might have been blown to bits,'' Viktor mused aloud, then seemed to shake off this hope of accommodation. ''And of course your map will be false. I have met other Albanians, Kraga. You settle into lies as a whore into a mattress.''

''Use your brains! Your story will close Tirana's file on Pal Kraga *only if that gold is where I say it is.*'' Kraga gave the big man a moment to ruminate on this. As Viktor was nodding to himself, Kraga went on: ''I cannot stay in this country now; thanks to you, and for the sake of my son, the boy must think me dead. And I must go elsewhere with still another name.'' He turned to Stu Ransome, who was silently tending the fire. ''Stuart, would you see to Mark's upbringing until he is of age?''

''I told you I would,'' Stu replied. ''That still stands, Justin.''

''There you have it,'' said the Albanian. ''If you refuse, your alternative is clear, Danilov: I shatter both of your elbows and deliver you to the American authorities with the entire story, including names and other particulars you have given me. The Americans will run me and my son through a much-improved relocation program after we testify in your trial, because that will be my bargain for our testimony. And if further attempts are made on Mark, the KGB will have to completely reorganize in this part of California. You will have done incalculable harm to the Soviet cause. If you have a family at home—'' A frosty smile, and a certain relish as he said, ''I happen to know how badly they will fare.''

The big man glanced toward Stu Ransome. ''And what of him and his story?''

''An amateur who ran from your Americans,'' said Kraga with an airy wave. ''You will say that he did not see me captured and cannot know your own affiliations. His story must be that I simply disappeared up here. That scenario should play to your people.''

Viktor touched chapped lips; nodded again. "May I know your cover while in Trieste? I was told that would clear up an old file, and as long as I interrogated you . . ."

"A name so common I did not dispose of it when I should: Alessandro Bellini. I interrogated many a Soviet pawn in those days. You will ask the name of my case officer next. Make up whatever name you like; it is what I would have done. It will be dark in less than two hours, and I have much to do. Decide now."

"Your concern for my welfare is not an Albanian's way. If the Americans would help you relocate, why not let them?"

"It is my son's welfare I am thinking of," said Kraga with some heat. "I would not have his life turned inside out as mine was, at his age. Decide now!"

"One thing only," said Viktor. "What do I say if you ever surface again?"

"Pray that no one ever finds me. I hold too many proofs of your weakness, and they will make headlines," he added, shaking Stu's little spiral-bound notebook in Viktor's face.

"To be a traitor, or a failure, a cripple, *and* a traitor? Very well; but only for the sake of my own sons," said Viktor. "I agree, Kraga. Hide yourself well, next time. By the way, you have left Grichanka up there too long," he added with a sidelong motion of his head. "Or do you care?"

"He will keep." Kraga stood up.

Viktor sighed. "And burying him among the stones is one of the things you must do, I take it."

"What made you think that?" Kraga's toothy smile was familiar to Stu now; it was his lying smile.

"When you said that I must report you dead," said Viktor. "That GRU *vawlk* will never agree, and you know the ways of wolves. Therefore, you intend to eliminate him."

Kraga, the smile erased, began to set the bindings on their remaining pair of snowshoes. "Perfectly correct, except that he is already dead. Your *vawlk* howled too soon, and the range was only five hundred meters. Stuart, let us tape his wrists. We would not want him to make a mistake now."

"Nor should you, Kraga. Be sure to get the car keys from Grichanka's pockets. I will need them, you know."

The sun stood low over Quartz Mountain as the three men forded the foaming creek, struggling against exhaustion with Stu in the lead. Here and there, sitzmarks revealed the reelings and falls of Ken Connor, who had somehow managed to continue with prolonged panic as fuel. Pausing to rest beyond the ravine, Viktor Danilov observed that he would have to stumble to the trailhead alone, and with his weapon. "You are dead, Kraga; I must begin the deception with the Connor brothers. I can say the American escaped on snowshoes."

"Hell, we should've thought of that," Stu muttered. "This is too goddamn complicated! We're going to slip up somehow, Justin."

"We have three minds to work on it," said the Albanian. "Danilov's future depends on this, and he knows it."

Stu withdrew the Ingram's long magazine and ejected a round from the chamber, emptied the magazine with repeated thumb flicks, then handed the weapon over. "Any reason why those scufflers might come after me in the future?"

"I can handle that," said Viktor. "But keep the Kraga boy out of sight for two weeks. It will take time for the death of Pal Kraga to go through channels. And for that gold to validate my claims."

"The information in the notebook could be leaked anonymously, and piece by piece," said Kraga. "It is in your interest to see that Mark and Stuart are no longer in danger. Stuart cannot repeat the answers you gave to me in Russian, and you have my word that I will not leak them if you keep your bargain."

"The word of an Albanian spy," Viktor said, his big chest heaving with mirthless laughter as he stamped his feet in wet shoes. "But I do what I must. And it is time for you to give me the car keys and that map." He watched as the Albanian tore a page from the notebook; studied it carefully. "A hundred meters below the Fierze road, then, in a cave, buried under bat droppings. No one but an Alb—'' He stopped, shook his head. "You are sure of these kilometer numbers?''

"Certain enough. Ten men could canvass those slopes in a day. I *want* it found, Danilov.''

Viktor folded the paper carefully and tucked it into a trouser pocket. He started downhill, his low-quarter shoes dragging through the shallow tracks. "Give me five minutes to collect the Connors. They must not see you, Kraga.''

Stu watched Viktor stumble ahead until he was nearly out of sight. "You think we oughta let him get five minutes ahead?''

"I am not an idiot, Stuart,'' said his friend, and began to follow Viktor Danilov. "He will have more ammunition in those vehicles. We must see what he does at the trailhead.''

Danilov looked back once while resting, saw that his pursuers had stopped within sight of him, and shook his head but made no other sign. "Maybe this will keep him honest,'' Stu murmured.

Kraga nodded. "He knows I have weapons that can baptize him from afar. My concern is that they could drive off and try to ambush us farther down the mountain.''

"So we camp up here tonight?''

"That was my thought,'' said the older man. "The heater in my Land Cruiser is quite good, and we can take turns as sentries.''

They resumed their walk, keeping well in arrears of the KGB man, never letting him out of sight for long until they drew within a half mile of the trailhead. The sun was a glowing sliver on the horizon as the two men separated, Stu carrying his pack and handgun, Kraga bearing the weights of the Galil and his scarred old Enfield. They heard Viktor Danilov calling through the dusk, and Stu hurried as fast as weariness would let him as he moved near the clearing.

With the fading sunlight, the temperature plummeted quickly. The mountain no longer seemed alive with the shedding of melted snow from fir and pine, and now the forest was silent. Stu made his way forward on bare patches of stone and humus, avoiding the crunch of his boots on snow. He pulled the rolled neck of his sweater up over his nose, hoping to make his frosty exhalations less obvious.

Before he had drawn within a hundred yards of the trailhead, he could see the looming masses of vehicles. The big Blazer had been driven back to the clearing and now he heard angry words, Viktor's low, rumbling, and indistinct; another man's ringing clearly. "I seen that roll you carry; pay us now!" A low, angry reply from the big man. Then Connor again: "The fuckin' feds go in bunches, and they don't shoot foreign hardware, and you guys weren't talkin' Italian!" There was more, and Stu crept nearer in the dusk intent only on hearing Viktor's responses.

The hard-edged "Move and you're dead, asshole," sent a wave of weakness and fear through him. Stu, crouched in the open while he moved toward closer cover, moved only his head. Thirty yards away to his left stood the elder of the Connor brothers, holding what appeared to be Viktor's submachine gun. Stu had emptied that weapon, and with false confidence he slowly stood erect, blowing on gloved hands as he stared over his shoulder at the balding man. "Sheee-it," was all he could say.

Turning his head slightly, still watching Stu, the man strode from behind a big pine and shouted, "Ken! I got me a live one!"

"I told you they'd try that," Ken Connor called back. "I think you was right, Al." Stu could not hear what the little man said next, but Viktor's hands went up and with them, his harmless weapon waved aloft. *So this one will be loaded*, thought Stu, still standing with his hands near his breast, wondering if Justin knew what was happening as he slipped one hand inside his jacket. He kept blowing on his left hand, hoping that his body hid the fumblings of his right.

"We can search 'em after, for the money," called Allen Connor. "You first."

A single shot, then another as Viktor Danilov fell. Stu's captor elevated the barrel of his weapon slightly, and in that instant Stu fired through his jacket, pulling the trigger again and again as he lurched forward, feeling surges of heat against his belly from the Beretta.

Allen Connor, unhurt but off-balance with astonishment, shied and leaped toward cover, spraying a burst from his Ingram as he ran, and an unseen force slapped Stu's pack hard enough to spin him. He staggered, fell on his back wrenching the Beretta from his jacket, and took deliberate two-handed aim between his raised knees. Allen Connor reached a tree, stuck the upper part of his body out to aim, and Stu began to fire again letting the Beretta's kick elevate its muzzle with each round, firing six rounds as fast as he could.

Allen Connor, blinded by the splash of bark in his face and creased by a ricochet, staggered sideways. Stu fired three more times without rising and saw Connor's body jerk from impacts as he crumpled.

Then, scrambling on all fours toward a hummock of granite, Stu called, "Take the other one out now!"

This was all Ken Connor needed to tell him that his brother's live one was still alive. Stu left his cover seeing the little man bolt for the Blazer. He shambled forward, still twenty yards from the trailhead when the Blazer's engine caught. Teeth bared, gasping from his exertions, he leaned against a tree near the body of Allen Connor and took dead aim through the rear window panel.

The Beretta was empty. A distant hammer of firing from the distance, and a cascade of flying glass from the Blazer's side windows as it roared forward. Stu cursed as the vehicle slammed down the trail and out of sight; even an Albanian, he decided, could miss in the dusk with an unfamiliar weapon. He took the stubby Ingram from dead fingers, but much too late to use it.

Kneeling beside Viktor Danilov, Stu found the big man trying to rise while favoring a useless left arm. "Twenty years without a wound, and now this," growled the KGB man as he pulled his right hand from inside his coat. The second slug had gone into his lower rib cage and featured an ugly exit wound with pinkish shreds of rib, displaced by Connor's heavy .45 slug.

Trembling with mingled cold and shock, Viktor Grigorovitch Danilov could still handle details clearly. He insisted that the bodies of Ray Nelson and Allen Connor be placed in the Lancer's trunk even though the process was not complete until full dark. "They will accept my failure to find the Greek," he said, as he levered himself into the Lancer. "But I must have the weapon that killed Connor."

Stu cursed and looked at his Beretta with a fondness he had never shown it before. "You're saying the KGB does autopsies and police forensics?"

"Both sides do, when they can," said Kraga. "He is right, Stuart. You dropped the weapon and fled at the lake. Danilov must show that he survived a mutiny by treacherous Americans, and yours is the only weapon that can prove him a hero of the Soviet Union."

"I will say that I faced them alone," said Viktor. "It would be Ken Connor's word against mine if he were questioned."

"And if you were so lacking in tradecraft that you would let him live that long," Kraga said.

"That detail has not escaped me. Nor will Connor, for long," said the big man. "And now the handgun, if you please."

Stu handed it over without much grace. "You sure you can drive like that?"

"When I cannot, I will stop," Viktor wheezed, watching without much interest as the Albanian, holding a pencil flash in his mouth, pawed under nearby humus with one hand for an astonishing cache of material. "If that damned Albanian can fight with a hole in him, I can continue with two."

Stu busied himself with retrieval of the yellow tent, moving at the pace of an octogenarian, never standing when he could lean, nor leaning when he could sit. "I like to leave a clean camp, Justin," he said at last, sweeping his own flashlight beam around the clearing. "But Danilov could bleed out."

"Neatness counts," said the Albanian, latching the Toyota's hood. "We will get him to the motel somehow. My key plate has the address." He turned to the man who had been his enemy. "Will that play, Danilov?"

"Under these conditions I would stop wherever I could."

"It is nearer than you think," said the Albanian in tones that were almost gentle.

"Wait," said Viktor suddenly. "Turn out your pockets to me, Kraga."

The Albanian cursed to himself, then hurriedly passed over the contents of his pockets, including the outsized wallet and Stu's spiral notebook from which he tore several pages before handing it to Viktor. He kept most of his money and unhooked two keys from his keyring. "You may guess that I passed my Toyota's key over to my American friend," he said to Viktor. "It will be in Stuart's possession."

"Not a good idea. An unnecessary complication," Viktor argued. "Let him return for your truck."

For a moment Kraga stood silent. "Perhaps a necessary complication, if we have further trouble," he said at last. He headed determinedly toward the old Land Cruiser. "Take the lead, Stuart. Show us how good those rally lights of yours are."

Slightly over an hour later, Stu cut his overhead spotlights as he reached the sudden lights and summer congestion of the Bass Lake perimeter road. Moments later he saw the Lancer veer into the parking lot of a roadhouse, stopping near a telephone booth that stood incongruously near the surrounding primeval forest.

Viktor was groggy but insistent. It took both men to help him lean against the kiosk, and the pair of revelers who left the roadhouse donated only a glance toward the drunks who glared back at them in silence while supporting the very large drunk holding the telephone. Viktor's long-distance connections were quite as good as Ma Bell's. He spoke haltingly in Russian and, holding a motel key before him in dim light, he read off its details before he fainted.

The Albanian replaced the receiver without a word, rubbed his left shoulder, and spent a moment muttering to himself.

Then: "Transfer your things to my vehicle, Stuart, and do not take off your gloves when you drive his car. I still must get this great lump of meat to Coarsegold without his blood staining his passenger seat and its footwell. It would raise unpleasant questions, so we will put him in my cargo compartment. His people will converge at the motel sooner than you think."

It was past eleven o'clock when Stu, holding his sleeve clear of the Lancer's blood-soaked door panel, followed the Land Cruiser to the motel on the outskirts of Coarsegold. Traffic droned past on the highway not fifty yards distant as the two men struggled with two hundred and fifty pounds of Viktor Danilov. Stu imagined that he was all too obvious while carrying two sniper rifles into the motel room wrapped in his mummy bag but these, said the Albanian, were two more loose ends to be knotted for the KGB. Kraga hurried back outside with the mummy bag, leaving Stu to pull the door closed with a gloved hand. By eleven-thirty they were speeding south on Highway 41 in the Toyota.

Stu, driving, watched his friend swallow caffeine tablets. "Hey, gimme some of those. Either that or bang on my head." He held out his free hand; popped two tablets. "I am absolutely blasted, Justin, but I'm scared shitless. Dammit, I *killed* a man this evening! I feel guilty that I'm not sorry. Does that make any sense?"

"Viktor Danilov killed him, Stuart. Ken Connor probably thinks the assassin did it. If you repeat that idea long enough you will come at last to believe it," said Kraga. "For example, I have come to feel affection for things Italian," he added.

"But in your guts you'll be Pal Kraga until you die."

"True. That surprised me, but it has kept me alive this day. Of course after tonight you must learn to think of me as missing and presumed dead. Ah, these damned details!" The Albanian put his hands to his face, exhaling long and hard, before he resumed. "You may be sure that the authorities will question you sooner or later. Always tell the same story, or none at all. They will want to know how you got my Toyota for Mark. It will be simplest if you admit that you found it at that trailhead.''

''Yeah? How did I know to look there?''

''M-m, yes. I must write you a note. You received it by mail, with two keys. You threw away the envelope. It bore a Coarsegold postmark.'' The older man thrust a hand into a trouser pocket.

''Not both keys, or you couldn't drive it up—''

''This is the second,'' Kraga interrupted, handing over a small key with a round barrel. ''To my safety-deposit box in Gilman. Its contents are yours and Mark's.'' A gentle laugh; ''I beg you, do not provide him too much luxury. I shall contact you both again, one day. Meanwhile, whatever he wants—including an education—make certain he helps pay his way. Youth must forge its own metal.''

Stu remained silent for some miles, and spoke only after noticing a road sign. ''You want the nearest hospital for that arm, or can you wait 'til Fresno?''

''I have no friends in Fresno,'' Kraga mumbled.

''Then where the hell am I taking you?''

Justin Paladino, alias Pal Kraga, sighed. Exhaustion thickened his accent; slowed his words. ''To San Jose, Stuart, though my son must believe the same story you tell everyone else. It breaks my heart, but Mark's safety depends on his own ignorance.''

Stu considered this for a moment, then nodded. ''Sooner or later he'd blab the truth to somebody he wanted to impress, I suppose. You're one tough-minded old fart, you know that? And your arm must hurt like a sonofabitch. You really intend to make it back to San Jose tonight?''

''It is you who must resume your life as though you had never been away, Stuart. I can drive if you cannot. That bullet did not hit the bone and I cannot be on record as a gunshot victim.''

At length Stu said, ''Danilov's got friends; well, you have one, too. I can patch you up at my place.''

Now Kraga was chuckling. ''And cross tracks with the GRU again? You underestimate Danilov's masters, Stuart.

You must take a motel room for me in San Jose and perhaps help me treat this damned hole in my arm. Park the Toyota where it will not be seen for a day or so and go home alone. To live your story perfectly, you must not try to contact me again. I disappeared somewhere above the Chain Lakes trailhead.''

Stu muttered a curse to himself and added, ''I've never lied to Mark. Hell of a start for his new guardian.''

''Americans mature—more slowly,'' said Kraga with a great effort at diplomacy. ''When my son is a man, he will understand. There is much that you must withhold until then.''

''I know it. I don't have to like it. Well, it's a long drive to San Jose. Brief me on the kid: allergies, whether he's had measles, all that stuff. It'll keep us both awake.''

Kraga's gift for remembered detail had never been so obvious as now, on the topic nearest to his heart. For hours, the Albanian recounted the events of his son's life; likes, dislikes, virtues and failings.

By the time Stu turned the Land Cruiser's nose up the Bayshore Freeway hours later, his companion was hoarse from talking. Not once had Kraga mentioned what must have been constant pain in his arm, and Stu felt an impending sense of great loss. ''It won't be long now,'' he said, approaching a motel district in San Jose. ''You've told me more lies than all the friends I ever knew, put together. And I guess I don't care. I'm going to miss you, Justin.''

''But you will curse me too,'' said Kraga. ''Let us keep that in mind. If I shed tears, let it be while you are probing into my arm.'' He spoke gruffly, humorously, with the tight throat of a man resisting his own emotions.

''It's a deal,'' Stu replied. ''Any idea where you'll resettle?''

''No,'' said the Albanian, with a show of teeth in the faint glow of the instrument panel.

''You really oughta do something about that grin, Justin,'' Stu said, and yawned as he slowed the Toyota. ''It says you've had another spot picked out for a long, long time.''

PART FOUR
AUGUST 1985

Chapter 25

WILEY Reed squinted against reflective concrete from beneath the brim of his old Stetson; touched a moisture-beaded bottle to his cheek as he squatted beside his camper in Karen Cavender's driveway. He spoke to the Birkenstocks that protruded from beneath the pickup: "It's been gimpy for nearly as long as I have, bubba. You can fix it some other time; hell, it makes me sweat just watchin' you."

Stu Ransome slid into sunlight on his back, using two flattened cardboard boxes as low-friction surfaces, and retrieved his beer from a patch of shade. "Yeah, well, mad dogs and shop teachers," he grinned, and stood up to guzzle, his eyes closed against the midday sun. He wiped a turned-up sleeve across his forehead and gestured with the bottle. "I had to know what parts we need. No sweat; plenty of replacement springs around. Mark can keep his eyes open for 'em while he's scaring up parts for the Toyota. He'll be back from the junkyard anytime now with his girl."

"Got a girl, has he? How's the kid doin'? Haven't seen much of him lately," said Wiley, following Stu toward Karen's kitchen door.

Karen, holding her telephone in one hand and its long cord in the other, did not stop talking as she saw the men enter. "—And Mr. Reed is highly experienced in divorce cases," she was saying as she stepped over to the refrigerator, pulling two more beers out, holding them at arm's length as she bumped the door closed with one hip. She gave them a smile to rival the noon sun, still talking. "I'm sure he'll give you a callback by three," she said, darting a glance at Wiley, responding to his heavenward glance, "or four at the latest. —You're welcome," she said, and pressed the disconnect. Turning to the men who were wrenching tops from bottles: "Better break out the long lens for this one," she said, passing a slip of paper to Wiley.

Wiley grunted and stuffed the slip into a shirt pocket without comment; hiding with a camera inside a sweltering camper, in August, in San Jose, was a prospect beyond commentary. Turning back to Stu, he said, "What gets me is how easy the kid bought old Paladino's fade-out. I still think he knows something he's kept to himself. I've thought so ever since you took him out of the slammer."

"Out of protective custody," Karen inserted, quick to defend a young friend with whom she had developed a close bond. "You know very well there were no charges filed against him."

"Whatever." Wiley shoved his hat to the back of his head and smirked at Stu as they took chairs. "I think maybe you're sittin' on the same thing, Stu. It's been in my craw for over a month now."

"I think Justin is alive," Stu said truthfully. "I know Mark thinks his old man is immortal, so he isn't worried on that score. Maybe he's just learning to keep his mouth shut. He misses Justin, sure; but I keep him pretty busy," he finished with a grin and another swig of Oly Gold.

"Restoring that old turd of a Land Cruiser? Shit-I-reckon," Wiley replied. "Prob'ly a lifetime job unless you find a pot of money. Speaking of which I gather Paladino, Kraga, whoever the hell he really was, stashed plenty of it in that safety-deposit box." He opened the bottle; waggled it suggestively to Karen. "More Gold, Ma'am?"

As she reached for the bottle, Karen's glance met Stu's, and they burst out laughing together. Pilfering from her refrigerator again, she shook the new bottle ruthlessly before handing it to Wiley. "Teach you to go easy on my booty," she said.

"And you go easy on the straight lines," Wiley grinned ruefully, holding the bottle, not opening it. "You wanta tell me what I missed a minute ago?"

Karen, with brows elevated, looked at Stu again. "I think you owe him that much," she said cryptically.

Stu leaned back with a sigh. "Yeah, but he'll only be chapped that I haven't told him before. You mentioned more gold, Wiley? Well, I've got it. I didn't even know I had it until a week ago. Maybe you can figure out what we do with it until—well, until Mark is ready."

Wiley had been teetering back on his chair, a questioning smile on his dark Indian features. Now he corrugated his forehead and leaned forward. "Not beer. You mean gold, like in *gold*," he said softly. "How much?"

Stu opened both arms wide. "That much. Mark doesn't know yet, and if anyone but the three of us found out, certain people could come for it. You remember Justin admitted he'd helped hide a fortune in German gold?" He waited for the nod and got it. "Well, I think he left some of it there, but he took one hell of a lot out. No *wonder* he risked his ass going back into Albania! He was bringing the stuff out with every trip, Wiley. Nearly half a ton of it. Must've taken him years."

Wiley whispered, "I'll be dipped in shit." More loudly: "And used his spook connections to get it over here? Wonderful! I once heard about a guy who shipped a jeep back, piece by piece, but—*half a ton*?"

"Not quite, but I may not have found it all yet," Stu laughed helplessly. "He had years to toy with it, beat it into layers, hide it in frame tubes. He was great with his hands. *Is* great," he amended. "And he's a bear for fine detail."

With a fingersnap, Wiley said, "It was in the friggin' Toyota!"

"Sure. The spare fuel tank under the passenger seat? This one takes maybe a gallon of gas. And it weighs three hundred pounds. The damn machine drives like a dump truck and needs fifty pounds of air in those six-ply tires. But tell me another way Justin could've made his assets more mobile than that." Outside, a distant slam of doors. Stu identified the sounds as those of his own yellow Baja Bug; leaned back; sipped his Oly as Wiley Reed began to stride around Karen's living room.

"It's obvious the old spook wanted you to find it," Wiley said, stopping to look out the big window. "You haven't told the kid?"

"Kids talk. I'll tell him when he graduates if he's ready to leave the nest then."

A low whistle issued from Wiley's lips. "I'll say one thing: he's already got an eagle's eye. You know what I think? I think the kid is developing adult tastes."

"Say again?"

"You've got eyes," said Wiley with a casual wave as Mark Paladino passed the window. In Mark's wake, following him through the door, walked a girl whose short blonde hair might never have felt Knox gelatin, whose long tanned legs might never have known a torn body stocking. She stood as tall as Mark, smiling at the familiar faces of Stu and Karen as she waited for an introduction.

"Hi, guys. Wiley Reed, this is Adele Nichols. Nothin' like a blonde in shorts to improve junkyard prices," Mark said with a wink at the girl as he moved toward the refrigerator. From the kitchen he said, "I got those linkages, Stu."

"Ohh yeah," said Wiley Reed, grinning, and turned toward Stu. "Great linkages. I'm with you, Stu. If I were Mark, I'd tell this young lady anything she wanted to hear."